106

W9-BLD-022

KILDAR

JOHN RINGO

Sci Fic
Ringo

KILDAR

This is a work of fiction. All the characters and events portrayed in this book are fictional, and any resemblance to real people or incidents is purely coincidental. This book and series has no connection to reality. Any attempt by the reader to replicate any scene in this series is to be taken at the reader's own risk. For that matter, most of the actions of the main character are illegal under U.S. and international law as well as most of the stricter religions in the world. There is no Valley of the Keldara. Heck, there is no Kildar. And the idea of some Scots and Vikings getting together to raid the Byzantine Empire is beyond ludicrous. The islands described in a previous book do not exist. Entire regions described in these books do not exist. Any attempt to learn anything from these books is disrecommended by the author, the publisher and the author's mother who wishes to state that he was a very nice boy and she doesn't know what went wrong.

A Baen Books Original

Baen Publishing Enterprises
P.O. Box 1403
Riverdale, NY 10471
www.baen.com

ISBN-13: 978-1-4165-2064-1
ISBN-10: 1-4165-2064-3

Cover art by Kurt Miller

First printing, March 2006

Library of Congress Cataloging-in-Publication Data

Ringo, John, 1963-
Kildar / John Ringo.
      p. cm.
"A Baen Books original"—Cover.
ISBN 1-4165-2064-3 (hc)
I. Title.

PS3568.I577K55 2006
813'.54—dc22
                           2005035468

Distributed by Simon & Schuster
1230 Avenue of the Americas
New York, NY 10020

Printed in the United States of America

10   9   8   7   6   5   4   3   2   1

KILDAR

KILDAR

CHAPTER
ONE

Night was falling and the snow getting thicker as the Mercedes skidded into the mountains, its traction control system constantly engaging to keep it on the roughly paved road.

Mike Harmon quietly cursed himself as he considered what to do. He'd made some stupid decisions in his life, more than one of which had been nearly fatal, but dying in the Caucasus Mountains in a blizzard was looking more and more likely. It would be a stupid and ignominious way to go out, all things considered.

Mike was a former SEAL who had, after leaving the teams, planned a quiet life. He'd been a student at the University of Georgia, not particularly happy but managing it, when he'd discovered a terrorist operation going on under his very nose. A series of choices had led him to a secret base in Syria where kidnapped coeds were being tortured and raped on camera to force the American government to withdraw from the Middle East. He'd been instrumental in breaking up the operation, freeing the girls and then holding the position until relieved by a SEAL team, after which airborne rescue forces captured the facility and extracted the girls. In the process he had been so badly shot up he nearly died, but he held his ground right up until passing out from blood loss.

He'd been paid a rather hefty reward for the operation and then wandered down to the Florida Keys to just . . . chill. With thirty mil in numbered accounts, a college degree suddenly seemed less necessary. Instead of a vacation, while enjoying himself in the Bahamas with a couple of lovely young ladies, he'd been asked to capture a nuke that more terrorists were smuggling through that country. Again, he'd succeeded, at least to the extent of preventing the terrorists from getting any further even *though* the nuke had been detonated in place. And, again, he'd nearly died from the wounds he suffered.

The Keys clearly being too hot for comfort, he'd wandered through Europe until in a whorehouse in Siberia he'd picked up the scent of *another* nuke. He'd followed it back through Europe, via the white-slave markets in Bosnia, and found it planted at Notre Dame, waiting for a papal mass. When the timer had gotten down to less than a minute and the French EOD unit was sure they'd never stop it in time he'd taken a fifty-fifty chance and sent a code to the bomb that would either temporarily disarm it or detonate it. He'd been lucky: Paris was still there. However, the French government was less than thrilled by his taking the choice in his own hands and declared him, or at least his cover identity, persona non grata.

This left him back in Russia, not sure what to do with himself and with every Islamic terrorist on the face of the earth pissed at this unknown who had broken up three major ops. Russia's winter was coming on, nothing to look forward to, and he decided to head south. Georgia had always interested him as a country and, just looking for somewhere to lay low, he'd headed that way.

Georgia, called the Switzerland of the Caucasus, was a mountainous country bordered by Russia, Azerbaijan, Turkey and the Black Sea. White people were called "Caucasians" because it was believed by some anthropologists that they had originated in these very mountains. A deep background study of world languages had indicated that the original "Caucasian" proto-language had about six different words for rivers and more than a dozen for mountains, which made sense given what he'd been driving through. The place looked a good bit like Vermont, but with higher mountains. It was renowned for its ski slopes and sudden avalanches.

The religion of the region was mostly Eastern Orthodox. Despite its Christian basis, the country had numerous security problems: Chechen Islamic terrorists that used its mountains as safe haven from their ongoing war with the Russians, a separatist movement in Ossetia, and internal stresses that dated back to the Soviet era. On the other hand, it was unlikely that anyone would notice just another wandering American tourist, much less make a connection between that tourist and the unknown American operative who had stopped three terrorist operations butt cold. And Mike had enjoyed skiing when he was trained in it by the SEALs. So to Georgia he hied himself, pleasantly contemplating a winter of hanging out in ski resorts and picking up ski bunnies.

Instead he'd found himself on this back road, totally lost, low on gas and in the early stages of a blizzard. He had no idea where he'd gone astray and the Fodor's map was next to useless without some road signs, which were notoriously rare in areas like this.

The Mercedes skidded through another saddle in the apparently endless mountains and, through the blowing snow, he saw a sharp right turn coming up. He braked carefully, following the road through a series of downward S turns until it, miraculously, flattened out. To his left he could see what might be the edges of fields while to his right was a steep slope. He consoled himself that any road led to a town eventually and kept on, driving carefully so he wouldn't be spun off the road into oblivion.

His lights suddenly illuminated a human figure in the middle of the road and he hit the brakes, hard, skidding to a stop, nearly sideways and only after a hard fight to keep the car from spinning out entirely. He had skidded right and the car was pointed directly at the small figure with a bundle of firewood over . . . her, by the clothes, back.

Mike put the Mercedes in park and stepped out, waving and smiling in his most friendly manner.

"Excuse me," he said in Russian. "Do you know where there's a town?"

The figure was covered in a heavy coat and a scarf and the reply, whatever it was, was whipped away by the blowing wind. The woman was bent nearly double by the bundle of sticks and Mike wanted to help her with it but he was pretty sure she'd take any approach negatively. The area was renowned for girls being stolen into prostitution and sexual slavery and there was no way for Mike to convince her he was just a lost tourist. Among other things, he didn't speak Georgian. Many of the locals spoke Russian, however, so he tried that again, stepping into the light so she could get a better look at him.

"Lost I am," Mike said, struggling for the Russian. He'd never studied the language; what he knew had been mostly picked up in brothels and bars. "A town? Petrol?"

The figure let go of the wood for a moment and pointed up the road, yelling something over the wind. It sounded like the word for six in Russian. Maybe six kilometers.

"Six kilometers?" Mike asked. "Thank you." He paused for a moment and then gestured at the car. "You need ride?" He made a motion for the firewood on her back and putting it in the trunk.

The woman backed up at first and then looked around at what was now, without question, a blizzard. She clearly was struggling with the fear of getting in a car with a stranger versus that of freezing to death. Finally she shrugged and hobbled forward.

Mike took the weight of the wood, which was at least eighty pounds, and popped open the trunk, dropping the large bundle in it. The woman was short and the wood must have weighed very close to her body-weight. Once he was in the Mercedes again he unlocked the far door and turned up the heater.

The woman got in and nodded at him.

"*Spasebo*," she said in a very small voice, sticking her mittened hands under her armpits and then removing one to point up the road. She had left on her scarf so Mike couldn't get a look at her face, but the eyes over the scarf were just lovely, a blue so dark and yet bright that they seemed to glow.

Mike followed her gestures carefully, including the ones to slow down as they came to curves. She clearly knew the road well. Fortunately, it was more or less level and only curved back and forth mildly. Mike couldn't get a look beyond about ten meters but it seemed as if this must be one of those wide valleys that were sometimes found in mountains. He'd heard somewhere that they were from glaciers, but he didn't know more than that about them.

The woman was clearly trying to pick out landmarks and suddenly made slowing motions, then pointed to the left, down a steep bank. There was a narrow road there, but it was a sharp descent. Mike considered it for a moment, then lined up the Mercedes and skied down the hill more than drove, ending up in a slight fishtail at the bottom. He lined out again, though, and followed the woman's directions through the snow to a house that was up another slight slope. He realized as he did that it was a good thing he'd happened on her; they'd driven nearly two kilometers and it was unlikely she would have made it home alive.

The house was long and low, made of dressed stone, with a roof that looked to be slate. There were very few windows and those small, with shutters, which were closed. From behind the shutters, though, light glowed. As Mike pulled into the yard in front of the structure a pack of dogs burst into a chorus of barks and surrounded the car.

The woman got out, yelling at the dogs, as the front door of the house opened. A man stepped out into the blizzard, shouting at the woman in turn. The woman replied at length as she got out the wood, stumbling with it to the door and waving with one hand at the car and Mike.

Finally, the dogs gotten under control, the man gestured for Mike to get out of the car and come in the house. Mike got out cautiously, surreptitiously checking his piece, and followed the man and woman into the house.

The first thing that he noticed was the smell, a compound of wet dogs and people who didn't bathe nearly enough overlain with wood smoke. The room was crowded with about ten people, adults and teenagers, and he could see the heads of older children peeking around a door. There was a large fireplace at the far end, near the head of a long table. Over the fireplace was a very moth-eaten tiger's head.

Dinner had been laid out on a long trestle table and it reminded him that he'd been getting hungry as well as annoyed at his predicament. He kept his eyes off the food, though, nodding at the man who had invited him into the house as the woman began divesting herself of layers of clothing. The man was tall and broad as a mountain with a shock of dark red hair. He was wearing a white long-sleeved wool shirt and blue jeans, but what caught Mike's eye was the heavy silver cross dangling from a chain. It was something like a Maltese cross with broad crosspieces that spread to look almost like an axe. It twigged something in Mike's memory but he couldn't quite place it.

"My name's Mike Jenkins," Mike said in Russian, using his current cover identity. "I'm American. I was headed for the Bakuriani Resort and I got lost. Is there a town around? My car's nearly out of petrol." At least, he thought that was what he said. His Russian was really rough.

Mike checked out the occupants of the room as he asked his questions. The first thing he noticed about them was that they were clearly peasants. Their clothing, the men's especially, was rough stuff designed for heavy work. Jeans, which were becoming internationally ubiquitous, and heavy wool shirts. Those looked as if they might be homespun. The women were in somewhat brighter clothing, wool skirts with colorful blouses.

The second thing he noticed was the similarity in looks; this was clearly either a very large family or an extended one all living in the same house. There was a fair number of redheads, which was fairly unusual in Georgia where the people tended to be black or brown haired. There were even a few blonds, also unusual.

The third thing, and it took a moment for it to fully sink in, was the overall good looks. There were two older women, who could be anywhere from thirty to eighty given the way that peasants aged, but they were both quite good looking for all their wrinkles. The men were all robust and handsome almost to a fault, like Hollywood extras chosen for their physical looks rather than any group of peasants Mike had ever seen. And the younger women were just lovely as hell. Slim faces ranging from sharp to heart-shaped, slim noses, high cheekbones, mostly Tartar eyes and beautiful hair even half covered by colorful scarves. The group was simply startling in its looks.

"Alerrso," the man said, waving up towards the road. He had the same family looks and was maybe fifty, with a square, hard jaw and hard eyes that were considering Mike carefully. "Six kilometers."

"*Spasebo*," Mike said, nodding at him and turning to the woman who had gotten her outer wear off to say goodbye. When he saw her, though, he froze.

The girl was no more than fifteen, probably younger, with the most beautiful face he had ever seen in his life coupled with those startling blue eyes and fiery red hair that peeked out from under her babushka scarf. He found himself mesmerized by her appearance for a moment until he physically shook himself.

"I hope you stay well," Mike said, stumbling over the Russian phrases and his lolling tongue. "Thank you for helping me."

"*Spasebo*," the girl replied, looking down suddenly. "Was far walk."

"You're welcome," Mike said, turning back to the man who was watching the two of them angrily. "I am sorry bother you. I go Alerrso. Thank you for directions."

"Good night," the man said, gesturing at the door.

Mike made his way out of the house and to the car in a daze, still entranced by the girl's looks. He had met many women in his travels but *none* as lovely as that girl. She was just exquisite. And he'd never meet her again.

"What did he say to you?" Eugenius said, grabbing Katrina by the arm and shaking her as the door closed. "What did you do?"

"Nothing!" Katrina said, lowering her eyes and shaking her head. "I was on the road. He nearly ran me down in the snow. It was very far; I didn't expect the snow so soon. I could tell he was lost, nobody like that with that car would come here. He asked me if I would ride with him and I knew if I didn't I might not make it home. I'm sorry, Father, but I would have died if I hadn't ridden with him."

"You are a disgrace," Eugenius said, shaking his head. "I should send you to town."

"She could have done nothing," Lena said, laying a hand on his arm. "Look at her; she was frozen when she came in. Nothing happened."

"It is a disgrace," Eugenius repeated, angrily. "We will all be disgraced by her!"

"Father," Dutov said, going to the table and taking his seat, "he was American. He would not know our customs. Come, sit down and let us eat. Katrina is . . . Katrina. Getting angry at a cat for preening is . . . silly."

"Father, I'm sorry," Katrina said, shooting an angry look at her brother. "I would have died in the snow if I had not ridden with him. And I kept even my scarf on. We did nothing but drive back here. And now . . . he is gone. Nothing has happened, nothing will."

"We must marry her off," Mother Lenka said, cackling. "Or sell her to town. I think she'd be happier in town anyway."

"Shut your fool old mouth," Eugenius said, pushing Katrina towards the kitchen and taking his place at the table. "Let us give thanks that we have food for the winter and eat. This matter is closed."

▲   ▲   ▲

The snow on the road was getting thicker and there were hidden patches of ice. Mike considered that fact as he looked up the road in the direction the man had pointed. The road, just beyond the farms, led up a narrow defile, twisting back and forth in parallel with a large, ice-choked stream. Fortunately, if he went off the road it probably wouldn't kill him and even in this weather he should be able to walk up to Alerrso or whatever. There was a narrow side road that went up the mountain to the east, but he was pretty sure that went nowhere and, given the conditions, he was in no mood to go exploring.

He engaged the transmission and headed for the first switchback, carefully. Normally, with a slope this steep, the only way to make it would be to get a run-up on the flats. But with the twists he was just going to have to hope the traction control and snow tires could give him some purchase.

The road headed upwards at about a six-degree incline, then bent sharply right. He made the turn, fishtailing only slightly but feeling the traction control reduce the power to the wheels as he slid. The more or less straightaway up to the right was, if anything, steeper than the approach and he pressed the pedal to the floor, feeling the traction control slip in and out as the car labored up the snow-covered road. He wasn't sliding much on that section but there were a couple of times when he thought he was going to come to a complete stop.

At the next switchback he backed and filled carefully, occasionally having to turn the control off to spin out of a hole, then lined up the next run. This time he backed up right to the wall of the switchback and gunned the engine, using the traction control to get some speed up before he hit the slope. This seemed to help but about half the way up the car started to fishtail, hard.

The traction control started to engage but he could feel the car spinning out to the left. On the right side was sheer cut rock and on the other about a fifty-foot drop. Instead of turning into the skid, which probably would have dumped him over the drop as the car went across the road, he increased it, turning the wheel slightly to the left. The maneuver caused a crunching sound as his right quarterpanel hit the rock wall, but the rebound from the "accident" pushed his rear end back onto the road and straightened the vehicle back out without either tossing him over the side or slowing him noticeably. The action was half instinctive but worked perfectly. The damage to the quarterpanel was hardly noticeable on the battered Mercedes.

Somewhat shaken, he made it to the next switchback and considered the next slope. The stream was to his rear, descending through a series of falls to the valley below and, at this point, actually running over the road. The ice of the stream meant he couldn't back up as far and get a run at the next rise but it didn't look as steep as the last two. He got a little speed up and hit the slope, pressing the accelerator down and letting the traction control handle the skids as much as possible.

Not only was that slope easier, it was somewhat shorter, and he quickly reached the top, not even slowing for the turn back to the left. He followed the road around, cautiously, finally reaching the top of the switchbacks.

There the road flattened out in either another upland valley or a pass. He couldn't be sure which since he only had about ten meters of visibility in the increasing storm. But he could vaguely see buildings ahead. Suddenly, with a swirl of wind, the barely glimpsed buildings disappeared. But he knew he'd found the town and drove forward, cautiously, since the road had more or less disappeared. In a few moments he began to see the buildings again and picked his way to the center of them, apparently driving down what passed for a main street.

The buildings vaguely visible to either side had the standard local look; most of them were one to two stories, built of dressed stone and looking as old as the mountains they inhabited. Most had trellis-covered porches to the side, currently covered in snow, and chimneys that belched a mixture of coal and wood smoke. From time to time he got a glimpse of the stream, which followed the line of the wooded hillside to the west. The oldest buildings were on that side of the road and seemed to follow the line of the stream. There were a few larger and more substantial buildings, including one that had a small sign indicating a branch of the Bank of Tbilisi and another that appeared to be some sort of store. A few of the houses had lights in the windows but nothing that looked like either a place to stay or get fuel.

At last he saw what was clearly the local tavern, its windows bright and a few rusted old cars and trucks parked in a small snow-covered lot bordering the stream. The building was two stories tall, dressed stone with a flat roof and apparently very old. By the parking lot, between the building and the stream, he could see a covered area with some tables. It wasn't in use at the moment, but it would be a pleasant place in better seasons.

There didn't appear to be anything along the lines of order in the parking lot so he just picked a spot not too far from the tavern and stopped the Mercedes, breathing deeply and slowly to get his nerves back. After a moment of that he shut the car down, shrugged on a heavy parka, grabbed his jump bag and headed for the tavern.

The door to the tavern was heavy wood and apparently stuck fast. He finally dragged it open and then closed it as fast as he could to shouts from the interior that quickly died. When he'd gotten it dogged back down he looked around the room, nodding to the locals.

There were about fifteen men in the room, most dressed in the rough clothing of laborers. They regarded him silently for a moment, then went back to talking in low tones of obvious surprise. It was apparent that the arrival of a half-frozen American in the middle of the night was soon to be the talk of the town.

The room was square with a serving counter on the left, a door to the rear and two doors on the left leading, presumably, to the kitchens. There were a few small windows on the walls but they were tightly shuttered against the snow. There was a fireplace on the far wall and a potbellied stove in the center. The seats by both were in use so Mike headed to the right side of the room, dumping his jump bag on an open table, then pulling out a rickety chair and sitting down. He was dog weary from the ride, the stress as much as anything, and he could feel it bleeding off. He wasn't sure if this was the sort of place that served you or if he should try to find the host or whatever, but for the moment he was willing to just sit in relative safety.

He looked up, though, as he heard rapid footsteps approaching and nodded at the woman in a dress and apron. She was in her forties, probably, not too bad looking but nothing compared to the people he'd seen in the valley. The phrase "rode hard and put up wet" came to mind; the life of running a tavern in the back country of Georgia probably wasn't conducive to maintaining youth.

"Food?" Mike asked in Russian. "Beer?" The beer in Russia was generally awful, but he'd never picked up the taste for either the local wines or vodka. Georgia wasn't noted for its beers either, but he could always hope.

"Stew," the woman said, nodding. "Or *sava*. Beer, yes. Bread, cheese?"

"Stew," Mike said, nodding. "Beer, bread, cheese. What is *sava*?"

"Is meat," the woman said, shrugging. "Is hit."

Mike wasn't sure what that meant but he nodded agreement.

"*Sava*," he said, his stomach rumbling.

"*Ruskiya*?" the woman asked, looking at him curiously.

"American," Mike said. "Traveling."

"Speak English," the woman replied, smiling broadly. "Little."

"Speak Russian," Mike said, grinning. "Little. No Georgian."

"Nobody speak Georgian," the woman said, smiling still. "Get food, beer."

"Thank you," Mike said. "Am very hungry, very tired."

"Is bed," the woman said, pointing overhead.

"I accept," Mike said, nodding. "Petrol?"

"Is down street," the woman said in English, pointing further into town. "Is close."

"Not tonight," Mike said. "Not with this," he added, waving outside.

The woman chuckled at that and left, headed for the rear. She took the door behind the serving counter so presumably the other door led to "bed."

Mike spent the time while she was getting his meal to check out the group in the room a bit more carefully. Most of the men were dark and burly from work, and appeared to be mostly drinking beer in tankards rather than wine, which was unusual in the area. There were a few plates around but the general intent seemed to be drinking as if there was no tomorrow. They were checking him out as well but they didn't seem unfriendly, just curious. They also were generally quiet, most of the talk in low tones.

The exception was a table at the back where a heavyset man with dark hair was holding forth apparently at the top of his lungs. Mike figured he was one of those guys who just always had to talk as if they were shouting from one mountain to another. The three guys gathered at the table had the look of toadies and nodded at everything the man said. He was a bit better dressed than the rest but didn't exactly look prosperous. Whoever the guy was, he was a pain in the ass. He was loud enough that it made it hard to think and Mike had a lot of thinking to do.

He wasn't sure where he was headed or what he was going to do. Being rich had always sounded great. And in plenty of ways it was better than being poor. But Mike had always had something that he was working towards. He was used to struggling, pushing his limits, excelling. Now he found himself in a situation where to excel, to stand out, was tantamount to a death sentence. Not only for himself but, potentially, for anyone he was involved with. He'd killed senior terrorists, foiled operations and done it outside the "normal" parameters. Generally, despite their effectiveness, special operations personnel weren't major targets except "in-country." Terrorists didn't, generally, track down and attack spec-ops guys, much less their families. But there were half a dozen fatwahs against him, personally, even if they didn't know exactly who he was. He needed something to *do* but at the same time he needed to go to ground. Somewhere that he'd be reasonably secure.

Georgia probably wasn't the place. The Chechens were starting to use eastern Georgia as their personal stomping grounds and the government was half in shambles. Terrorists, drugs, guns and sex slaves moved through the country in a constant stream. He'd be much better off in a place like, say, Kansas. But the only thing in Kansas was wheat. Okay, and spectacular blondes. But he liked wild countries like Georgia. They just had more soul than Peoria. Or New York, which thought it had soul but didn't realize it was butter substitute.

Maybe Nepal. Decent army, retired Gurkhas. Find some place like this and settle down until the terrorists either got reduced or found somebody else to target. If they ever forgot the guy called "Ghost."

The woman came back out bearing a platter covered with mugs and plates. She served the guy at the rear first, handing him and his three cronies mugs, picking up their empties and answering a question directed at her from the man. She answered it loudly enough that most of the people in the tavern could hear it and Mike caught the word "American" among the words.

After that she came over to Mike's table and set down a mug of beer followed by a bowl of stew and a platter with slices of dark brown bread and yellowish cheese.

"What your name?" the woman asked in English, sitting down and picking up a slice of cheese.

"Mike. What's yours?"

"Irina," she answered, considering him curiously. "How you come here?"

"Got lost," Mike said, shrugging and spooning up some of the stew. It was oddly seasoned but delicious. "Very good stew. Was headed for Bakuriana. Must have taken a wrong turn in the snow. Almost out of petrol."

"You lucky," Irina said, shaking her head. "Snow very bad."

"Very bad," Mike admitted, nodding. "Good car. Lucky."

"You stay?" the woman asked.

"Until snow clears," Mike said. "Roads clear."

"Hah!" Irina spat, laughing. "Spring."

"No plows?" Mike asked, surprised.

"Some," the woman said, shrugging. "Maybe couple weeks. Bad snow. More come."

"Crap," Mike said. "I guess I stay."

"Not much do," Irina said, gesturing around the room. "Get drunk. Talk. No talk Georgian."

"Used to being alone," Mike replied, shrugging. "Have books."

"I get *sava*," the woman said, standing up.

"Okay."

Mike ate about half the stew, then picked up the mug of beer, taking a sip. When he did he was pleasantly surprised, pulling it back and looking at it carefully. It was just about the best beer he'd ever had in his life, full and rich without being heavy or bitter. There was just a hint of something other than hops and barley in it but he couldn't quite place it. It was good enough that he took a deep pull and then set it down. Getting drunk his first night in town wouldn't be a good idea.

The *sava* when it was served turned out to be grilled strips of pounded meat, probably mutton, spiced and excellent, something like the meat you got in "gyros" in the States. He recognized some of the same seasoning as the stew. It was one of the better meals he'd had in the last few months.

Mike finished off all the food and the beer and realized he was exhausted. He knew he could keep going for days but it made more sense to get some sleep.

"You said you have a room?" Mike asked when Irina came back filling mugs from a pitcher.

"Upstairs," she repeated. "Small. Is okay."

"I think I'll head up," Mike said. "How much for the food and beer?"

"One ruble for food," the woman said. "Three rubles for room. You get bags?"

The combined sum came to about seventy-five cents. If the room even had a bed it was going to be a very cheap place to stay.

"I get bags," Mike said, pulling out some of the Georgian rubles he'd exchanged for at the border. He handed her five rubles and stood up. "For room and food. And tip. Thank you."

When he'd gotten his duffel, Irina showed him where the bathroom was and then his room. It was small, at the back of the building and both narrow and low, with a small shuttered window. It was also freezing; there wasn't any source of heat in the room and the stone walls radiated cold. The bed looked fairly comfortable with newly washed sheets but he knew it was probably filled with bedbugs. The door had a latch, which would last for about one kick. But one kick was about all he'd need if it came to cases.

After Irina had left he stripped the sheets and blankets off the bed and sprayed the mattress and sheets with bedding spray, covering all the surfaces until they were slightly wet and paying special attention to the seams. He then rolled out the small sleeping bag in his duffel on the mattress. He dumped his duffel on top of the bag and then sprayed the floor thoroughly with insect spray, hoping to get most of the fleas. He'd lived in enough third-world hovels in the service to know the creepy-crawlies you got in places like this. Last he pulled the pillowcase off the pillow, sprayed the pillow thoroughly and covered it with a case he carried. He'd gotten lice one time in Thailand and had a mordant fear of the damned things. Fleas and bedbugs just left you with bites; lice stayed around forever.

All that done he changed into a set of sweats and socks, slid his .45 under the pillow, slipped into the fart sack and drifted off to sleep in a haze of chemical protectants.

CHAPTER TWO

Mike had a hard time orienting himself the next morning. The room was dark and cold and there wasn't much in the way of sounds. There was a faint light coming from the cracks in the shutters, though, and after a moment he could recall the night before. He lay in bed for a moment, dreading the cold, then rolled out of the fart sack.

The stone floor was freezing, even through the wool socks he was wearing, but he ignored it, grabbed his money-belt, pistol and jump bag and headed for the bathroom.

The bathroom was small and intensely European. The shower was on a long hose with nowhere to hang it and all the fixtures looked as if they were from an American home in the 1930s, but he'd gotten used to that. He performed his morning ablutions, careful not to drink the water and washing his mouth out with a small bottle of bourbon after brushing, then headed back to his room. He considered repacking but given the weather report, and the brief glance he'd gotten out the window in the bathroom, he wasn't leaving anytime soon. So he dressed warmly, holstered his pistol, grabbed his jump bag and headed downstairs.

There was a young, good-looking girl—brunette and just starting to bloom—sweeping the tavern when he walked in. She was startled by his appearance, letting out a tiny squeak of surprise, then nodding and darting into the back room. Mike took a seat by the potbellied stove in the empty room and waited in hopes of service.

After a moment a short, slim man came out of the back, wiping his hands on an apron.

"I'm Stasys," the man said in Russian, shaking Mike's hand. "I own place and cook. You like room?"

"Very nice," Mike said, surreptitiously scratching where one of the fleas had gotten him despite his precautions.

"You want food?"

"Please," Mike replied. "Any coffee?" He could smell food and bread being cooked, but not a trace of coffee smell.

"Tea?" Stasys asked. "Bread?"

"Tea, bread and *sava*?" Mike asked. What he really wanted was three eggs, over medium, bacon and hash browns. But only Americans and Brits ate like that for breakfast.

"Yes, I get," Stasys said, going back in the kitchen.

The shutters had been thrown back and Mike could see the storm had passed over. There was still a light snow falling and it looked as if quite a bit had been dumped during the night. He wondered, briefly, about the additional snow Irina had mentioned. The way things were it looked as if he *wouldn't* be able to leave before spring.

As the tea, bread and *sava* were being served by the girl, the door to the room opened and a man in a long wool coat stomped in, kicking the snow off his boots and saying something in Georgian to the girl. He was tall and slender with a slim, intelligent face and wearing a uniform cap. When he pulled off the coat it revealed the uniform of the local constabulary and from the cut and tailoring Mike guessed he was a senior officer.

"Hello," the man said, coming over to Mike's table and sitting down. "You would be the American called Mike. I am Captain Vadim Tyurin, the constabulary commander for the Keldara." The man spoke excellent English with hardly any accent except of Oxford.

"Mike Jenkins," Mike said, shaking his hand. "Care for some tea?"

"Vyera is getting me a cup," Vadim said, smiling. "Coming right to the point, though, I don't suppose I could see some identification?"

Mike smiled back and dug in his pocket, pulling out his entirely false passport for Mike Jenkins. It was only false in that it wasn't his real name; it had been issued by the American government with all due forms.

"Sorry for that," Vadim said, handing it back after a careful study. "It's very unusual for us to get Americans, or any foreigners, in the Keldara. What brings you here?"

"I got lost," Mike said as the girl, presumably Vyera, brought out another cup and saucer and set it in front of the policeman. "I was headed for Bakuriana and I guess I took a wrong turn. I'm not even sure where I'm at."

"You are, in fact, nowhere," Vadim replied, shrugging and pouring tea. "The Keldara is pretty remote even in Georgia. With the exception of the Six Families it's rather sparsely populated. Which means the damned Chechens have the run of it. I'm *supposed* to be up here to disprove their ownership, but with only three subordinates that's rather hard."

"No funds?" Mike asked.

"Apparently not," the policeman said, taking a sip of the tea. "The Chechens run drugs, mostly opium, through the mountains and pick up many of their sex slaves in this area. Then they sell them in various places, use the money to buy guns and run them back through. They even force the locals to give them food and money. If they don't they burn down the farms and kill the farmers, taking the prettier girls for their sex slave rings. I've tried to form local militias, again no funds. It requires more than just giving them guns; if that's all you do the Chechens just 'inherit' them."

"Sounds frustrating," Mike said. "And a tad dangerous for the local police representative."

"Not so much," Vadim said, deprecatingly. "Since it is quite impossible, I simply don't try. Much safer all around."

"And if it was possible?" Mike asked.

"Oh, then I'd be quite interested," the Georgian said, narrowing his eyes. "The most frustrating aspect is the lack of authority and the responsibility. I'd *like* to discharge my responsibilities, but without the funding, it's quite impossible." He regarded Mike carefully and then shrugged again. "The subject has, I'm told, come to the attention of the American government. Russia has threatened to enter this part of Georgia and 'clean it up,' as if they could do any better than they have done in Chechnya. But the possibility of a border war with two countries that are nominal allies has the American government upset, or so I'm told. Which is why I wonder how you came here, really."

"Ah," Mike said, grinning. "I *really* got lost. I'm not a representative of the American government. Truly."

"Very well," Vadim said, sighing. "It was too much to hope, I suppose, that we might actually get some help."

"I'm just traveling," Mike said, shrugging. "Looking for someplace to settle for a while, I guess."

"You are unable to settle in the United States?" Vadim said, warily.

"Oh, I could," Mike said, hastily. "I just like . . . call it the wilder places. But a region that's about to have a border war with Russia might be a bit too wild. I'll probably just stick around until the roads get cleared, then pass on." He paused and frowned. "I met some of the people down in the valley, asking directions. They seem . . ."

"Unusual," Vadim said, nodding. "They're the Keldara, the people the region is named for. Georgia is a collection of many different peoples that have survived for thousands of years, protected by the mountains. Bits and pieces of dozens of cultures that were conquerors or driven out by the people that conquered the plains. There's no such thing as a Georgian, just many odd tribes like the Keldara. Did you see any of the women?"

"Yes," Mike admitted. "Spectacular."

"Very," Vadim said, grinning. "And they make the best beer in the world. You had some last night."

"I'd wondered where that came from," Mike said. "It was incredible."

"Secret recipes of the Keldara women," Vadim said, shrugging.

"How long until the roads clear?" Mike asked, looking out the windows. The sky had cleared, slightly, and the snow had stopped falling.

"A week or more," Vadim said, frowning. "There is another storm predicted for a day or two from now. If it clears for a time after that you might be able to get out. Until then I'm afraid you're stuck. Unless you can call in a helicopter."

"I could *afford* a helicopter," Mike said, looking back at the cop. "I'm not exactly without funds. But I'm not someone who can, for example, call Washington and get a helicopter sent in." Okay, a little white lie. He probably could do exactly that if there was a reason. "So what is there to do in Alerrso besides watch the snow fall?"

"Very little," Vadim said with a sigh. "There is a small brothel down the street and if you need money the bank can get it wired in. They are the only ones that have an internet connection, alas. They use a satellite, you understand? The phone lines and electric are spotty otherwise. There is no library. I have some books you could read but they are in Georgian and Russian mostly. A few military books in English that you might like. I don't know if you're a student of history or not."

"I *was* a student of history," Mike said. "I dropped out of university to form a company. The company was successful, especially after the war started. I sold out and now I travel."

"You have the military look," Vadim noted, dryly. "A soldier, yes?"

"Bite your tongue," Mike said, grinning. "I was a SEAL. But that was a long time ago. These days I'm a retired widget maker."

"You're young to retire," the cop pointed out. "And what is a 'widget'?"

"It's not anything, really," Mike said. "Well, there is something *called* a widget, a kind of box cutter. But it's really a term for any unspecified device. I made a communications widget for the military, for special operations units. I had the idea for it and got some guys who were smarter than me to design it. Then we got some capital and started a company making them. It was very small until the war, then there was big demand for them. There was a buyout offer from a major defense firm I couldn't resist. So now I'm retired. I used to do contracting work for the government on the same sorts of things. But I got tired of that. Sometimes I think the main reason I travel is so my former clients can't call me back."

"Or so you won't be recalled to the SEALs?" Vadim asked, raising an eyebrow.

"No chance of that," Mike said, darkly. "They don't want me back and I don't want to go back." He noted the look and shrugged. "I was an instructor for a long time. When I tried to go back to the teams there were problems. I got kicked off my team. After that I got out."

"And went into making widgets," Vadim said. "The money was better, yes?"

"Yes," Mike said, looking out the window, his face working. "But there are times I'd rather be back on the teams."

"Well, for now you are here," Vadim said. "Would you care to take a look around my town?"

"Your town?" Mike said, dropping a ruble on the table. "And I don't want to take up your time."

"There is no what you would call mayor," the cop said, shrugging again. "I am the police and also the administrative head.

So, yes, my town. As to taking up my time, there is not much to do in winter. Few move through the mountains during this season and when the Chechens aren't making problems we are a very quiet area."

Mike got his coat and followed the cop out of the tavern, getting his first clear look at Alerrso. The first thing he noticed was that the snowfall the night before was even heavier than he'd thought; the Mercedes was covered in a couple of feet of snow and the road was thoroughly packed.

The town didn't have more than a dozen or so buildings in it, all clustered in a small valley. The mountainsides were cloaked with heavy timber; most of it looked like oak and maple.

There was a solid ridgeline to the west rising to at least five thousand feet above his current elevation, but to the east the hills leveled off not much higher than the valley and he could see clearly along the slope of the western mountains. Right at the head of the valley, by the switchbacks he'd ascended, was an old fort of some sort occupying a ridge of land that jutted out from the mountains. It had a low curtain wall and a large building in the middle that looked halfway between a castle and a house. The area inside the curtain wall was extensive, which argued for gardens or something out of sight.

"The old caravanserai," Vadim said, noting his examination. "Nobody is sure when it was first built. This used to be a branch of the Silk Road so it dates back at least that far."

"The Silk Road was in use in the Roman times," Mike pointed out.

"Oh, it's not that old," Vadim said. "Probably to the time of the Mongols or the Ottomans."

"Is it occupied?" Mike asked, examining the sandstone walls. They looked in decent repair. Certainly there were no breaches.

"Not right now," Vadim said, sighing. "It's a long story and it's cold. Shall we walk?"

Mike nodded and they headed up the street, walking down the center of the road, which had been sketchily plowed.

"Georgian history is thousands of years old," Vadim continued. "This was the kingdom of Medea and, like Jason, one group after another has come here for riches or because we are a crossroads. The Greeks, the Byzantines, the Arabs, the Turks, the Mongols, the Russians, they've all invaded us and left their mark. In the bone the 'true' Georgian is a Medean, but we've so many little remnants, deciding who is 'true' Georgian is a full-time job.

"Of course the tsars conquered Georgia back in 1801," Vadim said. "It was more or less to keep us from being invaded by the Turks, again, but they took over against the treaty of friendship we had at the time. When they did, the tsar installed a local lord, a Cossack, and he took over the caravanserai for his home. At that time there was still some trade through here and he collected tolls for the tsars. That had been the pattern of the caravanserai as long as anyone could remember; that a foreigner from some distant king was installed in the caravanserai to control the area. There's even a name for the position: the Kildar. Then the Soviets took over and tried to make all their changes and installed a commissar in it to keep order. He had a small group of soldiers to enforce Soviet law but, really, it had little impact. During Stalin's time Georgia was much ignored and the various purges and pogroms mostly missed this little area. Then, with independence, there was the question of what to do with it. Eventually, it was sold to the Bank of Tbilisi along with a number of other parcels as part of 'privatization.' I actually lived there, briefly, when it was held by the government, then moved out when it was privatized."

"So the bank owns it," Mike said. "And nobody lives there?"

"The bank manager has a house in town," Vadim said, shrugging. "The caravanserai is a sort of mausoleum to conquest. And here we have the bank," he continued, pointing to a building which was heavily constructed of dressed stone. "Another very old building in a town of very old buildings. The original construction predates the Ottomans and may have been an inn of some sort."

Mike examined the building for a moment, frowning. The lintels of the heavy doors were marble supported by pillars that had once been carved. The stone was also excellently dressed. The building had not been hastily constructed and reminded him of Roman constructions he'd seen. But the Romans had never extended their reach to Georgia.

"And here we have the town square," Vadim continued, walking on. "On one corner we have the bank, across from it my small police station. On the other corner is our local brothel and on the last the local hardware, general sundries and apothecary. Down the street is the mill, which I won't inflict upon you. And, of course, there is a small church. Everything one small town needs," he added, humorously.

"How's the brothel?" Mike asked, examining the building. It was obvious Soviet construction as was the police station; simple buildings of poorly made concrete without any decoration.

"Being married, I, of course, only enter to ensure order," Vadim said, evenly but with a faint ironic smile. "The girls range from quite pretty to in one case very beautiful. Also quite young, which is generally unusual in such a small town. They are, however, somewhat infested by lice. A point my wife made rather sharply the one time I picked some up. From a hoodlum we'd arrested in there, of course. Certainly not from the young ladies. However, that is *why* I only enter to ensure order."

"Pass," Mike said. "Hate lice."

"Not as much as my wife," Vadim said with a sigh. "You'd have thought I brought home the pox from the way she went on."

"Is there anyone that rents rooms?" Mike asked, looking around. "Besides the tavern. The one they have me in is rather—"

"Small, musty and dark," Vadim said. "Not to mention infested by fleas, lice and bedbugs. I've had to arrest a few people who were using it and we usually use . . . what would you say, class four hazmat, yes?"

"Yes," Mike said, chuckling. "Seriously, are there any rooms?"

"I doubt it," Vadim said, sighing. "There has been no demand for such."

"What about renting the caravanserai?" Mike asked, turning

to look back at the small fort. The clouds had broken slightly and in the light the red sandstone gleamed. He wasn't even sure where the stone had come from; most of the stone in the area was granite.

"You could ask the bank manager," Vadim said, shrugging and walking to the bank. "But I find it unlikely that he will be allowed. With independence certain old laws were put back in place, one of which attends upon the caravanserai. I'm not sure it could be rented. And it would be very expensive."

"Old laws?" Mike asked as the policeman pulled open the door to the bank. The front stoop had been shoveled off but the door still caught.

"We'll speak to Mr. Mironov," Vadim said, waving him in.

Mr. Mironov turned out to be a small, spare man who occupied a large office at the rear of the building. The desk had the look of dating back to the Soviet era but there was a Georgian flag on one wall and a portrait of the current president behind the desk. The desk was mostly clear with the exception of a framed portrait. Its back was to Mike but he assumed it was of Mrs. Mironov.

"It is a pleasure to meet you, Mr. Jenkins," Mr. Mironov said as tea accompanied by small slices of brown bread was being served.

"Mr. Jenkins is interested in renting the caravanserai," Vadim said, taking a sip of tea and nodding at the young woman who had served it.

"Ah," Mironov said, sighing. "Renting is quite impossible, I'm afraid. The caravanserai is rather specifically entailed as they say in English. It cannot be rented and can only be sold with the entailed lands."

"Bit more than I'm interested in," Mike said, frowning. "I'm really just looking for somewhere to hang out until the snow clears. It looked interesting."

"It is quite interesting," Mironov agreed. "Some of the construction is clearly Ottoman, but the foundations are much older. The sandstone comes from a quarry in the valley that has been mined from time immemorial. It's the sort of place I'd like to show to an archaeologist or historian, just to get some idea of when it was originally built."

"Well, I was a history major, but I'm hardly a historian," Mike said, frowning sourly. "And the history program I was in wasn't very good in my opinion. One of the reasons I left."

"I would be interested in your opinion of the caravanserai, nonetheless," Mr. Mironov said, pulling out a ring of keys. "If Captain Tyurin thinks he can get up to it in his Range Rover."

"Possibly," Vadim said, taking the keys. "I'd certainly like to show it to Mr. Jenkins."

"Do you have a way to access accounts outside the Bank of Tbilisi?" Mike asked. "Specifically, if I wanted to get a draft on the Zurich Mercantile?"

"It could be arranged," Mr. Mironov said, raising one eyebrow. Mike had just as much as admitted to having a numbered account, which spoke of someone unusual.

"Zurich Mercantile is just easier to use overseas than an American bank," Mike said, shrugging at the looks. "Most of my funds are in Citicorp but I keep some of them in Zurich for walking around money. And some in American Express, for that matter. They manage most of my overseas investments."

"We have access to both," Mr. Mironov said, subtly changing his attitude to the American visitor. "And, of course, if you stayed for any time we'd be happy to open an account with the Bank of Tbilisi."

"I doubt I'll be staying that long," Mike said. "But thank you."

He and Vadim walked over to the police station and got in the latter's Range Rover.

"You think you can get down to the valley?" Mike asked.

"The road down should be plowed and sanded by now," Vadim said. "The Keldara do it. With horse-drawn plows, I might add."

"Must be a bitch getting up that hill with horses," Mike said, shaking his head. "Don't they have regular plows or tractors?"

"They have one tractor," Vadim said, pulling out of the station parking lot cautiously. The Range Rover had snow-chains but the road was still icy in spots. "It dates from Stalin's time. For everything else they have horses and oxen."

"Jesus," Mike said. "It really is poor up here, isn't it?"

"Very," Vadim said, sourly, as he approached the switchbacks. "Let us hope for good fortune in this endeavor."

The road, however, had been thoroughly plowed and sanded, and the Rover made it down to the valley easily. Mike noted that not only had that road been plowed but so had the road up to the caravanserai, which was another series of switchbacks.

"The Keldara do all of this?" Mike asked, surprised. A few of the valley's inhabitants were out in the snow, mostly gathering wood except for a group of children engaged in a snowball fight.

"They are responsible for the road in the valley and up the hills," Vadim replied as he turned onto the road up to the caravanserai. "And, of course, to the fort. It's a duty they've held for generations and they take it seriously. They take all their duties seriously. Fortunately, the commissars that held the area during the Soviet period were lenient; the Keldara can be very prickly about their rights and duties. And the way they maintain their farms fit well with the Soviet collective model. Even if the Keldara considered it just another form of fiefdom."

CHAPTER THREE

There was a small open area at the top of the slope and Vadim got out to open the gates. Mike got out as well to take a look around. From the spot it was possible to look across the entire valley and Mike realized it was much larger than he'd thought the night before, at least five miles long and a couple of miles across. There were four smaller valleys running into it, including the one that held Alerrso. Their streams, which were lined by trees in most places, joined in the basin and then drained down the road he'd approached on. The valley was mostly flat with a few small hills towards the northeast end with the road approaching from the northwest and running along a slightly elevated track on the west side. The homes of the Keldara were clustered on the south side near the town and directly across from the caravanserai.

Besides the villagers, who looked like ants from his elevated position, there were cattle and horses that had been turned out to look for browse. There were clearly distinguishable fields as well, most of them separated by stone fences. Mike guessed that the soil of the valley would be rather stony but it might be rich;

the rivers running down to it would bring a heavy load of soil with each spring flood. He could tell where the flood plains were and he realized that the Keldara homes were drawn well up above them.

He saw a flash of red hair on one of the playing children but even with the small binoculars from his jump bag he couldn't tell if it was the spectacular redhead he'd picked up. He used the binoculars to examine the area more carefully, especially the Keldara homes.

There seemed to be six distinct groups with about three houses and a barn or two to each. The barns were joined to the houses by low stone walls and there were a few covered walkways. The area around each of the houses had been plowed and shoveled carefully but it was the layout of the houses that bothered him. After a moment he realized what he was looking at; each of the separate groups had interlocking fields of fire between the houses.

Most of the houses were built into the side of the hill and from them the Keldara could lay down a withering fire on any enemy approaching from the valley. The thick stone walls and small windows made each house into a sort of bunker. They'd be vulnerable to artillery or mortar fire, or an attack from the south. But looking at that steep hillside and thinking about getting to it, Mike could understand why it would be ignored as a threat.

For that matter, there was a small drop-off between the houses and the valley that was hard to recognize at this angle. It might be natural but it had the look of something that had been built. Put a palisade on it and any attacker would be hard pressed to get to the houses from the valley at all. There were three breaks in the bluff, which he was sure was manmade, one running to the road, but dipping down to the valley first, and the other two to the fields. There might be a fourth, it was hard to tell from his angle, running east towards the southeast valley. The one that went to the road had a large stone fence running parallel to it that conceivably could have been a defensive wall at one point. Up above all of the houses, with a narrow track that might once have been a road, was an open bench that had rocks stacked on it that looked like old foundations.

"Seen enough?" Vadim asked from behind him.

Mike had heard him crunching through the snow so he wasn't startled.

"Pretty valley," was all he said.

"There used to be tigers in the mountains," Vadim replied, clearly disappointed that he hadn't surprised the former SEAL. "Or so it is said. The Keldara were called the Tigers of the Valley back then and it was the job of one of the Keldara to go out each year and kill a tiger. You can still see some of the skins around in the homes."

"Interesting layout," he said, putting the binoculars away. "Are the Keldara armed?"

"They have a few old guns," the policeman said. "About five if I remember correctly. None automatic. Bolt action rifles from the Great Patriotic War that a few of the men were allowed to bring home. They do some hunting with them. Why?"

"You said the Chechens sometimes attack farms," Mike said, turning to walk through the gate and putting his binoculars back in the jump bag. "I was wondering if they'd ever been attacked."

"Once," Vadim admitted. "But the Chechens had driven off by the time we got there. They lost a cow and one girl that the damned Islamics carried off."

"Driven away or been driven off?" Mike asked as they walked up to the caravanserai. There was a broad, flagged, courtyard beyond the gates with a fountain in the middle and gardens to either side. The main door had steps running up to it and a covered portico that was only lightly dusted with snow. On the north side the curtain wall ran close to the house with what appeared to be a graveled drive running between the two. Beyond the garden on the south side was a large yard that was heavily overgrown with weeds and even small trees. There was also a high wall on that side that extended out towards the yard; he couldn't see what was beyond it.

The ground floor of the house was about six thousand square feet or more from what Mike could see and while there were windows they were mostly small and deeply set. Too small for a person to climb in or out. The ground floor would be dark as hell. The second and third floors, however, had numerous windows, although most of the ones on the south side had decorative bars over them. On the sides the smaller second story gave on to a balcony, while in the center a domelike structure rose from the lower floor. The dome had numerous small openings on the side so there would probably be good light under it.

"Half and half," Vadim answered, negotiating the lock on the front door. The door was about ten feet high and made of heavy wood. "The Keldara said that they'd killed at least one of the attackers but there was no body. They'd pulled into their houses as soon as the Chechens were sighted driving down the road. The girl had apparently been out picking berries and couldn't make it back to the houses in time. The Chechens drove in, took fire from the houses, grabbed the girl and a cow and drove off."

Mike thought about driving into that open area in front of the houses and what even five rifles, well handled, could do and nodded.

The main door led to a hallway with another heavy door at the end. The floor was tiled in what looked like marble, some of it cracked and all of it worn. Mike noted that the walls were still stone and that there were a few windows with shutters on them that could look into the rooms beyond. The word "murder-holes" came to mind; the long, dark antechamber was intended for defense of the house from an attacker. There were coat hooks by the far door, which Mike and Vadim ignored; the house was as cold as the outside if not colder.

The foyer beyond was, in fact, well lit. It was high ceilinged and between large windows on the west side and lightwells on the east the room could be clearly examined. It was about nine hundred square feet with the ceiling held up by flying buttresses. The floor was more marble while the walls were dark wood paneling.

Directly across from the door was a huge fireplace with a setting around it including a few chairs and an antique sofa.

"There is a large dining room that way," Vadim said, pointing north through an arched opening, "and a massive kitchen adjoining it. My wife hated that kitchen but there's a smaller one on the second floor. There are two layers of cellars. Maybe more; that's as far as I got. There's a bunch of rubbish left down there from when the Soviets had it. There are two small bathrooms in the living areas down here and a few rooms for general use, but take a look at this."

Vadim led him to a door on the south side, then down a short corridor to another heavyset door with a locking bar on the house side. Beyond that was a long corridor with doors on either side that led to an open area that was more or less circular. There was a stairway spiraling up on the west side and a balcony circling the room with more doors off of it. On the south side of the room was a heavy door with metal filigree on it and barred windows following the line of the balcony. The floor was marble, in much better condition than in the foyer, and the walls were tiled in mosaics. Many of the tiles had fallen off but they appeared to depict pastoral scenes of woodlands and fields with wild animals and cattle browsing placidly. In the center of the room was a fountain but there was no visible furniture.

"Harem?" Mike asked after a moment.

"You figured it out," Vadim said, nodding. "It was the Ottoman harem quarters. The commissar used it for barracks."

"Silly commissar," Mike said, looking around. "Does the fountain work?"

"No, more's the pity," Vadim said. "The door leads to a walled garden. Very nice. Even has fruit trees. Needs to be cleaned up, though."

"I'm looking at it, not buying it," Mike said, turning back to the main house.

The second floor had the best bedrooms, fourteen in total, and four bathrooms, including the one off the master suite. The master suite was on the south side and had glass doors that led to a balcony. From the balcony Mike could look down into the garden of the harem and out across the valley. It was covered and fairly deep so there was only a light dusting of snow.

There was furniture in some of the rooms, but with the exception of the master suite it could better be described as "ruined" rather than "antique." And the few bits which were in good condition, including in the master suite, were Soviet era. From experience, Mike knew the beds and chairs would be uncomfortable as hell.

"Bit much for even a casual stay," Mike noted as they walked back down to the foyer.

"There are more bedrooms for servants on the third floor," Vadim said, shrugging. "And an attic that's packed with rubbish. The cellars are as well, as I mentioned. But it's awfully interesting, don't you think?"

"Very," Mike admitted. "You can tell it was renovated by the tsars at least. But the foundations aren't Russian or Ottoman. I don't know why I can tell that but they're not."

"No," Vadim said. "I think the building was originally more of a fort. Look closely at the windows on the ground floor; I think they were chiseled out at some point. Probably the upper stories were rebuilt or renovated by the Ottomans to make it more of a house."

"This foyer isn't Ottoman," Mike said, looking at the flying buttresses. There were six of them, made of sandstone that had been later reinforced in patches with concrete. But the base sandstone in places still had a trace of carvings. They had been very deep but time had worn them away, especially at levels where hands could touch. The best description he could come up with was "lace." They definitely weren't grape-vines although there were some bits of that in there. In a few places it was clear that something had been chiseled out and roughly sanded over. From the shape it might have been crosses.

Mike took a bit more of a look around, finding a large room in the south wing that was on the opposite corner from the harem. It had high windows that let in a fair bit of light and had once had fixtures on the walls.

"Library," Mike said, shaking his head. "Even the bookshelves were removed. I wonder why?"

"The Soviets probably didn't like the books," Vadim said, shrugging. "They might have cut up the bookshelves for firewood for that matter. And used the books for kindling."

Mike suddenly had a vision of the room filled back up with books. SEALs were generally thought of as slope-browed adrenaline junkies, but he'd found them to be well above the norm in intelligence. And he, personally, liked books. But he also could see using it for a workout room. He missed workouts; he hadn't been able to do any regular ones since leaving the states.

The place was way, way, *way* more than he'd ever need. He had no family and, given his security situation, no interest in starting one. And this was the home of a feudal lord, not a former SEAL. It was designed to hold dozens of servants and hangers on, not to mention guards.

On the other hand . . . it would be a damned good place to go to ground. Nobody would be looking for the guy named "Ghost" in this remote spot. And the place was *designed* for defense. The long yard on the south side would make an adequate pistol and short-distance rifle range. There was plenty of room for workout equipment. Weapons would be easy enough to obtain, legally or illegally, and if Vadim wasn't willing to be on the take he was a monkey's uncle. He'd turn a blind eye to anything short of a tank that Mike "obtained" and he might not even blink at a tank.

"How much . . ." Mike said, then paused and shrugged. "How much do you think the bank wants for this place?"

"A *million* dollars?" Mike said, his eyes wide. It was far less than he'd expect to pay in the states or western Europe, but in Georgia that was beyond a fortune. And the location was unusual to be asking that much money for a half-ruined fort.

"The caravanserai is entailed with the farms in the valley," Mr. Mironov said, shrugging. "It cannot be sold without including those farms."

"What about the farmers?" Mike asked. "The Keldara."

"They are tenants," Mironov replied, shrugging again. "They pay rent in a portion of the crops to the owner of the caravanserai. One of the reasons I'd like to get it off my books is that they're not very good farmers; the farms are not very productive at least."

"With nothing but horse-drawn plows what do you expect?" Mike asked disparagingly.

"I tried to get permission to purchase better equipment," Mironov said, defensively. "But the bank owners considered it just pouring good money after bad."

"Well, I don't want to be the lord to a bunch of sharecroppers," Mike said, shaking his head. "I don't know anything about running farms."

"There is an overseer," Mironov pointed out.

"I believe you met him at the tavern," Vadim said dryly. "Otar Tarasova. Large loud fellow. Hard to miss."

"I can imagine how well the Keldara work for him," Mike said, looking at Mironov. "I'm really not interested in becoming a gentleman farmer."

"It is a pity," Mironov said, sadly. "Frankly, the million is simply to clear the debts on the farm. We bought it as a lot with a number of other properties from the government and haven't been able to unload it. Among other things, the way that it's entailed it *cannot* be broken up. Buy the caravanserai and you get the valley. But nobody wants both."

"Hold on," Mike said. "The *whole* valley? For a million dollars?"

"Euros," Mironov pointed out. "But, yes. The whole valley."

Mike leaned back in his chair and steepled his fingers for a moment, tapping the balls and thinking. A million dollars was a lot of money to most people, but he had thirty mil, close enough, just sitting around. Okay, euros, say a million and a half. Most of it was invested here and there but the investments had been going well. In fact, he probably could close out everything and walk away with more than thirty mil. And it was a *bunch* of land.

But that led to the question of the Keldara. If he bought the land he'd feel a very real sense of responsibility about a bunch of red-neck farmers. But, then again, there was that one farmer's daughter. . . .

"Heh," he said after a moment, grinning faintly.

"What?" Vadim asked, curiously.

"In the U.S. military, one of the euphemisms for dying is 'bought the farm,'" Mike said, thinking. "I just used the phrase in my mind and realized what I'd thought. How big is that thing, anyway?"

"About thirty square kilometers," Mironov said. "Including the mountainsides which are useless except for the wood on them. Excellent woodstands; you could make money simply by lumbering them off."

"Last thing I'd do," Mike said distantly. "Although, there are a few spots that would make dandy ski runs."

"I think we're a little remote for a ski resort," Vadim said, watching him.

"I wasn't thinking about tourists, I was thinking about me," Mike said. "Just *how* stuck in their ways are the Keldara?"

"They can be *very* stuck in their ways," Vadim admitted. "But . . . I did mention that the caravanserai is generally owned by foreigners. The Keldara consider the current owner as their lord. Not one like Mr. Mironov, when he's working for the bank, but they even called the commissar the Kildar. They . . . tend to be more understanding about changes from the Kildar. He's just another in a string from their perspective. And, of course, you can toss them out on their ear if they anger you or don't do what you want them to. You even own the houses."

"Crap," Mike said, thinking about what he'd seen in those houses. "Those places are hovels."

"They're no worse, and in fact much better, than most homes in the mountains," Mr. Mironov pointed out. "And you have to be careful about changes; the Keldara are very prickly about debt. I suggested putting in gas heat and stoves and they asked how they were supposed to pay for it. They realized that it would mean being in debt to the bank and they flatly refused. The same thing happened with suggesting that they take loans to buy tractors. They have the right to cut wood in the mountains and some of their animals are their own, for which they have pasturage rights. They live within those constraints very carefully."

"Okay, so let me get this straight," Mike said. "You want a million euros for a valley with Neolithic, okay, medieval-style farms, a run-down castle and pig-headed farmers."

"There is a reason we haven't been able to move it, yes," Mr. Mironov said with a sigh.

"And let's not forget the security situation," Mike added, grimacing. "Vadim, any idea how well those guys can fight? Could *they* be a militia?"

"The Keldara rarely leave the valley," Vadim said, shrugging. "And they were specifically exempt from draft during the Soviet era; one of Stalin's odder legacies and one that was never explained. So there's no recent record to tell what they're like. However, during the Great Patriotic War many of them fought in the Red Army and acquitted themselves well. At least, so I've heard. There were quite a few Heroes metals sent home, posthumously, and a few that made it back with them. For what it's worth, the other groups in the mountains say they're the best fighters around. I don't know, personally."

"Say that again?" Mike said, shaking his head. "*Stalin* exempted them from draft?"

"Yes," Mr. Mironov said. "No one knows why. He wasn't even from around here."

"Okay," Mike said, blowing out. "Let me take another look around. I'm not too sure about this. Buying a farm wasn't on my to-do list this week."

He left Vadim with the banker and went out to get his Mercedes unburied. It took about fifteen minutes but he finally managed to get it out of the snowed-over parking lot and through the drifts thrown up by the snowplow.

He made his way back down the defile to the valley and drove along the road, looking out at the snow-covered fields. As he did he thought of the work that had been done to the road; it was an amazing undertaking if all they used was the draft horses he could see in the fields. And they were cleared before he and Vadim had driven down. Admittedly, he hadn't been up at dawn, but it was still impressive.

He stopped the car at the far end of the valley and turned around, driving back towards town slowly. As he reached the turn for the caravanserai he followed his impulse and went back up. He drove into the courtyard and looked around, for what he couldn't tell. There was something about the architecture of the lower floor that was bugging him. The blocks of stone were uniform, about a half meter long and a quarter meter high. Many of them had carvings, especially along the base. Near the stairs there was one that had what might have once been Roman numerals. He realized that what he really needed was some tracing paper and a carbon stick.

He walked into the caravanserai and through the foyer, examining the large formal dining hall and the massive, extremely messy, kitchen that supported it. He took a stroll through the harem quarters, just for the frisson. It would be easy enough to fill the quarters with girls from Eastern Europe. Not that he would; he'd come too close to his demons once. But it still had a bit of a tingle. The rooms had Soviet era military beds in them and Russian graffiti. Easy enough to fix. At least if he had a lot of visitors, he'd have somewhere to put them.

He realized he was thinking in terms of ownership and grimaced. Buy the farm. *Yeah, I bought the farm.* It just had the wrong ring to it. Like speaking from beyond the grave.

The house was wired for electric, which was something. The service this far out from major areas was probably spotty. Get that fixed with some big generators. Hell, there were three or four streams that would do for decent hydroelectric, which could be fed to the Keldara . . . And that lovely, lovely girl would finally have electricity. Maybe even running water.

He walked out of the house, whistling.

"I'll take it," Mike said after he'd been ushered into Mr. Mironov's office and the secretary had left. "I'd like some help and a few conditions, however."

"What conditions?" Mironov asked. "And how will you be arranging payment?"

"There's more than enough in Zurich Mercantile," Mike said, sliding over a slip of paper with his account number on it and a release code. "Go ahead and arrange a transfer of three million euros. One will go to pay for the farm, the other two into an operating account. I'll probably need more in time, but that will do for starters."

"Very well," Mironov said, looking at the number as if it were fairy gold.

"I have some arrangements to make, separate from the sale," Mike continued. "So until the final papers are signed, I'd like to keep my interest quiet. Will that be a problem?"

"Not in the bank," Mironov promised. "I'll have the papers drawn up this afternoon by Mrs. Chizhova; she's very discreet. When the transfers come through, the place will be yours."

"Until I'm ready, I'd like the sale to remain quiet," Mike noted. "I suppose I need to go talk to Captain Tyurin."

CHAPTER
FOUR

He eventually found the captain in the tavern, playing a game of cards with a few of the regulars. Tarasova and his cronies were already ensconced by the fire and well into their beer. Mike ignored them as he made his way to the captain.

"Give me a moment of your time, Captain?" Mike asked as the round drew to a close.

"Of course, Mr. Jenkins," Vadim said. "I was losing anyway."

"I'm shocked, shocked to find gambling in this establishment," Mike said, chuckling.

"You enjoy *Casablanca* as well?" Tyurin said, following him over to a table in the corner.

"I was wondering if you'd modeled yourself on Claude Rains' character," Mike admitted.

"A bit," Tyurin said with a sigh. "The price of being a powerless officer of the law is flouting the law. Even Inspector Renault had more forces than I."

"Well, good news," Mike said. "You've a new source of income."

"You're going to buy the farm, as you put it?" Vadim said, smiling sardonically.

"I am that," Mike replied. "But there are several things I'll need. Some of them are legal, normal and proper. Some of them *may* be legal and some I suspect are illegal."

"Let us start with the legal ones, shall we?" Vadim said, smiling again.

"I need a new overseer," Mike said, quietly. "One who knows the Keldara and who knows farming. Preferably modern farming. And not a loud-mouthed dirtball. I can tell I won't get along with Otar."

"Genadi Mahona," Vadim said, just as quietly. "He is actually one of the Keldara. He took his degree in agronomy at the University of Tbilisi then returned. He tried to get Otar to change some of his practices and got forced out of the homes. He works in the mill as a laborer at the moment."

"Figures," Mike said, sighing. "Okay, I am not an agent of the United States but I *am* a former SEAL. And a SEAL instructor moreover. I'm not going to just sit here and let the Chechens have anything they want. Besides working on the farms, I'm going to *try* to turn the Keldara into militia. For that I'll need arms."

"The problem is one of funding," Vadim said, shrugging. "I can register them as a legal local militia. But finding the funding for weapons is another thing."

"Funds are available," Mike said, dryly. "But what about obtaining them? How do we get them here?"

"You're serious?" Vadim said to a nod, "If you are, it is simple enough. I put in the order through the Georgian government for whatever you wish. You pay the supplier and it is shipped to us."

"Not through a central armory, right?" Mike asked. "I'd like to get everything I pay for."

"No, straight to us," Vadim replied.

"Anything?" Mike asked. "RPGs? Mortars?"

"They are a bit more sticky about heavy weapons," Vadim admitted, frowning. "Are you forming a militia or an army?"

"Say a well-armed militia," Mike said, grinning. "What about nonfirearm material? Electronics, uniforms, that sort of thing?"

"That will be less of a problem," Vadim said. "There is a very large surcharge on imports, but equipment for a militia is exempt. There is paperwork; I know how to file it."

"And what about farming equipment?" Mike asked.

"Again, it is exempt from import duties," the cop said, frowning. "How much are you planning on spending?"

"A lot," Mike admitted. "It's worth it to have a functioning farm and a functioning militia. With the sort of technology they're using, most of the men are tied to the farm. If I can bring in some equipment to free them up for training, especially serious training, it will be worth it. Speaking of which, can I bring in trainers? I don't want to do it all myself."

"That can be arranged, as long as they are not here to engage in combat," Vadim pointed out. "That would make them mercenaries."

"What about if *I* get stuck in a combat situation?" Mike asked.

"I think the American military puts it well," Vadim replied, smiling. "Don't ask, don't tell."

"And on that subject I believe we need to come to some accommodation?" Mike asked.

"A reasonable one," Vadim admitted. "A few hundred euros extra a month would be nice. But, frankly, just having the area somewhat secure would be wonderful. Anything they can do beyond that would be tremendous."

"You can't just secure a position like that," Mike said, shaking his head. "You have to know what is going on in a bubble around you. Which means intensive patrolling. I think that some of the changes I'm going to make will shake the Keldara to their core. But they'll be good changes. Where can I find this Genadi character?"

"Finding him will not be so hard," Vadim said. "He works at the mill and lives in a building at the edge of town with about a dozen other workers. Meeting with him without everyone in town hearing about it will be harder."

"Can you or one of your men, one that doesn't talk, pick him up and meet me outside of town?" Mike asked. "I'd say at the caravanserai but that would be a bit obvious."

"There's an old patrol house up the road at the pass," Vadim said, pointing south. "Around eight PM?"

"Works for me," Mike replied. "Thanks for the help."

"I don't care for Otar either," Vadim admitted.

Mike had a fire going in the stove by the time a battered police car pulled up. The drive up to the post had been much harder than down to the valley; he wondered that the old battered Trebia had made it at all. A man got out and looked around, then walked through the door of the small patrol post as the car pulled away. He was in his twenties, wearing old and soiled clothes and the weathered look of a farmer. But his light skin, blue eyes and bright red hair betrayed him as a Keldara.

"Siddown," Mike said in Russian, gesturing to a folding chair he'd brought from town. He'd been reheating tea on the stove and poured a cup. "My name's Mike Jenkins."

"Everyone in town has heard of you," the man said in passable English. "You got lost and Katrina saved you."

"Is that how it's told?" Mike said, smiling. "I didn't even know her name. And I think it was a matter of mutual help. I think she would have died in the storm."

"So do I," Genadi said, looking at him over the rim of the cup. "But you nearly got her in a lot of trouble."

"Why?" Mike asked.

"She was alone with a man," Genadi said, shrugging and setting down the cup. "She was nearly sent to town over it. That is what they call selling girls into slavery."

"Is she going to be sent to town?" Mike asked.

"Not over that," Genadi said, sighing. "Not yet, anyway. Do you understand why women are sent to town?"

"Because they get caught with men that they're not married to?" Mike asked, frowning.

"That is a direct cause," Genadi said, his brow furrowing. "But . . . I took an economics class in university and we talked about this. Women in low-tech agrarian societies, and that means all of the Georgian mountains and most of Russia, have very little economic worth. You know this?"

"I suppose," Mike said, interested. He'd sampled the fruits of the economic situation, but never really gotten into why so many women from Eastern Europe, of their own accord or not, ended up in the sex trade.

"They cannot do as much as men on a farm," Genadi said, shrugging. "So they don't bring in as much money. But they cost nearly as much in food and shelter costs as men. So they are . . . if there are too many women, they are excess to needs, yes?"

"If you say so," Mike replied.

"There are none of the usual jobs that women can do just as well as men," Genadi said. "And even where there are, men are preferred. So women have little worth both in the agrarian and industrial areas. But the Chechens that come here, they will pay what is very good money for the women. As much as a half a year's pay for a man. This is money that the farms need. So they sell their daughters. It is an old custom and so normal that no one in the mountains really thinks there is anything wrong with it."

"I do," Mike said. "I hope like hell they haven't sold Katrina or there's going to be words at the very least."

"She has not been sent to town," Genadi said, definitely. "I talked to her brother only yesterday. But I think she probably will be sooner or later. And maybe it would be for the best. Katrina is one of those that doesn't do well in the Families."

"Like you?" Mike asked.

"Oh, I did well enough," Genadi said, shrugging. "Until I told that bastard Otar that running wheat three years in a row on the same field was idiotic. I think I shouldn't have used that word."

"It's true, though," Mike said, frowning. "Even *I* know that."

"The valley is large but only specific fields are well suited to wheat," Genadi said, furrowing his brow. "He was being pushed for more income, and wheat is an income generator. But so is soy, especially now that there's a mill in Tbilisi. The transport cost eats up a bit, but not much. But he didn't want to listen. Wheat is what he knows, that and oats and potatoes. Even peas, though he doesn't have an eye for a good hybrid. Really, he's not a very good overseer. He just talks a good line to Mr. Mironov. And blames his failures on the Keldara."

"Do you think you could do a better job?" Mike asked.

"Is that what this is about?" Genadi said, raising an eyebrow. "A job interview?"

"And picking your brain," Mike admitted. "I want to buy the caravanserai. Unfortunately, it comes with the valley. I don't really need the valley, but if I'm going to buy a farm, I'm going to do it right. And I could spot a bullshitter from across the room. The question is, are you any better? I don't know a plow from a sickle so I don't even know the questions to ask. And I don't know what the Keldara will stand for."

"Well, they'll do most things that you ask in reference to running the farm," Genadi said, carefully. "If it cuts into their stores for the year, though, they'll balk. You understand the setup down there?"

"Not at all," Mike admitted. "Explain."

"The Six Families have worked the fields for as long as anyone can remember," Genadi said, frowning in thought. "And, really, there hasn't been much change in their methods since the late middle ages, I swear. The plows are a bit improved and they buy hybrid seeds, but that's about it. And even the hybrids they buy aren't the best, in my opinion. But they are cheap. They would be *willing* to work with modern machinery, but they have a deep belief that things like that are supposed to be owned by the land owner. Even the plows are owned by the bank, did you know that?"

"No," Mike said. "I'm not sure what I'm buying, am I?"

"No," Genadi said, sighing. "The land, the houses, the major tools, most of the livestock are all owned by the bank, by you if you purchase the farm. The Keldara own hand tools, their food, the furniture in the houses and the clothes on their backs. Oh, personal items as well. But everything else is owned by the bank. They buy seed on shares and owe shares of their output to the owner of the land. It works out to the owner getting about thirty percent of the material farmed and the Keldara getting the rest. They also have the right to farm small patches for themselves, three hectares per family, and to cut wood and gather certain items from the forests. They also have the right to run a few family-owned livestock out with the owner's. They have the duty of fattening two of the steers per family for the use of the owner and the butchering of same. There are various other minor rights and duties. Now, the point is, these are rights and duties as seen by the Keldara. Some owners, notably the commissars, forced them to provide different support, to change their rights and duties. But as soon as the commissars left, they switched right back to the original custom. They are very custom bound, are the Keldara."

"You say 'they'," Mike noted. "But they're your family, too."

"I was more or less cast out when I challenged Otar," Genadi said, shrugging. "If you hire me, I can work there. I can act as overseer. But I'm not, technically, a part of the Families anymore. That will make it easier in a way."

"What landmines do I really have to look for?" Mike asked. "Don't get caught alone with a woman, you said that."

"Well . . ." Genadi said, sighing. "If you buy the farm, things will be a bit different. Frankly, the older members of the family have been whining for a Kildar for some time."

"I'm not a lord or whatever," Mike said, definitely.

"If you buy the farm, you'll be the Kildar," Genadi said, just as definitely. "And don't discount that. The Kildar can get away with things that regular mortals cannot. If you make a mistake in dealing with them, they'll be immediately willing to overlook it for the Kildar. The Kildar is more than a landowner. In ancient times . . ." He paused and frowned, then shrugged. "Well, the Kildar is an important man to the Keldara. You get the similarity in terms, yes?"

"Yes, and they're not Georgian," Mike pointed out, wondering what Genadi had not said. "What about ancient times?"

"That's . . . not something I can talk about," the man said, rubbing at his chest.

Mike noticed that he had some sort of cord around his neck and wondered if his shirt hid an oddly shaped axe.

"So, landmines," Mike said, changing the subject.

"Debt," Genadi said, immediately. "The Keldara are very stingy and very loathe to assume any debt outside the Families. Even to the Kildar. And they won't take charity. If you buy farm implements, improve the houses, whatever, that is up to you. That is *your* responsibility. But . . . if the food runs short in summer, as it often does, they won't accept charity. And even if they are short, if they owe you foodstuffs they'll give them up rather than fail in a duty. That, to them, would be debt."

"What about medical support or public works?" Mike asked.

"There *is* no medical support," Genadi said, frowning. "The nearest hospital is Tbilisi. There's not even an infirmary. If anyone gets sick, they die."

"That's got to change," Mike said. "I'll see about that."

"You'll have a hard time finding a doctor that's willing to move up here," Genadi pointed out.

"I might be able to get more help than you think," Mike said. "Public works."

"Well, it depends on what you're thinking about," Genadi said, furrowing his brow. "What sort of public works?"

"I'm thinking of putting in a small hydroelectric dam and plant," Mike admitted.

"My, you *are* thinking big," Genadi said with a chuckle. "You'll have to pay the men to work on it. And I suppose you can work out some sort of an exchange if you intend to wire the houses."

"I do," Mike said. "But that is for later. That caravanserai is too big for one person to manage it. I'll need some help, a cook if she can learn to cook my way, at least a housekeeper and maybe some maids, a gardener, things like that. Can I draw on them from the Keldara?"

"They'd be insulted if you didn't," Genadi said. "But that doesn't fall in their shared duties so they'll have to be paid."

"Of course," Mike said. "What about forming a militia? From the sounds of what Vadim was saying, the Keldara aren't pacifists."

"Quite the opposite," Genadi said, chuckling. "They pride themselves on, well . . ." He paused again and shrugged. "They're not pacifists. In the spring they have tests of strength and wrestle to see who is best. The winner is called the Ondah and gets certain rights and privileges. Most of the men chosen to head the Families are former Ondah so people really strive to win. And there are old weapons stuck here and there. Sometimes we practice with them and we *really* practice with them. And you don't want to deal with an angry Keldara holding an axe. There is a technique to axe fighting and I think we may be the only people on earth that still practice it. If you wish to make a militia from the Keldara, they'll support it enthusiastically."

"It's more than just getting handed guns," Mike said. "I was an instructor for American commandoes, what are called SEALs—"

"Navy commandoes," Genadi said, his eyes narrowing. "I have heard of them."

"If, and I say *if*, I form a militia, I'll expect them to train to American methods and standards," Mike said, his face hard. "That's a cultural thing as much as anything. It might require change in the way they do things, how they think about fighting. For one thing, it requires being able to handle it when someone tells you

you're wrong and changing to the way that they tell you. Fighting and training with discipline. Will they be able to do that?"

"I think so," Genadi said, carefully. "The Keldara . . . I think they can, honestly. They *are* disciplined. They're prickly about their rights and duties, but not that way."

"Okay, I'm not going to promise anything to them," Mike said. "I don't think that it's good to make promises that you're not sure you can keep. But you can assume I'll make changes. The first is that you need some decent clothes. I'll take the cost out of your pay. And I've got to figure out how much to pay you and where to stash you until it's time to tell Otar he's redundant."

"Be careful," Genadi said. "The man can be vindictive."

"Well, I'm one person he won't want to cross."

Mike had stashed Genadi at the caravanserai, telling him to lay low, and settled back into the tavern in the meantime. The next evening he was contemplating his glass of beer, listening to Otar bragging, when he realized that there was one aspect of the village he'd neglected to check out: the brothel.

He dropped a ruble on the table and walked out into the night, crunching through the snow as he walked down the street to the building Vadim had pointed out. He paused as he was leaving the parking lot of the tavern, then doubled back to his car, getting some materials out of it and putting them in a bag. Then he resumed his evening walk.

When he got to the brothel he knocked on the door and was greeted by a short, fat man with a beaten look.

"Good evening," Mike said in Russian. "I understand that this is a place a weary traveler can find friendship."

"You must be the American," the man said, waving him into an entry hallway. "I am Yakov Belyayev. I have not heard your name?"

"Mike Jenkins," Mike said as the man opened the inner door.

The building was obviously a house since the entry area was a sitting room. There was one man in the room sitting on a couch with a gorgeous blonde on his knee. As Vadim had mentioned, the girls, three brunettes, a redhead and the blonde, ranged from very good looking to, in the case of the blonde, just spectacular. They also were, uniformly, young; the youngest looked as if she should be playing with dolls, not sitting around shivering in a teddy.

"Very nice," Mike said.

"You may have your pick," Yakov said, dispiritedly. "Business is very slow. It always is very slow."

"You have very pretty girls for a slow place," Mike said, looking the group over. The blonde looked at him and lowered her eyes demurely but he'd gotten just enough of a flash to know it was a total act. The eyes that had tracked to him were as cold as a shark's, cold enough that they were a little frightening. Not just resigned cold but the sort of look you saw on someone who'd seen too much combat and discovered they *enjoyed* killing people and breaking things. Mike occasionally saw the same look in a mirror and knew it was the outward expression of something he didn't want to get involved with. The blonde was a flat killer waiting for her chance.

"Most of the girls are local," the man admitted. "I could sell them to the Chechens, I suppose, and sometimes I think I should. They eat more than they make most of the time. But it is the only business I know."

"The blonde?" Mike asked, curiously.

"Katya," the man said, sighing. "She was on her way to Eagle Market. I don't know how she ended up here. The man wanted to sell her for too little money for me to pass up. Spectacular, no? She could make good money in Bosnia, but she is here where all men can afford is a few kopeks. I have tried to sell her before, for her own good, but no one would take her. I don't know why, she is beautiful. And quite well trained. You like her?"

"Pass," Mike said. "Besides she's with someone."

"That is Marat, my doorman," Yakov said with another resigned sigh. "Why I have a doorman I don't know; I always answer it."

"Being polite," Mike said quietly, turning away from the girls, "I understand there is a bit of problem with, well, body bugs."

"It is hard to keep the girls clean," the man said, shrugging. "Hot water costs money, you know. And the price they want for the shampoos, it is terrible."

"I see," Mike said, sighing. "Is there somewhere we can talk, quietly?"

"This way," Yakov said, walking slowly to the back, his head down. He led Mike into the kitchen, which was dirty and deserted. Mike wasn't about to eat anything cooked in the place, that was sure.

"I'm going to be staying for a while, as it turns out," Mike said. "The weather and all. And I'd like to have my ashes hauled, but not at the cost of lice and bedbugs and fleas. Not to mention the pox."

"No pox," Yakov assured him. "The girls all use rubbers."

"As you say," Mike said, not looking at the kitchen. "The point is," he said, starting to pull out stuff from his bag, "I'd be willing to front you the material to clean the girls up. Hell, I'll even pay you a few euros to make sure they have access to hot water and to make sure they *use* it. I'll be a major patron of your . . ." he paused and choked at the words "fine establishment," " . . . house. If the girls are clean. If not, I'll just stick to rosy palm and her five fingers." By this time he'd laid out six bottles of lice shampoo, bedding spray and pubic hair cream. "Do we have a deal?"

"You are giving this to me?" Yakov asked, frowning.

"Yes," Mike said. "And if I find out you resold it rather than using it, you won't have to worry about losing money. Do I make myself clear?"

"Yes," Yakov said, nodding dispiritedly.

"And make sure the girls have all the hot water they want," Mike said, pulling out a hundred-euro note. "This stuff works on first use. I'll be back in a day or two. If I see lice, I'll know you double-crossed me. You *don't* want to double-cross me."

"Some of the girls may be ... resistant," Yakov argued.

"You're a pimp," Mike said, standing up. "That's your problem."

CHAPTER FIVE

It was three days before everything was arranged. He picked Genadi up on the morning of the third day, having him wait in the back seat of the Mercedes while Mike went in the bank. It was a lovely clear day, the last storm having just cleared off and leaving the sky a washed blue.

In Mr. Mironov's office he found Vadim and Otar waiting, the latter looking puzzled.

"Mr. Jenkins," Mr. Mironov said, standing up as he entered. "All of the transfers have been verified." He pulled out a thick sheaf of papers and slid them across the desk. "This includes an up-to-date inventory of all the materials entailed on the farms. That includes, by the way, the Rover of the overseer."

Mike glanced at the inventory and then nodded.

"And the deed?" he asked.

"Here," Mironov said. "You sign here, taking possession, and I sign below, turning it over for the sum of one million euros. I took the liberty of escrowing that in one of our accounts and on your signature it transfers."

"Works for me," Mike said, thinking about the interest the bank had probably accrued. He doubted he was going to see it. He signed on the line and then slid the paper back to Mr. Mironov.

"And that is that," Mironov said with a sigh of relief. "You are now owner of the Keldara farm and all it entails, including the caravanserai."

"Thank you," Mike said. "Mr. Tarasova, Captain Tyurin, I think we should go inform the Keldara that they have a new landowner."

"You've bought the farm?" Otar asked, surprised. "I hadn't known you were even interested."

"It seemed like a good deal," Mike said. "Could you perhaps drive ahead? I'd like to talk to the Keldara."

As Otar left, Mike looked at Tyurin and shrugged.

"You're ready?" he asked.

"And eager," Tyurin said, grinning. "And thank you for the consulting fee. My wife appreciates it even more."

"I'm sure I'm going to be doing plenty of consulting," Mike said. He'd already arranged with Mr. Mironov to have five hundred euros a month drawn out and prepared for the police official. When in Rome . . .

They walked out to the parking lot and headed down the pass, Mike driving his Mercedes and Vadim his Rover.

By the time they got to the Keldara village, the people were streaming out of their houses and gathering in the open area at the center. Mike parked well to the rear and got out, leaving Genadi in the car.

"Keldara workers," Otar said, standing on a stone dais that looked like a mounting stand. "I have important news. The valley has a new owner." The overseer gestured grandly at Mike and raised his hand, getting a ragged and dispirited cheer. The day was clear and cold and nobody particularly wanted to be standing in the snow. But Mike sensed that they'd have been just as wary of cheering the overseer if he'd told them it was free beer and beef for the next year.

Mike stepped up on the dais next to him and looked around at the faces of the people. Most of them had put two and two together and knew he was the lost American that had picked up ... whatshername in the snow. With the exception of the children they looked ... wary.

"People of the Keldara," Mike said in Russian, since he didn't speak a word of Georgian yet. "I had merely intended to live in the caravanserai for a time. But with the caravanserai comes the valley. As you take your rights and duties seriously, I take mine seriously. And I will discharge one of them now."

He turned to Otar and clapped him on the back.

"Otar Tarasova, you have run these farms well for many years," Mike said, smiling. "You have done well by their owner and treated the Keldara with fair openhandedness." The latter had been tough to translate into Russian, but Genadi had helped him, laughing the whole time. "The years have been heavy upon you and you are worn by toil. Which is why I think it's time that you retire."

"But, Mr. Jenkins ..." Otar said, his face sliding from beaming smiles to ashen.

"Not with nothing," Mike said, reaching into his jump bag. "In the United States, it is a custom that when you retire you are given a watch. This is the best watch I could find in Alerrso and I hope that when you look at it you always think of the good days in the valley of the Keldara." He handed him the watch and then dipped into the jump bag again, pulling out an envelope. "And so that you can buy your own farm, here is a small token of my gratitude. Furthermore, you may keep the farm Range Rover in token of my esteem."

He helped the shaken man down and into the arms of Captain Tyurin. who led him over to the old, battered Rover.

"People of the Keldara," Mike said, loudly. "Three cheers for Otar Tarasova! Hip, hip, HOORAY! Hip, hip, HOORAY! Hip, hip, HOORAY!"

Mike kept the cheers up, dispirited as they were, until the

former overseer, accompanied by Tyurin, drove out of the compound and towards town.

"Now that that jerk is gone, I have another overseer you might recognize," Mike said, waving to the Mercedes.

There was a buzz of excited conversation as Genadi stepped out of the car and over to the stand.

"This is your new overseer," Mike said, waving at Genadi. "I understand that there is some water under the bridge. It's over as of now. Genadi, in matters related to the farm, speaks with my voice. I know nothing of farming. I was a warrior, a commando, for the American military. Then I was a maker of communications gadgets. When it comes to farming, I will trust in Genadi to make the decisions. If you seriously disagree, and can explain why, you may meet with both of us and lay out your reasoning. But it had better make sense to a five-year-old, or I'll go with Genadi's opinion.

"I spoke a moment ago of rights and responsibilities. I understand that you have your opinion of what those are. In general, we see eye to eye so far. But I will make a few statements. I am not a farmer, I am not a Keldara, I am not a Georgian. I am an American and I was an American fighting man. We have what *we* find to be our responsibilities. I can't think like a Kildar, whatever that is. All I can do is think like an American fighting man. So I'll lay down a few rules that are going to violate your customs as I know them.

"One: No women will be sent to town. I understand that sometimes there are too many women, that sons are needed to run the farms. Fine. We'll figure something out. But sending women to town violates *my* honor. You touch that honor at your peril. I have worked very hard to save women on occasion. I will not see any of the women of the Keldara sold to town.

"Two: No person will go hungry. Not the old, not the young, not the men, not the women. You fear debt. I can understand that. I will tell you a story.

"I had a friend whose grandfather was the owner of a store

in a small town like Alerrso. He died, as old men do, and my friend went to his funeral. After the funeral an old farmer, from a situation like your own, came up to him and told him that he was going to miss my friend's grandfather. 'Why once,' the man said, 'I was surely low on money. And I asked your grandfather for ten dollars as a loan. He told me he'd never ask for that ten dollars as long as I paid him a dollar a week. I've been paying him a dollar a week for the last few years and he never *did* ask for that ten dollars back.'"

Mike nodded as there were a few snorts. It appeared that not only was his Russian comprehensible but they had similar ideas of humor. Both were good signs. The faces of the people were beginning to thaw.

"The story was to show you that I understand your fear of being in debt," Mike continued. "But I'm not a commissar or a Kildar, I'm an American fighting man. I can only think of you as my troops. And you *do not* let your troops go hungry if you can avoid it. This, too, touches my honor. You will violate it at your peril. If I find that people are going hungry and I have not been told, I will take the most severe action. One way or the other, we will work it out. If I say there is no debt, there is *no debt*. If Genadi makes a mistake and there is too little food, there is *especially* no debt. I think that you'll find the changes we will make will ensure that no one will go hungry. But if we are wrong, *I* will assume the responsibility. And for that there is no debt.

"Third. Medical care. Right now there is none in this valley. I will see what can be done about that. But medical care, as of now, is *my* responsibility. For that, there is no debt. We will need to figure something out in the long term. But until we do, there is no debt. If anyone needs serious medical care, tell me and I will move heaven and earth to get it to them.

"A wise old general once said that you should never promise your troops anything you can't guarantee. I think you'll see some changes for the better but I promise *nothing*. You will have to see what I deliver and make your minds up about me on the basis of that. It's cold and you've been standing out here too long. I'd like to meet with the senior members of the Six Families as soon as possible, preferably in one of the houses where it is warm. I thank you for listening to me and hope to get to know each of you as time goes by. Now let's *get inside!*"

The men gathered around the table ranged from probably in their fifties to one that looked to be seventy. But he was a tough old bird, short but as hard-looking as the mountains that ringed the valley. He'd taken the seat at the far end, opposite Mike, as his due as senior.

"Genadi," Mike said to the overseer at his right. "I think introductions are in order."

"This is Father Makanee," Genadi said, pointing to the man on his right. "He is head of the Makanee family." Father Makanee was medium height with brown hair and eyes and broad shoulders. He was just about the youngest of the "elders." His hands looked like hams. He nodded at Mike warily.

"Father Devlich," Genadi said, pointing to the man to Mahona's left. This was the man Mike had met on the night of the blizzard. He, too, was watching Mike warily, but nodded.

"Father Devlich I've met," Mike said in Russian. "But we weren't introduced. A pleasure to see you again."

"Kildar," the man said, nodding again.

"Call me Mister Jenkins," Mike said, smiling.

"Father Mahona," Genadi said, pointing to the man on Mike's left. He had short-cropped blond hair shot with gray and a graying beard. Another nod.

"Father Shaynav," Genadi said, continuing to the man across from Devlich. He was in his sixties with red hair gone almost completely gray and a gray beard that hung to his chest. He watched Mike with interest, though, out of bright blue eyes. Mike noticed that he looked more like Genadi than the man who had the same last name. Either there was some fooling around going on or he didn't understand the family structure.

"Father Kulcyanov," Genadi said, leaning over to point to the second to the last man. Kulcyanov had once been hugely big, Mike could tell, but time and age had shrunk him. He looked in worse health than the man at the end of the table.

"And Father Ferani," Genadi concluded, pointing to the septuagenarian at the end of the table.

"Pleased to meet you all," Mike said. "First things first: Within my duties, which means responsibility to equipment and the homes as I understand it, is there anything that you need?"

The men looked at each other for a moment, then at Father Ferani.

"One of our houses needs the roof repaired," Ferani said in Russian, eyeing him warily.

"What do you need to do that?" Mike asked. "And do I pay you to do it or farm it out or what?"

"We need nails and roofing materials from the store," Ferani said, frowning. "And our men should be paid. We will do the work."

"Any other roofs that need repair?" Mike asked.

"Two of our houses leak," Father Kulcyanov said, wheezing slightly.

"Genadi, get a list, take a look at full replacement for all the roofs," Mike said. "Next."

"We have two plows that need to be much repaired or replaced," Father Devlich said, frowning at the apparent largesse.

"Pass," Mike replied. "I won't promise new equipment for the spring, but it's likely. I'll be looking at that with Genadi. Next."

"Our well has to be redug," Father Mahona said. "We will do the work, but it's the responsibility of the Kildar to provide for the wells. The Kildar owns the water. We should be paid."

"Can you do that in winter?" Mike asked, frowning.

"With difficulty," Genadi replied. "The ground is hard."

"What are you doing for water now?" Mike asked.

"Melting snow," Mahona said, shrugging. "What else?"

"Genadi, put that at the top of your list," Mike replied. "Figure something out. If it has to be redug by hand, it has to be redug by hand. But if we can get equipment in to do it, get the equipment."

"I'll look into it," Genadi said.

"Next."

The meeting went on for about an hour and it was apparent that the bank had been neglecting its duties, at least from the point of view of the Keldara.

"I'm not going to guarantee to get all of this fixed this week," Mike said as the list grew. "Or even this month. But it will all get worked on. If there is anything that you can do by yourselves, do it and bill me. If there is something that needs fixing that falls in my duties, get it fixed. Work out the payment and arrangements with Genadi. There is a large operating account with the bank for just this sort of thing. We should be able to cover everything that needs doing. Now, a few things that I need. I'm going to be moving into the caravanserai but the place is so huge I'll need servants. Notably, I'll need a cook, a housekeeper and some yard help. The housekeeper may need some help as well and there are repairs to do on the grounds and on the interior. I'd also like to get some of the junk moved out of the cellars, especially since I have materials I'm going to be moving in. I would prefer the housekeeper be capable of reading, writing and basic bookkeeping. I'll also need some foodstuffs. All of this, obviously, will be paid for."

"We can do all of this," Father Ferani said, nodding. "What is the planting schedule for the spring?"

"That will be up to Genadi," Mike said, firmly. "I think you'll find that we will be buying more, and more expensive, seed than you are used to. If any of you find this excessive, I'll be glad to take up the slack. Again, I'm not promising anything, except to promise that there will be changes. On that note, I'm bothered by the security situation. I intend to fund a militia with both arms and training. Is this going to be a problem?"

"No," Father Kulcyanov wheezed. "Give us the guns and we'll show you what we can do."

"There is more to it than giving you the guns," Mike said. "Some of you might have been soldiers or talked to soldiers. I'm a professional. And there are going to be changes I *know* you won't like. Among other things, I'll be bringing in female soldiers to train the women."

"What?" Father Mahona snapped. "You're mad!"

"No, I'm a *professional*," Mike snapped right back. "Women, by and large, aren't good field soldiers. But they can hold fixed positions just fine if you give them training. And *that* is how this militia is going to work. The men won't just be sitting on their butts but patrolling and finding the enemy before we're struck by them. Then they'll maneuver in the field and strike them from the flanks and behind while the *women* hold the farms. That's the way to *win*, not just survive. I intend to make this region a no-go zone for the Chechens because that means they never *get* to the farms. But if they do, they'll find them bristling with guns, guns served by *women*."

"In the Great Patriotic War many women fought alongside men," Father Kulcyanov wheezed. "And the women of the Keldara have always been the last line of defense of the homes. This is nothing new."

"There will be new things," Mike promised. "But the training, weapons and equipment that they get will be top of the line. There's no reason for it not to be. If you're in agreement, and Captain Tyurin already is, I'll begin rounding up trainers, weapons and equipment immediately. For the time being, we'll store it in the caravanserai."

"As you wish, Kildar," Father Mahona said. "But if you think women can be taught to fight, I think you are mad."

"What about Mother Lenka?" Father Devlich said, grinning.

"I was thinking that she would make the Kildar an excellent housekeeper," Father Mahona said.

"Woe is the Kildar!" Father Shaynav moaned.

"I think there are better choices than Mother Lenka for a housekeeper," Genadi said, firmly. "Almost *any* other choice."

"Who is Mother Lenka?" Mike asked, smiling at the interplay.

"Mother Lenka is . . . Mother Lenka," Genadi said, sighing. "She is a force of nature. I think you will like her, but not as a housekeeper."

"You will be staying here," Father Ferani said. "Not returning to America?"

"I am not unwanted in America," Mike said, frowning. "Okay, honesty time. I have enemies. It is one of the reasons I want to train you as militia. Not to defend me, but to defend yourselves if my enemies come for me. But, for now, this is a good place for me to be. It is out of the way and defensible. And with Captain Tyurin's tacit approval, I can purchase weapons for my defense. I can do this in America as well, but this place, I think, is better." He paused and grinned. "Even with the friends I have in America, and they are powerful friends, if I kill a bunch of ragheads there will be questions and problems—"

"And here we have shovels," Father Kulcyanov said, then choked and laughed.

"And here we have shovels," Mike said with a nod. "And it is a reason for me to get a backhoe. Be joyous."

"It is good there is a Kildar again," Father Ferani said, considering him carefully but smiling. "And you are a good Kildar for us. Better than you can know."

"We should bring you to each of the houses if you will, Kildar," Father Shaynav said. "I understand you have a taste for beer. You should try each Family's brew and decide which is best."

"I don't think my first day on the job I should get hammered," Mike pointed out. "But I'll try a bit."

"We shall start here," Father Kulcyanov said, raising his voice in Georgian.

The meeting had been held in the main room of the house with everyone chivvied out except the elders. Now the rest of the Kulcyanov family began pouring in from the back rooms where they must have been packed in like sardines.

"Bring food and drink for the Kildar," Father Kulcyanov said in Russian. His tones were formal and for once he managed to not wheeze, sitting straight in his chair, his face firm. It gave him a trace of what he must have once been and Mike was sorry he'd never met that man. "We greet our new Kildar. Let him be proud of the peoples he now leads. And let us give thanks to the Father of All that a true Kildar has returned."

The women began to prepare food as the younger men of the household lined up to be introduced. Mike had a hard time keeping up with all the names but he figured he'd learn them in time. There were four married men in the household, some of them old enough that their sons were of marriageable age. One of the younger ones, Oleg Kulcyanov, hadn't fallen far from the tree. He was a monster, at least six foot six and broad in proportion, heavily muscled and blond with clear blue eyes. A couple of others had the same general build and look.

The meal was simple and light, bread, cheese and a little *sava*, which seemed to be the local equivalent of a hamburger, probably because everyone knew he was going to be visiting the other families. And he was given a small tankard of beer to sample. He thought it would be much the same as the beer in the village, but when he tried it he was amazed. He'd thought the beer in the tavern was good until he tried this stuff.

"That's great," Mike said, setting down the tankard carefully. The beer was a trifle more bitter than that in the village, but excellent. And, again, with a hint of something he couldn't quite place. "Do you all brew your own beer?"

"The women of the Families brew the beer," Father Kulcyanov answered. "Each family has its own recipe. Every spring they have a contest to see who has the best."

"I can't imagine any of them being better than that," Mike said, shaking his head. "Who is the brewer?"

"I am," one of the older women said, curtseying. "I am Mother Kulcyanov."

"You have an excellent house, Mother Kulcyanov," Mike said. "And a fine brew."

"Thank you, Kildar," the woman replied, curtseying again. "But I know that I do not make the best beer in the valley," she added, sighing. "That would be Mother Lenka. The witch."

"If Mother Lenka's beer is better than this, she *must* be a witch," Mike said, shaking his head.

Through the rest of the day Mike was taken from house to house. In each he had a small meal and tested the beer. After the first two he realized he was never going to be able to tell which was better. He just praised them all to the heavens. He met dozens of men and a few of the women. In the latter case, he was introduced to married women only, generally the family "Mother." It was apparent that the Families were more like small clans. He wasn't sure what the total population of the valley was, but there were enough young men to make up at least a company of infantry.

The last house they visited was the Devlich household, the one that he'd come to in the blizzard. Father Devlich seemed the most unsure about him but Mike could handle that.

He was seated at the end of the table while the women served and was handed the usual glass of beer. He was a bit tipsy by that point, but he tried it cautiously. And then he shook his head.

"This must be the house of Mother Lenka," he said, grinning. "I'd been warned that Mother Lenka's brew could make an alcoholic of any man." The beer was flat-out fantastic. Strong, full and rich—it was truly "liquid bread."

"Hah, you've heard of me already!" one of the older women said with a cackle. She still had a trace of great beauty buried in a mass of wrinkles, and her hair was still black with only a trace of gray.

"Of your amazing beer and great beauty," Mike said. "Also that you're a meek and kind individual."

"Who has been lying about me?" the woman said. Her Russian was excellent; he knew enough to detect a trace of a Leningrad

accent, and Mike suspected she was not from the Families originally.

When he was finished with the meal and beer at the Devlich
house, Mike and Genadi stumbled out to the Mercedes and made
their way up to the caravanserai. While he'd been being introduced, a group of the Keldara had already headed for the castle
and when Mike arrived, wanting nothing more than to have a
brief nap, the house and grounds were full of bustle with the
courtyard filled with colorfully painted wagons.

"Kildar," a woman said as he entered, "I am Mother Savina.
If you accept my services, I will be your housekeeper." Mother
Savina was a short woman with black hair gone mostly gray and
a strong face. "Mother Griffina would be your cook. She is in the
kitchen, cleaning. Would you like to meet her as well?"

"Not at the moment," Mike admitted. "Right now, I'd just like
to lie down and sleep off the food and beer. And what beer!"

"I will ensure that there is beer in the house," Mother Savina
said with a smile. "Will you be wanting dinner?"

"The way I'm feeling now the answer is no," Mike said. "Maybe
something light. Are there any beds available?"

"The master suite has already been cleaned and the linens
changed," Mother Savina said, nodding. "Please rest. We will try
to keep the noise down."

CHAPTER
SIX

When Mike awoke he just lay in bed for a moment, thinking and working his joints. He'd taken some ibuprofen and drunk a bottle of water before lying down and that helped with the hangover. But it didn't help, much, with the joints and they were frozen as usual. Between his time in the SEALs and some of the stuff afterwards, he had massive damage to his body; he couldn't just roll out of bed anymore.

But what kept him in bed at the moment was the situation. There were a billion things to do, both from the point of view of making the caravanserai livable and getting the farms prepared for the spring planting. He wasn't sure what you did for that, but he knew that if you were going to do it right, it would require equipment. Tractors, trucks, a harvester. He wasn't sure how much any of it cost, but he'd run across something about a harvester being a quarter of a million dollars. He had no idea what a tractor would cost. For that matter, he was vaguely aware that they came in different sizes and he wasn't sure what size was the best for the farms.

At the least, each of the "Families" would need a tractor of their own. Maybe one harvester for the valley. A couple of trucks for each family. No, a truck and an SUV. Both could double for use of the militia.

And that was another question. He was going to need equipment, weapons and trainers. He knew where to get the equipment but he was going to have to shop for the weapons. Not a bad thing, in and of itself, but he wasn't sure how to do it in this remote area. If you were forming a militia, did arms manufacturers send you reps? He smiled at that and then rolled painfully to his feet.

The house was still cold; he added a delivery of fuel oil for the furnace that ran the radiators to his list of things to do, then thought about a more modern heating system. Could you run forced air through stone like this?

The stones of the floor were bare and he made a note that he needed some carpets. Gads, this was going to get expensive, quick. He needed an internet connection. He needed to know if DHL delivered out here. He was almost out of bedding spray, he needed lice shampoo. Medicines in case something went wrong out here in the back of beyond. Trainers . . .

By the time he'd gotten out of the shower he had a general list of things he needed to do and get and his joints were working again. He did some stretching exercises to work out the last kinks, added workout equipment to the list, again, realized he needed something to write on and added general office supplies. A computer. Gads.

He made his way downstairs and passed one of the Keldara, a girl in her teens, who was dusting the rungs of a chair. She was half bent over and the outline of a very shapely ass was visible under her skirt. That reminded him that he was back in a serious lackanookie situation, while being surrounded by beautiful women. Not good.

The girl didn't hear his soft foot treads until he was almost past and then turned around and straightened up with a frightened squeak, bowing to the new boss. He winked at her and was given a blush in return.

Despite being the local baron or whatever, he was painfully aware that the Keldara women were off-limits. Which was too bad; they were real lookers.

He found Mother Savina supervising the girls working on the lower floors and she led him into a small parlor near the harem quarters where a fire was cheerfully warming the room. She served him tea and bread, the bread still fresh from the oven, and he nibbled on that as he listened to her recite what had been done and what needed to be done from her point of view.

"I would like to replace the tile in the foyer," Mother Savina said, diffidently. "But we do not mine marble so we'll have to either replace it all or get some that matches. And it will be expensive."

"I'll add it to the list and figure out a budget," Mike said. "I've barely gotten a look at the cellars. Do you have any idea what is down there?"

"Oleg checked it out for me," Mother Savina said, shaking her head. "There is broken furniture. Some of it can be repaired and used. Maybe in the servants' quarters. Most of it is good for no more than firewood. There are also many boxes and crates. He opened one and it had papers in Russian, I think documents from when the commissar was here. That is as far as I know."

"We need to sort out what is worth keeping and get rid of the rest," Mike said. "I suppose there is some scholar somewhere who could make something of documents from a minor commissar. If he finds anything that appears to predate the Soviets, I want to see it. Anything broken, throw away or burn. Any military equipment, set aside for me to inspect. Anything the Keldara think they can use, take it. As long as it doesn't pre-date the Soviets."

"Very well, Kildar."

"On the subject of general cleaning," Mike said, clearing his throat. "I hate vermin. Fleas, lice, bedbugs, especially. Buy whatever cleaners you need to get rid of them. I sprayed down the bed upstairs when I knew I was going to be sleeping in it. But wash all the linens and keep them separate to ensure they don't get reinfested. And anyone working in the house on a regular basis needs to take a bath or shower, and use lice shampoo, to get rid of lice and bedbugs. Clean clothes, to get rid of fleas. Okay?"

"Of course, Kildar," Mother Savina said, nodding.

"Um, about the people who work in the house," Mike said, carefully. "I'm a heterosexual male and I haven't been getting a lot lately. You'll probably need some help, but . . ."

"Older women?" Mother Savina said, smiling faintly.

"Unfortunately," Mike said with a sigh. "Happy as everyone seems to be to have a 'real Kildar' whatever that means, I don't think they'd be nearly as happy with pregnant daughters."

"You should have a woman in the house, though," Mother Savina pointed out. "That would make the problem . . . less."

"And a woman I was close to would be a hostage to fortune to my enemies, if they ever find me," Mike replied. "I'll make some arrangements eventually. Clean up the girls in town. Import a professional from time to time if nothing else. Is there a room that can be set up for an office? And have you seen Genadi?" Mike added, changing the subject.

"Genadi is still sleeping the afternoon off," Mother Savina said. "And there is a room that would be a good office. On the ground floor to the rear. It is not well lit . . ."

"That's what lamps are for," Mike said. "Show me."

The room was, if anything, a bit too large for an office and had only one window, high on the rear wall. But with the stone walls it would make an excellent room for secure conversations and it had a fireplace, which would be nice. He added setting up some secure links to the mental list. He hoped he wouldn't need them, but with the way things had gone since he got out of the teams, it was more likely than not.

Speaking of which, he really needed to check in.

"I'm going to be going up to the balcony of my room," Mike

said. "I'd prefer that I not be disturbed and that you keep people out of the area. I need to hold a private conversation."

"I will assure it, Kildar," Mother Savina said.

Mike walked back to his bedroom and pulled his sat phone out of the jump bag. The sat phone was the size of the old "brick" cellular phones with a thick antenna. He had a more elaborate one in his duffel, but this would do for the conversation.

He went out on the balcony and made sure he had a good signal from the satellite, then hit the speed dial.

"Office of Special Operations Liaison," a man said when the call connected. "United States Navy Captain Folsom, how may I help you sir or ma'am?"

"Go scramble," Mike said, punching in his combination.

"Scrambled."

"This is Jenkins," Mike said. "Checking in. I'm going to be spending some time near a town in Georgia, the country not the state, called Alerrso. Alpha, Lima, Echo, Romeo, Romeo, Sierra, Oscar."

It was just before four PM local time, seven AM in Washington. His usual contact was generally in by then, but he might be preparing for a briefing.

"Confirm Alerrso," Captain Folsom said. "There'd been a query out on you, sir. What is your situation?"

"Nominal," Mike said. "I've bought a house and intend to stay here for the foreseeable future. I'd appreciate security updates if there's a major issue in the area."

"Alerrso is in a heavy Chechen area of Georgia," Folsom said after a moment. "The security situation is poor."

"There's a local group I'm going to support in forming a militia," Mike replied. "I'll do that through my own contacts and methods. But if there's major intel on the local security situation, I'd appreciate being apprised. I'll keep the secondary line on standby for data dumps. Right now, given the meteorological conditions, the security situation is stable."

"Roger that. I'll pass on your situation and intent. Take care."

"Will do," Mike said, cutting the connection.

The Office of Special Operations Liaison was the group that briefed senior members of the government on Spec Ops missions and plans. Mike had become associated with them during his first post-team mission when Colonel Bob Pierson had been his "control" and communications point. Since then he'd continued to maintain contact through them and had been "asked" to keep them apprised of his current location when out of the States. It was a pain in the ass, but made up for itself in having a Big Brother to call when the shit occasionally hit the fan. Of course, in at least one case the call had gone the other way and he'd ended up shot to ribbons. But in that case, Uncle Sammie also picked up the medical bills and cleaned up the mess.

He put away the handphone and set up the larger sat phone on a chest of drawers, careful to ensure that it could get reception through the stone walls and roof. The laptop sized sat phone could download secure documents and had a headset for longer conversations, not to mention general laptop capabilities. It used a proprietary software, unfortunately, which was even buggier than Windows. But it usually worked.

With commo put in, he headed downstairs to find out what trouble the Keldara had gotten into.

With the sun setting and clouds presaging more snow, most of the Keldara had left by the time he got back downstairs. The foyer was deserted although there was a fire going in the fireplace, and Mike wandered around until he found Mother Savina and, he presumed, Mother Griffina in the kitchen.

He'd checked the kitchen out on a previous visit and been horrified. Whoever used it last, presumably the Soviets, had left it in a state of total disaster. Every cooking surface was covered with grease and food residue and most of the counters were just as awful. Not to mention the patina of dust mixed in. The floor didn't bear description and he'd had to scrape his shoes off after leaving. He hadn't dared look in the Soviet-era refrigerator.

The place hadn't been raised to perfect standards in the short time the women had had to work on it but it was much better. The tile floor was visible in spots and the counters had been cleaned. The stoves had been scrubbed, but it was evident that there was more work to do. Savina and Griffina were apparently discussing that in low tones when he entered. A few of the remaining girls worked on the floor; he had a hard time keeping his eye off of them. The only way to get the floor clean was to scrub it with brushes, on their knees. The girls had pulled up their skirts to keep them from getting ruined and their lovely legs were exposed. The way they pulled the skirts up also tightened them across gorgeous asses. It was a sight to drive a guy nuts. Or down the road to the brothel.

"A mess, isn't it?" Mike said, startling the women. He didn't *mean* to move quietly; it was just the way he moved. There was a reason he'd been given the team name "Ghost."

"Kildar," Mother Griffina said, bowing. "I am sorry, you should not have to see this. It will take a day or two to get the kitchen properly prepared."

"I saw it before you did and I should have warned you," Mike said. "Where'd you bake the bread? Not in here, I think."

"There is a smaller kitchen upstairs," Mother Griffina replied. "If you would like something to eat . . ."

"I'm fine," Mike said. "I'll be getting back in shape and I'll eat enough to satisfy you then. But when I'm not working out, I eat light. I ate *way* too much today. But there are a few dishes that, when the kitchen's in better order, I'd like to show you. Americans eat . . . different than most other people. We eat bacon and eggs for breakfast, for example."

"I will get bacon and eggs," Mother Griffina said. "I will have them ready to prepare in the upstairs kitchen in the morning."

"Don't sweat it tonight," Mike said. "It's not that big of a deal. And I don't usually eat that heavy when I'm not working out. Savina, we need to get the furnace working in this pile. It's freezing in here."

"There is no fuel oil for the furnace," Mother Savina said,

nodding. "I have sent word to order some. There is a man in town who delivers. He will deliver tomorrow, I hope. I had the men bring in firewood in the meantime. Uncle Latif is the yard man, he and his son Petro. Fires have been laid in all the fireplaces except in your room. I had one lit in the foyer and in the parlor."

"Works," Mike said. "Skip the foyer usually; there's no way to actually warm the room with it and I don't expect I'll be sitting out there much. Mother Griffina, don't get too attached to these antique stoves; I'll probably be getting new ones. Christ, there's going to be a bunch of work to be done."

"We will get it done, Kildar," Mother Savina promised. "Why don't you go to the second floor parlor and I'll bring a snack?"

"I'll do that, since there's no furniture in the office," Mike said, yawning. "Get Genadi up, if you would, and have him meet me there. We have a lot to talk about."

Mike was sipping tea and working on a list when Genadi came in the room. The second floor parlor was nearly adjacent to the master bedroom and also overlooked the harem garden. At the moment all that could be seen was leafless trees and equally leafless bushes Mike assumed were roses. But it would be pretty in spring.

"The more things I realize I want, the more I come up with," Mike grumped as Genadi came in. "But we need to talk about the farms. For starters, I want a big pickup for each family and an equally big SUV. The pickups should be four-door and long-bed. But we need to talk about tractors and combines."

"That is a lot of money, Kildar," Genadi said, surprised. He sat down on the couch across from Mike and shook his head. "Very much money."

"Money I've got," Mike said. "Unless we're talking in excess of ten mil. In which case, we'll need to discuss it. I'm probably going to be spending more on arms and equipment; you have no idea how much top-line weapons and commo cost. Not to mention the pay for the trainers. Speaking of which, it's late January. When does planting start?"

"Usually around April," Genadi said. "The ground is not warm enough before then. Some of the gardens will put in cabbage and beets earlier."

"So we have a month and a bit," Mike mused. "That means I can't get everything in place before planting season. Tell me how that goes."

"First there is a thaw," Genadi said. "Then we pick the rocks from the fields. After the rocks are picked it is time to start planting, usually. The old ones wait for signs, certain birds to return and the time of the moon. I'll be testing for soil temperature but I might let them go a day or so on the basis of signs. Frankly, it works out about as well. Then we plow and plant the first crop. With some of the hybrids I'll be getting, we may be able to do a second crop of some of the plants. Turnips go in early, but we won't do much of that, cabbage as well and there will be at least one field of cabbage. I have plans on which fields should take which plants, I've been thinking about it for a long time . . ."

"Up to you," Mike said. "The main point is that I'll need about a two-month period when the men are freed up to an extent. And assume that they'll have machinery to help with what it can help."

"If there are tractors and machinery, many of them will be free even during planting," Genadi said. "Not all the young men, but many of them. By around the first of May."

"I'll take a look at manning later," Mike replied. "But do you think we can squeeze, say, seventy percent of the men from seventeen to thirty-five, starting sometime in May?"

"Easily," Genadi said. "If we have machinery."

"Okay," Mike said, nodding. "I want you to move down to Tbilisi for the time being to get the machinery we'll need. I'm not sure they'll have everything we want in stock. How do we get you there? I don't want to be driving back and forth."

"There is a bus, I can ride that," Genadi said.

"Works," Mike replied. "That way. You'll need an SUV or pickup, your choice, for getting around. Get that first. I've got an account with the Bank of Tbilisi. I'll set up another that you can draw on. Get everything in place and we'll move it up in one load if we can. By late March, I want to be able to dump a gigaton of machinery on these folks. Let's figure out what we need, want and desire."

It took about an hour to draw up the list. Some items could be put off and a few could be rented for specific periods, but Mike erred on the side of purchase. The final estimate was a pretty fair bite, running right at a million euros.

"A million here, a million there and before long you're talking real money," Mike muttered. "While you're in Tbilisi, find out if there are any IMF grants for this sort of thing. Grants not loans. Check with the American Embassy as well; I know there's a fair amount of foreign aid going to Georgia. But nothing with a lot of strings attached. With Americans, there are always strings."

"I will, Kildar," Genadi said, nodding. "This is very much money."

"I can afford it," Mike noted. "But I'd prefer to afford as little as I can. See about a lawyer as well. A good one. They're generally up on things like that. Check with your old professors, all the usual. Use your head. On the trucks and whatnot, if it's about the same price or even a little more, get Fords if they're available. F-350s for the big ones."

"Why Fords?" Genadi asked. "Mercedes makes . . ."

"I like Ford," Mike said, cutting him off. "And they're bigger than the Mercedes vehicles in the same cost range. Oh, and all of them need to be four-wheel drive with the roads around here."

"As you say, Kildar," Genadi replied, sighing.

"I need to make some phone calls," Mike said. "Get packed and head to town tomorrow. Get yourself a cell phone when you get there and contact me so I know where to reach you."

▲   ▲   ▲

Mike went back to the master suite and got the larger sat phone, bringing it into the parlor when Genadi was gone and setting it up. It had a good connection and he used the limited internet pipe to do some searching. He got a few good hits off of Google and started making calls.

Three hours later he'd learned more about the international arms business than he liked. He was going to need an end-user license from the Georgian government, which he assumed Tyurin could arrange, and a bunchaton of money. After talking to a few brokers he'd cut to the chase and called Skoda Arms. The Czech company had been formed during the Soviet period and, even then, was noted for its high quality of manufacture and design. They still made some of the best weapons in the world and were more than willing to sell to anyone with cash and a reasonable set of documents. They'd even offered to broker secondary weapons they didn't make and ship the entire load in one shipment. He still wasn't sure what his total manpower looked like so he started doodling on a notepad until he figured it was after lunch and he could call Washington with a fair chance of getting ahold of Pierson.

"You said you bought a house," the colonel said when the scrambler was in place, "not a fucking fortress."

"I take it you've been talking to NRO," Mike replied, referring to the National Reconnaissance Office, the guys who ran all the satellites for the United States.

"That we have," Pierson said. "Nice place. The President's impressed."

"It's going to take a fair bit of work." Mike sighed. "It's so old nobody knows who built it to begin with and the interior looks it. But what I called about was the local militia, or lack thereof. This area is apparently lousy with Chechen terrorists and support structure. I'm going to try to form a tiddly little militia to cut down on that. If I do, it will take some of the heat off of Georgia with regard to the Russians. I know a border war has been a real worry in Washington for a while; any chance Uncle

Sammie could, quietly, defray some of my costs? I've been doing equipment lists and, before the cost of the trainers, I'm looking at two to four mil in gear. That's a nasty bite. Then there's ongoing training costs."

"We might be able to swing something," Pierson said, musingly. "You'll need to work through the local military attaché but we can keep your connection low-profile. A word in the right ear and all that. What are the Georgians going to think of an American warlord in their rear area?"

"The local police chief thinks it's fine and dandy," Mike said. "I'm not too sure about the central government. I'll probably have to cross a few palms."

"Just dialing back the Chechens should make them happy," Pierson said. "But you never know about local governments."

"It's not like I can stage a coup," Mike pointed out. "Not with one company, more or less, of light infantry."

"How high you going to train them?" the colonel asked.

"As high as I can," Mike admitted. "I'd like them to be at least Ranger quality in a year. The basic material is there, I'll have to see if they can really take to the training. I've got a start on the TOE, I need to start rounding up trainers."

"Have fun."

"I'm buying guns, gear and soldiers," Mike said, chuckling. "Other than women, what's more fun to buy?"

CHAPTER
SEVEN

"Frog Gear."

"This is Mike Jenkins. I'm an advisor to a local militia in Georgia, the country not the state. I need gear. Lots and lots of gear."

In the previous two weeks, things had started to shake out. The house was improving; there was heat at least and the whole place was now spotless. The cellars were still being emptied out, but Mike was keeping some of the stuff. There were some interesting metal trays he suspected dated to the period of Ottoman occupancy and wooden boxes of books in Russian, Arabic and even Greek that he was itching to figure out. The Keldara had turned out to be excellent craftsmen and he now had shelves in the library again as well as a desk.

And he'd gotten a handle on his potential militia manpower. There were a hundred and twenty of the Keldara who were in the age and ability range to make decent militiamen. He suspected a few of them wouldn't have the right mindset to make the sort of soldiers he wanted, but most seemed to. The Keldara were very disciplined, but after watching a couple of fights he'd come to the conclusion that was necessary rather than normal. Aggression was the first necessity for a soldier, the rest could be trained. And the Keldara had *plenty* of aggression. They were *very* serious about how they settled arguments.

He'd taught a few of the women to take measurements, given them a list of Keldara who were designated for the militia, and set them to work measuring them. So he had full measurements for the entire group. Putting them all in an e-mail had been tedious, the sort of reason he wished he had a staff, or even a clerk. But the order was ready to go. And after he got the weapons and equipment, he could start introductory training.

In addition to the male fighters, there were about forty females he thought might make decent fixed-position soldiers. The Keldara women were beautiful and, on the surface, remarkably oppressed. But there was a lot of fire there. He'd seen one of the Family mothers berating one of her sons and it sounded like a drill sergeant dressing down a recruit.

But the time had come to start putting in serious gear orders. And Frog Gear was the place, in his opinion. They could supply everything from boots to batteries with all the electronics gear, uniforms and rucksacks that would be needed in between.

"How are you going to be paying for this, sir?" the saleswoman asked.

"I'll mail you a check from Citicorp," Mike said. "I want to set up the order, then I'll mail you the list. It's probably going to take a container to ship it all."

"That much?" the saleswoman squeaked.

"That much," Mike said. "I'm outfitting a light infantry company and I'll need both mobile and fixed communications gear. So give me an order number and I'll send you the list. You figure out how much it's going to cost, including shipping, and I'll send you a check. Works?"

"That will work, sir," the saleswoman said, cautiously.

"Just to give you an idea," Mike said. "I'm looking at three hundred sets of uniforms, a hundred and fifty combat vests, an equal number of NODs, etcetera. Delivered to Georgia. And, given the quantity, I'm going to want at least some discount."

"Adams."

"I heard you retired Ass-boy," Mike said. "It's Jenkins. How you doing?"

"Jenkins, huh?" the retired master chief replied. "Nice handle. Where the hell are you?"

"Georgia," Mike said. "The country, not the state. What are you doing these days?"

"Watching the grass grow," Chief Adams grumped. "I've been looking for a job but what in the hell does a retired SEAL do for work?"

"There are plenty of companies that could use you in sales," Mike said, grinning. "But I've got a contract offer you might be interested in."

"What are you doing, headhunting?" Adams asked, warily.

"No, this is for me," Mike replied. "I bought a farm in Georgia. It came with retainers. They need training. Lots and lots of training."

"Georgia, huh?" Chief Adams said. "The wife is going to love that."

"You old goat, what is this. Number six?"

"Five," Adams said. "Going on six."

"The girls are gorgeous and the beer is fantastic," Mike said. "And the base material is outstanding. I figure six months with some time off when they have to work on the farm. Not just you, I'll need a team of fifteen or so. Maybe, probably, more. Twelve instructors for the males, three for the females, a few specialists, notably commo and rifle, you for senior NCO and an OIC. Frankly, I'd like you to pick an OIC for it; you're more connected these days than I am. Spend six weeks taking a class in Georgian, a month or so getting to know the people, basic training period, then some stick around for advanced training. I'll need at least three females with combat experience since I'm going to want to train some of the women as well."

"Direct fire only?"

"No, I got permission for mortars," Mike admitted. "You think you can round up some special forces heavy guys? Oh, and there are some civil works projects I think we can throw in the mix. See if you can get a couple of SFers with real engineering and electrical training."

"I know some people," Adams admitted. "This is on the up and up, right? I want to be able to come back to the States."

"Fully supported by the government of the land of the free," Mike said. "At least as long as the current government is in place. Next year's elections are going to be interesting."

"That they are," Adams said. "Okay, I'll start rounding up a team. What's the pay?"

"Two hundred kay for six months for the OIC," Mike said. "One-seventy for you. One-twenty for all the other trainers. Room and board provided. And, of course, seventy kay is tax free."

"In that case I'll get right on it," Adams said. "How soon do you need them?"

"Soon," Mike admitted. "I've been running behind the eight ball getting things in place. So the sooner you can get a team over here and learning Georgian, the better."

"Will do," Adams replied. "See you soon, Mike."

"Look forward to it," Mike said, cutting the circuit as Mother Savina came in the office with a distracted expression on her face.

"There is another truck," Mother Savina said, shaking her head. "A large truck from DHL."

"Workout gear," Mike said, happily. He went to the front and, sure enough, the usual DHL driver was standing outside his truck looking dyspeptic.

"There is many parcels for you, Mr. Jenkins," Tolegeon said in broken English, shaking his head. "Very heavy. Very much."

"I'll get a crew," Mike replied in a mix of Georgian and Russian.

He was picking up the former more or less by a process of osmosis while his Russian was getting, if anything, more fluent. Albeit with some odd loan words. "Mother Savina, get Petro and he and I will start. But call down for a few strong backs; we'll be at this for a while."

"You should wait until Keldara get here," Mother Savina said, shaking her head. "Kildar should not unload trucks."

"The Kildar has done worse in his time," Mike said, going around to the back of the truck.

He, the DHL driver and Petro had barely gotten a third of the way through the truck when some Keldara made it up the hill. Despite the climb the farmers immediately started unloading, toting the gear to the cellar room Mike had designated for a weight room. He'd decided to leave the library as a library and use one of the many rooms in the cellars for workouts.

The truck took about an hour to unload, since most of the packages were heavy enough it took two to lift them. But finally it drove away and Mike was left looking at a room piled with large and small boxes.

"This is going to take a while to assemble," Mike said, shaking his head.

"You want help?" Vil Mahona asked. He was one of the Keldara Mike had mentally designated as a militiaman and given his normal initiative and "can do" attitude, Mike suspected he was going to be one of the officers or NCOs.

"I could use help," Mike admitted. "If anybody wants to stick around, feel free. And, yes, you'll get paid."

The Keldara had a brief discussion and Vil and two of the others stayed as Mike went to work opening the boxes. One problem that was immediately apparent was that although the assembly instructions were "international," the various languages they were printed in did not include Russian, much less Georgian. Which led to another question.

"Vil, can you read?" Mike asked as well as he could in Georgian.

"A little," the Keldara admitted. "We are taught some reading by the mothers. But not well. Are not many books." Vil was using a mix of standard Georgian with some Keldara words. The Keldara spoke a dialect of Georgian that was very nearly a different language. Fortunately, most of the older members spoke Russian and all but the youngest could get by in standard Georgian. However, the "Georgian" Mike was picking up was mostly Keldara.

"Fortunately, most of the instructions have pictures," Mike said, looking at the instructions for the Nautilus equipment. "But even with the pictures, I'm lost. I'm not the world's greatest mechanic. And we'll need tools."

"I get toolbox," one of the other Keldara said. Mike thought his name was Dutov and from his looks he was a Devlich. If he remembered correctly, he was Katrina's older brother, although with the Keldara it was hard to tell.

Mike pulled out parts to the weight bench and started laying them out on the floor as Vil started doing the same with one of the Nautilus machines. The third Keldara, who was in his mid-teens, scratched his head for a second, then started in on one of the other Nautilus machines.

"What are these?" Vil said after looking at the instructions in confusion.

"They are machines for building muscles," Mike said, then looked up at their expressions of surprise. "Look, I know you guys pick rocks and throw bulls and stuff all day. But, first of all, I don't. I'm stuck in this house doing other things. Second, with these you can target-build specific muscle groups so you don't *just* have muscles for picking rock and throwing bulls. When I have the time I like to use these machines for about four to six hours a day." He'd had to use a fair bit of Russian to get that across and Vil was forced to translate some of the words, in some places obviously looking for phrases when Georgian and Keldara gave out.

Dutov shortly came back with a toolbox and the four of them went to work. It quickly became apparent that Dutov had quite a bit more mechanical aptitude than the other three, especially after Mike ended up assembling half of a Nautilus backwards.

"This is for muscles?" Vil asked, holding up a padded part. "How?"

"That's a pec device," Mike said, holding up his arms bent at the elbows and moving them inward. "You push your forearms against the pads. There's a bar you hold with your hands," he added, pointing at one of the parts. "The one . . . son, what's your name?" Mike asked the teen.

"Erkin, Kildar," the boy said.

"What he's working on is a leg machine," Mike said, pushing with his legs. "For building strength in the legs."

Dutov said something fast in Keldara and Mike couldn't quite catch it but the other two laughed.

"What?" he asked, curiously.

"He said you should try using a plow all day," Vil said, flexing thighs that were thick as trees. "And climbing the mountains."

"That I do," Mike said. "Climbing, that is. But this is for doing what is called circuit work. Trust me, it's better than general farm work and, as you pointed out, I don't do that. Although I'll probably help some, just to get a feel for it. It reminds me of a joke, though."

"You have good jokes," Dutov said in broken Russian. "Try it."

"Hmmm, you know anything about American football?" Mike asked.

"No," Vil said. "I've heard of it, but I've never seen it."

"Well, take my word for it, it takes big, really strong guys," Mike said. "Oleg *might* make a decent pro-player, but he's one of the only Keldara I've seen that's big enough."

"Oleg is an ox," Dutov said, frowning. "Football players are bigger?"

"And stronger," Mike said. "Trust me. Pro players are fucking monsters. But the joke goes like this. Up until, say, when Father Kulcyanov was young, there were still people in the U.S. that used horses and plows. There was this one team that had *really* big guys on its line, the guys that have to be really big and strong but don't have to be smart."

"Oleg is smart," Vil said. "Don't let him fool you."

"He hasn't," Mike said, smiling. "But the joke about how the team got those guys is that the coach, the boss, would go driving around in the country. When he saw a big guy behind a plow, he'd ask him the way to the nearest city. If the guy stopped plowing and pointed, he'd drive on. He hired the guys that picked up the plow to point."

"Yes," Vil said, laughing. "Even Oleg would point."

"Shota would point the plow," Erkin said, shyly.

"Then we must get Shota on a pro football team," Mike said. He thought he knew which one Shota was, a red-headed monster even bigger than Oleg but with a very placid nature. He moved well, though, and he looked fast.

"Dutov," Mike said, standing up and stretching his joints. "I hereby promote you to assembler of Nautilus machines. I'm going to go find out what crashing emergency has occurred while I've been down here. Don't work on this too late, and expect to come back tomorrow to finish, okay?"

"Yes, Kildar, is very okay," Dutov said, looking up at him with a grin.

"I like the Kildar," Erkin said after Mike was gone.

"So do I," Vil admitted. "But I'm interested in finding out what will happen that he will not promise."

When Mike made his way back up to the ground floor, he found Mother Savina waiting for him.

"Was a call on your satellite phone," Mother Savina said. "Colonel Pierson. He asked you to call him back."

"Thank you, Mother," Mike replied, sighing. "I wonder what he wants now?"

▲   ▲   ▲

"What now, Bob?" Mike asked when the scrambler was in place.

"You sound tired," Pierson said. "Too many women?"

"None at all, unfortunately," Mike admitted. "Seriously, what's up?"

"A little bird suggested that you take a ride over to Tbilisi, tomorrow," Pierson said. "There's a meeting tomorrow with Ambassador Wilson, ours, Ambassador Krepkina, Russia, our military attaché, the Russian military attaché and a couple of Georgians. The Russians just intercepted a big group of Chechens that were planning on replicating Breslan. And they intercepted them exiting Georgia. Actually, although the Georgians don't know this, the Spetznaz team was on the Georgian side of the border. The Russians are getting ready to do a Cambodian invasion on Georgia, and the Georgians are making big talk. I think your intent to form a militia group in the area can *possibly* calm things down. At least it's something."

"Would the little bird be a black guy of Jamaican extraction?" Mike asked. "Or a cowboy from Texas?"

"Both," Pierson replied. "The Russians are taking their new preemption doctrine to consider Georgia fair game. In a way, I don't blame them; Georgia *is* a haven for the Chechens. But it's not Georgia's fault; they're trying. They just don't have the funding, the training or the manpower."

"Bob, all I'm forming is a company of light infantry for local defense," Mike pointed out. "I can't solve the Russians' problems for them."

"But you *are* intending to shut down Chechen operations in your area, right?"

"To the extent that I can," Mike said. "Yes. I don't like any Islamic group, you know that and you know why."

"Just tell them what you intend," Pierson said. "That may mollify the Russians enough to get them to back off. They don't really *want* to have a border war with Georgia; they've got too much on their plate in Chechnya. If they can see *any* glimmer of hope, they'll probably snap at it. Even if they don't appear to at the time, we'll be dropping hints in their ears at higher levels. Just go to the meeting, okay?"

"Okay," Mike said, sighing. "I don't have a suit, though."

"Just be yourself," Pierson said, chuckling. "You've talked to the President in shorts before, a Russian ambassador is nothing."

"The President *expected* shorts," Mike pointed out. "And you *know* I'm not diplomatic."

"Just be yourself," Pierson repeated. "You'll do fine."

CHAPTER EIGHT

Mike had had to get up at o-dark-thirty to make the nine AM meeting in Tbilisi. He'd brought Vil, who said he could drive the Mercedes in case he had to have it move around. As he pulled up at the gates of the embassy, just short of nine, he shook his head.

"I don't have a way to contact you," he said.

"I wait here," Vil replied. "If you leave, I follow."

"Just make sure the protection guys know that," Mike said, as they pulled up to the gates of the embassy.

The American Embassy to the Republic of Georgia looked like half the American embassies in the world. It was an old house, very large and rambling, that had been fortified with solid concrete barriers all around. Getting to the gates required driving through a serpentine series of turns and when they got there, they were surrounded by armed guards. One of the Marines, in dress greens, carrying a clipboard and wearing a side arm, stepped up to the door as Mike rolled down the window.

"Mike Jenkins," he said, handing the Marine his passport. "I've got a meeting with Ambassador Wilson at nine. This is my driver, Vil, a Georgian citizen."

"Yes, sir, you're on the list," the Marine lance corporal said. "If you don't mind, could you pop the trunk for inspection?"

"Got it," Mike said, hitting the latch.

In a few minutes the car was passed through. He carefully followed the Marine's directions to a parking area and slid into a spot designated for Distinguished Visitors.

"You're going to have to wait at the car," Mike said as he got out. "It might be a long time. Don't go wandering. I'll try to get someone to come out and tell you where the can is and stuff."

"I'll be fine," Vil said, sliding over to the driver's seat and reclining it. "Very comfortable. Better than working the farm."

Mike went to the front entrance where another Marine escorted him to a conference room. When he got there, there were two men in suits and one Army colonel in dress greens already present.

"Mr. Jenkins," a short, pleasant-faced man said, stepping over to shake Mike's hand. "I'm Ambassador Wilson."

"Pleasure to meet you, Mr. Ambassador," Mike said, nodding. "Sorry about how I'm dressed but I didn't expect to be doing diplomatic work." He'd dressed in jeans and a safari jacket for the meeting, just about the most formal clothes he had.

"Not a problem. Your reputation precedes you," the ambassador said, cryptically. "Let me introduce Colonel Osbruck and Mr. Steinberg. Colonel Osbruck is the senior military attaché to the embassy and Mr. Steinberg is our intelligence representative."

"Gentlemen," Mike said, shaking hands. "Pleasure to meet you."

"I see the SEALs are on the case," Colonel Osbruck said, smiling. He was a tall, slim officer with cropped hair and a straight back.

"I'm just a common citizen," Mike replied, shaking his head. "Don't get all hoo-yah on me."

"Yes, of course," Mr. Steinberg said with a slight New York accent. He was a tad taller than the ambassador, with dark hair and eyes and a hooked nose. "As the ambassador said, your reputation precedes you."

"I hope not," Mike replied, his face hard. "If it does, I'm going to be very pissed at some people in Washington. Define reputation, if you will."

"We were simply told that at times you've done significant service for the United States government," the ambassador said, placatingly. "Specifics were not mentioned. What was mentioned was that quite often you tend to have an effect that is . . . how was it put? An effect that is far greater than could be anticipated. We *hope* that such will be the case here."

"Mr. Ambassador," a man said, sticking his head in the room. "The Russians are here and so is Colonel Kortotich and Mr. Svirska."

"The colonel and I need to go greet them," the ambassador said. "Mr. Jenkins, if you'll take the assigned seat we'll be right back."

Mike took the seat indicated by Mr. Steinberg as the two left the room and shrugged.

"I think this is ritual dick-beating, am I right?"

"Maybe," Steinberg said, grabbing his own chair. "But . . . your reputation precedes you with the Russians. I'm not sure what *these* Russians know, but Putin, at least, knows about the Paris operation and that you were the primary operator on it. And from what I've been told, he has at least told these guys that you're not just some Joe-Schmoe. I don't think the ambassador or the colonel knows that and I haven't been told they have need-to-know. The call from the secretary of state was probably enough for both of them."

"Interesting," Mike said. "Especially since the secretary and I are not mutual admirers. He considers me a bit of a loose cannon."

"You *are* a loose cannon," Steinberg said. "But you're remarkably targeted for a loose cannon. As long as you keep that up, people will think you're golden. Screw up once, though, and you'll find yourself out in the cold in a heartbeat."

"Thanks for the pep talk," Mike said dryly.

"I was told you were a no-bullshit kind of guy," Steinberg replied. "I can blow smoke up your ass if you'd prefer."

Mike just chuckled and stood up as the door opened.

There were four men with the ambassador, one in Georgian uniform, one in Russian uniform and two guys in suits who could have been twins. They didn't look alike facially, but their expressions, build and suits were identical.

"Ambassador Krepkina, Deputy Secretary Svirska, Colonels Kortotich and Skachko, Mr. Steinberg, the embassy's intelligence officer, and Mr. Jenkins, an American citizen currently resident in Georgia," Ambassador Wilson said.

"Am pleased to meet you," the Russian ambassador said, shaking Mike's hand. "President Putin has good things to say about you as does Colonel Chechnik of the president's office."

"How is he?" Mike asked.

"Very well," the ambassador replied. "He sends his regards and hopes that you can in some way improve the situation."

"That's what we're here to talk about," Mike said, cautiously.

"Something must be done," Colonel Kortotich said, darkly.

"Gentlemen, let's take our seats before we begin arguing, shall we?" Ambassador Wilson said as the Georgian colonel darkened.

"I could do a long preamble," Wilson said when everyone was seated. "But I won't. What I'm going to do is let Mr. Steinberg explain why Mr. Jenkins' plans may, and I stress *may* have a salient effect on the current situation. Mr. Steinberg?"

"Mike, you got any idea what a functional militia in your area will do to the Chechens?" Steinberg said, standing up and going to a map on the wall.

"No," Mike admitted. "Let's get something straight up front. Okay, apparently most of the people in the room know that I've got some enemies. Specifically among Islamic terrorists. I settled where I settled because I liked the area and I *especially* liked the little fort I bought. I'm going to form a militia because the people in the area need some relief from the Chechens, who are apparently running rampant. And because I could use some gun-bunnies around. But I hadn't planned on crushing the Chechen forces in the area. The Red Army can't do that in Chechnya and the Georgian army can't do that in Georgia."

"The Chechens are not running *rampant*—" Colonel Skachko said, angrily.

"The hell they aren't," Colonel Kortotich snapped back. "You have no control over the eastern—"

"Wait," Steinberg said, holding up a hand and looking at the Georgian representatives. "Let's get something straight. We're here to talk reality. The Chechens use eastern Georgia, and especially the Pankisi Gorge, as a safe base. We know it, the Russians know it, the Chechens know it. That is a fact and all the posturing you can do in the world won't change it. By the same token, you're unable, not unwilling, *unable* to change that fact. Georgia doesn't have the funds or the resources to comb them out or even cut down on their movement. We know it, the Russians know it, the Chechens know it. In Russia's case, they can't gain full control of Chechnya, so you guys," he said, nodding at the Russians, "need to keep in mind that with fewer resources, the Georgians aren't in a position to do more than you have done. The U.S. has been helpful in training Georgian special operations, but we can't fund the entire Georgian army; we've got too many other irons in the fire and too many political constraints. Also facts. What we're here to discuss is what Mr. Jenkins can do about those facts and why, by a stroke of luck or genius, he picked a very good place to do it. Can I continue?"

"Go ahead," the Russian ambassador said, evenly.

"As I said, the primary Chechen bases are in the Pankisi Gorge," Steinberg said, pointing to the deep rift in southeast Georgia. "From the Gorge they can move into Chechnya through a series of old smuggler paths. But the Gorge has no industry and damned little in the way of agriculture. So they have to get all their support from elsewhere, notably by moving it through Georgia."

"We have tried to stop this..." Colonel Skachko said with a sigh.

"How hard?" Colonel Kortotich snapped.

"Gentlemen," Ambassador Wilson said, sharply.

"You have tried to stop it," Steinberg admitted. "But you've had the same lack of success that the Russians have and for the same reasons. I won't get into the reasons at the moment—"

"Because when you hit a checkpoint if you pass the guards a few rubles they wave you through," Mike said, folding his arms. "I think you said something about no bullshit."

"And you can change this?" Colonel Skachko snapped.

"I don't know," Mike admitted. "But it's going to be interesting the first time one of the Keldara does it. For him."

"The point is that while there is effective control over Chechen movement, in general, in the Tbilisi valley," Steinberg continued, calmly, "there is very little control over areas outside the central authority's region. A great degree of the reason for this is simply lack of forces, rather than low-scale corruption. But the amount of material that has to move, drugs and women out for sale and then guns back using both currency from the sales and external sources of funds—"

"And when are the Americans going to get the Saudis to stop *funding* these fucking black asses?" Colonel Kortotich asked, angrily.

"After we've changed regimes in Iran and Syria," Mike said. "At a guess. If you want the timetable moved up, you might suggest to your government that when we target a country, they *help* rather than hinder. Not mentioning any names, *Iraq!*" he added with a cough, covering his mouth.

"Mr. Jenkins," the ambassador said, sternly.

"Look," Mike replied, angrily. "I told everybody and their brother I'm not a fucking diplomat. Maybe I can be of some help. But I'm not going to promise anything and I'm tired of ritual dick-beating. Let Steinberg finish his dog and pony and I'll get back to *doing* something. Okay?"

The Russian ambassador held up his hand to stifle the colonel and then nodded at Steinberg. "Please, continue."

"If you look at this series of valleys leading from the Gorge," Steinberg said, pointing at the map, "you'll notice that they funnel towards Alerrso. Mike, did you know that that pass you're in has been a caravan route since time immemorial?"

"I'm living in a caravanserai," Mike pointed out, dryly. "It's fairly obvious."

"Until the major road was built to Tbilisi, Alerrso was the primary route through Georgia," Steinberg said. "And it's, currently, the route of choice for Chechen movement. If you set up a functional militia, that regains control of that area, you'll be cutting their throats."

"And they'll respond," Mike said, frowning. "I'm going to be six months forming a militia up to the point I think they should be. We're *not* going to be doing a lot of interdiction during that time. And I'm only looking at a company of light infantry who are going to be part-time. I'll choke what I can, when I can, but I'm *not* going to guarantee to stop everything. And what I'll be doing, the Russians will never see." He looked over at the two and shrugged. "I mean, all you'll be getting is negative data. Some attacks will still come through and every attack that gets through I don't want you guys blaming on *me*."

"You said that we should speak honestly," the Russian ambassador said after a brief pause. "And so I will speak with 'no bullshit' as you said. My government is...I was going to say 'extremely concerned' but in honesty they're more like extremely tired of the Chechens using Georgia as their base."

"We..." Colonel Skachko said and then stopped as Undersecretary Svirska held up a hand.

"Please continue, Mr. Ambassador," the undersecretary said, nodding.

"Yes, we all know why," the ambassador said. "But it does not change the fact. And, yes, my government is considering armed incursion into Georgia, even knowing that it will lead to a border war. Which will simply create chaos and probably make it easier for the Chechens to move. I have argued against this but the decision will not be made at my level. The Americans have argued against this and that is perhaps why it has not yet occurred. But if there is nothing done to stop the Chechens, or at least slow them down, we will be forced by the circumstances to invade. For our own defense. Mr. Jenkins, honestly, what do you think you can do?"

Mike thought about the terrain and looked at the map. He hadn't been giving any thought to the strategic situation, but he could see Steinberg's point.

"What about going south to Azerbaijan?" Mike asked.

"There is support through that route as well," Steinberg admitted. "But they don't have the markets there for sales. Mostly what we're concerned about is the trade to Eastern Europe. Weapons are available from Azerbaijan, especially being funneled by the Iranians, but not in the quantity, quality or cost that they can get them in Eastern Europe."

"It will take months to get the Keldara to the point they can do more than local defense," Mike said. "But by . . . say autumn, I'll have them patrolling. The point to that is to see anything coming before it gets to us. But the *effect* will *probably* be to interdict movement through the area. To an extent. I won't guarantee that we'll get everything. I need something from both the Russians and the Georgians, though."

"What do you need?" the undersecretary asked, sighing. "Money, unfortunately, is not available."

"I've got some money," Mike said. "But the end-user license is being held up somewhere. I need that expedited."

"Done," the undersecretary said, nodding. "I will ensure it is done this day."

"I'm going to be bringing in trainers," Mike said. "American and possibly Brit. They're not mercenaries, but they may end up engaged in combat, given the way the Chechens move. If they do,

I want it kept very quiet and I don't want the Georgian government coming down on us."

"Guaranteed," Colonel Skachko said. "I will ensure this through my office; I have the authority."

"From the Russians the main thing that I need is an intel feed," Mike said, looking at the two. "If you have concerns on something that you suspect or know is moving through my area, tell me. You should be able to get data on my secure link through American sources. If you have an issue, call me. I'll do *what I can* to handle it. Okay?"

"Yes," the ambassador said, nodding.

"I've got limited manpower, which is currently untrained," Mike said, sighing. "And I don't actually know what they're going to be capable of. But on my honor, I'll do my best to cut out Chechen movement through my area of operations. For the reasons we've discussed and because I fucking hate Islamic terrorists. I would *appreciate* it if Russia gave me a year to see what I can do. I know that's a long time in a war, but it's going to take at *least* that long to get a full grip on the area."

"I will present that to my government," the ambassador said, nodding.

"I want to make a last thing perfectly clear," Mike said, frowning. "I am *not* an agent of the United States government. I never have been. All I am is a retired SEAL. Don't go hanging CIA or NSA or any other tags on me. I'm a free agent. I'd just intended to make a tiddly little militia. I'll do what I can to keep two countries from going to war. But I make *no* guarantees and I'm getting dick all of support. This is all on my dime. Keep that firmly in mind."

"And you made your money from a communications company nobody has ever heard of," Colonel Kortotich said, smiling thinly.

"No," Mike said, working his jaw, "I made my money from killing people and breaking things. Specifically terrorists and their operations. Your point?"

▲   ▲   ▲

He had about a million things to do, but none of them were as urgent as getting a cup of tea from the kitchen and cadging another look at those lovely girls. They were still cleaning the kitchen, even now, and quite frequently on their knees with their lovely butts up in the air.

When he got there, though, the girls were up on their feet. Well, three of them were, while the fourth was sitting at the kitchen table, bent over in pain.

"What's wrong?" Mike asked.

"Irina has a bellyache," Mother Griffina said, frowning. "I think it is just gas."

"It *really* hurts," the girl said, her face working in pain.

"Lay her down on the table," Mike said, looking at the girl's face. She was sweating and pale.

The two old women helped her onto the table and Mike watched as the girl bent to favor her right side.

"Okay, I'm not doing anything wrong," Mike said, sliding his hand behind her neck. "Think of me as a doctor. This much I think I know about." She felt extremely warm but Mike didn't have a thermometer. Yes, he did, come to think of it.

"One of you," he said, looking at the girls who were standing around. "In my room there is a large black bag. There are three pouches on the outside. In the top pouch, there is a small purple plastic case. Get it."

"Stay still," he said to the Irina, laying his hands on her abdomen. "Does this hurt?" he asked, pressing her near the stomach.

"No," she said. "Maybe a little."

"You'll know when it hurts," Mike said, putting his hands on her left side and pressing near the kidney. "Does this hurt?"

"No," Irina said.

"This?" Mike asked, pressing into her right side.

The answer was a cry of pain and the girl arched forward.

"Sorry, had to check," Mike said, shaking his head as the girl he'd dispatched ran in with the plastic box.

The case was supposed to be a holder for soap, but Mike had used it for small breakable items he didn't want to be without. One of which was a small mercury thermometer. He shook it down and inserted it under the girl's tongue then took her pulse. It was nearly a hundred and a bit thready. He pulled the thermometer out; she was running a hundred and four degree temperature.

"Okay, we have a serious problem," Mike said, thinking about the long drive to Tbilisi. "We need to get Irina to a hospital as fast as we can. I'll need one friend, a good friend, and I'll take Genadi since he has to go to Tbilisi anyway. You," he said, pointing at the girl who had brought the thermometer. "Go back up to the room. There is a black box on the top of my dresser. Close the top, unplug it and put it in the small black bag. Then bring them both down here. You," he said, pointing to the next one. "Go get Genadi. Tell him he has three minutes to pack and be out front. You," he said, pointing to the last, a really beautiful blonde. "You're coming with us. She'll need somebody to hold her hand. This is going to get very bad."

"Kildar . . ." Mother Savina said.

"You have to stay here and finish getting the house prepared," Mike said. "So does Mother Griffina. Get her mother headed to the hospital tonight if you can. In the morning if you can't. Get a taxi or a car or something. There is a bundle of euros in my top drawer, use those. But we have to leave *now*."

"Very well, Kildar," Mother Savina said, shaking her head.

"Let's go, Irina," Mike said, helping the girl off the table. "You're going to have a very long, very unpleasant ride."

The girl he'd sent for his jump bag was standing in the doorway holding it carefully when he headed that way.

"Follow us to the car," Mike said. "Then run and get some bottled water. Where in the hell is Genadi?"

"Here, Kildar," the man said, looking at the girl who was bent over double in pain.

"We're going to Tbilisi," Mike said. "Right now. She has an

inflamed appendix, I think. There's a couple of other things it could be," he continued, making his way through the foyer. "Mother Savina, have clothes for both girls sent with Irina's mother. Tell the elders she's gone to the hospital. And pray we get there in time."

CHAPTER
NINE

Mike had given Irina two tablets of hydrocodone and three of Keflex when they got to the car. He then roared out of the compound with the two girls in the back and Genadi up front.

"Kildar," Genadi said as the Mercedes took a corner at dangerous speeds. "You might want to slow down. Killing all of us will save nothing."

"There's only so much time," Mike pointed out. "And it's, what? Four hours to Tbilisi?"

"There is that," Genadi said, sighing. "Are you sure it's the appendix?"

"I'm not a damned doctor," Mike said. "But I was on a mission one time when one of the team came down with it. I talked to the team medic about it and when you get that sort of reaction it's pretty much a given. He also said that once they burst, you're in huge trouble."

"This I understand," Genadi said. "But we are in huge trouble anyway."

"My driving isn't that bad," Mike said, chuckling.

"No, that is not it," Genadi sighed. "Kildar, we are two unmarried men in a car with two unmarried females."

"Oh, give me a break," Mike snapped. "If she didn't go to the hospital, she'd die."

"You should have brought Mother Savina or Mother Griffina," Genadi said.

"Fine time to tell me, now," Mike pointed out, then shook his head. "I think Savina tried to tell me but I cut her off. How much of a screw-up have I made?"

"For you, very little," Genadi said, quietly. "For Lydia and Irina, perhaps much."

"Kildar, it is okay," Lydia said, from the back. "You are the Kildar, you can do as you will."

"Don't tell me things like that or we *will* get in trouble," Mike replied. "I'll fix it. Don't worry about it."

"Kildar . . ." Genadi said.

"I'll *fix* it, Genadi," Mike snarled. "If I have to, I'll make them eat it raw. But they are not going to send Lydia or Irina to town because of *my* mistake. Get that straight. The absolute *worst* that happens is I'll take them in myself. But *nobody* mentions that option, understood?"

"Yes, Kildar," Genadi said.

"Thank you, Kildar," Lydia replied.

"How is Irina?" Mike asked.

"Asleep, I think," Lydia said. "At least very sleepy and quiet. What did you give her?'

"Enough Loritab to put her under," Mike said. "And enough Keflex, I hope, to slow down the infection until we get to the hospital. The Loritab has Tylenol in it, so it should get the fever down a bit. I'm not sure what I'm doing, but I'm trying."

"It is very cold in here, Kildar," Lydia said. "Could you maybe turn on the heat?"

"The colder it is, the harder it is for her body to let the fever run out of control," Mike said. "We're just going to have to put up with it."

The rest of the drive was mostly made in silence except for when occasional really bad bumps would wake Irina up. Finally they got to Tbilisi after midnight and Mike followed Genadi's directions to the hospital.

At the receiving dock for the emergency room, an armed guard waved them away.

"Right, I'm going on full ugly American mode," Mike said. "Genadi and Lydia, get Irina out. I'll handle the rest."

Mike got out of the car and stalked over to the guard who reacted by pointing his AK at Mike's chest.

"Get that out of my way," Mike said, slapping the barrel aside. "We have a medical emergency here. Where's a damned doctor?"

"You cannot park here!" the guard said, trying to swing the weapon back.

"Like hell," Mike replied. He pulled the AK away from the guard, dropped the magazine and disassembled the weapon before the guard could even reach for it. "Where is a damned *doctor*?" he snapped, grabbing the guard by the collar and lifting him off his feet.

"Inside," the guard gurgled, pointing to the doors.

"Thank you," Mike replied, setting him down. "I'll move my car in a bit. If you have any questions about this little encounter, contact Colonel Skachko at the Office of the President and he will put it in perspective."

Mike grabbed his jump bag and still made it to the doors before Lydia and Genadi had gotten the shaky Irina to the door. He held them open and then strode into the admissions area.

"Where's a doctor?" he asked the woman at the first counter.

"You will be having a seat," the woman said, pointing to a set of folding chairs.

"Nope," Mike said, leaning over until he was inches from her face. "We have an inflamed appendix. Onset was better than four hours ago. We need a doctor and we need him now. If I have to wake up the president of Georgia, and I can with one call, I will. But you had better get me an internist, one that is sober, in no more than ten minutes or I'm going to make sure you spend the rest of your life in a cheap brothel in Turkey. Do I make myself clear?"

"I am Doctor Platov. What is the problem?"

The doctor was about fifty and clearly tired, but Mike couldn't smell any alcohol on his breath.

"Possible inflamed appendix," Mike said. "Pain from palpation on the right side, fever of 104 plus, Fahrenheit. She's had fifteen milligrams of Loritab and seventy-five milligrams of Keflex about four hours ago. Onset was slightly in excess."

"Get her to an examination room, now," the doctor said to one of the orderlies that had accompanied him. The orderlies were large and male and Mike figured they had two purposes.

"She comes from a very strict mountain society," Mike said as the orderlies brought out a gurney and helped Irina into it. "As long as possible, her friend should be with her," he added, indicating Lydia. "And a female nurse is going to be required."

"The first thing that is required is payment," Dr. Platov sighed. "I can confirm your diagnosis, but to open her will require assurance that the bill will be paid. I assume she has no insurance if she is from the mountains. And I cannot, *cannot*, operate without assurance of payment."

"Give me an estimate," Mike said, "and I'll give you cash."

"You do not understand," the doctor said, tiredly. "Even in this country, such things will be expensive. At least a thousand euros."

"Where's the cashier?" Mike asked as two policemen came in the doors.

"I believe you threatened her with being sold into slavery," the doctor said, dryly.

"Fine," Mike said. "Just one thing. I know that there are local medicines and foreign and the foreign are more expensive. They're also better. Use the foreign. I'll pay for it."

"You, stop right there," one of the policemen said, placing his hand on his pistol.

"If you draw that, you'll end up on a border post shaking down Chechens," Mike replied, glancing over his shoulder. "I'm quite serious. If you think I'm not, you'd better wake up Colonel Skachko at the office of the President of Georgia. Right now, I'm going over there," Mike said, pointing at the functionary at the desk, "and I'm going to pay her for the services this doctor is about to perform. Come on over. We'll talk about whether I'm under arrest over there, okay?"

The doctor looked at them and nodded, then gestured at Lydia to accompany him as the gurney was wheeled away.

"Hi," Mike said, smiling at the woman who was looking at him with a mixture of wariness and anger. "Sorry about all that, I was just trying to get through to you." He dipped into the jump bag, ignoring the police at his back, and pulled out a thick bundle of euro notes. "The doctor estimated that the operation will be a thousand euros," he said, opening up the bundle and counting. "That's fifteen hundred. The extra is for good medicines. I'm, personally, good for any additional treatment. Is there any question?"

"What is she, your whore?" the woman asked, eyeing the money on the desk.

"No, she's in the nature of a retainer," Mike said. "As far as I know, she's a virgin. She'd better be one when she leaves the hospital. Pass that around.

"Right," he continued, turning to the cops. "Mind if I pull out my cell phone?" he continued, ignoring them as he did just that. He hit the speed-dial list and held the phone up where they could see it. "That is the personal, home, number of the Georgian Undersecretary of State for Military Affairs, Vladimir Svirska. Would you like me to hit Send?" he asked, hovering his finger over the button.

"No," the policeman in the lead said, holding up both hands. "Not a problem."

"I was on a medical emergency," Mike said. "You might talk to the guard and explain to him the term 'medical emergency.' I will now go move my car so that ambulances can pull up."

"Are you okay?" Mike said, sitting down by Lydia. He'd sent Genadi off with some money to arrange a hotel room with instructions to get a suite at the Hilton. Be damned if he was going to stay in any fleabag.

"She wouldn't wake up," Lydia said. "The doctor was very concerned. I left when they started to undress her. It was women doing it. The doctor promised there would be women present at all times, but I had to leave. She was very hot and she moaned but she wouldn't wake up."

"She had a lot of painkiller in her," Mike pointed out. "It hits some people that way. She'll be fine." *As long as they don't screw up the anesthetic from her having Loritab in her. Or bungle the operation. As long as the appendix hasn't burst already and she doesn't die from peritonitis.* Bad thoughts that he set aside.

"Will it be very long?" Lydia asked.

"Probably not," Mike said. "Pulling an appendix is a very straightforward operation. In fact, a doctor once did it to himself."

"How?" Lydia asked. "And why?"

"Traffic in Cairo is very bad," Mike said. "The doctor knew he had a swollen appendix and was going to the hospital but he got caught in a very bad traffic jam. So he removed it himself and then drove to the hospital. Now, I don't know that *I'd* want to do that, it would probably hurt like hell, but it has been done. So, you see, it's very straightforward."

"The Fathers will be very angry," Lydia said, looking at the floor. Mike desperately wanted to hug her, hell, he wanted to screw her, but he refrained.

"Because this puts the Family in debt?" Mike asked. "Or because I screwed up and didn't bring a chaperone?"

"Both," Lydia admitted.

"Well, on the debt thing, I warned them," Mike said. "I should have brought Father Kulcyanov in earlier, so we can get his heart checked. He's got a case of congestive heart failure if I've ever seen one. And as for the other, they can kiss my ass. If they're that worked up about it, I'll sell the land back to the bank at a loss and go find some other insular society to bug. And then they won't be able to throw their hands up in despair and say 'The Kildar!'" Mike finished, throwing his hands up in exasperation.

Lydia smiled at that and ducked her head.

"You are very funny, Kildar," she said, looking up after a moment. "And very kind."

"I'm just trying to get you in bed," Mike said, then clapped his hand over his mouth. "Sorry, sometimes things like that just slip out."

"I am promised," Lydia said, primly. "To Oleg."

"Well, Christ, now I'm in trouble," Mike replied, thinking of the massive Keldara. "He's gonna break me in half!"

"He will not," Lydia said, patting him on the arm in comfort. "He likes you. He wants to be a leader in the militia."

"Well, I'm gonna see you two married if it's the last thing I do," Mike replied. "And with a passel of kiddies. See if I don't."

"Perhaps in summer," Lydia said, shaking her head, sadly. "There are problems."

"We'll work them out," Mike promised. "One way or another." He looked up as the doctor came in the room, still stripping off his gloves, which were spattered with blood.

"It is good," Dr. Platov said, nodding. "It was an inflamed appendix, yes, very bad. But it had not burst. She should be well. There is no infection of the bowel. Peritonitis, yes? None of that."

"Good," Mike said, more relieved than he was willing to admit. "Thank you, Doctor."

"She will stay here overnight for observation," Platov said. "Then can be moved tomorrow, perhaps tomorrow afternoon. I have placed her on what we call a priority regimen," he added, smiling ironically. "This will increase the cost, it uses German medicines instead of Russian, but you can be sure the bottles have drugs in them and not distilled water."

"I can afford it," Mike said. "When can we see her?"

"She is in recovery and it is well after visiting hours," the doctor said, yawning. "I would suggest that you find a room in town. Come back tomorrow not before eight. She should be awake by then."

"We'll see her tomorrow, then," Mike said, standing up. "I'm unsure of the customs and I hope this is not an insult. Is a gift in order? For a life?"

"Always," Platov said, nodding. "Make sure she is not sold to town by the damned Keldara. I did not work on her as hard as I did for her to be a whore. But if you are talking about money, no."

"Kildar, this is too much," Lydia said when they were shown to the suite. It really wasn't much from Mike's point of view. A small living room and kitchenette with bedrooms on either side. The furniture was 1970s chic. It looked freshly made, which meant some designer somewhere needed to have their head examined.

"Don't worry about it," Mike said, yawning. It had been a long day. "Genadi?" he called.

"In here," Genadi said from the left-hand room. He popped his head out and grinned. "I'd missed television."

"The boobtube will rot your brain," Mike said. "But I wonder if they get ESPN? I might be able to catch a game." He thought about the time of year and shrugged. "Never mind, the Superbowl's even over. Lydia, you get that one," Mike continued, pointing to the right-hand bedroom. "I'm sure the door locks. Lock it. There will be a bathroom and all that. Get cleaned up, long day tomorrow. Then get some sleep. We'll be getting up in about..." He glanced at his watch and blanched. "Two hours. So get some sleep fast."

▲   ▲   ▲

Mike was sitting on a chair down the hall from Irina's room when Ambassador Wilson entered the corridor, followed by a couple of functionaries including one of the hospital administrators.

"Hi, Mike," the ambassador said, sitting down next to him. "Really, Administrator, I'm just here to talk to my friend."

"If there's anything we can do for you, Mr. Ambassador . . ." the administrator said.

"Not a thing I can think of," the ambassador answered, smiling. "I'm just going to talk to Mike for a bit and then head back to the embassy."

"If you need anything," the administrator said, "have one of the nurses call me. If there are any problems at all . . ."

"I will," Wilson said, smiling. "We'll be fine."

When the administrator had left, Wilson looked over at the former SEAL.

"So, any problems you need fixed?" he asked, chuckling.

"Why do the words 'follow the money' come to mind?" Mike asked.

"Because we dumped about six million dollars into this place three years ago," Wilson replied. "Most of it went down the usual corruption rathole, but some of it stuck. The surgical suite your friend was fixed up in for example. And we've got an ongoing cross-training program for doctors. They like us very much, yes?"

"Yes," Mike said, smiling faintly.

"So, how's the Keldara militia going?" Wilson asked.

"Slowly," Mike admitted. "I've got the equipment. I'm waiting on the trainers. Time."

"Napoleon," Wilson replied. "'Ask me for anything but time.' Did you really beat up a guard?"

"Took away his peashooter," Mike admitted. "And, okay, lifted him up by his collar. I didn't *hit* him, though."

"All good," Wilson said. "Spreads the myth of the American. In general it's a problem, but in places it's quite useful. You should have tipped the policemen, though."

"Arrange it and bill me," Mike said, tiredly.

"And the president wants to meet you," the ambassador added.

"Just what I need," the former SEAL said with a groan. "Georgia's I take it?"

"Svasikili," Wilson agreed, nodding.

"I still don't have a suit," Mike pointed out, hanging his head in his hands.

"There are tailors in Tbilisi," Wilson said. "Hey, that alliterates."

"I've seen the suits they make," Mike said, sitting up. "Yours is nice, where'd you get it?"

"Harrowgates on Bond Street," Wilson said, turning out the lapel.

"Think they do house calls?" Mike asked, yawning.

"You look like hell, Mike."

"Two hours sleep," Mike said. "And the sort of stresses I'm not used to. And I can't believe a bed in a God damned Hilton would be that uncomfortable. The designers should be shot. No, that's too good for them. Hung up by their balls over a shark tank and handed a rusty knife."

"Get some rest," Wilson said, standing up. "If you haven't got your health, you haven't got anything."

"An ambassador who watches *The Princess Bride*," Mike said, smiling. "Will wonders never cease."

"And I can walk and chew gum at the same time," Wilson said, nodding as he left.

Mike was half asleep when he heard a throat clear.

"Kildar?" a woman said.

Mike looked up, rubbing sleep out of his eyes, to see a Keldara woman loaded with parcels standing in the corridor. She could have been anywhere from thirty to sixty but she still had some of the same lean good looks as Irina overlaid with years of stress and wear.

"You would be Irina's mother?" Mike asked, standing up and yawning.

"Yes, Kildar," the woman said, nervously.

"I'll take the bags," Mike replied. "She was awake the last time I checked. She's down the hall, second door on the left. I'll take the stuff back to the hotel. When you get thrown out, visiting hours are almost over, get a taxi and come to the Hilton. I'll arrange for the doorman to pay for it. Do you understand?"

"Yes, Kildar," the woman said.

"On the being alone with Irina and Lydia," Mike said. "I'll take it up with the Fathers. There will *not* be a problem or there's going to be a *huge* problem. For them. Don't worry about that."

"Very well, Kildar," the woman said, unhappily.

"I'll see you at the hotel."

"Thank you for calling Harrowgates of Bond Street, how may I help you?" a chipper female voice said.

"There are problems in life that cannot be solved by throwing money at them," Mike said, philosophically. "And then there are problems that can. I'm trying to figure out which this is. I'm in Georgia, the country not the state, and I need a suit to meet with the President of Georgia day after tomorrow. How much money do I need to throw at that problem to get one of your suits by then?"

"Sir," the woman answered, tautly, "we have a number of clients and at the moment our wait time is . . ."

"Ten thousand euros?" Mike asked. "For one suit? I'll arrange a business jet to fly in one of your tailors or whatever . . ."

"Haberdashers, sir, please," the woman said. "And, frankly, some of our suits *sell* for ten thousand euros . . ."

"I'll skip the bidding and go straight to thirty, then," Mike said. "I'm medium build. Around a forty-four-inch chest, about thirty-four waist. Thirty-inch inseam and sleeves, more or less. I'll put him up at the Hilton. Fly out, get me fitted, fly back. Anything you have around my size and in decent style. Thirty thousand euros. And I'll need some more, I guess. Figure that out later."

"I think we can arrange something sir," the woman said after a moment's pause. "If I could have your name and how you're planning on paying for this . . . ?"

CHAPTER TEN

"President Svasikili," Mike said, shaking the President of Georgia's hand. "It is a pleasure to meet you." The president was a round man, slightly shorter than Mike, with a firm handshake and affable smile that stopped at his eyes. Typical third world politician in a nominal "democracy" one each.

"And you as well, Mr. Jenkins," the president said. "Might I present General Umarov, the Chief of Staff of the Army."

The meeting was taking place at the presidential palace, an ugly structure that dated to the Soviet period. Since the president of Georgia regularly had to travel in a massive convoy to prevent assassination, it was a security and ease measure for him.

The American ambassador traveled in nearly as large a convoy, but he was, apparently, more expendable. As was Colonel Osbruck, the senior American military attaché. They were both present and everyone nodded then proceeded into the conference room.

"Do you think there will be a thaw, soon?" the president asked Mike after everyone had gained their seats and tea was served. The woman doing the serving was a serious looker, like a supermodel, and had a sway to her that said that more than tea was available. The tea was served in traditional glasses with metal holders. These were silver and transmitted the heat of the tea straight to the handle making it too hot to hold. It was a silly design and Mike had always wondered what idiot came up with it in the depths of time.

"You'd know better than I, sir," Mike replied, quickly setting his tea down and waiting for it to cool. "This is the first time I've been to Georgia."

"I do hope it warms up soon," the president said. "My old bones hate the winter. When I retire I'm going to move somewhere very warm."

Possibly straight to hell if an assassin gets through, Mike thought. Svasikili had run on a platform of cleaning up the graft and ending the war in Ossetia. Since then negotiations had been stalled, the Ossetians were terrorizing western Georgia, the Chechens eastern Georgia, and taxes seemed to disappear into a black hole. The hole, of course, was called "Svasikili's cronies" and funds to prop up his primary voting base, which was among organized labor. The military, despite the conditions, had just sustained another cutback. At least part of that was in fear that they'd attempt a coup. It wouldn't work out, it never did, but Svasikili had to know that if the military took over, he'd be lucky to leave with his shirt.

"But in the meantime, I'm forced to try to make bricks without straw," Svasikili said, sighing. "This country is impossible to govern. Dozens of different interests, all vying for power, the clans in the mountains always feuding, the Ossetians, the Chechens, just impossible."

"Lovely place, though," Mike pointed out. "It's why I decided to settle here. And the people are very nice as well. The Keldara are grand fellows."

"So it was the beauty of the country that caused you to settle here?" the president asked.

"And the women," Mike admitted, smiling at the joke. "The Keldara beer isn't half bad, either."

"I can call for a beer if you would prefer," the president said, waving at the untouched tea.

"This is fine, sir," Mike said, picking it up despite the handle and taking a sip while glancing at the ambassador. He wasn't trained or interested in diplomacy at this level but he was afraid he'd just insulted the country of Georgia by not sipping the damned tea. "I've become quite a tea drinker since moving overseas."

"The question, of course, is *why* an American would want to settle in Georgia," the president said, nodding at the comment. "There are less than a thousand American ex-patriates in the country and almost all of those are here for one company or another. There are a scattering of people who just find this country conveniently inexpensive. But you are not short of money. Your ambassador has assured us that you are not wanted by any international agency. So the question is why you would want to settle down here. Especially in that forsaken wasteland of the Keldara. Then there's the question of why you are forming a little army out of them."

"Hardly an army," Mike pointed out, glancing at the ambassador again. He should have been briefed on what this meeting was about beforehand but he felt a general trend. "They will constitute about a company in size and be designed for small-unit operations. Just a mountain militia."

"A remarkably well-armed and equipped mountain militia," General Umarov interjected. "When the request came through to expedite the end-user license we, of course, complied. We are as worried about conditions in east Georgia as the Russians. But when the actual *lists* started arriving we became . . . somewhat concerned. Your simple mountain militia will be better equipped than the Presidential Commandoes."

"I discovered when I was a SEAL that good equipment helps," Mike said. "It's not everything, though; you have to have good training. And, I'm sorry to point out, they're probably going to be better trained than your commandoes as well." He didn't have to look to know that the ambassador had just winced. "I don't think that it would be fit to do less and they're going to need that training to do what they'll have to do to suppress the Chechens.

"However," he added, as the general opened his mouth, "they are, as I said, less than a company. And they are training for open field, small unit actions. I know that there is always a fear that a particular group will . . . oh, become the tail that wags the dog as we say in the United States. The Keldara are going to be training in a way that makes that *fundamentally* unlikely."

"Explain," the president said, holding up a hand to cut off the general's retort.

"There are, essentially, three types of forces in the world," Mike said, picking his words carefully. "Field forces, regime protection forces and show forces. Show forces are very good at parading. They are trained to look good, pretty much period. Some excellent combat units are also good at showing off, don't get me wrong. The Rhodesian Selous Scouts were bloody peacocks and marched better than the Coldstream Guards. But show forces are only there for show.

"Next, there are regime protection forces," Mike said, trying not to look at the Chief of Staff of the Georgian army. "Regime protection forces are, essentially, very large police forces. They are trained to suppress resistance to the regime, to break up riots, to ferret out guerillas and so forth. They're, really, peacekeeping forces in countries where peace is shaky. Due to the nature of their training, they're very good at coups. They're used to moving to specific places in cities and, for example, taking over broadcast stations or buildings that are important to a coup.

"Last, there are field armies. Field armies are designed to meet other forces on the field of battle and defeat them. That can be small unit or large unit, but that is their training. They may march well and they may be able to occasionally be used to keep the peace, but they're not fundamentally trained for either. Field armies are designed to destroy other forces and when used in a coup tend to break much more than they should. They also make various mistakes, like firing into crowds indiscriminately, that make the succeeding regime, even if the coup is successful, very unpopular. The vast majority of the American army is field forces. The only units that are not are Civil Affairs and MPs."

"I see," the president said, nodding. "And what type of training are the Keldara getting?"

"Field force training," Mike said, definitely. "They're also being trained for open field combat, not urbanized combat. The Keldara, frankly, would be bloody useless in a coup. And given their training and the fact that they're only a company, trying to *stage* a coup would be insane. I take it, now, that that is the subject of this discussion?"

"One of them," the president admitted. "And I wanted to see what you were like."

"And what am I like?" Mike asked, suddenly weary. He missed his boat in the Keys.

"Blunt," the president said, laughing. "As I was warned. Not the diplomat at all. This is good. A person as blunt as you would, yes, be very bad at staging a coup. What do you think of the Georgian army?"

"I haven't seen much of it," Mike said. "From what I have seen, it's trained as a regime protection force and not very well trained at that. It's underpaid, so all the troops are on the take, which means anything can slip through your checkpoints with a little cash. The officers don't understand leadership; all they understand is discipline and that badly. And for a little extra money you could have gotten much better equipment; the boots, especially, are horrible."

"I see," the president said, his face frozen.

"Yes, I am blunt," Mike replied. "And you asked. If you don't want to know the answer, don't ask me the question. Now, do I get to train my Keldara so I can do something about the Chechens in the area or do you want me to pack up and leave?"

"Oh, I think you can train your Keldara," the president said. "If for no other reason than the fact that if they're going to be

as well trained as you say, if there *is* a coup, I'll have somewhere
to run."

"Great," Mike said. "And you can feel free. I'll make sure you
get somewhere safe. But if we can cut this short, it'd be great. I've
got *another* meeting pending and it's going to be even tougher
than this one."

"Tougher?" General Umarov asked. If he was upset at Mike's
bluntness, or his opinion of the Georgian Army, it didn't show.
In fact, he had a twinkle in his eye.

"The Keldara can be rather stuck in their ways," Mike
admitted.

Mike sat at the head of the kitchen table as the elders filed in.
He had "asked" Captain Tyurin to pick them up, since for the
time being he was the only one in the valley with the wheels and
Mike wasn't about to have Father Kulcyanov walk up the hill.

He waited in silence as the Six Fathers took seats and then
hooked his feet on a convenient rung under the table and tilted
his chair back.

"In case anyone's interested," he said, "Irina is doing fine. She,
Lydia and her mother are in a hotel in Tbilisi. It will be a few
more days before she can be driven back safely. With that out of
the way, go ahead and say the rest."

"Kildar," Father Mahona said after a series of looks were
exchanged. "You have to understand that among the Keldara, if
a woman has been alone with a man she is considered . . . not
eligible for marriage."

"Spoiled goods," Mike said, nodding. "Unclean. Fit only to be
sent to town. She's your daughter, and I assume we're discussing
Lydia, here, but I understand she's promised to Oleg Kulcyanov,"
Mike said, looking over at the old man. "What does the Family
of Kulcyanov say?"

"Lydia is a good woman," Father Kulcyanov replied after a
moment. "And Oleg cares for her very much. But there is the
problem of . . ."

"Of a medical emergency," Mike said, dropping his chair to land hard and leaning forward. "Okay, I screwed up. I was in full American mode. In the U.S., there would have been no thought of this. I needed to get Irina to the hospital or she would have died..."

"The money..." Father Shaynav said.

"NO!" Mike shouted, slamming his fist on the table. "I said there would be NO debt for medical treatment! You touch on MY honor with this! As to Lydia," Mike continued, more calmly, "nothing happened. Not in the car, not in the hotel. Think about this, Oleg *is* going to be one of the leaders of the militia. I will have him at my *back* with a gun in his hand. How *stupid* would I have to be to fool around with his woman? Do you *really* think I'm that stupid?"

"It is a matter of custom, Kildar," Father Mahona said, tightly.

"Yes, it is," Mike replied. "It is a matter of control of reproduction. I can lecture on it for hours. I probably understand it better than you do. There are pills and things to do it in more advanced cultures. But in your culture, for thousands of years, the only way to control reproduction was to control the body of the woman. The only way that worked, at least. But Lydia is still in the same condition as when she left. So is Irina, for that matter. In the future, I will be much more careful. You'll have to chalk this up to the Kildar not knowing your customs as well as I should. I have been here for a very short time. But, I will *not* have Oleg pissed at me because I tainted his marriage, much less ended it! That is *final*. Is this clear?"

"Yes, Kildar," Father Mahona said, angrily.

Snow still covered the ground thickly, but the roads were plowed so Mike used those for his morning run. He'd gotten severely out of shape but between the weight machines and running in the morning some of the old form was coming back. Every other day he'd started laying off the run and taking a heavily weighted ruck up the paths in the mountains. The first week he'd barely been able to make it a few hundred meters, but at the end of three weeks he was climbing all the way to the summit of the western mountains. The first day he made it to the top he'd had to just sit up there in the blowing cold and breathe for a good half hour. The air was noticeably thinner and the ruck march had worn him to the point he wasn't sure he could get back down. It was late afternoon before he made it to the caravanserai and he'd been in no shape to work out the next day.

This morning he was coming back from a light ten-mile jog that had taken him up and down the hills to the north. He turned into the road up to the caravanserai, speeding up and really pushing the muscles up the switchbacks until he reached the gate, then slowing down and trotting around the gardens to the south. He was breaking snow at that point so he slowed to a walk and continued around the caravanserai until he got back to the front door.

It felt good. The run had been long and not particularly slow and some of the hills to the north had been steep, not even mentioning the damned road up to the caravanserai. But he still felt good. Back in form. Yakov had even gotten the girls in town cleaned up, if not the house, and Mike was back to getting his ashes hauled on a regular basis. Life was good.

He dropped the sweats on a table in the foyer—it was nice having servants—and headed up to his room in sweat-soaked shorts and a T-shirt. After a shower and shave he got into jeans and flannels and headed back downstairs.

He'd taken to eating in the kitchen, much to Mother Griffina's initial shock and horror. But at this point she'd gotten over it. By the time he made it back downstairs the sweats had been whisked away, coffee was brewed and Mother Griffina was ready to serve up his "barbarian" breakfast of eggs, bacon, hash browns and biscuits with gravy. It helped that he'd gotten various German appliances shipped in, at exorbitant cost. The kitchen had all new stoves and an industrial refrigerator and freezer. In the attached cellars there was a zero degree freezer he intended to fill up during the year as meat and vegetables became available. He'd also gotten a couple of sets of washing machines and dryers so Mother Savina and her helpers wouldn't have to do all the laundry by hand.

"There was a call from a shipping company," Mother Savina said as he entered the room. "There are two containers on the way, both full. They should be here a little after noon."

"The militia's equipment arrives," Mike said, sitting down at the kitchen table and nodding to Mother Griffina in thanks as she poured coffee. "We're going to need a bunch of strong backs."

"And Genadi called from Tbilisi and asks that you call him back," Mother Savina added.

"I'll call him after breakfast," Mike said, as Mother Griffina set the heaping plate in front of him. Between the cold and the run he was famished.

After breakfast he took a cup of coffee to the office and dialed Genadi.

"Kildar," the farm manager said when he answered the phone. "It is good to hear from you."

"What's the situation?" Mike asked. When they'd last spoken the local Ford dealer only had two models that they needed. They'd placed an order for the rest.

"All of the trucks are in," Genadi said. "And the SUVs are supposed to be on the next ship. When do you want to start delivery?"

"What about the tractors and sundry equipment?" Mike asked.

"I've gotten the entire list rounded up," Genadi said, happily. "They can be delivered at any time."

"Monday," Mike said. "The militia equipment is coming in today. I'm going to store it in the cellars for the time being. Bring it in on Monday and we'll make an event of it. There's not much going on at the moment."

"The weather report expects a thaw to start next week," Genadi said. "There will be the floods starting maybe. We can use the time to train people on the equipment."

"The trainers are going to be arriving week after next," Mike said, thoughtfully. "We're not going to start serious training until we have some idea how the new equipment works with the planting."

"We will work it out," Genadi said. "Can do."

"Can do," Mike replied. "Schedule delivery of all of it for Monday. And don't forget *my* SUV. The Mercedes is awfully comfortable but I'm tired of not being able to drive anywhere but paved roads."

"I won't," Genadi said with a chuckle.

"Later," Mike said, cutting the connection. "Come," he added at a knock on the door.

"The Keldara will be here a little before noon," Mother Savina said.

"Ask Mother Griffina to prepare to feed them, if we have the food in the house," Mike said. "I'd like to take every opportunity to feed them when I can. That cuts down on the stores they have to draw on."

"I'll pass that on to Griffina," Mother Savina said, nodding.

"There are about twenty people arriving next week," Mike said. "We're going to have to lay in stores for them as well. Make sure there's plenty of beer; most of them are going to be beer drinkers. Get some wine as well. And get the upstairs rooms cleaned up, most of them will be housed in there. They will be staying for some time. I'll get some helpers for you while they're here; I'm not sure I want to mix Keldara women in with these guys until I get a better read. I need to go talk to Yakov."

Mike found the pimp in his usual spot, hanging out by the door hoping for customers.

"Mr. Jenkins," Yakov said, happily, as he opened the door for the former SEAL. "It is good to see you in the house again."

"Glad to be back," Mike said as they walked into the main

room. It was early so the girls were probably still in bed; the room wasn't occupied anyway.

"I can wake up Inessa," Yakov offered. The redhead was Mike's "regular" although he switched around to keep all the girls in spending money. Even the cold-eyed blonde who *was* good in bed, but a maven for tips. The problem with screwing her, though, was every time Mike got it stuck in he was half afraid there'd be a razor waiting for him. The girl was just trouble. He'd seen it in how she treated the other girls and even Yakov, who apparently had no control over her.

"Not right now," Mike said. "The reason I stopped by is that I'm going to have some visitors. They're going to be staying for a while. Now, I could send them to town for the joys, but I'd rather not. Nothing against your house; it's a security issue. What I'd like to do is *borrow* some of the girls for the time they're here."

"You mean rent I hope," Yakov said, his eyes narrowing. "Borrow is a different meaning."

"Rent then," Mike said, sighing. "And they're going to have to help with some stuff around the house, especially with everyone that's going to be there. Actually, I'd like to leave just one with you, maybe Katya, and take the other four."

"If you take Katya it's a deal," Yakov said. "I'll keep Esfir. If your friends get tired of the other girls, you will perhaps send them up here?"

"Be sure of it," Mike said. "The guys are arriving week after next. Go ahead and send the girls over middle of next week."

He left the brothel whistling. Having the girls around would keep the troops happy and he wouldn't have to go visit the girls in this crappy "house." He should have done this a long time ago.

He stopped whistling as he realized he was going to be letting Katya in his house. That wasn't going to be fun. But he could handle her. And if she couldn't be handled, well, there was a backhoe arriving on Monday.

▲   ▲   ▲

"Father Kulcyanov," Mike said, shaking the old man's hand, then going on to the other elders. "It is good to see you," he continued, louder, looking over the crowd of Keldara gathered outside the houses, "all of you."

There was a cold wind blowing but not as cold as it had been, and it was blowing from the south. The temperature was well above freezing and the ground was slushy and nasty. But it was Monday. He stepped back onto the dais so he could see the whole group and nodded.

"When I first spoke to you, I said that I would promise nothing," Mike said, reaching down and hitting the transmit button on the radio at his side twice. "I said you would have to see what I would do. Last week, the men of the Keldara helped unload two containers of material. This gear is now housed in the caravanserai until trainers arrive. But they could see what was in the boxes. Uniforms, boots, ammunition vests, communications, guns and ammunition. All of the things that we will need to make this valley secure from any threat."

He paused as there was a brief buzz and didn't look over his shoulder as the buzz got louder and people began pointing behind him excitedly.

"But there is more to this valley than its security," Mike continued as he heard the sound of truck engines revving on the flat. "This is a farm, first and foremost, and a farm cannot function without tools. So now you see the other side of what I have not promised, but have been able to deliver."

He stepped down as the first of the tractor trailers negotiated the turn into the valley and then kept going down into the flats. He'd had the Keldara plow and gravel a large area, completely mystifying them, but it now gave the six tractor trailers room to maneuver into place.

Two were car carriers loaded with pickup trucks and SUVs, red diesel F-350 flaresides and black diesel Expeditions. The others were loaded with tractors, including one monster for pulling a combination harvester. The combine was going to be delivered later since there hadn't been enough trucks to bring everything at once. There was also a large container truck that pulled in next to them.

Mike joined the group of Keldara that crowded forward to see the arriving equipment and smiled at their talk. The equipment was a big hit.

He smiled even more broadly when Genadi pulled up in a big black Expedition.

"Good to see you, Genadi," Mike said as the farm manager got out of the SUV.

"Yours is the first to be unloaded," Genadi said, pointing at one of the car carriers as the driver got out and started undoing the chains.

"Just getting this stuff unloaded is going to be a chore," Mike said. "Especially the container vehicle."

"There is a forklift in it," Genadi said, smiling. "The equipment is on pallets. A bit more expensive but we should be able to get it unloaded quickly."

There was more than tractors on the flatbeds; they were loaded down with attachments. As it turned out, even with the willing help of the Keldara it took more time to unload the flatbeds than the rest of the material combined and when all the equipment was down off the trucks and the trucks were gone, Mike shook his head.

"I need to see the elders," Mike said. "And Oleg for Kulcya-nov."

When the group was gathered Mike waved at the equipment.

"There is one forty-horsepower tractor for each family," Mike said. "Most of them have a forklift attachment, a dozer blade, a bush-hog, a hay cutter and a couple of other minor attachments. Spread them out to your houses and barns. The big tractor is for the farm in general; there will be a harvester and some planting devices delivered next week. Each family gets a truck and an SUV. The SUVs are for the fathers so they can move around and they can let people use them as they wish with one exception:

they are also for the use of the militia when we get it going. The militia has first call on the SUVs. The pallets have general tools that Genadi thought would be of use. There are shovels, hoes, axes, chainsaws and other items. Distribute them equally among you. Yes, I own them, but you are to use them as you would use your own tools. Use them to cut wood until we can do something better for heat, use them in your gardens. Do not think that this is debt; you will surely use them in service of the farm in general as well."

"Kildar," Father Shaynav said, nodding at him. "We thank you for these items."

"If the farm has good tools, good seeds and good people, it will prosper," Mike said. "There was no way that we'd be able to make anything better without the proper tools. Next week the trainers will be arriving. They will take a few weeks getting acquainted and looking at the land to figure out where to do training and some projects I have in mind. With the tractors many of the young men will be available for training even during planting. When the trainers get here I'll come up with a schedule and get it to you. While we are still unable to work the fields, however, we'll start introductory weapons training with some of the Keldara. I'll run it, starting tomorrow," he said, handing Oleg a sheet of paper.

"That is a list of the first group to be trained," Mike said. "I would like to see those men at the caravanserai tomorrow morning about nine. Genadi has another list of Keldara who will start training with the tractors tomorrow. Put the gear away today and I will meet with those men tomorrow."

CHAPTER
ELEVEN

"Oleg, Vil, Pavel, Sawn, Padrek, Yosif," Mike said, shaking hands with the group when they got to the caravanserai. Each was from a different Family and each had shown enough intelligence and initiative in the time he'd known them that they might make good leaders for the militia. "We need to get some gear and set up some stuff. Petro has some wood to set up target boards. For today, we'll probably just work on setting up the range up here. Oleg, you brought the Kulcyanov tractor with the posthole attachment and a wagon?"

"I did," Oleg said, his normally somber mien breaking into a grin for a moment. "I liked driving it."

"We rode up in the wagon," Vil added. "I felt as if I was being lazy."

"There will be work enough today," Mike said.

There was a cargo door to the cellars on the north side and Mike led them down to the cellars, then over to it.

"Oleg, get the tractor and bring it around," Mike said, looking at the pile of material he'd gathered near the opening. "We'll start hauling this stuff up."

"What is this?" Vil asked as he picked up a large and heavy cardboard box.

"Steel target system," Mike said. "You'll see. I should have gotten Dutov up here."

They loaded up the tractor, then hauled all the material over to the long lawn on the south side.

"I'm going to want to berm all these walls eventually," Mike said, directing Oleg over to the wall. "But this one will be first. It's going to take a beating in the meantime."

He started setting up the range, occasionally consulting a layout he'd drawn. On the west side he dropped steel targets for a pistol range along with the materials for a rolling target system, then set out more target materials for a rifle range on the east. The rifle range was only going to be about sixty meters long, which wasn't nearly enough, but it would do for "around the house" practice.

Using the posthole digger attachment on the tractor they set up wooden target stands and settled the bases of the steel targets. Both of them they set in concrete from bags of Quikrete Mike had gotten from the hardware store. It took most of the day to finish setting up the range to Mike's satisfaction, including having Sawn and Padrek set up shooting tables from raw boards. As with any project, they had to go back to the house for stuff Mike had forgotten and at one point he sent Pavel to the hardware store for more Quikrete and nails.

By the end of the day, though, they had a decent fixed range to shoot at.

"Okay," Mike said as the sun was going down. "Back here tomorrow at nine to start classes in weapons."

"We can be here earlier, Kildar," Vil pointed out. "We are up at dawn."

"So am I," Mike said. "Running. Nine."

▲   ▲   ▲

Mike was shaved, showered and fed when the Keldara turned up. In addition to the six that had been there before, Oleg had brought another Keldara, an older man, maybe forty or fifty although it was difficult to tell with the Keldara, who was thin and hard looking.

"Lasko has some experience with shooting," Oleg said. "I hope you don't mind me bringing him. He is very good."

"Most of the time you have to retrain people who think they can shoot," Mike said. "But we'll see. Let's head down to the cellars."

Most of the weapons were still in boxes and Mike had dragged a couple out of the locked storeroom where they were secured.

"This is the basic weapon that the militia will be issued," Mike said, cracking the seal on the wooden box and opening it up to reveal some silver pouches, each with the outline of an automatic rifle. "They used to ship these things in Cosmoline, which is a bitch and a half to take off. Fortunately, just about everybody's gone to vacuum pack these days."

He pulled out one of the pouches and slit it, pulling out an AK variant.

"This is the Skoda AKMS," Mike said, jacking the slide back and checking the barrel. "Anybody know what I just did?"

"Checked to see if there was a bullet in it," Lasko said.

"A round, yeah," Mike corrected. "A bullet is the little lead and copper bit that kills. A round is the shell, propellant and bullet. Any time you get handed a weapon, the *first* thing you do is check the breach." He closed the breach and tossed the weapon to Oleg.

Oleg lifted the weapon in interest and started to rotate it.

"Oleg," Mike snapped. "What's the *first* thing you do?"

"You didn't find anything, Kildar," Oleg said, puzzled.

"It doesn't matter," Mike said. "Check. The. Chamber."

Oleg jacked the slide back and a round came flying out.

The Keldara muttered a curse that Mike didn't quite catch and looked at the Kildar angrily.

"I palmed a round and dropped it in when I was closing the chamber," Mike said. "It's a very old trick. But I bet you'll never forget to check it again. Everybody grab one of the rifles and get them out of the foil."

The other six got their weapons out and Mike was pleased that *all* of them checked the chambers as soon as they were clear of the foil.

"Okay, set them down for now and let's get some ammo," Mike said.

The ammunition was stored in another locked room and Mike pulled out a couple of cases of 7.62x39 along with a case of magazines.

"Let's go," Mike said when they had all the materials.

They headed up to the range and loaded mags, then laid the guns out without mags in the well.

"The way the military teaches about weapons is to have you learn everything about them first, live with them, sleep with them, strip and clean them and then, maybe, they let you shoot them," Mike said. "I think they go about it all wrong. Earplugs," he said, handing them out. "Always wear earplugs if you can; shooting will take away your hearing in a heartbeat. Now, one thing you *have* to do with a weapon is zero it. Everybody shoots differently, so every weapon has to be zeroed to their particular form. Oleg, you first."

Mike showed him how to take a good solid shooting prone position on a tarp he'd laid out, then walked him through trigger squeeze and sight alignment.

"Okay, slip the magazine in the well like this," Mike said, showing him the proper sequence. "Jack back the slide and take your first shot."

Oleg followed the directions and lined up the target. It was a standard five point shooting target at twenty-five meters. He took his first shot and it was high and left.

"Do two more," Mike said, watching the shots through his binoculars.

Oleg put two rounds in close to each other and the other was a flyer.

"Okay, you're high and left," Mike said. "The second shot was a flyer, you flinched or jerked the trigger, I can't tell which."

He zeroed Oleg and the other "leader" types, then got to Lasko.

"I can zero," Lasko said, getting in a prone position.

He took three shots, slow, and all but the first seemed to miss. But as the Keldara adjusted his zero, Mike took a closer look at the target through the spotting scope. He could swear the hole looked too large for a 7.62.

"Did you just put all three shots through the same hole?" Mike asked, quietly.

"Yes," Lasko answered, just as calmly. "I am adjusted, now. May I continue shooting, Kildar?"

"Go," Mike said.

Lasko fired five more shots, all of them making a single large hole in the bull's-eye.

"Okay," Mike said, nodding. "You're good. Very good. Where'd you learn to shoot?"

"I am the family hunter," Lasko said. "We hunt, a little. I am the best shot in the Keldara," he added with quiet pride. "This gun is not so accurate, though."

"No, it's not," Mike said. "Okay, troops, you go ahead and blaze away. Lasko, give pointers. Stay on semi-auto; the first guy that goes full auto gets kicked out of the class. I'm going into the house for a couple of other weapons."

Mike went back to the cellars and got a couple of gun cases and cases of ammo. One of the cases was heavy enough and awkward enough, he had to put it in a rucksack to carry it back.

"How's it going?" Mike asked Lasko when he got back.

"They are fair," the older man said. "They have much to learn."

"Well, we'll see if you do," Mike said, setting out the cases and ammo on the rifle range. It was still too short for what he wanted to do but it would work for zeroing. "Come on over here, Lasko."

He opened up one case and pulled out a Mannlicher 7mm sniper rifle with a 10x scope, then opened up the other and set out a Robar .50-caliber bolt action with a 20x scope. Last he set up a spotting scope.

"Start with the Mannlicher," Mike said, showing the Keldara how to set up the bipod and take a good position, including setting up the straps. "Bolt action, five rounds. Comfortable with the scope?"

"I love it," the Keldara whispered. "May I load, Kildar?"

While the other six were blazing away, Mike showed the Keldara how to zero in the scope and use the spotting scope. It turned out that Lasko was a fucking artist with the Mannlicher. After he was comfortable with the weapon, Mike went back over to the others. He corrected a few bad habits they were developing and then ran them through alternate shooting stances. He moved them off the shorter range and over to the longer, pulling up the steel targets and having them engage those.

"Okay, everybody," Mike said. "That includes you, Lasko. I'm going to show you why you don't go on full auto."

There were three silhouette targets that had been set up at fifty meters. Mike had Oleg take a standing position with his AK.

"Okay, Oleg, I want you to use a full magazine to engage those targets," Mike said. "Single fire, the whole magazine. Shoot one for a bit, then the other, then the other."

"Yes, Kildar," Oleg said, puzzled.

"Try to do it fast," Mike added.

Oleg lifted the weapon and engaged the targets, firing fast but keeping on target. When he was finished with the course of fire, Mike walked the group down to the targets and patched them. Twenty-five of the thirty rounds in the magazine had hit the targets.

"Okay," Mike said when they were back at the shooting tables.

"Now, I want you to take the weapon and put it on full auto. I don't care how you hold it, just blaze away at the targets."

"Very well, Kildar," Oleg said, grinning a bit. He put the weapon to his shoulder, set it on full auto and hammered out the whole magazine in about two seconds.

"That was fun," Oleg said, smiling faintly.

"Sure is," Mike said. "Now set the weapon down and let's go find out how well you shot."

When they checked the targets, there was one round center of mass in the left target, another in a shoulder of the same target and the other two hadn't been hit. They patched those and went back to the shooting tables.

"When you fire, the muzzle climbs," Mike said, picking up one of the weapons and demonstrating without firing. "When you're on full auto, the muzzle climbs out of control. You may get one round on target, maybe two or three if you train for it, but if you fire off the whole magazine you're going to hit damned little."

"I see that," Oleg said, frowning.

"There's a way to fire on auto," Mike said, picking up a magazine and inserting it. He lined up the left-hand target, leaning into the weapon. He hit all three targets with quick three round bursts, moving back and forth until all the rounds were expended. "Let's check the targets."

When they got to the targets, they counted the holes and thirty out of thirty were in the targets. All of them, moreover, were in a narrow area from the upper chest to the head and the pattern of the bursts was clear, neat, triangular shots.

"Father of All," Vil said, breathing out.

"One of them was a nick," Mike said, shaking his head. "I'm way out of practice. But the point is, if you just blaze away, you miss. Stay on single shot. We'll practice burst, but in general, stay on single shot. The other point is, you're not going to be sitting in the houses with your ammo. You're going to be moving and you have to carry it on your back. And there aren't any helicopters to bring ammo from God. If you go blazing away, you're going to shoot yourself dry. Conserve your rounds, service your targets and make every shot count."

"Is the bigger gun a machine gun?" Vil asked, pointing at the Robar.

"No," Mike said, shrugging. "I probably shouldn't have gotten it out. But . . ." He considered the targeting possibilities and shrugged again. "Oleg, grab the box of ammo, Vil the Robar and Lasko the spotting scope. We're going to need more range to zero it."

He took them back to the house and up to the balcony overlooking the harem garden.

"This will do," he said, setting the Robar on a table and unfolding the bipod. "Lasko, spot my rounds on the third zero target." Mike loaded a magazine in the weapon and took a good sight picture on the target. The scope was strong enough that the bull's-eye filled most of it.

"Right, high," Lasko said at the first round. "Low, left, just outside."

Mike took five rounds to get the weapon zeroed in to where his last two went perfectly through the X ring. He replaced the magazine and loaded, then swiveled the weapon to look down into the valley.

"What time of year is it?" Mike asked, noting a small group of deer down by the stream. "Spring. Any hunting laws around here?"

"You're looking at the herd?" Lasko asked, looking through the spotting scope. "That is nearly two kilometers away."

"Which one?" Mike asked. It was a *long* time since he'd shot at this level and he wasn't sure he could make the shot. But he was sure enough to try. Even *close* would be impressive at this range.

"The bigger darker one on the left," Lasko said, quietly. "That is the buck. He has nothing to do for the rest of the year but eat. He's skinny now, though. He'll be very tough."

"I'm making a point," Mike said. "You can have the meat if I'm on."

Mike looked down into the valley at the trees and tried to gauge the wind. About seven knots from the southeast. Range . . . if the deer was a meter and a quarter or so at the shoulder he was 1500 meters based on the measurements in the scope. Mike wished for a moment he'd gotten a laser range finder out. There was one sitting in the equipment room but he hadn't expected to need it. He adjusted the scope and considered his target. Even with the 20x scope the deer was small at this distance. He took a slight breath, breathed out, drew back on the trigger and timed the last bit of squeeze for when his heartbeat was off.

The Robar cracked and Vil sighed.

"Missed."

"Wait," Mike said. A moment later the deer took a step forward, then fell to his knees and over on his side. The slush beyond him was red with blood. The other deer sniffed at it for a moment and then trotted away in confusion.

"Vil and Lasko," Mike said, straightening up. "Get the Expedition and go pick up my deer, please. Dress it and present it to Father Kulcyanov with my compliments and apology for it being so tough."

"Yes, Kildar," Vil said, quietly.

"Right through the fucking heart," Vil said that night at dinner. "Right behind the shoulder."

"Formidable," Lasko said, nodding. "Very formidable. I look forward to what he can teach me."

"We have a real Kildar again," Father Shaynav said, nodding. "Not some fat commissar or corrupt policeman, but a warrior as the Kildar should be."

"I think he should be brought into the mysteries," Vil said, boldly. "He is equal to them."

"It is early to decide that," Father Shaynav said, sternly. "We have not seen him tested in struggle and he still does not know our customs. When he stands the test, when he has been one of us longer, we can consider if he should be brought into the mysteries."

▲   ▲   ▲

"Ladies," Mike said as the four whores filed into the foyer and looked around in interest. They were each carrying small bags, probably all they owned. "If you'll follow me, I'll show you where you're going to be staying."

The harem quarters had been cleaned up but the rooms were still Spartan in the extreme. He showed them to the four rooms he'd chosen for them, had them drop their bags there and then showed them to his office.

"Here's the deal, girls," Mike said. "I've been trying to figure out how much money you're making in the bordello. I'm still not sure but it's not more than ten euros a day, average. Anybody disagree?" he asked, looking at Katya.

"I've made more than that," the blonde said, sadly. "Is that what you're going to be paying us?"

"You've *made* more from time to time," Mike said. "And I'm talking about after your split to the house. But on average, you don't. There are days when you don't have *any* customers. So. What I'm doing is paying Yakov ten euros per day to, well, 'rent' you. But you'll be earning thirty euros a day, working."

"That I can live with," Katya said, raising one shapely eyebrow.

"Yeah, I bet," Mike said. "However, besides what you're experts in, you'll be expected to act as general house help and hostesses. There are going to be about twenty people staying here for several months. We can get help from the Keldara for cleanup, especially heavy cleanup, but you're going to be doing some of that, for sure. Notably, room cleaning of the visitors, making beds, things like that. Then there's being general party girls. You're getting paid a flat rate, don't go fishing for tips," he added, looking at Katya who raised her eyebrow again.

"Room and board will be provided; there's no kickback. And the board will be better than at that fleabag you're staying in. On the subject of fleabags, you know how I am about vermin; don't get a lice attack started. Shower *every* day, check yourselves for lice and treat yourself as needed. If you suspect bedbugs, see Mother Savina and she'll work on it. If you see fleas, expect a major assault. This place is clean, now, keep it that way.

"Your rooms aren't particularly pretty," Mike continued. "And you don't have much in the way of possessions. There are some catalogs around that have room furnishings, pictures, things like that. There are others that have clothes, including lingerie. I'll set up two funds. Each of you will be allowed to order from the catalogs to the limit of your funds each month. The first month you'll have about six hundred euros, apiece, to buy things for your rooms. Those will be staying. You'll also have about five hundred euros to order clothes. Shipping will not be included. After the first month it will go down a bit to two hundred for stuff for the room and two hundred for clothes. If you don't use one month's, it rolls over to the next. But use it or lose it; when you leave you don't get what's left to have as cash."

"For that I will gladly stay here for some time," Katya said, raising an eyebrow. "What about jewelry?"

"That falls into the clothes budget," Mike said. "Anything you'll be leaving with." He looked at the girls and shook his head. "I'm going to rename you all. Expecting troops to keep up with Katya and Illya and Latya will just be too tough." He turned to Latya, a young brunette, and pointed.

"Flopsy," he said, then pointed at Illya the slightly "older," all of sixteen, brunette, "Mopsy, and . . ." He looked at Katya and smiled. "Cottontail. I know you are."

"Very nice," Katya said, smiling thinly. "A nursery rhyme?"

"Something like that," Mike said.

"What about me?" Inessa said, raising an eyebrow and ducking her head coyly.

"Bambi," Mike said. "She was a good friend and so are you."

"Bambi," Inessa said, wrinkling her brow. "I like that." One of the things Mike liked about Inessa was her simple approach to life; as long as she didn't have to think too hard, she was happy.

That and the fact she could suck a golf ball through forty feet of cheap garden hose, kinks and all.

"Okay, go get settled in," Mike said. "All of you except... Cottontail. I need to talk to her."

When the others had filed out he looked Katya squarely in the eye.

"Katya, you're one hard, cold bitch," Mike said, frowning. "And you've been a pain in the ass to everyone who's tried to keep you. You know it and I know it so don't deny it."

"I won't," she said, raising an eyebrow and looking at him coldly.

"I don't have time for it," Mike said. "I'm going to have enough on my plate as it is. I'd put you in charge of the girls, except you'd make their lives more of a hell than you already have. And I won't have it. I want *happy* young ladies in this house, or at least a semblance of it. You've got two choices, a binary solution set as they say in math. You can go with the flow for while you're here, or I'll put you down like the rabid bitch you are. I won't beat you, I won't rape you, I won't make you clean the floor with your tongue. I'll put a bullet in the back of your head and dump you in a grave. Am I clear?"

"Yes," Katya said, with a voice like ice.

"But I'll throw you a bone," Mike said. "What do you *want* in life?"

"What?" Katya asked.

"What do you *want*?" Mike asked. "You're smart; you couldn't be as dangerous as you are without being smart. So you've got to have an idea what you'd rather have in life than this. What is it?"

"I never want to spread my legs for another man," Katya said.

"Can't oblige you right now," Mike admitted. "I need you. But *how* are you going to do anything without spreading your legs, have you thought about that?"

"Yes," Katya said, warily. "I need to go to school. Get a job."

"You'd kill your boss," Mike said. "You're going to have to think bigger than a job. Okay, you need to get educated. Stick with me for a while, until I've got things a bit more settled, and I'll either send you to a school or, more likely, get a tutor. You're not socialized enough for most schools; you'd lose your temper and get kicked out. But you have to work with me or all bets are off and I'll put you in a grave, understand?"

"I won't step out of line," Katya said.

"That includes tormenting the girls to get your kicks," Mike said. "I need them happy and joyfully ready to jump in bed. And I need you to at least play the part. I may not be able to get a tutor until sometime in the summer, maybe even the fall. Just bide your time in the meantime. Can you read?"

"A bit," Katya said.

"There's a library," Mike said, shrugging. "It's not much of a library, but it's got some books in Russian. Knock yourself out. When you're not otherwise busy. Being able to *really* read is the first step to learning."

"Good to see you again, Chief," Mike said as Adams came up the steps.

He'd sent some of the less insane Keldara drivers into Tbilisi to pick up the trainers. The group had been staying in Tbilisi taking a Berlitz course in Georgian. They'd have to get used to the Keldara dialect, though.

"Good to see you, Mike," Adams said, shaking his hand. Mike and the chief had gone from BUDS to the same platoon when they started off as SEALs, New Meat as they were called. After Mike left the teams to be an instructor they'd halfway lost touch. On the other hand, the chief had been on the platoon that went into Syria where he'd recognized his old team-bud "Ghost." Since then they'd kept in a little better touch.

"This is Colonel Nielson," Adams said, introducing the short, slightly paunchy man who had followed him. The man had black hair and green eyes that were bright with intelligence and maybe a hint of mischief. "He's got good background for this. Former SF officer, Civil Affairs experience."

"Pleased to meet you, Mr. Jenkins," the colonel said.

"Likewise," Mike said, grinning. "I'm going to be dumping a load of work on you. I hate paperwork,"

"And I'll find someone else to dump it on," Nielson replied, smiling back.

It was only marginally cool today and most of the snow had melted. There was still ice in shadow patches but the air felt balmy after the winter and the trainers looked as if they had caught the spring fever. Or maybe it was the girls lined up behind Mike, holding trays loaded with mugs of beer.

"Welcome to the valley of the Keldara," Mike said, looking the group of trainers over. They looked as if they had seen the elephant, one and all. Given the way the U.S. military, and especially special operations, had been used for the last two decades, finding people with combat experience wasn't hard. None of them were young; the youngest was a former Marine NCO who was twenty-seven. But most of them were still in shape. The exception were a couple of big guys who looked as if they couldn't run but they could carry an M-1 Abrams around on their backs.

"The Keldara know where you're going to be bunking," Mike said. "So dump your gear on them, grab a beer and follow me."

He led them to the dining room, his office being too small, and got them settled around the table.

"Anybody a teetotaler?" Mike asked. "There's water and some different sodas. Also tea or coffee. Ask."

"I'd prefer a cola," one of the females said in Georgian. "Barring that, water."

"Mopsy," Mike said.

"Yes, Kildar," the girl said, nodding and hurrying out.

"Servants," Adams said, grinning. "You're going up in the world, Ass-boy."

"So have you," Mike said, looking around the table. "Okay, first of all, rations and comfort. Meals will usually be served here unless training dictates otherwise. Mother Griffina is the cook. She's going to be getting some Keldara girls to help her out. Eat as much as you'd like but it will probably be Dutch choice; that is, there will be food on the table and that's what's for dinner. Breakfast is the usual eggs to order and all that. Or cereal, although most of those are European; getting American out here is damned near impossible. You're bunked upstairs, mostly one to a room but some of the juniors will have to double up. They're pretty Spartan, but you can fix them up how you like. We can order stuff in from catalogs. In that case, we can get some stuff from the States. I've set up one of the parlors as a dayroom. There's a keg in there for as-preferred serving. If any of you can't handle the sauce, you'll be out on your ass. This is the usual training thing; keep your partying away from the troops except on special occasions.

"On the subject of partying," Mike continued, looking up as Mopsy came back in and set a glass of Coke in front of the female who'd asked for it. "The young ladies here present are *on* limits. For convenience sake they're named Flopsy, Mopsy, Cottontail and Bambi," he said to chuckles, pointing to each. "They've been hired for the duration to ensure your comfort. There's four of them and about twenty male trainers: handle that. Getting into fights over comfort providers is unprofessional." He nodded at the girls and they discreetly left.

"For the ladies," he continued, looking at the three females and shrugging. "You'll have to make your own arrangements. For a dozen obvious reasons, stay away from the Keldara men. That pretty much means if you have needs find your outlet in the team. Unless, of course, you go the other way. I don't frankly care but if you do, make your arrangements with the girls. Questions?"

"Not from me," said the one who'd asked for a Coke. "I've already made arrangements." She was a slim redhead with a hard face, about forty probably but looking a bit older from time in the sun.

"I dunno," one of the big guys said, shrugging. "That Cottontail is a looker, Sandy."

"We're good," one of the other females said. "We'll make arrangements. And I have to agree, that blonde is a looker."

"Cottontail is one vicious bitch," Mike said. "I tried to avoid bringing her in, but she's here. If she gives anyone trouble, tell me, I'll handle it. But, for general info, she'd just as gladly slide a knife in as anything else. Don't let her fool you. On the other hand, she can fuck like a mink. Have fun. I'll take Bambi any day."

"I take it they're getting paid for this," Sandy said.

"Very well by local standards," Mike said. "And various comfort items to make them happy. Flopsy, Mopsy and Bambi will be happy as clams as long as Cottontail doesn't screw with them too bad. They're all bunked in the extremely convenient harem quarters. You guys are upstairs. They'll handle stuff like bedmaking. If you don't like the job they do cleaning up, explain it to them. I haven't had time."

"What's the training schedule?" Colonel Nielson asked.

"In a week or so the ground will be soft enough for rock picking," Mike said. "That's an all-hands evolution. After that comes planting. That used to be all hands but with the equipment I've brought in there will be spare hands. I want to use that time to get to work on some projects. Notably I want to see if we can build a small hydroelectric dam. We also can start doing some work with specified leadership types and work out the training schedule. After planting there's a period when they usually repair winter damage. I understand there's a bit of a party to celebrate spring. I think the day after the party would be a good time to start training," he finished, grinning evilly.

"Be nice guys until training time," one of the trainers said with a strong British accent. "Then evil bastards?"

"You got it," Mike replied. "I'll just make one comment now on training. Generally in U.S. mil training they use the 'show then tell then do' method. I'd prefer that you use, to the greatest extent possible, 'do then show then tell.' Carefully instruct them *as* they set the demo charge, then let them blow it, then give them the class."

"Keeps them interested," Colonel Nielson said, nodding. "And experience is the best trainer. Will do."

"There are a hundred and twenty guys and forty females," Mike said. "Training the females is going to be tricky. The Keldara don't, in general, think much of women. The usual back country story. But I've convinced them that the women have to be trained to hold fixed positions. Most of that training will have to be done by the female trainers since they're also really picky about having males around the women. But I've got some push I can use there. Questions, comments, concerns?"

"What's with the feudal lord look?" one of the younger trainers asked. "I'm not trying to be challenging, sir, but it's pretty odd."

"It is that," Mike said, sighing. "This culture is odd. Some ways it's like every third world rat hole you've ever dealt with. Other ways . . . it's not. The Keldara are a small little insular tribe. In a lot of ways they act like the tribes around them and in other ways they don't. They sure as hell don't *look* like most of the people in the area. Bottom line is that the guy who's held this castle always seems to have been a foreigner, at least foreign to the area. They call the owner the Kildar, which doesn't have any clear etymology I'm aware of. Doesn't mean baron or duke or sheriff, just 'Kildar.' Obviously it's related to Keldara, but how I'm not sure. I think the answer might be somewhere in this fort. The construction is odd, especially on the lower floors. It almost looks Roman or Greek, but I don't think the Romans and Greeks got this far."

"Byzantines might have," the heavier trainer who had been bantering with Sandy said. "They extended up this way for a while if one of my college classes is being recalled right. Have you taken a good look around?"

"Not in the cellars," Mike admitted. "The first two levels are okay. The lower one isn't lit and looks a little shaky in places. If you go exploring out of boredom, take a buddy and tell somebody."

"Will do," the guy said. "Doubt I'll be bored, though, I'm your engineer and general electronics mate. Don Meller."

"In that case, you're going to be busy as all get out," Mike said. "We have to build everything, ranges, barracks, warehouses, storerooms, ammo bunkers."

"Don's the electric expert," the other heavyset trainer said. "I'm the rest of it guy. Charles Prael."

"Roads, bridges," Mike said, smiling. "You're going to be busy. And the rest of you guys are mostly shooters, I'd guess."

"Shooters, MPs, a couple of shooters with mortar experience," Adams said. "One intel and commo specialist."

"Here," one of the trainers said, his hand shooting up. He was a short, stocky guy with blond hair from a bad dye job. His natural shade looked to be brown. "Sergeant Vanner reporting for duty, Kildar!"

"You're going to be spending some time with the women," Mike said, smiling faintly. "I'm figuring they're going to be doing the fixed commo. Teaching them will be . . . interesting. Don't *ever* spend significant time alone with one of them. Not unless you *want* a shotgun wedding."

"Got it," the guy said, nodding.

"I don't suppose you speak and read Russian?" Mike asked.

"You'd suppose wrong," the guy answered in Russian. "And Arabic and Farsi and French and German. Oh, and Spanish. And Latin. And a little Greek. Archaic. Smattering of ancient Egyptian, some Chinese . . . two dialects Fusian and Mandarin . . . enough Thai to get laid . . ."

"Most of the team is polylingual," Colonel Nielson said in Russian. "It indicates that they can learn other languages easily. It was one of the criteria I used. Most of them are single other languages, however," he added, smiling.

"It might help with Keldara," Mike said. "It's not exactly Georgian although you can get along in it."

"I noticed that the drivers were using a very strong dialect," the intel guy said. "Very odd one, too. Lots of loan words from Russian with some words that sounded suspiciously like Greek. I'm going to have fun sorting it out."

"Vanner started as a translator," Adams said, shrugging. "Then intercept. Spent some time with No Such Agency. Marine. Go figure."

"Well, until the militia training starts in earnest, I'm going to expect everybody to pitch in," Mike said. "With setting up ranges, if nothing else. Who's a real shooter expert?"

"Here." The trainer was medium height and build with brown hair and a very sharp face.

"Praz Ebowsky," Adams said. "Sniper instructor, Army rifle team, President's One Hundred rifle, took second . . . how many years? At Perry."

"Three," Praz said, frowning. "Damned Marine I swear could *will* his rounds to the target beat me out each time."

"Got a guy named Lasko you're going to *love* to meet," Mike said. "But your first job is to walk over the area I've figured will be the main firing range and stake it out. Can do?"

"Can do," Praz said, nodding. "Been there, done that. KD, pop-ups, what?" KD referred to Known Distance whereas pop-ups were automatic targets that "popped up" when the shooter was ready to fire then fell down if hit.

"Both," Mike said. "I want them to be able to shoot for target *and* engage for combat. Can do?"

"Can do," Praz agreed. "I'm not sure about pits for the KD, but I can do work-arounds. And I can do pop-ups as long as we've got the targets."

"We'll probably have to go with manual initially," Mike said. "We don't have the juice for electric until . . . Don works his magic."

"I dunno about magic," Meller said. "But it's amazing what you can do with a bulldozer . . ."

"Pain in the butt," Praz said. "But I can do it."

"Tonight we party," Mike said, lifting his beer. "Tomorrow, bright and early, we PT. The rest of the day you guys get a look around while Adams, Nielson and I figure out what you're going to be doing. Now, let us drink!"

CHAPTER
TWELVE

"I'm a fucking engineer," Meller said, bending over and ralphing by the side of the road. "I ride bulldozers. I run AutoCAD programs. I quit running when I got out of SF!"

"Easy run," Vanner said, trotting by. "Easy."

"Fuck I hate this shit," Prael said, pulling up to bend over by Meller, breathing hard. "Fucking SEALs."

"Don't mind us," Sandy said as the three females trotted by. "Just headed home to wash up and put on our makeup. Told you you shouldn't have had all that beer!" she added as they headed up the path to the caravanserai.

"Fuck," Meller said, walking painfully up the path.

He had to admit, though, that he'd only been the first to fall out. Half the trainers were straggled along the side as he climbed up the switchbacks. Most of them, including Prael and, to his disgust, the three women, made it in before him.

"Very nice," Mike said as the group straggled in. He was hardly sweating. "I think we're going to have to break this down into groups. Vanner, you weren't supposed to hang with the big dogs. You're an intel puke."

"Love to run, sir!" Vanner shouted enthusiastically to groans from the fallouts.

"Praz, Praz, Praz," Mike said, sadly, shaking his head at the marksman. "You did so well up until the hill!"

"I sit in my hole and shoot people," Praz said, gasping. "I move *very* slowly. Running only makes you die tired."

Mike glanced at the back of the sweatshirt of one of the shooters who had fallen out on the hill.

"Killjoy?" he asked.

"Sorry, sir," the trainer said, gasping. "No excuse, sir. Quit running when I got out of Recon. I'll get in shape."

"You don't look very tired," Mike said to the Brit. His sweatshirt said "Scotty."

"Girlie run," the man said, shrugging. "Bit of a warm-up but when are we going to do some *real* running?"

"We'd been running in Tbilisi," Adams said. "But nothing like this." He'd broken a solid sweat but wasn't dead on his feet like most of them. Given that he had most of them by a decade, he'd done well.

"Ah, weeell," Mike intoned. "We will get the shooters into shape. And even Vanner. Tomorrow, engineers and Praz run with the ladies. That's not a dig, you've got a point. You guys don't run that much in your jobs and won't have to with the troops. I expect Praz to do some ruck marching, though."

"On it," Praz said, nodding. "Where are the rucks?"

"Currently in the cellar," Mike said. "We'll do issue tomorrow. Fall out for shit, shower and shave. See you later."

"Okay, Colonel," Mike said when he, Adams and the colonel met at nine. They were in his office drinking coffee as he slid a file folder over to the officer. "This is lists of all the potential recruits, what I've ordered for TOE, general sketches of where I think ranges and barracks can go in and what Genadi, my farm manager, thinks are times people will be the most free to train and build. At that point, I'm stuck. I can write a SEAL training schedule. I can do SEAL training in my sleep. I don't know how to set up a base for nothing or how to set up the force structure. I'm not even sure what I don't know."

"Lots," the colonel said. "But you'll be learning, too. I take it you're going to be operational with this group?"

"Probably," Mike said. "But I want the leadership types to be trained up to full tactical ability to lead their teams. When we do multiteam exercises is when I'll come in. I've mentally broken the teams down by the Families. The good part to that is there's automatic cohesion, the bad part is if a team takes heavy casualties, it will hit the Family hard. It might make more sense to split them up."

"Split them," the colonel said, automatically. "The other problem is that if a team is operational when there's something to be done around the farm, that Family will be hardest hit for workers. Okay, let's look at this." He picked up the paper and then extracted a pair of glasses from his shirt pocket. "You're sure about the hundred and twenty?"

"Close enough," Mike said. "They haven't been physicalled."

"We've two SF medics," Adams said. "We'll get 'em all checked."

"Assume the hundred and twenty," Nielson said, looking at the paper. "Six teams, one team leader from each team. Twenty people including the team leader. Team leader and an RTO. The RTO is going to need something that carries in these mountains, maybe satellite if you can afford it . . ."

"Can," Mike said.

"Two medium machine-gun teams," the colonel continued. "Gunner, AG and ammo bearer. Two snipers, two five-man teams. It works out."

"Okay," Mike said, looking at the TOE list. "If we put twelve medium machine guns in the teams, we're short at the houses. I'll either need to order more or get heavies. What about the mortars?"

"They'll stay at the houses," Nielson said. "The women will run them."

"That's going to go over great," Mike said, grimacing. "How about women and older men?"

"Works," Nielson said, shrugging. "You got one-twenties. The women are going to have to be *strong* to service them."

"They're farm girls," Mike said, shrugging. "They're lookers, but I've seen them toss around some pretty heavy loads. I think they can hang."

"This will be fun," Nielson said, looking at the sketchy map of the area. "No better maps?"

"Not currently, sorry," Mike said.

"I'll get Meller and Prael to do a survey map of the area," the colonel said, humming. "That will keep them out of mischief. Don't know what to do with the rest for the time being, but we'll find something, we will. Idle hands are the devil's doing and I do so love training. . . ."

"That's the river I think would make the best one for hydro," Mike said, bringing the Expedition to a stop short of the foaming white-water. The river, still rich with snowmelt, was running at the top of its banks. It dropped through a steep gorge to the flats, running over large rocks as it reached the bottom and then through a deeply cut channel through the fields. Behind them, they could hear a low, deep song as the Keldara worked at picking the numerous stones from the fields. The stones had been brought down by this and other rivers ages ago, and dropped by sheets of ice along with the rich dirt of the valley. With the freeze in winter, the rocks were pushed up through the soil and had to be picked out to prevent damage to the plows. The soil was black and deep, but it had the price of the rocks. "I'm told it won't start to go down until April."

"Oh, there are things we can do now," Meller said, getting out of the SUV and looking at the slope. There were ridges to either side and they were very steep, but the one to the south was slightly lower and covered in trees. He pulled himself up the incline, using the trees and sideways shoved feet, and started up the hill.

Interested in what he was looking for or at, Mike followed. The engineer kept climbing, though, following the course of the stream. He climbed for about an hour and then stopped where two streams ran together.

"Okay," the engineer said, looking from side to side and then climbing to the top of the ridge, "how much demo do we have?"

"Lots," Mike said. "And I can get more. How much do you need?"

"A lot," Meller admitted. He slid down to the stream and then shook his head. "Should have brought a rope." Despite the speed of the current and the water being freezing ice-melt he waded in, working his way across carefully, holding onto large rocks that jutted out, until he reached the north side of the gorge. That side was lower and he climbed to the top of that ridge, looking to the far side.

"Meet you down at the bottom," he called to Mike.

When they got to the bottom, Meller wandered off to the north. Mike watched him for a moment and then got back in the Expedition, driving down to where there was a barely fordable point and crossing the stream. When he got back by the edge of the valley he found the engineer considering another gorge. This one was, if anything, steeper than the first, a very narrow, tree-choked V, with a small stream flowing out of it.

"Do you know if that stream is really important to the Keldara?" Meller asked, distantly, as Mike walked over.

"No," Mike admitted.

"How about this field?" Meller continued, looking around and then squatting down and looking around closer to ground level. "What do we have in the way of earth-moving equipment?" he asked, getting down in a leopard crawl position and spinning in place, looking outward.

"Not much, yet," Mike said as the engineer leopard crawled backwards to the treeline and looked from side to side. "We can get it. Backhoe?"

"Steam shovel," the engineer said, pushing up and looking at the ground. "Definitely steam shovel." He stood up and brushed off his hands. "I'm going to need a bulldozer, a big Cat or equivalent, or one hell of a lot of strong backs. Something to mix concrete. Cement and sand. Sand we can get here. You know if there's any good clay around?"

"No," Mike admitted. "And I don't know if this field is important."

"It's okay," Meller said, wandering over to the ravine. "I can route it along the base of the hill with some rocks."

"What in the hell are you talking about?" Mike asked, puzzled.

"That gorge isn't as good for a hydro dam as this one," Meller replied, looking at him as if he was a moron. "We'll build one over here."

"There's only a trickle of water," Mike pointed out. "And that's intermittent."

"There won't be when we route the main stream over here," Meller said. "That's why I was asking about demo."

Meller showed Mike and Genadi what he was contemplating on the rough map of the area supplied by the Georgian military. It had apparently first been done by the Soviets, and it was both poorly surveyed and horribly out of date. But it showed both gorges, even if the elevations were wrong.

"We'll build the dam in the north gorge," Meller said. "I need to survey it really carefully, but I'm virtually certain it's going to make a better dam. Much more rise to it with less expanse."

They were considering the map while parked by the north gorge. The day had brightened up and while it was still cool, the thaw was definitely in place. That was evident by the mud that coated the Expedition as much as anything else.

"You can get higher water for a shorter dam?" Mike guessed.

"Got it in one, Kildar," the former SFer said with a grin. "Shorter it is, less likely to fail all things considered. Also, it's not overrun with snow-melt so we can get started as soon as the ground thaws a little more. We'll build the dam, then blast a channel from the previous river over to the new gorge. We'll have to do that in stages so it doesn't get a hard flood, but we can work that out later. Drop some of the rubble into the current gorge, build a smaller dam up there, with a relief overflow, and you have the river running into the new gorge and the old one is just a trickle except in spring when it will overflow into the old gorge. The river will come out of the new gorge, go down a channel we'll cut, and join the old river. The flow of the land works that way, anyway. Might not even need to cut the channel."

"That looks like one hell of a lot of work," Mike said, shaking his head. "I hadn't realized how much work it was going to be."

"Ah, it won't be all that much," Meller said. "This spot also has a couple of places where there are what looks like old logging roads. We can improve those and run trucks up them to dump onto the dam area for material. We'll need a bunch of rock, various sizes, dirt in quantity and most important, some good impermeable clay."

"There is clay where the Kildar wants to put in the rifle range," Genadi said. "Lots of very tough clay. That is why it is pasture and not fields."

"I'll have to check the permeability," Meller mused. "All clay is not golden."

"What about electric?" Mike asked.

"Simple enough," Meller said. "Set up a controllable culvert weir with a turbine. There are turbines like that you can get from GE or Siemens. Automatic diverter system, a condenser coil, some transformers and you've got power to the whole community. Enough, for sure, for the Keldara and the caravanserai. If you build up the turbines, you might have enough for Alerrso."

"What do you need?" Mike asked. "That we don't have."

"Hmmm..." Meller hummed, rubbing his chin. "I don't *need* anything until I get to the electric part. But the shovel and a dump truck would speed things up a lot. And a good concrete mixer. I'm going to need various numbers of people at different times. Oh, and lots of sand and lots of gravel, good gravel, rock and cement."

"There is a gravel pit," Genadi said, pointing up the southeast valley. "Up in here. From the Soviet days. We don't have gravel-ling machinery. We can break it with hammers like we usually do, but..."

"We'll get gravelling machinery," Mike said. "And a small bull-dozer for up there. Bigger than a Bobcat, but small."

"Those rocks they've been picking," Meller said. "Are they granite?"

"Mostly feldspar," Genadi said. "Why?"

"Never mind," Meller replied. "I was thinking we could gravel them, but not if they're feldspar."

"You're losing me," Mike said.

"Granite is what most of the mountains are made of," Meller answered. "It's really hard. There's other rock in there, since these are folded mountains, but most of it is granite. Feldspar is softer."

"There is some granite," Genadi said.

"Not worth sorting out," Meller replied. "Not if we have a gravel pit already. We should get that as soon as possible. Lots of uses for gravel. Some of these roads could really use gravelling."

"For that we can even use the draft teams," Genadi pointed out. "We haven't had the heart to put them down, yet."

"Don't," Mike said. "Don't breed for them, anymore, not much. But don't put them down. If I recall correctly, most of them are mine anyway. I'll pick up the tab for keeping them."

"They are expensive to feed in winter," Genadi said, nervously.

"They'll only last another, what? Ten years maximum?" Mike asked. "We'll get by. And there will be occasional uses for them, like this. Oh, the oxen you can stall and feed up and we'll slaughter.

But not the horses. And not any of the oxen that people really think of as pets."

"I don't think anyone thinks of the oxen as pets," Genadi said, darkly. "You have never had to deal with oxen."

"Genadi, get one of the Keldara who is sharp at bargaining and finding things to help Meller find some gravelling equipment," Mike said, nodding in thought. "Try to get used. This whole thing is costing like the dickens."

After Meller and Genadi left in the latter's Expedition, Mike drove over to one of the nearby fields where teams were slowly picking rocks.

"Kildar," Father Makanee said as Mike pulled up. He was in there with everyone else, lifting the rocks from the black earth, but he stopped and came over to Mike's vehicle, letting the rest get on with it. "It is good to see you. You are looking at the dam site?"

"Meller has an idea how we can get started early," Mike said, watching the rock pickers for a minute. Even girls were out in the field, picking up small rocks, up to the size of a person's head, while the men lifted the larger ones. They stayed behind the tail of the pickup, lifting them from the ground and throwing them in, where other men moved them forward to a growing pile. There was a wagon or two out as well, since there were more pickers than trucks. "We might have it in by midsummer, God willing."

"That would be good," the Keldara elder said. "What do you think?"

The total expanse of fields that would be plowed was evident with the snow gone. There was at least a thousand acres and Mike wondered how they ever could have plowed and seeded it all with only horse-drawn plows. One day at a time, he guessed.

"I think it's going to be a good year," Mike said, nodding, then getting out. "I'm not going to do this for long, but I think I should do it for a while."

He could see Erkin, who wasn't up to his full growth, struggling with a boulder that was trapped by heavy soil. Mike bent and pulled at it along with the teen until the rock broke free and then helped him heave it into the truck.

"Christ," he said. "I can't see doing this all day."

"It is backbreaking," Erkin said, shaking his head. "The worst chore of the farm. But even with the new plows, we have to pick the rocks."

With rocks that weren't so trapped, the pickers were working in a rhythm, some of them calling out a long series of syllables.

"What is that?" Mike asked Erkin as he bent to pick up another rock. It was at least seventy pounds and he could lift it easily, but he could see that this would get wearing after a very short time.

"The cry of the picker," Erkin said, shrugging. "It is what we always chant. Ah Syllio!" he called, bending for another rock then: "Casentay!" as he heaved it in the truck. "Ah Syllio!" he repeated as he bent for another. "It is the cry of the spring. When we harvest, there is another cry."

"But what does it mean?" Mike asked.

"Nothing," one of the older men answered. "It is just what we chant. It makes the time go by."

Mike couldn't quite bring himself to join in, not all of the men were singing anyway, but he listened to it as he picked rocks and he found that the time did go by. The cry was hypnotic, sounding up from the fields in a regular rhythm as the chanters got in beat, echoing from the surrounding mountains.

He had just heaved a huge stone into the truck when Erkin waved at him as he bent.

"Time to break," Erkin said, waving at an approaching cart. "The women bring beer and food."

"I could eat," Mike admitted, wiping sweat from his brow. The day was cool but he was sweating from the effort. He needed to get some of the trainers down here to learn what real work was. He was dogged by the hour or so he'd spent at this and the Keldara would be at it all day.

"You need to pace yourself," the older Keldara told him. "If you tire, don't dip with every cry. Work to your body's pace, this is the only way to make it. And you don't lift well; use less back."

"I'll keep that in mind," Mike said, grinning. "I guess I have a lot to learn."

"It is good that you help, Kildar," the man said, nodding formally. "It shows that you care for the land, as a Kildar should. But you have other duties to attend to."

"I'll stay for lunch," Mike said as the women began unloading from the cart. "Then I'll head back."

The women of the Keldara were, as always, beautiful. But never so beautiful as when they were bringing beer. Most of them had buckets in their hands with beer packed in snow and Mike was as eager as anyone for some.

As he stepped forward, though, he saw Katrina swinging a bucket in front of her, a pout on her face. He realized that there was a protocol to who got beer from whom, and for some reason Katrina was being, effectively, shunned.

"So what did you do now, Katrina?" Mike asked, walking over to her and plucking one of the bottles from the bucket.

"It wasn't my fault," Katrina said. "It was Vasya's!"

"And who is Vasya?" Mike said, struggling to get the bottle open. They were old glass bottles sealed with wax and a cork and after trying to pull the cork out, he cut the wax with a folding knife then pulled the cork out with his teeth.

"He's my cousin," Katrina said, shrugging. "I didn't start the fire!"

"Not in the house, I hope," Mike said, sternly.

"No, in the paddock," Katrina said. "He wanted to see if horse manure would burn . . ."

"Was it dry?" Mike asked, wincing.

"Yes," Katrina said with a sigh. "And it turns out it burns very well. We should use it for fuel!"

"And your part in this was . . . ?" Mike asked, raising an eyebrow.

"I knew where there were some matches," Katrina said, her head bowed and face working to try to pout. "But *I* didn't light them!"

"Hmmm," Mike mused, taking a sip of beer. "Let me ask one last question: How old is Vasya?"

"Five," Katrina said in a very small voice.

"And were you supposed to be watching him and keeping him out of trouble?" Mike asked.

"But . . ."

"But, but, but," Mike said, shaking his head. "But you bring me Mother Lenka's beer, and I don't believe anyone was harmed, so you are forgiven by the Kildar."

"Thank you, Kildar!" Katrina said, her head coming up and her face shining.

"Your mother and father on the other hand," Mike said, shaking his head. "They have to make their own decisions."

"Oh," Katrina said, frowning prettily. "You're teasing me."

"A bit," Mike said. "But since I'm talking to you nicely, everyone will know that you're forgiven by the Kildar and that will make them less likely to punish you. More. But you have to start to *think*."

"I do," Katrina said. "All the time. Most of the time very fast and very well. But sometimes I get . . . strange."

"Thoughts feel like they won't connect?" Mike asked, cautiously.

"Yes, like they are running around like horses in spring," Katrina said. "Very many of them, but none make sense. I feel crazy at times like that. And sometimes I get very sad. Usually there's a reason, but sometimes there isn't any. I just don't want to do anything but sleep and mother gets very angry with me. They all call me lazy, then. I'm afraid I'm going to become like Aunt Anjelike. I don't think you've met her. She was very fun for a long time, my favorite aunt. Now she is . . . not right in the head."

"Sounds like you need your meds adjusted," Mike said, smiling. "Have a beer."

"They say I'm a witch," Katrina said, quietly, but smiling. "That I can be one, at least."

"I've got a few friends that are witches," Mike said. "Back in the States. Most of them, admittedly, are nuts. But that's what medication is for. And *they* have access to psychiatrists."

"I see things," she said, looking around. "In my dreams. I told my mother just before you came that I had a dream of ice and a beautiful man who would be a great leader for us. She told me I was crazy, but here you are."

"Well, there was snow," Mike said, smiling. "I suppose that counts for ice. But you screwed up on the beautiful part."

"You are very beautiful, Kildar," the girl said, then ducked her head. "I am sorry I said that."

"It . . . wasn't a good thing to say," Mike admitted. "You have your life and I have mine. I might be able to change yours, a bit, with everyone else's. But you need to be careful or you'll be in the position of being sent to town. I'll prevent that, but if you make enough trouble, your life will be hell. You know that."

"Yes," Katrina said, quietly.

"Go spread your beer around," Mike said. "I'm going to go put my empty in the cart and head back before I get you in trouble."

"I will not get in trouble for talking to the Kildar," Katrina said, smiling at him shyly. "Not out here in public, anyway."

"You just wait," Mike said, shaking his head.

CHAPTER THIRTEEN

Mike pulled the Expedition to a stop as he heard the sound of a chainsaw going full blast.

The spring thaw had passed and planting was well underway, with all seven tractors out on the fields breaking ground. The heavy tractor was drawing a single system that plowed, harrowed and planted while the other tractors were simply plowing. After plowing they would change to harrowing and planting devices.

Normally there would have been at least ten plows going at this time with more teams harrowing and planting behind them. The tractors had freed up a good bit of manpower but so had other devices. As Mike made his way through the woods to the sound of the chainsaw, which was in an area he thought they weren't clearing, he saw one.

The chainsaw turned out to be attached to a wooden device the Keldara had knocked together under the direction of Prael, the "other" engineer. They had the chainsaw attached vertically to a solid platform and were using it as a band saw to slice raw timber into planks. Most Keldara construction that used wood had been heavy timbers made by splitting and adzing logs. Using the field-expedient sawmill they could get dozens of planks where they had only gotten one thick timber before. And making that heavy timber would have taken a Keldara most of the day. As he watched, two of them used a swinging crane to lift a massive log into the sawmill and started cutting it up. In a few minutes', admittedly hard, work they had a thick timber member and a litter of planks. They stopped at that point, setting the thick member on a pile of similar ones, about eight by eights, and getting another large section of oak log.

"Going good, huh?" Prael asked.

Mike had heard him sneaking up even over the sound of the chainsaw and shrugged.

"What, exactly, do we *need* all this lumber for?" Mike replied.

"Every time we take a look around there's another project," Prael said, pouting slightly at not having surprised the Kildar. The word had apparently gotten around that he was a sneak special- ist and the various trainers had been trying to surprise him on a daily basis. It never worked, but they kept trying. "The planks are mostly for forms for the dam, but I'm also going to use them to build a couple of wooden bridges over the Keldara River so they don't have to keep using the fords. Then there's repairs to the buildings, forms for bunkers, all sorts of things. The only thing we need more than lumber is concrete."

"How's that coming along?" Mike asked, walking back through the woods to his Expedition.

"We've got material coming out of our ears," Prael said. "The gravel pit is working well. We've been using the horses for sand mining on the river so we've got plenty of that. And there was a big delivery the other day of cement. The big bottleneck is mixing; we've got two small gas-powered mixers and after that we're down to doing it by hand. But we're not going to be really slowed by it for another week; that's when Meller thinks he'll be done working out the foundations of the dam."

"Get a concrete truck?" Mike asked. "Rent one or get a contractor if we can find one?"

"Might be a good idea," Prael admitted. "It'll make building the bunkers easier, too."

"I'll look into it," Mike said, getting back in the SUV. "Have fun. And, by the way, if you try to miss every little leaf you're never going to learn."

He decided to skip the dam workings for the time being, heading over to the range area. It was at the north end of the valley, right up against the range of tree-covered mountains at that end, and was coming along nicely. There was a pistol and sub-gun range installed already, with another for pop-ups underway to the side. The last range, the farthest to the east, was for long-range rifle. That one used heavy metal targets and had been laid out but wasn't being worked on yet.

He followed the graveled road up to the end of the range under construction and waved at Praz as he arrived. The rifle instructor waved back, then walked over to the Expedition after a word to the Keldara doing the pop-up installation.

"How long?" Mike asked.

"Another week for the basic installation," Praz said. "A couple of days for the long-distance range."

"Need more bodies?" Mike asked. "Meller won't need half his bodies in a couple of days when they get finished on the foundations."

"I'm good," the rifleman admitted. "More people would just require more supervision. If I get some people I'd like Killjoy and he's working on bunkers."

"The basic bunker installation is going to be done pretty soon," Mike said, frowning. "If you get slowed down, talk to the colonel and he'll shift some people your way." Mike looked around and smiled. "A decent range will be nice for a change."

"Well, this one will be pretty decent," Praz admitted.

"Onward and upward," Mike said, waving back to the valley. "Gotta go check on the dam."

He made his way back down to the south, passing one of the plowers on the way and returning a wave, until he reached the small valley chosen for the hydro dam.

The trees and brush had been cleared out from the base of the defile and most of the dirt dug away to reveal bedrock. On both edges of the defile a narrow trail had been graded and blasted up the hill to positions over where the dam was going to go in. As he pulled up, the fifty or so Keldara who had been doing pick and shovel work were making their way into the open and getting behind the backhoe that, so far, had been their only major equipment.

"Hold up here, Kildar," one of the Keldara said, walking over to the Expedition as Mike pulled up. "Sergeant Meller is about to set off a charge."

"Works," Mike said, shutting down the SUV and getting out. "How big, you know?"

"Small," the Keldara said. "Getting rid of a cell of rock. A big stone, really. It's in the way for getting to the rock on the south side. Once it's out of the way we can finish leveling the foundation. He thinks it will take more than one blast, though."

"Hey, Kildar!" Meller said, coming around the edge of the defile. Where the trees and scrub had been was an area of rock that was mostly flat until it hit the slope. The small stream now ran down a narrow rock channel. "Hang on a second," he yelled again, holding up an electronic detonation device. "FIRE IN THE HOLE!"

There was a sharp crack and a blast of dust in the defile and Meller looked up and around.

"The sky didn't fall!" he caroled, walking back into the valley before the dust had even settled.

"Got to go," the Keldara said, hurrying in that direction.

Two of the farm trucks roared to life pulling forward, Keldara swarming on the back for the short ride, with the backhoe following more slowly.

Mike pulled forward as well, driving the Expedition actually into the stream to avoid the line of Keldara and bumping up the streambed until he could see the center of the workings. The dirt had been dug out and rocks blown down to create a fairly broad level area. He could see the final obstacle they were working on, an irregularly shaped boulder about the size of the Expedition, which had been cracked on one side and nudged out from the wall of the valley. The *remaining* mass was about the size of the Expedition; the portion that had been blasted off was about the size of a Volkswagen and now lay strewn around the workings.

"Hey, Kildar," Meller yelled as Mike pulled up. The Keldara had already set to work lifting smaller rocks into the back of the trucks as the backhoe moved into position to lift the heavier material.

"How's it going?" Mike asked, getting out of the Expedition.

"Pretty good," Meller admitted. "There's no problem with the position and the Keldara are the hardest workers I've ever met. Once we get this rock out of the way and level out the position we'll start making forms. After that we'll pour the foundations and the main weir. It'll take about two weeks for that to set enough to start work on the rest."

"What are you going to need for that?" Mike asked.

"Just a lot of dirt at first," Meller said. "I can move that with wagons and stuff, but it would be better to get a couple of dump trucks and the steam shovel. I'm going to need to dig dirt out from the channel to bring the water back to the main stream and anywhere else I can find it that won't get in the way of planting. I'll run the trucks or whatever up there," he said, pointing to the roads that had been blasted up the hill, "then dump it in position. It'll have to be tamped down, I'd like to get a compressor for that, and we'll lay it down in layers until the dam is built up to the proper level. Then we'll front it with clay from over by the ranges."

"Is it . . . what you said about permeable, enough?" Mike asked.

"Permeability," Meller said, nodding. "It's *impermeable* enough.

I did a field expedient test. I probably should be doing more soil tests, but this stuff is good material from what I've seen; not too much organics to it but it will compress really well. I've built dams this large before in Afghanistan and Iraq and this one should be fine. I'm really overbuilding it, but better overbuild than underbuild."

"What about seepage?" Mike asked.

"That's why we're preparing the foundations," Meller said, grinning. "If you want to bring in an engineer with a degree and everything to check it out, I won't mind."

"You got plans?" Mike asked. "I can just find a firm and send those over to see what they think."

"Hand drawn," Meller said. "You don't have AutoCAD on the computers at the caravanserai."

"Order a copy," Mike said. "Do up the plans and I'll get them vetted. Or you can send them to a firm if you know one. But, yeah, I'd like a guy with a degree in this stuff to say it will work. Do that before you start pouring."

"Will do," Meller said, frowning. "It'll take me a few days, though, not counting the time to get the program. There are some smaller packages that I can download that will do for showing it to an engineer. But I'll have to work on that by itself."

"What you're doing here any of the trainers with blast experience can do," Mike said, shrugging. "Hell, I can take over if you want. It's just blowing this rock out of the way and leveling after it's gone, right?"

"Yeah," Meller said, shrugging. "You want to take over?"

"I haven't had a chance to blow anything up in years," Mike replied, grinning. "Well, okay, a year and a half."

"Don't use too much," Meller said, carefully. "You don't want a *crater*."

"I won't," Mike said. "Take one of the Keldara with you who can drive and head back to the caravanserai. I'll get this thing out of the way while you work on the plans. Suits?"

"Suits," Meller replied.

"Who's your straw boss?" Mike asked watching the Keldara work. There didn't appear to be anyone supervising but the Keldara were expert at moving rock. They even did it in a reasonably safe manner, but he mentally added steel-toed boots to the list of materials these people needed. Every time he turned around there was one more "vital" item someone required. He'd taken a look at the spreadsheets last night and *capital* costs on the militia and infrastructure equipment had gone over four million dollars. Ammunition and pay for the trainers was going to easily go over another million. Fuel, food, the very low pay the Keldara were getting for all these projects, the whole damned thing was costing like crazy. And he didn't see any way to recoup it.

"Sawn," Meller said, pointing at the Keldara. He had the brown hair and short, broad look of Father Makanee, who it turned out was actually his uncle. He was pitching in just like the rest, tossing boulders nearly the size of his barrel chest into the back of the truck.

"Isn't that rock granite?" Mike asked.

"Yeah," Meller answered. "And the trucks will take it over to the gravel pit."

The backhoe dumped its load into the back of one of the trucks and then the majority of the Keldara backed up as it scraped the ground, clearing the last of the rubble. There was a small mound at the base of the hill that a few of the Keldara set to work on with shovels as one of the trucks drove away with its load and the backhoe began working its way out of the defile.

"It's time to set the next load," Meller pointed out. "I'll show you where the demo shack is."

A small, reinforced shack had been set up down on the flats and Meller opened it with a key to reveal a reel of detcord, a stack of Semtek cases, a box of detonators, wire and receiver modules.

"Semtek's not the best material for this sort of work," Meller said. "And I really should be drilling the rock. But that would have to be done by hand so I'm just putting in charges and tamping them with sandbags."

"I can work with that," Mike said. "But have you considered shaped charges?"

"I could make a couple," Meller admitted. "But . . ."

"I was thinking of the RPGs," Mike pointed out. "They'll dig a small diameter hole in the rock if you use the HEAT rounds."

"Now that's thinking outside the box," Meller pointed out.

"When you get to the house get an RPG and send it back with the Keldara along with a few rounds," Mike said. "About twelve. I'll have to experiment some." He thought about it for a moment and then shrugged. "Take Sawn and have him stop and find Genadi on the way back. There's a pump around somewhere and we'll use it to cool the holes."

"This is getting complicated," Meller pointed out. "Why not just tamp?"

"I'm bored," Mike admitted.

"Don't set the pump up, yet," Mike said as he crossed the small stream, carrying the RPG and three rounds. "And everybody back up and put your fingers in your ears; this is going to be noisy."

He set the rocket-propelled grenade launcher across his knee and loaded in one of the bulbous rounds, rotating it to lock the head in. Then he inserted earplugs and lifted the weapon to his shoulder, flipping up the sight. The distance was about fifty meters, just over arming distance, but that should work. He checked his backblast area, to make sure none of the Keldara had wandered behind him, and flipped the weapon off safe.

The rocket flew straight and true to impact on the side of the rock, impacting with a large explosion and one hell of a bang. But when the smoke had cleared there didn't appear to be any damage to the rock.

"Kildar," Sawn called, smiling, "we will be here a very long time making gravel that way."

"Look again," Mike said, leaving the RPG and rounds in place and crossing back over to the rock. The Keldara gathered around in a crowd and shook their heads at the small hole drilled in the rock.

"I'm going to need a small, straight, piece of metal or wood," Mike said, frowning. "I need to see how deep that is. And we'll need some clay. Somebody head down by the ranges and dig some up. Just a few bucketsful will do."

Sawn detailed one group to go get the clay while a few of the younger men went to the pile of debris from clearing to look for a long, straight piece of wood that would fit. Mike, in the meantime, crossed back over the stream and continued to shoot into the rock, keeping low on it now and circling around to the east side. Each of the impacts caused a small diameter hole and he stopped when he had six.

By that time a suitable piece of wood had been found and he explored the first hole with it, noting that it was still extremely hot. The hole turned out to be only a meter and a half or so deep.

"Tum tee tum," Mike hummed as the truck got back from the ranges with the clay. He wandered back to the demo shack and loaded up with gear, then headed over to the diggings.

"Set up the pump," he told Sawn. "Fill each of the holes with water. If they flood out, that's fine. But keep filling them 'til they cool down."

"Yes, Kildar," Sawn said, obviously confused.

Mike pulled out three blocks of Semtek and broke them up, using the hood of the truck to roll out narrow cylinders. He then hooked up detonators to sections of detcord and headed over to the diggings.

He'd considered two ways to blow the rock and settled on the more reliable, using the detcord to slide the narrow cylinders of explosive to the bottom of the wet holes. Then he used the stick to pack clay down on top. It took him about an hour to fill all the holes. What he was left with was six holes with detcord sticking out of clay plugs. He then "daisy-chained" the detcord ends together and led a string of detcord out from the rock.

"Okay," he said, waving everyone back. "It's about ready to go. I'd suggest you back up a bit more than usual; I'm not as precise as Meller."

When everyone was back around the scrap of hill, he hooked a detonator and module up to the detcord daisy-chain and walked down onto the flats himself.

"Let's see what we get," he said, looking at Sawn and grinning as he hit the firing button.

The sound was much more muted than Meller's detonation and there was less dust. But when they walked back around the hill he saw that the rock had been shattered along one side deep into its mass and was now sitting on a narrow base. More rock had been thrown outward, ready to be picked up, but Mike held up his hand as the Keldara moved forward.

"Let's break it up some more, first," Mike said. "Sawn, time to learn how to use an RPG. Everybody on the other side of the stream."

This time he walked the Keldara through the loading and firing sequence, showing him how to check that he had enough back-blast area and explaining why it had to be clear both of people and obstructions. He had the leader fire two rounds, then picked out another Keldara at random to fire the next couple until he'd expended all his remaining six rounds. One had missed so he only had five holes to fill this time, scattered over the upper mass of the rock. One reason that he'd fired rather than having the Keldara start clearing was that he was unsure the rock was stable enough, but it had taken five hits from an RPG and hadn't fallen over so that was good enough.

By the time he'd completed the second demolition it was late afternoon and he called a halt.

"Go ahead and start heading home," he told Sawn. "I'll break up a couple of these smaller rocks, then head home myself. I'll see you tomorrow and we'll break up the last bit and clear the area."

"Yes, Kildar," Sawn said, nodding. "Weapons can be used for more than killing, apparently."

"A weapon is a system for applying force," Mike said. "Force like that can only be used for destruction, but sometimes you can use it for stuff like this, yes."

Mike was placing a quarter pound of Semtek under a rock the size of a recliner when he heard light footsteps coming up the path.

"You were supposed to go home," Mike called.

"You have not had dinner, Kildar," Katrina said.

"And it's nearly dark," Mike pointed out, straightening up and turning around. The girl had a basket that probably held food and a bucket with three beer bottles in it. "You're going to get yourself in trouble coming out into the dark with a man you're not married to."

"I was sent out," Katrina admitted. "But I asked when the men came back. You should eat."

"I was going to when I got back to the house," Mike pointed out. "That's why I have a cook."

"I called Mother Griffina," Katrina said, opening up the box and laying out a colored cloth, then pulling out food. "You have been working all day and you did not eat lunch. You will eat."

"I'm going to wash my hands first," Mike said, uncomfortably. The girl was about fourteen if she was a day. Not to mention bloody gorgeous. And in her society, being alone with a man was tantamount to admitting you weren't a virgin. And if you weren't a virgin, you could never get married. He couldn't imagine Father Devlich simply letting her come out here to have dinner, even if it *was* with the Kildar. It was literally unimaginable. On the other hand, there was no way she could have prepared a supper like this without permission; the Keldara were far too careful of their food use.

By the time he got back to the little picnic, Katrina had laid out a plate of cold chicken and potatoes with a small mess of spring greens. A bottle of beer was open and sitting next to it.

"And what are you going to eat?" Mike asked.

"I'll eat when I get home," Katrina said, archly.

"Don't think so," Mike said, sliding the plate between them. "Eat. So tell me how you *really* managed to convince them that you should come out here."

"I simply pointed out that you hadn't had lunch and that you were going to be late for dinner," Katrina said.

"And you'd been watching what I ate?" Mike asked, pulling a drumstick off the chicken and handing it to her.

"Everyone knew that," Katrina said, accepting the chicken diffidently. "The old women had been clucking about it half the day."

"Oh," Mike replied, uncomfortably. He knew the Keldara watched him, but he wasn't aware that the scrutiny was that intense. "And they just let you come out here?"

"Yes," Katrina said then sighed and shrugged. "I probably would have been sent to town this year if you hadn't said no one would be. No family will have me. I'm too—"

"Different," Mike said. "Hardheaded and all that, too. But mostly it's that you don't fit the Keldara mold. You're damned pretty, though," he added, then realized what he'd said and cleared his throat.

"Pretty doesn't matter," Katrina said, a touch angrily. "I know too much, I think too much. And I say too much," she added, sighing again. "Usually at the wrong time. So . . . coming out here was not such a . . . loss to the Family. Whatever anyone thinks. Besides, I'd already been with you. In the car. Remember?"

"Vividly," Mike admitted. There was just something about snow, even if you thought you were going to die in a blizzard, that was romantic. "So what are you going to do with your life?"

"I'm probably going to be the old aunt that does all the work," Katrina admitted, shrugging. "Or I'll run away to town. I'm not sure I can handle being the last woman my whole life."

"Don't run to town," Mike said, sliding the plate closer and handing her the fork. "Bad as it is here, it can be infinitely worse in the hands of the slavers. Some of them aren't all bad, but you don't get to pick and choose in advance."

"There's another choice, of course," Katrina said, taking a small bite of potato and handing the fork back. "The Kildaran."

"I take it that means the wife of the Kildar," Mike said, surprised at her boldness. "Ain't gonna happen."

"Actually, it's the woman of the Kildar," Katrina said, taking a small bite of chicken. "Not the wife. I'm not sure of the right name for you."

"Concubine?" Mike asked. "Mistress? Katrina, there are reasons I don't have people close to me. You *don't* want to be one of them."

"You're wrong in that, Kildar," the girl said, setting down the chicken and looking him in the eye. "I know you have enemies. But I'm strong and I'm the right woman for you."

"You're a girl," Mike said, shaking his head. "In my country, even *thinking* about fooling around with you is a capital crime."

"Latya, the one you call Flopsy, is younger than I am," Katrina said, evenly.

"I'm not terribly happy about that," Mike admitted.

"And you like Inessa," Katrina continued, remorselessly. "Because she looks like me, I think. Is it that I'm too smart? Too . . . headstrong? You like weak women?" she ended angrily.

"No," Mike admitted, unwilling to meet her eye. "But I don't want you getting hurt. Either by being here, with me, or by living with me and being a target."

"I am a *woman*, Kildar," Katrina shouted. "This year I would be *married* if it weren't for nobody *wanting* me! And you *do* want me, I know that!"

"Yes, I do," Mike said, finally looking at her, his eyes hot and face hard. "But I'm sure as hell not going to take you here on the grass. If the time comes, if it is *right*, I will consider it. But until then, you'll have to *wait*. Understand? Can you do that? You're an impatient bitch."

"What's a promise from a man worth?" Katrina asked, bitterly.

"From one that's *not* trying to get in your pants, usually a lot," Mike said. "And it was anything but a promise. Let things get stable and we'll *discuss* it. But right now, it's out of the question."

"I'll wait," Katrina said, furiously. "For a while, Kildar. But only for a while. You have shown that you will do things even that you don't promise. For that, I will wait."

"Hey, Kildar," Killjoy said as Mike walked in the caravanserai. The former Marine was sitting in the foyer area with Flopsy curled into his side and a glass of beer in his hand. "This beer is fantastic, you know that? You ought to sell it."

"They make it in small batches," Mike said, absently. "You using Flopsy at the moment?"

"No," Killjoy said, giving the girl a slap on the rump. "Up and to your master, little one."

"You want me, Kildar?" Flopsy asked.

"Very much," Mike said, taking her by the wrist and leading her to the stairs. "If anybody wants me, I'll be busy for a while."

CHAPTER
FOURTEEN

Mike pulled up to the police station and got out wondering why he'd been called. All that Vadim said was that he needed to talk and not over the phone. Although Mike could call the police station on his sat phone, the local phones used a party line and were less than secure.

"The season starts," Vadim said, walking out the front of the headquarters as he was throwing on a light jacket. He waved for Mike to get back in the Expedition. "Please, Kildar, it is probably the best place to talk."

"Are we going anywhere?" Mike asked.

"Up the road," Vadim said, waving south. "You have weapons with you, yes?"

"Yeah," Mike said, frowning. "Do I need them?"

"No longer," Vadim said, sighing. "At least probably not. A farm was attacked by the Chechens. At least I assume it was Chechens. The farmer was seen talking in a tavern with some Chechens yesterday. Today there is a home burned, dead bodies, all the usual. It is very annoying."

They drove up over the pass to the south, climbing close to the treeline at the top, then down into a series of narrow valleys. Mike took a turnoff on one of the dirt roads that led up into the mountains, grateful that he'd brought the Expedition instead of the Mercedes, and finally stopped at a clearing.

It was a small mountain farm like many in the area, a cleared vegetable patch next to a small stone house. Across the road, and a stream, was a larger area that was green with some plant. There should have been goats and maybe an ox in the paddock to the side, some children playing or working around the house.

Instead there was a smell of fire and two policemen picking up bodies and dispiritedly loading them into the back of a truck. The paddock had been broken down and the door to the house was shattered and half burned.

"There were nine who lived here," Vadim said, shaking his head and getting out of the Expedition. "Viljar Talisheva, his wife, a brother and six children. There are four bodies. He had a teenage daughter and one that was just short of teen."

"And those are the bodies missing?" Mike said, his face hard.

"Indeed," Vadim said. "This is what I'm to prevent, but I'd like to know how."

"With more people you know who is moving in the area," Mike said. "You intercept the Chechens before they do stuff like this. Simply keeping them from moving through town will cut down on it; you can't move through this region without moving through Alerrso. Not north and south. Do you think they moved north?"

"No, they fled back to the south," Vadim said. "They will bribe their way past a checkpoint and be gone. I have put out the word on this, as you would say, and I am told they will be found. I doubt it. Honestly, south of the pass there are a dozen ways they can go. They might still be in the area, waiting until we are no longer looking for them. They might have passed the food they took to a mule train that will take it to Chechnya over the mountains. Maybe done the same with the girls or simply kept them for their own uses."

"We're going to have to patrol heavy," Mike said, shrugging. "As soon as the militia is trained. It's going to be a pain in the ass, but I'd rather this not happen in Alerrso or the Valley. And I'm sure the news about what's happening in the valley is getting out. We're going to have to keep a close eye out for movement in the area even before the militia gets formed."

"I'd love to know how," Vadim said, dispiritedly. One of the bodies was very young.

"I'll see if we can get the phone system in Alerrso upgraded," Mike said. "If anyone moves through the town, we can set up a signaling system. Maybe put out some hide positions using radio. Even without the militia, there's a tiddly strike force in the trainers. If they strike first through the roads we'll have warning."

"Do what you can," Vadim said. "I'll stay here to clean up. It's all *I* can do."

"That's the situation we're dealing with," Mike said, shaking his head. He'd called Adams and Nielson into a conference as soon as he'd gotten back. "While we're training, we need to keep one eye on the security situation."

"I don't want to just put guns in the hands of the Keldara," Adams said, frowning. "They're smarter than I'd hoped, but I don't think that would be a good idea."

"Agreed," Nielson said, setting his laptop on the desktop. "But the trainers can start carrying, heavy, from now on. The work they were on is winding down as I'd planned as we get closer to the planting festival. Planting's done, by the way; what are they waiting for?"

"It's scheduled for a particular day in the year," Mike said, shrugging. "It's more of a spring festival than a strictly planting festival. But I still think we should wait until then to start training; I don't want to interfere in their festivals and for a few weeks after there's not much to do around the farm the women and older men can't handle."

"I can work with that," the colonel said. "We can start pulling back a small strike team, five or so, in the event that something goes wrong. Keep an SUV up here for them to move in."

"Create a ground-floor weapons room," Mike said, nodding as the plan took shape. "There's a small utility room by the main entry corridor. Start storing personal weapons there. I'll get a couple of Keldara to set up weapons racks."

"That will handle any minor attack," Adams said. "But I'd like some recon and a warning net."

"Some of the Keldara are hunters," Mike said, musingly. "Give them over to a pretraining team and set them out, two-man teams, as eyeballs north and south. Nothing we can do about the tracks in the mountains right now, but we can keep an eye on the road. Get Vanner setting up the main commo shack and train them in on the radios. Scatter some radios in Alerrso. Lay in a secure line to the Keldara commo center or put it up here."

"Up here would work better," Nielson said, definitively. "It's the most secure location and we can put an antenna farm up on the roof that will link through the whole area easily. We've got the satellite radios for longer range; only thing that will work in these mountains. I'll set up the training teams. Probably send out a trainer with the hunters for some makee learnee. One trainer and one hunter per team for the time being."

"Give me the names and I'll start rounding them up," Adams said. "And the back-up strike teams. We should rotate that."

"I'll get it to you by the end of the day," Nielson said, frowning.

"I'll get some Keldara up here and get them started on the gun-rack," Mike said, nodding. "Anything else?"

"Not that I can think of at the moment," Nielson said.

"I can," Adams said. "Some of the Keldara are bound to get shot up doing this stuff. The medics are going to designate some of them for basic medical training, maybe more with some of the women. But we're still a long damned way from the hospital. Any way that we can get a chopper for extraction?"

"Unlikely," Mike said, shaking his head. "As far as I know

the hospital in Tbilisi doesn't even have one." He looked at the chief's face and frowned. "Damnit, you want me to buy them a *chopper*?"

"One that we have first priority on," Adams said, nodding. "Yes. And they'll probably need help, for the first year at least, with support and pay for the pilots. Keep in mind, you might be the guy that needs it."

"Christ," Mike said, shaking his head. "This is getting expensive enough it's noticeable. Okay, okay, I'll think about it."

"Then that's all," Adams said. "I'll get with the Keldara about the gun-rack; you don't know diddly about building a gun-rack."

Mike was down in the weight room, pushing his way through a punishing pect workout with E Nomine cranked up on the speakers, when the door opened to reveal one of the Keldara women. She immediately shouted something he couldn't catch over the booming industrial.

Mike stepped out of the Nautilus machine and turned off the stereo, cocking an eyebrow in query.

"There has been an incident in the village," the woman said. "A Keldara woman has been taken by Chechens. They were seen driving down the hill this way."

Mike thought rapidly about how long it would take them to make it out of the area as he grabbed a towel and ran up the stairs. He could hear the duty squad throwing on their gear but he didn't bother; the vehicle would be out of the valley before they could even make it out the door fully rigged. Instead he kept climbing, running up to the second level and into his bedroom.

He'd laid in a gun room next to his room, a little security blanket in case everything went to shit. Among other weapons in the room was a Barrett. The Robar was more accurate but the M-82A1 was a better light material gun.

He grabbed the Barrett and headed for his balcony, looking down into the valley. He could see the road clearly from his position and there was a white van heading down the valley road at high speed. They must have gotten the impression they weren't welcome or maybe they were just really stupid drivers.

Mike moved rapidly but with care, throwing the Barrett up onto the balcony railing, sliding in a magazine, arming the weapon and then snuggling in to look through the scope.

It took him a moment to acquire the speeding van but when he did he slid forward, laying the crosshairs on the engine compartment and then leading it. In the mild spring air he could see the round crackling through the rippling air and it impacted forward of the van, gouging up a spurt of dust that was lost in the dust of the van's passage. He pulled back a bit and the second round cracked into the side of the vehicle, uncomfortably close to the cargo compartment. The third of five rounds cracked into the driver's area and the van swerved wildly for a moment then straightened out. Killing the driver was nowhere in his plan so he led the van, which was getting out of range, a bit more and let go with the fourth round. He couldn't figure out where that one went but he followed it up with another and was professionally pleased to see the van's muffler start streaming blue and the van slowing to a stop.

He dropped the Barrett, then stopped by the gun room just long enough to pick up a fully-loaded silenced M-4. He still made it out the front doors just after the last member of the duty squad.

"Over," Mike snapped, slipping in the door of the Expedition.

"God damnit, Kildar," Russell said. He was one of the Rangers with the group, a pure shoot trainer, a real freak of nature, too. He pumped more iron than any normal human should and looked like a walking tank. Loaded down with his weapon, body armor and spare ammo he looked even worse. "You're not even in *armor.*"

"Shit happens," Mike said. "Go!"

No one had gotten out of the van when they reached it. It was parked on the side of the road, near the southwest end of the valley. A few Keldara who had been in the fields had drifted that way but Mike waved them back as he unloaded from the Expedition and moved forward in tactical present.

As he neared the back door he could hear the rest of the team moving out to either side and noticed a bit of movement by the back window. Suddenly the back door opened up and a man was revealed holding a gun to the head of a girl. Mike noticed in passing that it was Katrina. Figured. She looked more pissed than scared but she was sitting still. There was a large red mark on her face and her blouse was torn, revealing an amazingly good chest for a fourteen-year-old girl. Mike figured somebody was just going to *have* to pay for that.

"If you or your men move closer I'll kill her," the man said in heavily accented Georgian.

"Go ahead," Mike said, glancing past him into the van. There were seats in it and he couldn't figure out how many girls were in it, but it was close to full. "I've been in this situation before. One guy walked away alive. He was the one that let the bitch go. I don't really care if you kill her, pussy in the mountains is in overabundance. But if you do you won't be walking away." The M-4 was sighted for 150 meters, so at this range, due to parallax, the round would tend to track up. Mike dropped the sight to just below the guy's chin and worried about the shot. The problem with the M-4 was that the 5.56 round was bound to pass through the target. If there was a girl on the other side of him, and Mike was pretty sure there was, she was liable to take a round in the back. "Hey! Girls in the van! On the floor if you please!"

"Shut up!" the man shouted. "I will kill her, I swear!"

"You're clearly not listening carefully," Mike said, dropping to a sitting position and leaning over a bit so he was now targeted to go through the guy's head and upward. "You can let her go and walk or . . ."

The top of the man's head lifted up and sprayed blood and brains into the interior of the van accompanied by screams from the girls on the interior.

As soon as the man's hands went flaccid, Katrina rolled out of the van and onto the ground, lying flat. Mike darted forward to cover her as the rest of the team went for the other doors. There were more screams and a crunching sound as women started to pour out of the side door.

"Sorry about that, boss," Russell said as Mike walked around the driver's side of the van. Russell was holding the driver by the wrist and the guy was sitting on the ground, trying very hard not to move; his hand was at a forty-five-degree sideways angle. "I guess I pressed a little too hard when I jerked him out."

"Works for me," Mike said, walking over to the man on the ground. "Hurt?"

"Yes," the man whispered, his face white.

"Good," Mike said. "Your van's all shot up, but we'll get you a splint and a ride back to Chechnya. Then you tell your buddies that the valley of the Keldara is *off-limits*, clear? You try to take our food, you try to take our women, you try to fight us, you're going to end up very dead. Is that clear?"

"Who are you?" the man asked, looking around. "You're Americans."

"*I* am the Kildar," Mike said. "These are some of my friends that I asked over to help out with the security situation. American and British Spetznaz. They're going to be working on the security in the area. And training the Keldara to do the same. So unless you *want* to get the shit kicked out of you, stay far, far away."

"Patch him up," Mike said, looking at Russell and switching to English. "Tell doc to just splint it. I'll get Vadim to find a ride for him back to the border."

"Will do, boss," Russell said.

"Boss?" Thompson said, walking around the side of the van. "We've got the girls unloaded, what do we do with them?

"What the fuck *do* we do with them?" Mike asked, looking at the nine girls lined up by the roadside. They'd mostly stopped crying and now looked at the men with guns in fear. They also were covered blood and in some cases vomit.

"Clean 'em up and fuck 'em?" Thompson suggested. The former

SFer shrugged at Mike's expression. "Just a thought. I mean, they were on their way to being whores anyway, right?"

Mike had to admit that under the mess some of the girls were damned good looking. Not as good looking as Keldara, but still damned good looking. On the other hand, some of them were . . . pretty young.

"We'll take 'em up to the caravanserai for now," Mike said. "I'll call Vadim and get his read on the situation. They all came from farms, maybe they can go back."

"They were all 'sent to town,'" Vadim said, after entering Mike's office. The girls had been turned over to Mother Savina with orders to get them some clean clothes and a bath. "Most of them are from farms down the road to the south. Various places between here and the Gorge."

"So can we send them back?" Mike asked.

"Assuming we can find any of the farms, probably not," Vadim said, shrugging. "Generally, none of these girls have been more than a kilometer from their homes and don't really know where they are. I'll send one of my men out to see if they can figure it out. But even if we can *find* the farms, girls get sent to town for a reason. Generally, they're of no more use. And if you send them back, they're just going to be sold again."

"So what the hell do I do with them?" Mike asked, angrily.

"I dunno," Vadim said, shrugging. "Clean them up and fuck them?"

After Vadim was gone, Mike sat at his desk and rubbed his forehead in thought. For good or ill, he'd apparently inherited a harem. The *honorable* thing to do was to figure out some way to send them off to a school, preferably female only, until they were old enough to find jobs. But half the time even women with training in countries like this ended up as "bar girls," whores in other words. There just weren't enough jobs for all the men, and women got hired last. Even when women could find decent jobs, it was usually at the cost of putting out to the boss. He thought about the "secretary" or whatever who served tea at his meeting with the president. It was unlikely that she only typed for her pay.

Hell, it was unlikely that he could find a school that would take them. None of the girls were going to speak English so sending them to somewhere in Europe would be out of the question and one in Georgia would probably reject them. Boarding schools in countries like Georgia were for the well-to-do. Period. Country peasants need not apply. There might be a school run by nuns or something that would take them in. Unlikely, but possible.

The easiest thing would be to simply keep them here as a harem. He considered that for a moment. The biggest problem the girls would face, even if they were "of age," say eighteen or so, would be education. He could get a tutor. Get them educated to high school level and they could get into a university. If they needed money for that, well, he had money.

He had to admit that the thought had a certain something. Poor, almost assuredly virginal, waifs. What to do? Clean 'em up and fuck 'em seemed to be the general consensus. It was what they knew was coming, anyway. Okay, and get 'em a tutor and take care of 'em until they were old enough to find a real life.

Conscience salved and decision made, Mike got up to go explain the facts of life to the girls.

"Good evening, ladies," Mike said, looking the group over. He was holding the meeting in the atrium of the harem quarters, sitting on the still nonfunctional fountain. The girls had been cleaned up and clothing found for them. There wasn't enough actual clothing available in their sizes so they were in whatever was available. In a couple of cases that meant robes and one of the ones in robes had a magnificent set of hooters that were showing a good bit of cleavage. He tore his eyes away from it and looked around at the other girls. Most of them were mid-teen but ranged from about seventeen down to one he was afraid might be twelve or so. She was a sweet-looking thing with black hair and an elfin face. And blue eyes that were watching him nervously.

"You all know why you were sent to town," Mike said, firmly looking away from the girl's eyes and the various breasts that strained clothes. "The good news is that you're not going to be turned into whores. The bad news is that there's not much else to do with you."

"Could we stay here?" one of the girls asked, nervously.

"That's the way it's trending," Mike admitted. "But, and there's always a but, you can guess under what conditions. The term is concubine. You'll be housed, fed, tutored and given a small salary. You'll clean house and provide other comforts. To be precise that means warm my bed and sometimes the beds of visitors I designate. Anyone who can't handle those conditions I'll have taken to Tbilisi and dropped off with some money and clothes. You can make your way from there. But you know damned well how you'll be making your way."

"That is fine," the little girl with the blue eyes said. "We heard that the Kildar had returned even where I lived. I do not mind being a woman of the Kildar." She actually seemed eager, which blew Mike's mind.

"I think you're nuts," Mike said, shaking his head. "And you'll be waiting for a bit; in my culture you're way too young so for the time being you'll just be helping around the house, little lady. Later we'll discuss the rest. As for the rest, when you're old enough to make it in the world you can go forth with an education under your belt and enough money to get a start. That I can do."

"Where are we going to stay?" the girl with the hooters asked, pulling her robe closer.

"Here," Mike said, waving around. "It's the old harem quarters. Convenient, no? We need to get you clothes. A tutor. An understanding tutor. Sheets for the beds . . ." He stopped and shook his head, sighing.

"Kildar," one of the girls said, standing up and coming over to sit by him. "We will speak to Mother Savina and tell her that we will be staying. And the rest that you said. There should be others to take care of that."

"What's your name, girl?" Mike asked. She was pretty but not beautiful, with long brown hair and brown eyes. She'd borrowed a dress from one of the hookers, Flopsy's if he recalled it correctly, and it fit her like a glove. Since she wasn't wearing a bra, she bulged out pleasantly. She also apparently had a longer torso since the dress, which was designed to fall to mid thigh, was hiked up to where it just barely covered her assets.

"I am Klavdiya," the girl said. She was on the upper end of the age range, probably about seventeen.

"You're hereby appointed straw boss," Mike said, sighing and trying not to stare down the dress. "Until I can get a harem manager. Tell Mother Savina that we'll need more house outfits."

"There are many rooms," the one with the hooters said. "Which one do we use?"

"There are four in use now," Mike said, pointing down the corridor. "Other than those, I don't care. Choose."

"We don't have to share?" Klavdiya asked, surprised. "Bless you, Kildar, I have never had a room of my own!"

"This is a sick culture," Mike muttered in English.

"What is that?" Klavdiya asked.

"Nothing," Mike said. "Yes, you can each have your own room, your own bed. And you'll be given a stipend to fix it up. Money to buy clothes of your own. You are the women of the Kildar. You cannot go out in public in robes," he said, gesturing at hooters. "What's your name girl?"

"Tinata," the girl answered, shyly. She was probably about sixteen, at a guess. On the spot he made the decision that that was the cut-off age. The twelve-year-old and the one that he was pretty sure was fourteen or so were off-limits until older. Sixteen he figured he could live with.

"Mind if I just call you Tina?" Mike asked. "There is an outfit that I got made for the other girls who are helping out. You'll each get a couple of those and you'll be given money that you can use to order more clothes. The deal is you get six hundred euros to order stuff for your room, all there is in them now is a bed and a night stand, and five hundred for clothes. That's for the first month, it goes down after that but it's still fair. I'll add some money every month for play money, that will be cash. When you leave, you can take any clothes that fit, jewelry, what have you. The furnishings stay."

Most of the girls were looking at him as if he had two heads, but one had clasped her hands over her mouth and bowed her head. She appeared to be crying.

"What did I say wrong?" Mike asked, looking at the crying girl and then Klavdiya.

"Most of us were . . . sold for less money than that," Klavdiya said, looking at him in disbelief. "You are going to give us this?"

"You keep the clothes and jewelry and whatever," Mike said. "The furnishings stay. And you keep the money, yeah. What's the problem? It's a good deal."

"It's wonderful," Klavdiya said, throwing her arms around him and giving him a kiss on the cheek. "I've never had money in my hand, before."

"There's the whole sex thing, too," Mike pointed out, trying to avoid a pair of extremely firm breasts pressed into his arm.

"You seem gentle," Klavdiya said, drawing back since he was clearly uncomfortable. "And we were to be whores. None of us were to have a husband. Now we are to be women of the Kildar! And paid too! This is too wonderful to describe!"

"I did mention the sex thing, right?" Mike asked, confused. Most of the girls were looking at him as if he was God. "Hey," he added, to the girl who still had her head down, "could you quit crying? It's a real turn-on. By the way," he said, turning back to Klavdiya, "I'm not the nicest guy in the world. I can be pretty rough."

"But you will not beat us to make us do things," Klavdiya said. "Will you?"

"If I *have* to," Mike said. "For that matter, I enjoy it. But I won't do it at random. And I generally either need a damned good reason or permission. Some girls enjoy playing with pain. However, yeah, if you get out of line I'll beat the heck out of you. Not as my first reaction, but don't push it, okay?"

"I won't," Klavdiya said, swallowing.

"And I won't be rough the first time," Mike said. "It ruins the young lady's approach. Speaking of the first time," Mike continued, looking around and shaking his head, "the one requirement I'm going to make here is that I'm first. I figure I'm paying for it, I might as well get first crack. But slowly, come up with a list. Actually, just get the girls' names and I'll figure it out. Can you write?"

"No, Kildar," Klavdiya admitted.

"Learning's going to be a bitch," Mike said, sighing. "I'll get one of the female trainers in here to set up the logistics. After I have a list I'll figure out who goes first."

"I volunteer," Klavdiya said, her jaw working nervously.

"Okay," Mike said, shrugging. "You seem pretty balanced and hopefully the rest will be less worried if you give a good report. Later, though. I've got things to do."

"Very well, Kildar," the girl said, slightly crestfallen. She'd obviously screwed up her courage to volunteer.

"And tell Mother Savina to tell Uncle Latif that I want this fountain working," Mike said, standing up. "Sheets on the beds, get clothes, get a list of the girls and fix the fountain. The rest can wait."

CHAPTER
FIFTEEN

"I heard we had some excitement today," Adams said, coming into Mike's office after a knock.

"This is getting out of control," Mike said. "I just picked up seven more waifs. The only thing to do with them is kick them out or make them concubines. I thought about trying to just keep my hands off them but that would make things weirder in the long term."

"You're due, buddy," Adams said. "Something about fifty college coeds if I recall."

"Forty-nine," Mike said, sadly. "Forty-nine."

"Yeah, well we got forty-nine out," Adams said.

"Besides, I screwed twenty of the forty nine," Mike admitted.

"*Twenty?*" Adams shouted. "Damnit, I only got six!"

"*Six?*" Mike snapped back. "When the hell did you get six?"

"Well, there was the hotel in DC," Adams said, ticking off on his fingers. "Two there, separate times, mind you. Then there was the party at the Kappa Alpha house, that was three..."

"Yeah," Mike said, shaking his head. "I heard about that one."

"Those Kappa Alphas can *party*," Adams admitted. "Then there was the visit I made later. That was the last one, a Chi O, but then there were two more of her sorority sisters over the weekend . . ."

"Christ," Mike said, shaking his head. "You were bent on taking over UGA weren't you?"

"Dude, it was only a plane hop away," Adams pointed out. "And all I had to do was get one of the girls to introduce me as a SEAL and it was pussy city. And you got *twenty*. Don't give me any shit."

"Well, it took most of a month," Mike admitted, grinning. "But I think I potted all the girls that were recovered enough. It was fun. Good for them, good for me. But that doesn't cover the present problem. I wasn't planning on having a harem."

"Wah," Adams said. "Not a problem most guys want to listen to somebody complain about."

"Well, if a certain team name ever gets tagged to me the area around me is going to get really exciting," Mike pointed out. "Having a bunch of potential hostages around is not my idea of a good plan."

"You've got the Keldara around you," Adams pointed out. "Both as defenders and as potential hostages. A few more bunnies running around won't matter."

"I suppose," Mike said. "But doesn't it bother you a *bit*?"

"Nah," Adams replied. "You always overanalyzed. Go get it stuck in and forget the rest. It won't matter in a hundred years anyway. But you need to get you a harem manager, you know that."

"I can just see that advertisement," Mike pointed out. "Wanted, harem manager for group of teenaged concubines. Must be female. Send photo and resume."

"Mike, I've *had* teenaged daughters," Adams said. "Well, step-daughters. You don't want to put up with them most of the time. They should be raised in a barrel. Oh, the screaming fits and the sulks and the pouts and the whines. Get a professional."

"And where, exactly, does one find a professional harem manager?" Mike asked, smiling.

"Uzbekistan comes to mind," the chief said, seriously. "We were there for a refit in between jobs in Afghanistan. The team had a night off so we went down to the local club. Some dude with heavies was sitting in the corner with a girl about thirteen on his lap and another that looked like a damned model, maybe twenty-three or so, sitting next to him. Turned out he was one of the local sheiks and the twenty-something was his harem manager. There were about ten girls out on the dance floor shaking it, all in a group, not one over seventeen I swear. The harem. That's what you're shooting for, man, trust me."

"I'm not so sure," Mike said, frowning. "Sounds fun, but I'm sure there are headaches. Besides the dealing with teenaged girls. I've noticed that if they're getting laid on a regular basis they're less prone to the sulks at least."

"Braces come to mind," Adams replied, shaking his head. "You're going to be going through a ton with an orthodontist, if you can find one in Tbilisi."

"Braces," Mike said, wincing. "You had to mention those."

"Okay," Adams replied, shrugging. "So they're a turn-on. This is a good thing."

"Klavdiya," Mike said, sticking his head in the girl's room after knocking.

"Yes, Kildar, is it time?" the girl said, standing up. The bed had been made up but the room was still awfully Spartan, no more than a bed and a nightstand, not even a chair.

"I've been called out of town," Mike said, shaking his head at her expression. "Try to keep your hands off the trainers while I'm gone, okay?"

"Yes, Kildar," the girl said, nodding.

"Is Cottontail giving you any trouble yet?" he asked.

"No, Kildar," the girl said, looking at him in a puzzled manner.

"Odd, that," Mike said. "I guess she's biding her time. I may be gone for a week or so. You just listen to Mother Savina. She'll manage things 'til I get back. If there are any questions she can't answer, get ahold of Sergeant Heard, she's the senior female militia trainer. Questions?"

"No, Kildar," the girl said.

"Good girl," Mike said, sighing. "I need to get going."

"Chatham Aviation, Gloria speaking, how may I help you?"

"Hi, Gloria, it's Mike Jenkins again," Mike said. "I don't know if you recall me chartering..."

"It's been the talk of the office for the last year, Mr. 'Jenkins,'" the receptionist said, giggling. The quotes on the name were evident in her voice.

"Great," Mike said. "I hope it *stayed* in your office. Look, I need another charter. I don't suppose Captain Hardesty is available?"

"As a matter of fact he is," Gloria said. "And as far as I know the discussion hasn't left the office. I certainly haven't talked about it; our clients' actions are considered privileged for very good reasons. Your travels were rather... interesting, however. Other than that, I won't discuss it over the phone."

"Maybe another time," Mike said, chuckling.

"Where are you this time?"

"Georgia," Mike said. "The country not the state. I'll pick up at Tbilisi Airport and be going to Uzbekistan. A layover there and then back. I need to see a man about a harem manager."

"In your case, Mr. Jenkins," the receptionist said, the humor in her voice evident, "I won't even bother to guess if that's the real reason you're going to the Stans. When do you need the jet?"

"Yesterday?" Mike asked. "In other words, as soon as possible."

"Captain Hardesty will be in the air in an hour or so," Gloria said. "Always a pleasure, Mr. Jenkins."

"The same, Gloria," Mike replied. "Nice dealing with professionals."

▲   ▲   ▲

"Steinberg."

"Jenkins," Mike replied. "Go scramble code seven."

"I'm on," Steinberg said. "What can I do for you, Mr. Jenkins."

"I need a very discreet conversation with your opposite number in the Uzbek embassy. Can that be arranged? I'll add that it's a private matter rather than purely business."

"Sure," Steinberg said. "What you need to start learning is that at this level, personal and business are interchangeable. Want him to call you or vice versa?"

"If he could call me, soon, that would be good," Mike said, stuffing the sat phone into his jump bag. "I'm hoping to head to Uzbek sometime today."

"Any *business* reason you're headed for Uzbekistan?" Steinberg said, curiously.

"Nope," Mike assured him. "Purely personal. I'm hoping he can arrange a discreet conversation for me with someone there. I need some advice and contacts."

"I'll call him as soon as we get off the phone," Steinberg said. "But you've got me curious."

"It's a *long* story," Mike said. "And one that needs to stay very close to the vest for the time being. In other words, not to be discussed with your bosses. Personal, as I mentioned."

"Okay," Steinberg said. "Talk to you later."

"Come on out to the house," Mike said. "We'll hoist a few."

"I've heard of Keldara beer," Steinberg said. "That's a pretty good invitation."

Mike was in the middle of discussing with Nielson what had to be done while he was gone when the sat phone rang.

"Jenkins."

"David Wangen," a male voice said. "Scrambler code nine, please."

"Go Scramble," Mike said, punching in the code.

"Mr. Jenkins, I'm the intelligence coordinator for the American embassy in Uzbekistan," Wangen said. "Bob Steinberg suggested that you needed something and indicated that it was worth my time to help."

"I don't know about worth your time," Mike said. "It's purely personal."

"Anyone who can pick up the phone and call the President is worth helping, Mr. Jenkins," Wangen said, chuckling.

"I haven't talked to the boss in . . . months," Mike said. "And for reasons that are going to be really obvious this is something I'd rather never get to his ears. So, Mr. Wangen, exactly how discreet are you?"

"If it's not a matter of national security I can be very discreet," Wangen said, curiously. "What's the problem?"

"I inherited a damned harem," Mike said, rolling his eyes at Nielson who was grinning. "The reasons are complicated and I'll explain it when we're together, if you want. But I need a harem manager. One of the guys I got for training the locals said that there are a couple of guys around Uzbek that have traditional harems. I need to talk to one of them about where in the hell you get a harem manager. I'm not going to try to keep a bunch of teenage girls in line myself. I don't have a big enough club around the house."

"My heart bleeds," Wangen said, chuckling. "My wife is pushing fifty and going through the 'change.' But I know a guy that fits the profile. I'll give him a call. When are you planning on coming out?"

"I've got a plane on the way from England at the moment," Mike said. "I figured I'd be there by tomorrow morning. Sometime tomorrow work?"

"Probably," Wangen said, hesitantly. "I'll have to call the sheik and check on his schedule."

"I can hang out for a day or two," Mike said. "I just need to be back by Saturday."

"That can be arranged," Wangen said. "Let me give the sheik's people a call and see what I can arrange."

"Thanks," Mike said, hitting the disconnect. "The plane's on the way. Given how long it takes to get to Tbilisi I probably should be leaving," he continued to Nielson.

"We've got it handled," Nielson said. "Take off. You realize you're running away from a group of teenage girls?"

"Oh, certainly," Mike said, standing up and folding away the satellite phone. "Women are the root of all evil. And teenage girls haven't learned to use their power for good. There is a reason that harem doors had bolts on the outside."

"I need to get a helicopter," Mike muttered as he bumped over the road to Tbilisi.

"Pardon, Kildar?" Vil said. Mike had brought the Keldara along to drive the Expedition back to the caravanserai. But he wasn't about to trust him to actually drive with Mike in the car. The Keldara had many traits Mike had come to admire, but their driving style was pure third world.

"I said I need to get a helicopter," Mike replied. "This road is awful. But maintaining the damned thing in the valley would be a pain in the ass. And taking the Expedition means the reaction team has to use one of the Family's. Stop by the Ford dealer and tell him we need two more SUVs. They don't have to be Expeditions, Explorers would do, but they have to be four wheel. And black or red."

"Yes, Kildar," Vil said. "May I ask a question?"

"Always," Mike said.

"I know you intend to use the vehicles for the militia," Vil said, hesitantly. "Black I can understand, but why red?"

"Red is nearly as hard to see in the dark as black," Mike said. "Not that with their reflective coats they're camouflaged or anything. But that's why red or black. You guys ready for issue and zero on Friday?"

"Yes, Kildar," Vil said enthusiastically. "We're looking forward to it. The Keldara are farmers, yes, but at heart we are warriors. We have been kept from the warrior path for too long."

"I won't get into the difference between the warrior and the soldier," Mike said. "These days the definitions are getting a bit blurred, anyway. But to be a true modern warrior requires learning to be a soldier. At the same time, being a soldier will not be enough, I want all the Keldara to make the jump to modern warrior, a fighter who can both use initiative *and* obey orders."

"We will try, Kildar," Vil said uncertainly.

"I sort of hit the difference, there," Mike said in explanation. "A warrior fights for honor and glory and to show that he has courage. He takes rash chances so that he can stand out. A soldier fights for the honor of a cause and, in the heat of battle, so that he doesn't let his comrades down. They don't take chances but, on the other hand, they'll soak up the casualties if that's what it takes to perform the mission, and they don't run.

"Warriors tend to have plenty of reasons to leave the battle and tend to get whacked when they don't. They don't work well in teams, don't think of their fellow fighters as worth taking chances for, so they tend to fight badly. The mujahideen are warriors. They hit and run and when they try to stand up and fight they get slaughtered by soldiers and modern warriors.

"Most American forces fall into the category of modern warriors. They fight for all the reasons of soldiers, they fight well in teams and stand to their salt when the chips are down but they don't have a problem going the extra mile. If they see a better way to achieve the objective they'll use initiative and courage to do so. They don't take stupid chances but they don't have a problem taking the hit if it means the mission gets accomplished.

"That's what I'm hoping to find in the Keldara. You find it in some tribes around the world, the Kurds and the Gurkhas are the best known. The Keldara seem to have that same basic ethos. I hope I'm right because what we're going to try to accomplish will require that you guys be beyond good."

"I think I see," Vil said, nodding. "There are things about the Keldara . . . I think we will be good for this. Give the Keldara guns and an enemy and the problem will be holding us back.

We have a great hate in us and more courage than you might think for farmers."

"And plenty of things you're not discussing with your Kildar," Mike said, apparently paying close attention to the twisting mountain road. "Like what that cross you wear actually means. It's not a standard cross. It looks one hell of a lot like an axe. Maybe a hammer, but that would be really odd."

"An axe would not?" Vil asked, carefully.

"There's a tribe in southeastern Georgia that has various practices," Mike said, shrugging. "Among other things, they have a spring festival that celebrates something like the story of the Golden Fleece. Medea was near here, it's possible that they're a remnant of the Medean tribe. You're familiar with the story of the Golden Fleece?"

"Yes, Kildar," Vil answered.

"Interesting," Mike said. "I'd love to hear your version. 'This asshole from Greece and a bunch of his drinking buddies showed up one day, seduced the king's daughter, killed her pet dragon, stole the Fleece and made off with it and the girl. Then he dumped the girl, the bastard.' But the point is that they also have an axe that is a symbol of authority. That path probably traces through the Greeks or the Medeans. A hammer, though, that's pretty unusual. Assuming a Greek descent it would relate to Hephaestus, the Greek god of smiths. But I've never actually seen that motif in ethnology. Now the *Norse* used an axe as a symbol, especially in reaction to Christianity. Not like yours, but similar. However, the only Norse that got down here were the Varangian Guard of the Byzantine emperors. And I've scanned a couple of online sources and they don't have that particular motif anywhere. For that matter, Constantinople is a long damned way from here. Most of the hammer symbols were late Norse. Early Norse hardly had any specific god symbols at all. The Gallic tribes used an axe as a symbol of authority for a while, but that's a pretty long shot. And while you guys have some evidence of Norse characteristics, they're awful muted. Cultural memes can hold out for a long time in isolation, I suppose. I'd love to get a gene typing of you guys, though. You're either classic Caucasian types, the very base of the Aryan gene pool, or you're some very odd transplants. I haven't figured out which. On the other hand, I have figured out that *you* know, or think you know. Close?"

"Very," Vil said, uncomfortably.

"You've got your secrets; I've got mine," Mike said. "Don't expect to find mine out any time soon. I don't expect to find out yours."

"Mr. Jenkins," Hardesty said as Mike got out of the Expedition. "It's good to see you. Will you be changing names again?"

"Not this time," Mike said, grabbing his bags out of the back. "Nice simple visit to Uzbekistan. We may have to sit around for a couple of days."

"I'll attempt to restrain my enthusiasm," Hardesty said, smiling faintly.

"Been to the Stans, have you?" Mike asked. "Vil, head back to the valley," he continued as the Keldara took the keys to the SUV. "Don't forget to stop by the Ford dealership. And get the oil changed and whatnot if you've got time."

"Yes, Kildar," Vil said, getting in the driver's seat.

"And don't ding it," Mike shouted as the Keldara sped away.

"You have a minion," Hardesty said as Mike boarded the Gulf-stream.

"I do indeed," Mike replied. "Minions, actually. Which is a different kind of headache than I'm used to. But now we're away to Samarkand and I get to forget the minions for a while."

"We're preflighted," Hardesty said. "If there's nothing keeping us."

"No," Mike said. "Get me out of here before someone figures out a reason I have to stay. Let us waft to storied Samarkand."

"You haven't been in Uzbekistan lately," Hardesty said, chuckling.

"*Au contraire*," Mike replied, sitting in one of the front seats and buckling in. "But I can hope it's improved."

CHAPTER
SIXTEEN

It hadn't.

Samarkand of fable and legend was a city originally placed across the Great Silk Road, the ancient caravan trail from the Mediterranean to China. It had grown from a village to a powerful city, fat with tolls from the caravans, famous for its snow-packed melons, then been overrun by the Mongols and subjected to one of the more professional jobs of "rape, loot, pillage *then* burn." It was rebuilt by the Mongols and subsequently captured by the Turks, the Persians, the Uzbeks and finally the Russians, although the order was often disputed. Each had left their mark on the city but the Russians had managed to do the most damage. If it were still in ruins from the Mongols, it would look better than what fifty years of Socialism had done to it.

The Samarkand of fable from Marco Polo's travels had been a city of gardens, narrow alleys, romantic caravanserai and red-walled fortresses. Admittedly, it had probably been lacking in plumbing, but Marco Polo was no rose by the time he got there. The Samarkand that the Soviets left behind was a city of straight roads, ugly monuments and crumbling concrete. Uzbekistan had been officially "democratic" and "capitalist" for better than two decades, but the various presidents had all been kleptocrats and public improvements were low on their list of priorities. For that matter, land locked, virtually without mineral or oil wealth and having nearly zero industry, in the modern world Uzbekistan was the backwater of backwaters and one of the poorest nations listed in the CIA worldbook.

At least it had been prior to September 11, 2001. With the attack by the Al Qaeda on New York and Washington, the need to remove the Taliban in Afghanistan was self-evident. There were two ways open to attack Afghanistan, another land-locked country. The easiest would be through Pakistan, which had high quality roads and railroads and the port of Karachi to supply through. But the Pakistani people, especially those in the northern territories, were closely linked to the Taliban-supporting tribes in Afghanistan. Pakistan could provide a small measure of support, but it would be minimal, and safe basing was out of the question.

Uzbekistan, however, had already entered into various agreements with the United States prior to 9/11 and many of the forces fighting the Taliban were related to the Uzbeks. When it became evident that using Pakistan was impossible, the U.S. had, instead, poured its military wealth into this flat, land-locked, country. Special operations and air force bases had been built, contracts had been let and servicemen and women had poured into the country. In short order, the number-one employer in Uzbekistan had become Uncle Sam either directly, by hiring people to work on the bases and construction contracts, or indirectly by providing goods and services to off-duty soldiers and airmen.

And fabled Samarkand had become the target of choice for those off-duty service personnel. If for no other reason than the quality of its whores.

Mike remembered spending one seriously drunken four-day weekend in Samarkand. Despite being a Moslem country, the influence of the Uzbeks, one of the many tribes of "Mongols" that had overrun the Middle East in ancient times, was strong. Liquor was legal and prostitution was considered just one of those things. Girls from Russia had flooded into the country to supply "services" to lonely American lads and Mike had taken full advantage. The team had just come off of nearly two months of straight combat ops and, at the time, it was all TDY. The TDY pay-out had been . . . sizeable. And he'd blown damned near all of it on booze and girls. At something like five bucks for a blowjob and twenty for around the world, he'd screwed himself silly. And barely been able to remember it for all the booze.

Good weekend.

In response to the increase in business, Hilton had, thank God, built a hotel. Mike considered that as he looked out the windows of the hotel at downtown Samarkand. The last time he'd been here he'd ended up staying in some really lousy bordello the whole four days. Literally lousy; he'd had to thoroughly de-louse when he got back to the base. In a Hilton that worry wasn't an issue.

The Hilton was close to the center of downtown and fairly new, which meant that something had been destroyed to put it there. Mike hoped that it was one of the horrible Soviet six-story tenements that infested the city. The decaying tenements were perfectly square, at least in design—no Soviet builder could actually make something perfectly square—and unadorned. So was Bauhaus architecture, but it used pleasing lines to create something that was only mediocre. The Soviets had managed to create buildings of oppressive ugliness without really trying. Unfortunately, they were generally ringed around the center, though, so it was more likely to be some traditional building or buildings.

Samarkand had one notable feature that was post-Soviet: the Mosque. For some reason, Islamic countries had gotten into a battle over who could build the mosque with the highest minaret and onion dome. Not to mention the most surpassing ugliness. Aesthetics definitely took a back seat. The Samarkand Mosque was a grotesque building that dominated the view. The older houses, shops and mosques that huddled near it were dwarfed by the thing. It looked as massive as the Great Pyramid, although Mike knew that was an exaggeration. Baroque in the extreme, covered in murals, most of them made of rather cheap ceramic, and "gold" that was mostly anodized aluminum, the thing was a monument to tasteless excess. It was the perfect counterpoint to the Soviet block architecture that was its antithesis in style. With each equally ugly in amazingly different ways, the circle of ill-conceived architecture was complete.

Mike wondered what the Keldara would make of all of this. As soon as countries became "independent," whether of Soviet domination or theological domination or Western domination, they jumped into capitalism with both feet. And their heads up their butts. They created the shape of capitalism in skyscrapers and ... well, big mosques even. But they couldn't create the social base. Uzbekistan had various positive factors that could permit it to grow and thrive. Hong Kong had done so with less, although they were anything but landlocked. But the concept of simply digging in and doing was foreign to so many cultures. The "Protestant work ethic" was a rare thing indeed. In cultures like this one, actually doing work was considered a social abasement. Management was one thing, getting your hands dirty another.

It was the main reason, after the Islamic influence, that east Asian countries were firing away on all cylinders, with admittedly some boo-boos, but countries like Uzbekistan were stagnating. In east Asia, everyone understood the concept of working as hard as you could to make a dime. In west Asia, it was *verboten*. And they still had the "command economy" idea in their heads from the Soviets. As if that had worked.

He was wondering if the Keldara could make less of a hash of things when his moody reflections were interrupted by the buzz of the sat phone.

"Jenkins."

"Mr. Jenkins, this is David Wangen from the embassy, how are you today?"

"Fine," Mike said, wondering why Wangen didn't go on scrambler, then realizing he was probably using an unsecure line.

"I've met with Sheik Otryad and he is willing to meet with you," Wangen said. "This evening at his compound outside of town. Are you available?"

"Yes," Mike said. "I've seen Samarkand before so I can skip the sight-seeing trip. How do I get there?"

"I'll have a car sent from the embassy," Wangen said. "They'll know how to get here. About five?"

"Works," Mike said, frowning. The ways were being greased big-time and he didn't know why. His negligible connection with the President was unlikely. Far more likely, someone wanted something.

"I'll make sure the car is there."

At a bit before five Mike was down front in one of his new Harrowgates' suits, a briefcase in hand containing his sat phone. Precisely at five a Cadillac limousine pulled up front and an American riding in the front passenger seat got out and opened the back door.

"Mr. Jenkins?" the man said, nodding.

"The same," Mike replied, stepping into the rear of the limo. The divider was down and he could tell the driver was an American also. "Why'd I get diplo protection guys?"

"Uzbekistan has a very limited terrorist problem," the person riding shotgun said as he got back in the car. "Just a small security measure."

"Did Mr. Wangen set this up?" Mike asked, leaning back and watching the minor sights of Samarkand pass. As he did, he did a rear check and, sure enough, there was a trail car, a Chevy Suburban.

"Actually it was at the orders of the ambassador," the driver said.

"The last time I was in Samarkand . . ." Mike said, then paused.

"Well, let's just say that I handled my own security. And I'm not, as far as I know, a high profile target."

"There's only so much one person can handle," the shotgun said. "Just sit back and enjoy the ride."

"There's another side to it," the driver said. "With us covering you, Otryad knows you're connected. Being connected is a necessity in Uzbek society."

"This is one hell of a lot of money being spent on a personal mission," Mike pointed out.

"From what I've heard, you've earned it," the shotgun replied. "Nothing specific, but when the secretary of state suggests that the ambassador roll out the red carpet, it means you've earned it. And I doubt it was from contributions to the presidential election campaign."

"Oh, I've done those, too," Mike said, shaking his head. "I really *really* wish SecState hadn't even heard about this particular mission. It's . . . delicate."

"As you say, sir," the driver replied.

"What's the read on this guy?" Mike asked.

"Former Sov apparatchik," the shotgun answered. "Used his position to snap up a couple of factories and some farmland after independence. Tight with the current president, the last two for that matter. Has a position as undersecretary of the interior, more or less permanent post rather than an appointee, that he uses to squeeze a king's load of graft, mostly in roads contracts. Gives to all the right Islamic charities and parties like there's no tomorrow. Real taste for young womenflesh. Has a harem of about sixteen girls at present and none of them are over eighteen except the harem managers. And the harem managers are fricking gorgeous. He goes into town every weekend to party with his girls so he's a known face around town."

"I take it he doesn't go into the office much?" Mike asked.

"No," the shotgun said. "If you need to meet him you meet him at his house. He only goes into town for shopping and partying."

The drive was fast, the road getting better if anything as they got out of town. In fact, it was just about up to western standards and Mike wondered about that until he saw an F-16 take off in the distance. The road had probably been upgraded with American money and contracts. Five times the graft of doing the same road in the U.S., and still less than half the cost and time.

Samarkand was placed on the Zarafshan River but they were headed in the opposite direction. The country around the city was flat as a pancake but in the distance there were hills and they seemed to be heading in that direction. The spec ops base Mike had been at was in the opposite direction and he'd never been in this part of Uzbekistan. As they approached the hills, though, he had to admit they looked like everything else in the desert belt that circled the globe; they were basically denuded of vegetation, and erosion had exposed the underlying rock. It seemed to be mostly red sandstone, which caught the descending sun rather prettily.

They took a turnoff from the main road up into the hills and the quality of surface dropped markedly; once again Mike was being beaten by third world surfaces and it made him yearn for one drive in the U.S. Even the roads in California were better than those in the third world. Not by much, admittedly, but better. Well, except for portions of L.A.

The road wound into the hills and after about a half hour of that they made a sharp turn into what looked like another road. This one was a bit better paved but it wound even more sharply, climbing the side of one particular hill. As they rounded a corner Mike could see a hilltop fort and realized they were approaching their destination.

"The sheik does himself right," the driver said, gesturing to the fort. "Very nice place."

"Looks a lot like my house," Mike said. And it did. The style of building was very similar, at least to the upper portions of the Keldara caravanserai.

"You live in a place like that?" the shotgun asked.

"Yep," Mike said. "Great for seeing if anybody's coming to call."

"Point," the shotgun said, looking over his shoulder. "The sheik's pretty particular about personal safety. If you're carrying you'd be best to leave it with us."

"Worse than flying commercial," Mike said, sighing. But he drew his .45 and set it on the seat.

"That it?" the shotgun asked, curiously.

"That's it," Mike said. "Half a dozen guns is for wankers or very special situations. By the time you need your backup you should be using the other guy's stuff. A pistol is only good for getting a shotgun which is only good for getting a long gun."

The gates to the fort were open and the limo pulled to a halt in front of the main doors of the house. A houseboy, actually a man in his twenties, immediately darted forward and opened Mike's door.

As the former SEAL got out he glanced around professionally. The sheik certainly was serious about his security. There were guards on the walls of the fort as well as a couple of serious heavies, really heavy, they had to weigh damned near three hundred pounds and not much of it fat, carrying MP-5s by the door. On the other hand, the HKs were the wrong weapon for the situation. If the sheik was really worried about getting hit by a ground attack they should be carrying AKs or M-4s; the MP-5 had lousy range and take-down capability.

The main door opened and Mike was escorted into an entry hallway by another heavy. If anything this one was larger than the ones by the door. Halfway down the man gestured for him to stop and waved a wand over the former SEAL, stopping at a couple of articles. He considered the folding knife for a moment and then handed it back without expression. Mike couldn't see any security watching the procedure but there were two very small and discreet cameras in the decorations near the far door. He figured if anyone got froggy there were at least two more heavies with weapons standing by. And for the few guests who might take offense it was sufficiently private that they could ignore the implied insult.

Security satisfied, the man opened the inner door into a foyer not unlike the one in the caravanserai with the exception of the domed ceiling. This one had high ceilings and opened directly onto an interior garden. Two men were waiting for the visitor, one of them an obvious American, blondish, balding and about fifty, and the other presumably the sheik. The sheik was a rotund guy, about five six, with black and very cold eyes. He looked a lot like the president of Georgia except for a slight epicanthic fold.

"Mr. Jenkins," the American said. "I'm David Wangen. A pleasure to finally meet you in person."

"Likewise," Mike said, shaking the intel officer's hand. "Bob Steinberg sends his regards."

"And this is His Excellency Sheik Abdullah Otryad," Wangen said in Russian, gesturing to the host.

"A pleasure to meet you, Excellency," Mike replied in the same language, bowing slightly. "Your fame, wisdom and knowledge is renowned throughout the world."

"As is yours, Mr. Jenkins," the sheik said, bowing in turn. "I welcome you to my house and invite you to take refreshment with me."

"I gratefully accept," Mike replied. "The hospitality of the sheik is as famous as his wisdom." Mike had a hard time with the last word in the sentence and substituted what he thought was the right Arabic instead.

"You know the language of the prophet?" Otryad asked, waving the two of them towards the garden.

"Only a bit," Mike replied in Arabic. "Very little."

"We will continue in Russian, then, if you don't mind," the sheik said. "My English is much like your Arabic."

"I am sure you surpass me in every way," Mike said, looking over at Wangen and rolling his eyes. He knew that the higher you got in Islamic cultures the language got more and more florid, but he was running out of buttery phrases.

"I am told you live in Georgia," the sheik replied, gesturing for them to take seats around a hammered brass table. Mike had seen things like it in bazaars but even in the most ornate homes they were only decorations. From the stains, it seemed the sheik used it as a regular table. There was an ashtray on the table and the sheik reached into his suit to pull out a pack of cigarettes. They weren't the ubiquitous Marlboros, Mike noticed, but a brand he'd never heard of, Nat Shermans, American or British at a guess.

"Do you smoke?" the sheik asked, offering the cigarettes.

"A cigar from time to time," Mike said. "I run too much for regular smoking."

"Then we must get you a cigar," the sheik said, clapping his hands.

There was a fourth spot at the table and as the sheik pulled out a cigarette and snugged it into a holder, a fucking vision entered the garden through a side door. The girl was in her mid-twenties and so beautiful it was scary. Long blonde hair pulled up at the back to reveal a long neckline, high cheekbones, heart-shaped face, tartar eyes, lovely legs and magnificent breasts. She was wearing a long blue dress just a shade lighter than her dark blue eyes. She was accompanied by two men who carried a tray of coffee makings.

"Anastasia, cigars for our friends," the man said, not looking around.

The girl looked at one of the men and then leaned forward to light the sheik's cigarette, taking a seat next to him. The two men laid out the coffee and then retreated as she began to serve.

"Georgia is a lovely country, or so I've heard," the sheik said.

"Very high mountains," Mike said, trying not to frown. In American society not introducing the lady would be the height of insult but he respected he was just supposed to ignore her. "Very wild in a way. Much wetter than Uzbekistan, obviously, very green. If it weren't for the mountains it would be a breadbasket. As it is, it's mostly small farms. A small seacoast on the Black Sea. I've never been there but I'm told it's pretty."

"Do you live in Tbilisi?" the sheik asked, picking up a small cup of coffee and sipping at it.

Mike lifted the coffee that was offered to him by the girl and sipped at it as well. It was incredibly thick and sweet, more like a syrup than coffee.

"No, my home is much like this," Mike replied. "I happened on it, got lost in a snowstorm if you can believe it. Rather liked the old fort and it came with a farm so I bought it."

"A small farm?" the sheik asked. "They are rarely profitable."

"Errr," Mike temporized. "Rather large, actually. Right at a thousand hectares. One of the larger valleys, quite fertile. There's a small town next to it and some tenant farmers. The caravanserai is much like this house; I felt right at home as soon as I entered." Mike noticed that the girl looked up at that and frowned. He wasn't sure what he'd said wrong.

"There's a serious security situation in Georgia, I'm told," the sheik said. "I, of course, am more interested in internal matters of Uzbekistan, but I hear rumors, read the news."

"The Chechens are a problem," Mike admitted. "The Ossetian problem doesn't really touch on us; we're on the other side of the country."

"The Chechens are a scourge," the sheik said, shaking his head. "They use Islam as a shield for the most vile of crimes. Breslan was an atrocity."

"They've killed more people than that in Georgia," Mike said. He paused as one of the servants came back in the room bearing a cigar box. Mike didn't recognize the brand but did see the word "Cuba" on the side. The girl extracted two cigars, snipped them and started them with a lighter, then gave one to Mike and the second to Wangen. "They say they're freedom fighters but in Georgia they're more like bandits. I'm trying to do something about that in my area, forming a small militia from the tenants who work the farm." Mike puffed on the cigar and found it to be incredibly strong. He caught the smoke in his mouth and let it back out carefully, unsure of exactly how you smoked something this strong. And foul. He preferred much lighter cigars.

"Such men rarely make decent soldiers," the sheik said, shaking his head again. "What do peasants know?"

"As you say, Sheik," Mike replied, shrugging.

"You disagree?" the sheik asked.

"The Keldara are an old tribe," Mike said, picking his words with care. "And they are warrior stock, that is evident in . . . well a lot of things. And I'm not just handing them guns; right now there are about twenty former American and Brit spec ops troops preparing to train them. For that matter, I've poured about two million dollars into equipment. If they can't outdo the Chechens with that level of training and equipment, well, I'll go find some Gurkhas to replace them."

The sheik chuckled at that, leaning back and handing the cigarette holder to the girl.

"You have your own security concerns I think," the sheik said as the girl replaced his cigarette with a fresh one.

"There are people who would very much like my scalp on their wall," Mike said, shrugging again. "Thus far they haven't managed. Generally it's been the other way around."

"You are capable?" the sheik asked.

"Competent," Mike answered.

"Let me interject if I might," Wangen said. "In American culture, understatement is the norm when you are trying to make a point. To say that you are competent means you are, in fact, very good. Mr. Jenkins is more than competent; he is among the very best in the world at what he does."

"Among the very best?" the sheik asked, raising an eyebrow.

"There are some CAG that are better," Mike said, shrugging. "Those guys are freaks of nature."

"CAG?" the sheik asked, looking at Wangen.

"Delta Force," Wangen translated.

"And, let me be plain about something," Mike said. "I occasionally do favors for the American government. Sometimes I do those favors before they know they need them done. But I'm not a general contractor."

"That is understood," the sheik said. "Your house is much like this one?"

"Except for entering directly on the garden and the fact that the foyer has a dome, practically identical," Mike admitted. "I suspect that it's much the same layout. It's been rebuilt a couple of times. The last major rebuild appears to be Turkish."

"And it is well guarded?" the sheik asked.

"At the moment it's guarded by American and Brit former special operations personnel," Mike said, smiling. "I think their reputation precedes them. When they are gone, it will be guarded by the Keldara or better. And then, of course, there's me," he added, smiling faintly. "We had a recent problem with the Chechens not getting the word that there was a new sheriff in town. They learned the error of their ways."

"And you had a hand in that?" the sheik asked, interestedly.

"Mostly in stopping their van," Mike said, shrugging. He looked over at Wangen and raised an eyebrow. He received a nod in return. "It was headed down the valley. Catching it would have been a pain in the . . . would have been a problem. So I took it down from the caravanserai."

"How far?" Wangen asked, interested in spite of himself.

"About two klicks when I got the engine block," Mike said. "The angle was pretty steep."

"A moving van?" Wangen asked, raising his eyebrows.

"Doing about forty," Mike said, shrugging. "Barretts are good at light material engagement." He had to put that in English since it went outside his Russian.

"I didn't catch that," the sheik said.

"The gun is good at killing vehicles," the woman said, quietly. "The Ba-rette."

"Ah," the sheik said, nodding. "The American .50 caliber rifle. I have one myself. But . . . two kilometers?"

"He is, as I mentioned, very good," Wangen noted.

"Formidable," the sheik said. "And does this formidable American have ladies to keep him formidable?"

"That was what the van was carrying," Mike said, shrugging. "Girls who had been picked up from farms to be sent to town as they say. To be whores in other words." He looked at the woman for a moment, then averted his eyes. "It's nearly impossible to find their farms and the families would not accept them back anyway."

"Of course not," the sheik said, frowning. "Are these the women you intend to make up your hareem?"

"Nothing else to do with them," Mike said, shrugging. "We hit the impact point of our two cultures. In your culture they are considered damaged goods. In mine they are considered specially protected. I intend to land somewhere in the middle. I considered various things to do with them. The most obvious, from my perspective, is to bring them into my household as concubines." He'd used English for the word since he hadn't figured out the right Russian term.

"Keeping teenage girls is not easy," the sheik said, smiling and handing over his finished cigarette again. "I suggest the stick on regular occasions. It reminds them who owns the home."

"I will take the suggestion to heart," Mike said, smiling faintly and taking another sip of coffee syrup. "However, neither Georgian culture nor my own has a background for exactly what I've ended up with. There are whore masters, of course, but . . ."

"Pimps are unworthy to approach a true hareem," the sheik said, shaking his head. "The hareem is a place of peace and contemplation; pimps would turn it into a place of sex, pure and simple."

"Well, I'm not going to discount the sex aspect," Mike said, wrinkling his brow.

"Of course not," the sheik said. "But the hareem is far more than sex. A hareem that is well run is where the lord goes to regain his sanity from the day of stress. There is much that he can delegate, but the ultimate responsibility lands upon the lord. That is day-to-day stress that, also, is unknown in your society. Very few have that sort of stress laid upon them. For the lord must not talk about his problems to his followers, lest they lose faith in him. He must hold it all in, all upon himself. The hareem is where he goes to escape that. It is only in the hareem that he can discuss his problems, for the women of the hareem are closed from the outside. They do not talk outside the hareem and thus the fears and problems of the lord stay safe. Thus the women of the hareem must be trained in far more than simply sexual arts. They must be trained to soothe and please their master, to remove the stress, not add to it. Thus, we have the problem of teenage girls, who are a problem all of their own."

"That they are," Mike said, thinking about Katya and then inserting Katrina in addition.

"You need an assistant," the sheik said.

"Agreed," Mike replied, raising an eyebrow. "I seek your wisdom in that."

"Anastasia?" the sheik said, looking at the woman. "You are over time to leave the hareem."

"Yes, my lord," the woman said, nodding and keeping her eyes down.

"This would be a good choice for you, I think," the sheik said. "You will go with him."

"Yes, my lord," the woman said, nodding.

"It is done," the sheik said, waving his hands. "Go and prepare to leave."

Mike started to open his mouth and then froze at a small gesture from Wangen. It seemed like a hell of a cold way to get sent out of the only life the girl had known for . . . probably a decade at least.

"She will be ready to leave shortly," the sheik said, dismissing the girl with another wave. "Her replacement has already been trained. This is better for her, I think. She is educated, but after living in the hareem it is hard to adjust to the outside. She would probably have found work managing girls for a pimp in some brothel. This is much the better course. She is old, of course, but she will be adequate for some time to come."

"My thanks," Mike said, letting out a breath that held much unsaid.

"I may have need to call upon you at some time," the sheik admitted. "Nothing that the American government would find amiss, I assure you. But I have my own security concerns, concerns that also concern the American government. Having a man who is . . . good with his hands, who owes me a favor is useful."

"A friend in need is a friend in deed," Mike said, noncommittally. "I take it you have my number."

"I do," the sheik said. "And American military scrambler codes."

CHAPTER SEVENTEEN

Mike wasn't sure of the protocol when Anastasia came out the door but he boarded the car, first followed by the girl, then Wangen. Her bags, three, had already been loaded in the trunk so they pulled out with a last wave to the sheik.

"Back to the Hilton, Tom," Wangen said, letting out a breath as the car cleared the gates. "Drop Mr. Jenkins and his friend off, then to the embassy."

"Airport," Mike said, getting out his sat phone. "I have to get back to Georgia. If that's okay?"

"Fine," Wangen said. "It's closer than the Hilton. What about your luggage?"

"I had it sent to the plane," Mike said. "I'm on a bit of a tight schedule."

"Problems at home?" Wangen asked, curiously.

"A festival," Mike replied, shrugging. "Then we're starting training on the militia. They're starting issue today. Nielson and Adams have that well in hand, but I'd like to be around in case there are problems. And I definitely need to be there for the festival."

He called Hardesty and made sure they were ready for a late take-off, then leaned back in the seat as the limo bumped over the roads to Samarkand.

"What can we talk about?" Mike asked.

"I dunno," Wangen said. "How much are you going to be discussing around your new harem manager?"

"Otryad wants to be president," Anastasia said. "He knows that he'd get American backing if the choice is him or Dulmaa."

"Probably," Wangen admitted. He looked at Mike and shrugged. "Dulmaa is . . . well, he runs as an Islamic fundamentalist, but not as fundamental as, say, the mullahs in Iran. He's more of a conservative in the local sense. The usual riff about cleaning up the corruption but he's as deep in the take as anyone. But he's *not* a friend of the U.S. He'd be hard pressed to toss us out, but he could make things harder for us. We'd much prefer Otryad over Dulmaa."

"I'm not going to take out a major presidential candidate," Mike said, shaking his head. "Ain't gonna happen. Wouldn't be prudent."

"Otryad is not going to ask for help with that," Anastasia said. "Dulmaa has to live. But he is closely supported by others, including the Dar Al Islami party. Their head is Farhad Bazarhuv, also untouchable. But they are a front for the Islamic radicals. It is *those* he fears and wants help with."

"Islamic radicals I do," Mike said, breathing out. "I take it you're not going to assign Delta or Army of Northern Virginia on it?" ANV was known by a half dozen acronyms, all of them false, but it was the blackest of black ops units, existing in a nebulous world somewhere between the military and CIA. Mike had ended up in its hospital, twice, a place where the patients didn't even have a name, just a number. The personnel for ANV were drawn from the military, but after they left they never returned. Even Deltas came back in when they had too much rank for the relatively small force. ANV operatives just disappeared into the night and fog.

"No way," Wangen said. "Maybe if we get a sniff on somebody like Rabah Batatu; he's connected with Al Qaeda or at least a supporter. And he's probably connected to the Dar Al Islami in some nebulous way. But the radicals that Otryad has a problem with are internal matters to Uzbekistan. They're not in our sights at the moment. Even for a 'friend.' Not even for ANV."

"Dulmaa will use the radicals to disturb the election," Anastasia continued. "They will intimidate candidates and attack rallies. There are a few key members, Ju'ad Puntsag comes to mind, who are better off dead. Certainly from Otryad's point of view."

"Puntsag we've got a sheet on," Wangen said, nodding. "More of a street thug than a terrorist, but nobody would miss him, not even his mother. But since he's a street thug and not a terrorist, he's definitely not in our sights. CAG and ANV is out."

"Otryad has his own people," Mike pointed out.

"They are big and can hold guns," Anastasia said, shrugging. "I don't know that they are . . . formidable."

"Christ, all I wanted was a damned harem manager," Mike said, sighing. "I take it this didn't get discussed at the highest levels in a very specific 'didn't' way."

"Absolutely not," Wangen said. "I definitely did not get a disk delivered by courier from the NSA discussing the ramifications of you meeting with Otryad."

"Great," Mike grumped. "God damn that bitch. If they want to do black ops they have plenty of people available."

"But it won't be as black as this," Wangen pointed out. "The U.S. government has absolute deniability on it. Real deniability. We gave you a ride to meet the guy and an intro. What happens from there is not our deal."

When they reached the plane it was already warmed up. With the copilot's help they got Anastasia's luggage loaded, and boarded with a last wave to Wangen.

"Have a seat," Mike said, waving the girl into one of the front seats. "After we take off we can get a bite to eat and chat. I need to make a call, right now."

"Very well, Mr. Jenkins," the girl said, nervously. She fumbled with her seatbelt for a moment and then got it closed, cinching it down firmly.

"Call me Mike," Mike replied. He pulled out his sat phone and called the embassy in Tbilisi.

"Lieutenant Timmons, Duty Officer, U.S. Embassy to the Republic of Georgia, how may I help you sir or ma'am?"

"Hey, LT, this is Mike Jenkins. Is Colonel Osbruck around?"

"No, sir, he's gone home for the day."

"Any chance you could call over to the Ministry of Defense and ask if I could borrow a helicopter sometime late tonight? I am *really* not looking forward to riding back to the caravanserai tonight."

"Yes, sir," the lieutenant said. "I'll give them a call for you, sir."

"My sat phone number should be on the embassy rolodex as much as you guys call me," Mike said. "Call me back if you can scare something up. Sorry to dump this on you."

"Boring night, sir," the lieutenant said. "Glad to have something to do. And it lets me practice my Georgian."

"Thanks, LT," Mike said. "Come on out to the house some time, I'll feed you some real beer. I've even gotten some decent steaks laid in."

"Will do, sir. Thank you."

"Take care," Mike said, cutting the connection just as the jet began its rollout. "Ever flown in a corporate jet?" he asked Anastasia.

"No," the girl said, clutching the arms of the seat.

"They take off at a pretty high angle compared to an airliner," Mike said. "And they fly higher. You can get a pretty good view from forty grand."

"Forty grand?" the girl said, uncertainly.

"Forty thousand feet," Mike said as the jet turned onto the threshold. "Less turbulence up there."

"We are going up to forty *thousand* feet?" the girl squeaked nervously.

"Anastasia," Mike said, gently, "have you ever flown before?"

"No," she said, panting slightly.

"It's all right," Mike replied, sighing as the jet started to roll. "Just lean back in the seat and we'll be up and level before you know it." He leaned back into his seat as the jet rocketed forward. Corporate jets were designed for higher acceleration on take-off than jetliners and Hardesty was a former fighter pilot; he liked to squeeze every bit of performance out of the plane. They pushed down the runway at what Mike figured was about three Gs and then the plane pointed up at about a thirty-degree angle.

"Is this normal?" Anastasia said, in a frightened tone.

"When Hardesty is flying," Mike said. "Don't worry, he's really good. We'll stay like this for a while and then it will feel like we're falling for a bit; that's when he slows the engines down at altitude. Don't panic at it: it's perfectly normal."

"I will not, Mr. Jenkins," the girl said, struggling to be calm and composed.

"Please call me Mike," Mike said, hitting the intercom. "Barring that, Kildar. Captain Hardesty?"

"Sir?" the pilot replied, happily.

"As it turns out, Miss Anastasia has never flown before," Mike said. "So let's not get into any acrobatics. And give us some warning when you level out."

"Is she okay?" Hardesty asked.

"She will be," Mike said. "As long as you tell us when you're going to level out."

"Will do, sir," Hardesty said.

"There," Mike continued, cutting the connection. "He'll warn us when we level out."

"What is this you said," Anastasia asked. "The term?"

"Kildar," Mike said, sighing. "It's what the land owner in the valley is called. Sort of like sheik or baron or something. Anyway, if you can't handle calling me Mike, call me Kildar. Mr.

Jenkins . . . isn't my real name anyway. And don't ask what the real one is."

"I won't," Anastasia said, looking over at him.

"Mr. Jenkins," Captain Hardesty said over the intercom. "Preparing to level out."

"Not a big deal," Mike said as the whine from the engines dropped and the plane seemed to drop a bit. He saw the girl's reaction and reached out a hand. "It's fine and normal. We'll be level in a bit."

The sensation of change stopped after only a moment and Anastasia nodded.

"I had not wanted you to know I hadn't flown before," the girl said, unhappily. "I'm sorry I showed my emotions like that. It was unprofessional of me."

"You handled it fine," Mike said, then chuckled. "Sorry, reminded me of a guy I knew in jump school."

"What is that?" Anastasia asked, curiously.

"Where they teach the Army to jump out of planes," Mike said. "You have to get cycled through it for SEAL training, even though you spend the rest of your time free-falling. Anyway, was this guy in the stick I was in that had never flown in a plane before he went to jump school. He did all five jumps without landing, so I don't know when he actually landed in a plane."

"Do you . . . jump from up this high?" the girl asked.

"No," Mike said then paused. "Okay, I know one group that did, but it was a special case. Most jumps are under fourteen grand, fourteen thousand feet. That way you don't have to use oxygen. High altitude is twenty thousand to thirty. Very, very few people have ever jumped over thirty thousand. Go ahead and look out the window," he said, unbuckling and getting up to cross the plane. "It's too unreal to feel high," he added, pointing out the small window.

Anastasia looked out for a moment, then turned away.

"It still looks very high," the girl said. "And very big."

"It's a big world," Mike said, gently, sitting down next to her and taking the window seat. "I take it you didn't do a lot of traveling in the harem?"

"No," Anastasia said. "Or before. I grew up on a farm in Russia. A scout for Otryad saw me at a fair and arranged the marriage with my parents. I went from the farm to the household and have been there ever since."

"May I ask how old you are?" Mike said, carefully.

"Twenty-six," Anastasia said, closing her eyes. "I have been from the farm to the house and occasionally to Samarkand. I was a girl in the harem until I was seventeen. Then I was brought into training to be a manager. I took over as assistant manager at nineteen and full manager at twenty-one. I have managed his harem ever since."

"And never been in a plane," Mike said, a touch angrily. "Has Otryad ever traveled?"

"Yes," Anastasia said. "But it wouldn't be . . . right to take his women with him. It would be unseemly."

"Not to me," Mike said. "If I have to travel, you can figure on coming with me. Unless you really don't want to."

"Oh, I would like to," the girl said, breathing out finally. "I have wanted to see the world. But I'm afraid of it as well. I have been . . . inside for so long. Not only in a house, but like being trapped in a cage. Like the tiger in too small a cage, I pace and pace, but if the door is open, I'm afraid to walk out."

"Well, the door in my house is always open," Mike said. "I'm hiring you, not buying you. You're free to go any time. You're a full adult and have some training in people management if nothing else." He saw her fearful expression and sighed in exasperation. "That's not kicking you out, damnit. I'm just saying you're free to be whoever you want to be. If you don't like working for me, I'll find you another job. The door to my harem is always open. For one thing, I don't think of the girls as just mine. I have people who work with me, friends who visit, and if the girls want to mess with them, they can feel free. For that matter, four of the girls currently in the house are rented hookers. They are, very specifically, for the comfort and support of the trainers who have quarters in the house. The rest of the girls . . . I'm not so sure."

"If you would take my advice," Anastasia said, diffidently, "they should not be given to other men. Girls of the hareem are not whores. There is a great deal of difference, in the head if nothing else. They may be gifted to subordinates as wives, especially as they age. This is traditional in Uzbek society at least. But they should not be passed around like . . . sweetmeats at a party."

"I'll keep that in mind," Mike said, grinning. "And, yes, that's exactly what I wanted you for. How much are you supposed to get paid, by the way?"

"I had a small stipend from Otryad," Anastasia said, shrugging. "To buy clothes and jewelry. And he would give me gifts."

"That's it?" Mike asked, shaking his head. "Well, that won't work for me. The *girls* get that. I'll figure out a salary. He said something about education. You can read and write, right?"

"Yes," the girl replied. "And do mathematics. I can read and write in Russian, Uzbek, Arabic, German and English. For that matter," she continued in not badly accented English, "I can speak all of them as well."

"And he kept you locked up in a harem," Mike said, shaking his head. "What a fucking waste. Pardon my language."

"The master need never apologize," Anastasia continued in English. "In fact, it is a sign of weakness that the girls will exploit."

"Hmm . . ." Mike said, thinking about that one. "I think we might have some differences in approach and we'll have to see how it works. For one thing, this harem will not be entrapped except by situation. And I'm not going to be married to any of them, or you for that matter. On the other hand . . . Western militaries handle their soldiers differently from most of the militaries in your area; had you noticed that?"

"Not really," Anastasia said, frowning. "I do not associate with soldiers."

"You're going to be associating with a bunch of them as early as tomorrow," Mike pointed out. "But in developing nations, the troops are treated like dirt and the officers don't even *think* about talking to them as equals. In American militaries officers, good officers, treat their subordinates like humans that have their job to do. Officers have the job of making or expanding decisions for their unit and they give the troops their orders. The troops have the job of expanding on those orders to the limit of their position and ability but they don't see the officer as God or something. They treat him with respect and the good ones with admiration. But they don't hesitate to bring up alternatives if asked and if an officer has screwed up, he'll admit it and work on ways to change that."

"And this is how you would treat the girls in your hareem?" Anastasia asked, frowning. "I'm not sure how they will respond to that."

"I don't understand *any* of their responses," Mike admitted. "I thought when I brought up them staying as . . . concubines they'd freak. Most of them looked as if they wanted to get on their knees and give me a blowjob right then and there."

"I think I can explain that, at least," Anastasia said after a pause. "They were girls from small farms in the area, yes?"

"Yes."

"And they had been sold by their families to be whores," the girl continued. "The house you live in is much like that of the sheik, you said. They had been taken from their small farms, where they had to work very hard for very little good in their life. They had very little of their own, maybe only their clothes and those are usually from older sisters, and they lived in a place that was very . . . rough. They had thought they would be whores, to be used by any man who had the money and sometimes in very bad places. Instead you offer them security in what to them is a palace. I can understand it very well. I was sad, very home-sick, when I had to leave my family. But to live with the sheik was . . . paradise." She stopped and shrugged at his expression.

"My greatest fear in life was what I would do when I grew

too old to be with Otryad anymore. He had discussed finding me a husband but anything would be a step down from being his hareem manager; I was not going to find a *rich* husband, you understand, not in Uzbekistan. I would be the wife, maybe not the first wife, of someone less important than Otryad. My...status was not high enough to get better. I was not a virgin, among other reasons. Otryad is very good about sending his women out into the world; he tries to find them husbands and if he cannot he sets them up with money of their own. But he likes young girls; I was only still in the hareem because I was a good manager. But Darya was old enough to take over while still being younger, and fresher, than I."

"Well, I didn't see the rest of his hareem," Mike said, using her term. "But if he was kicking you out of his bed he was an idiot."

"There are women aplenty in the world to a man with money," Anastasia said, shrugging.

"Not many that are as good looking as you," Mike said, then frowned. "Okay, except among the Keldara, I'll admit."

"These are your retainers?" Anastasia asked, curiously.

"I don't know what to call them," Mike admitted. "I hate just calling them tenants. I suppose retainers is a good word. The men are generally pretty damned handsome and the women are fucking outstanding. The beer's good, too. Great place to live. Not that I wouldn't mind going back to the States some time. But, for now, the valley's a good place to live. I'm doing good work there, getting them up to speed on modern farming, I got them equipment so they could retire their horse teams, and I'm training them so they can defend themselves. Not much of that, yet. That's why I'm hurrying back; training starts on Monday after this planting festival."

"You will be training them?" the girl asked, curling up in the seat and leaning forward to listen.

"Not day-to-day," Mike said. "But I'm going to be out there for specific items. I'll probably have to lead them in some of the stuff they're going to be doing. So I'll probably show up for each new item, prove I can do it, and then retreat. If I demonstrate my ability when they're just getting introduced to it, it should look like I'm such a fucking master they won't believe it. Take running; I'll probably lead the first run. After they're fully trained, there are probably a few that will be better than me; they're mostly younger for one thing. But if the first time they go out, the Kildar smokes them, well that will stick in their mind. The Kildar can run, the Kildar can ruck, the Kildar can patrol and the Kildar can shoot. That way when we go out to actually do something, they'll be confident in my abilities, even if by then some of them are better than I am."

"It sounds like it's a good thing I'm an expert in massage," Anastasia said, smiling.

"Oh, I'm pretty dialed in," Mike said. "I've been working out since I got there; the muscles are as good as they're going to get with all the damage. I won't mind having somebody to help me get out of bed in the mornings, though."

"You have trouble with that?" the girl asked

"Bad joints," Mike said, shrugging. "Mostly a legacy of beating them to death on the teams. Any time I stay still for a long period of time, and I don't move much when I sleep, they freeze up. So getting out of bed is a pain. It passes after a while. Mostly," he added, rubbing one elbow absently. Ever since getting caught in an unpressurized wheel well on a mission he'd had trouble with that joint. "So, I hate to ask about the sex thing, but where are we on that? From one point of view you're an employee. As far as I'm concerned, you could be married to someone else and do your job . . ."

"I think not," Anastasia said, carefully. "You are my master."

"Be careful with that term," Mike said. "That has a very specific meaning in sexual relations. Unless you meant it that way?" he asked, glancing at her.

"You are the master of the hareem," Anastasia said, cautiously. "But, yes, I'm aware of the meaning of the term. I don't know you well, hardly at all . . ."

"I don't even know your last name," Mike said. "Is it Otryad?"

"I have not been married to Otryad for more than twelve years," Anastasia said, frowning. "My last name was changed to my maiden name when I divorced: Rakovich. He keeps four wives, as the Koran dictates. All the others are concubines. He marries and then, when it is time to get a new wife, divorces and keeps the girl in his harem. This way he can approach families with an offer of marriage."

"Personally, I've got problems with that," Mike said, his jaw working. "But that's his society."

"He is not unpleasant about it," Anastasia said, sighing. "But it is hard, knowing you are but a temporary addition to his household. However, you are the master of the harem and my job is to manage the harem and provide you with sex in addition. I do not have a problem with that, in fact I look forward to it; you are very beautiful."

"That's the first time anyone's said *that* to me," Mike said, laughing. "Be aware, I'm used to either dating for sex or buying hookers. I'm not sure how to handle this relationship."

"Try not to treat me as a whore," Anastasia said. "Think of me as a wife whose job is very specifically to provide sex. But . . . I have needs," she added, carefully.

"I'm generally considered decent to good," Mike said, glancing at her again. "But I tend to be a bit rough by preference."

"Rough is good," Anastasia said, sighing in relief. "Very rough is very good."

"Really?" Mike asked, raising an eyebrow. "How rough?"

"As rough as you can manage," Anastasia answered. "Do you know the term masochist?"

"You're serious?" Mike said. "In that case, we need to negotiate carefully. Rough is a very broad term."

"The rougher the better," Anastasia said, looking at the floor of the plane. "Otryad was not . . . rough enough. And there was never enough sex with so many girls in the harem. I was lucky towards the end if I had one night a month with him. And he was never strong enough with the whip."

"O-kaaay," Mike said, with a whistle. "I can see where this is going. I don't have a bondage dungeon set up *yet* but it can easily be arranged."

"That would be *wonderful*," Anastasia said, delightedly. "I had access to the internet, yes? I saw some of the bondage dungeons on there and they excited me very much. I would love to have you take me to a bondage dungeon and treat me roughly as a slave to be trained."

"But you're already trained," Mike pointed out.

"I could be bad," Anastasia said, glancing at him out of the corner of her eye. "They had a terrible time with me at first; I was often bad just so that I would be beaten. When the hareem manager then, that was Shahla, realized what was going on she was very angry. After that I was good, just so that I could be properly beaten from time to time. Shahla was very good with the whip; I miss her. After she left Otryad had to do it and he never really had the same touch."

"Yeah, but we still need to negotiate," Mike said with a sigh. "I don't know that . . . experienced as you are, you were in the hareem. The rules are different on the outside. For example, what about being whipped in front of people you don't know very well? A scene as they call it. Or play 'sold' to another man? Have you ever been butt-plugged and then put in a submissive position and auctioned off?"

"No," Anastasia said, breathlessly. "But it sounds terribly exciting!"

"Oh, good God," Mike said, flipping up the seat arm. "I need a blowjob and I need one now."

"Yes, master," Anastasia said, leaning over and unzipping him. With her teeth.

Mike leaned the seat back and closed his eyes as she began to slowly lick his member like a lollipop to be savored. After a moment he snorted.

"Master?" Anastasia asked, lifting off of him.

"Never mind," Mike said, slapping her lightly on the back of the head. "Get back to work."

The snort was for the situation. He was in a private jet being blown by a fucking expert. One that looked like she should be making a million a year as a supermodel. It had been a long damned route to this moment.

And Anastasia was an *expert*. She'd started by licking him and pumping him to get him fully engorged then taken him in her mouth, slowly stroking at first. Despite not using her hands, it was one of the best blowjobs he'd ever gotten. She had tremendous suction and her lips pressed around his dick as firmly as fingers. As she continued she sped up, stroking up and down so far that he could feel his dick entering the back of her throat. She alternated with taking him all the way down, right into the throat, and swallowing so that the muscles sucked his head down her throat.

She sped up slowly, finally going into a long continuous stroke at high speed that had him right on the edge of bursting. At which point he realized he'd forgotten to negotiate one thing before starting. On the other hand, to hell with it; she was a harem slave. With that thought he started pumping in her mouth.

Anastasia caught it all, choking a bit at first and then sucking him dry.

"Was that good, master?" she asked, straightening up and tucking him away.

"You can do that any time you'd like," Mike said.

"Good," the girl said. "I like giving blowjobs. Otryad did not like them that much but he would let me give them since I enjoyed it. That is why I tried to learn to give them well, so he would enjoy them also."

"You're great," Mike said, leaning back in the seat. "Very, *very* good, and I say that as a guy who has gotten a fair number of them in his life."

"Is there any wine?" Anastasia asked, cautiously. "I like the taste of cum, but the aftertaste is ... not so good."

"In the back," Mike said, thumbing over his shoulder. "There's a wine cooler with white and a rack with red."

"Would you like a glass?" Anastasia asked, getting up and looking to the rear of the plane.

"No thanks, I'm a beer drinker," Mike said. "On second thought, see if they have a Johannesburg Riesling. I could do with a glass."

"Then you will go to sleep, yes?" Anastasia asked, walking back to the gallery area.

"I could sleep," Mike admitted. "It's been a long day."

CHAPTER
EIGHTEEN

As it turned out, Anastasia slept. Mike reclined both of the seats and the girl had snuggled down next to him, arms held vertically over her breasts so her hands were folded under her chin, pushed in hard against his side and in a few minutes was fast asleep. It had been a long, tough day for her too, Mike figured. Torn away from the only home she'd known since she was twelve, flying for the first time, possibly being with the first man other than Otryad that she'd ever had sex with. She seemed comfortable, though, content. She wasn't having bad dreams, at least.

She was so fucking beautiful, it made Mike angry to think about her life. He knew that he had a blind spot when it came to beautiful women. Plenty of them, even in the West, had lousy lives. But a creature as visually perfect as Anastasia would have been able to write her own ticket in the States. Instead, she'd been sent off to be a harem slave. And she considered herself lucky, with reason. The whole developing world was awash with girls like Anastasia, ranging from her situation to the girls in the Alerrso brothel.

Without the economy and culture to support equality, women came out a distant second in the war of the sexes. Even the "lucky" ones who found husbands had lives of unremitting toil, popping out one baby after another until their bodies were worn out. The rest filled the brothels of the developing countries. The luckiest ones were the girls near Western military bases; the worst actions of the Western troops, by and large, were the norm in other cultures. American troops mostly just wanted to get it stuck in or sucked off. The few of them that were into pain paid for the privilege instead of thinking of it as a right.

But even those didn't have much of a life. After they got old and worn, at all of twenty or so, they'd be shipped off to lower quality brothels, slipping down the ladder rung by rung. The bottom of the barrel were places around the Mediterranean waterfront, especially Istanbul. Trying to find a good-looking whore in Istanbul was like looking for gold in a tarpit.

Mike wasn't sure how long this gig in Georgia was going to last, but he knew damned well that *none* of his girls were ever going to wind up in a whorehouse in Istanbul. Not even Katya, although she deserved it.

Mike got up carefully at a chime from the sat phone, trying not to disturb Anastasia. She muttered but stayed in place.

"Jenkins," he said, putting in the earphone.

"Mr. Jenkins, this is Lieutenant Timmons," the duty officer said. "There will be a Georgian military helicopter at the airport in Tbilisi at two AM."

"Thanks, Lieutenant," Mike said. "Not looking a gift horse in the mouth, it has room for two and some luggage?"

"It's a Blackhawk converted for distinguished persons transport," the lieutenant replied. "Plenty of room."

"Great," Mike said. "Thanks for the help. Hope the rest of your duty goes well."

"All I have to do is stay awake," the lieutenant said, chuckling.

"What duty officer stays awake?" Mike asked. "That's what enlisted men are for."

"Ones that work at embassies," Timmons said, somewhat bitterly. "It's not like regular SDO work. And guys on duty at SOCOM and the Pentagon for that matter. Norad, Cheyenne . . ."

"Got the point," Mike said, smiling. "Well, come on out for a beer and some steak some time; I owe you that at least."

"Will do, sir," Timmons said. "Two AM."

"Works," Mike replied, "Have a good night."

Mike covered Anastasia with a blanket, then pulled out a copy of the training schedule. Since he wouldn't be staying over in Tbilisi, he'd be back for equipment issue. That was a two-day affair with basic uniform and field gear issue being in the morning and weapons issue the next day. Normally troops would get their weapons and then rack them. In normal militaries they'd spend a few months learning to clean the damned things and field strip them before they ever got to shoot them.

With the Keldara, Mike was taking another tack. They'd be issued on Friday right at the range. The only pretraining they'd get was on safety and aiming. Then they'd zero in the weapons. After that would be the class on stripping, cleaning and reassembly. One reason for that was that they were bound to mess up the cleaning. That meant nice dirty weapons to rag on them about come Monday and regular training. A weekend with a little grime here and there wasn't going to ruin the guns. Hell, knowing the way that the Keldara did things, the weapons were probably going to be spotless.

Mike might or might not do a demonstration for the range day. The Keldara were only going to be firing on a twenty-five meter range for zero. The time to do that was when they did the full Basic Rifle Marksmanship class later in the training cycle. They were taking the Marine approach to that one, training them on marksmanship on the Known Distance range, then going to pop-up targets.

Marksmanship and combat engagement were two different mindsets, but the one was important to support the other. Training on pure marksmanship meant that the soldier was actually paying attention to the target. The two problems with that were he then tended to see the target as a human and not just a target and he tended to take too long in engagement. With the latter, he was paying attention to his shooting rather than the fact he was in a combat engagement. With the former he ended up more stressed by taking a human life. Training to simply engage pop-up targets and consider the shapes that the soldier engaged as nothing more than those tended to reduce both problems.

He put the training schedule away when he began to yawn and curled up next to Anastasia. He had to admit there were worse ways to fly.

"Mr. Jenkins?"

Mike had woken up the moment the cockpit door opened and now opened his eyes, to look at the copilot. He'd assumed the pilot was on his way to the rear for a drink so he hadn't bothered before, just tracked his movements by sound.

"Yeah?" Mike asked, shifting upwards. Anastasia was still out like a light so he gently lowered her down so her head rested on his thigh.

"We got an in-flight advisory that we're suppose to taxi to the military side of the Tbilisi airport and await a Follow-Me," the copilot said, quietly. "Captain Hardesty thought you should know."

"Thanks," Mike said. "I should have told you guys I was picking up a helicopter for the rest of the trip. That's all it's about."

"Okay," the copilot said, nodding. "We'd . . . wondered."

"No great adventures on this trip," Mike said, grinning. "Maybe some other time. How long?"

"We'll be beginning our descent in about a half an hour. Be on the ground in about an hour."

"I'd better wake Anastasia up," Mike said, nodding. "Thanks for the heads up."

Mike looked at the girl on his lap after the pilot had gone and decided to let her sleep a little longer. She looked worn out by the day and flying in the chopper was probably going to unnerve her a good bit.

As it turned out, the power-down and dropping feeling woke her up instantly.

"Are we okay?" she asked, sitting up hurriedly and wiping her eyes.

"Fine," Mike said. "We're on descent to Tbilisi airport. There's a helicopter waiting for us there."

"Okay," the girl said, her eyes wide as the plane bumped through some turbulence.

"That's normal, too," Mike said. "Pockets of thicker or denser air cause the plane to go up and down a bit." Mike thought there must be a front in the area since the plane lurched again. "Lean over here," he said, sliding sideways and putting his arm around her. "It'll be okay."

Mike leaned over and looked out the window and was surprised to see that the air was clear. You got clear air turbulence from time to time, but rarely this severe.

"Captain?" he said, keying the intercom. "Are we following someone down?"

"Spot on, sir," the copilot answered. "We're behind an Airbus. I think we're probably too close, frankly, but nothing we can't handle. And this is where Tbilisi control wants us to be."

"Back off a bit if you can do it discreetly," Mike said. "The ride is getting a little rough."

"When a plane passes through it disturbs the air," Mike continued to Anastasia. "It settles out pretty quickly, normally, but if you're close to other aircraft it makes this happen; the plane goes up and down."

"Will it make us crash?" Anastasia asked.

"Not hardly," Mike replied. "These business jets are built very tough and very maneuverable. And Hardesty is a great pilot. This is not a problem."

"Okay," the girl said, sighing. "It's all new."

"And a bit scary," Mike said. "More than just the flight. You'll be okay, I promise."

Hardesty greased the landing and was careful on the braking, obviously keeping in mind his junior passenger. Tbilisi airport had been built to support Soviet bombers during the Cold War and it had plenty of runway for an easy brake. About halfway down the runway he took a right, instead of the normal left to the terminal, and followed a series of turns to stop not more than seventy meters from a Blackhawk with its rotor already turning.

"This is your stop, sir," the copilot said, coming into the main cabin.

"Up we get, dear," Mike said to Anastasia.

The luggage was secured in an underside compartment with a door behind the left wing. As the copilot opened the door, a Georgian lieutenant gestured for an enlisted man to help.

Between the three of them, the copilot, Mike and the Georgian soldier, it only took one trip for the bags. Mike, frankly, could have humped them all himself, but he wasn't about to get in the way of the dance. He ended up with just his briefcase and personal bag.

He led Anastasia over to the helicopter and started to strap her into one of the comfortable chairs in the center of the chopper's cargo bay, but she pointed to one of the jump seats.

"I would like to look out, if I may," she said, diffidently.

"Sit wherever you'd like," Mike said, leading her over to the seat and strapping her in. Unlike the passenger seats, the jump seat had a four-point restraint system and when hooked up it hiked her skirt all the way up to the top of her stockings. She discreetly pulled it back down on the sides, but there wasn't any way to cover up the inner thigh.

"Perhaps I should . . ." she said, waving at the regular passenger seats which had normal "airline" seatbelts.

"I like the view just fine," Mike replied, picking up a headset and putting it on her and then following with one for himself. "Pilot?" he asked in Georgian.

"Yes, Kildar," the pilot replied. "Are you ready for us to take off?"

"At your leisure," Mike replied. "Thanks for the ride."

"It is an honor, Kildar," the pilot said.

The rotors increased in speed and Mike looked out to see if they'd form a halo. Sometimes, when the dust was just right, static discharge would form on the rotors. It would slide down to the edge of them, like little lightning bolts, and the effect would look exactly like a silver halo on the ends of the rotors. Not this time, alas. Anastasia would have liked it. However, it was also a sign of increased rotor wear, so he thought he should be thankful.

"Are you okay?" he asked as the bird lifted into the air. There was an intercom control on his seat panel and he'd switched it so that he was only talking to the girl.

"Fine," Anastasia squeaked, nervously. But she leaned forward and watched as they lifted. "This is beautiful. I had thought I'd be afraid, but I am only a little. This is very interesting to watch."

The bird spiraled up to about two thousand feet above ground level and then headed southeast towards the valley of the Keldara. The moon was only a quarter, but once they got away from the city lights and their eyes adjusted, it lit up the landscape like day.

"This is so beautiful," Anastasia whispered. "There are so many trees. I'd forgotten how much I like trees. It must be very green in the day."

"It is at the moment," Mike said, looking out for himself. "The trees are just coming out in their leaves and it's greening up nicely. The tops of the mountains, though, reach above the tree line. Some of them are snow-covered year round."

"Where I came from there were many trees," the girl said, quietly. "But no mountains."

"Lots of mountains in Georgia," Mike said. He'd noticed that the helicopter was on a continuous fair climb, even after the upward spiral, but as it approached the mountains it turned south into another spiral, fighting for altitude.

"We are going very high," Anastasia said, breathing deeply in incipient panic.

"High mountains," Mike pointed out. "We'll be fine. These things are rated for ten thousand feet with a load of troops. This is easy flying."

As they headed into the mountains, below the peaks, the helicopter began to buffet in the crosswinds and Anastasia squeaked and closed her eyes.

"This I don't like," the girl said. "I think I am getting a little sick."

"Try opening your eyes," Mike said, rummaging around in the seats until he found an airsick bag. The package was paper with a plastic bag on the inside, which he extracted and handed across to the girl. "If you have to go, go in that."

They crossed through a saddle, with tree-covered slopes on both sides that seemed close enough the rotors should have hit the branches, then started to descend, banking through a series of turns as the helicopter followed the complex angles of the valleys. The crosswinds had settled down, though, and while the chopper was banking, it wasn't going up and down so much. With the change of motion, Anastasia seemed to get over her sickness, sitting with the bag in her hand but a rapt expression on her face as the chopper banked past the hills. At one point it practically stood on its left side, letting her get a close look at the ground below and leaving her hanging in her straps.

"This is fun," she said in surprise as the chopper leveled back out.

"That it is," Mike admitted. "I really need to get one for a dozen different reasons."

"You can buy a helicopter?" Anastasia asked.

"Well, a Blackhawk would be a little out of my range," Mike admitted. "They're damned expensive. Good birds, but overpriced. The Czechs sell a Hind variant for executive transport and medical evac that's only about six hundred grand. And there's something like ninety percent parts compatibility with regular Hind-Ds.

And Hinds are all over the place. The only reason the Georgians have these Blackhawks is the U.S. government gave them five and support the parts."

As he finished, the Blackhawk banked one more time into the valley of the Keldara and Mike realized he'd forgotten to get anyone to lay out an LZ.

"Pilot," he said, switching back to the general intercom, "I forgot to tell anyone I was coming so there's no LZ laid out. You want to hang up here while I call or go in on an unmarked?"

"I'd prefer marked," the pilot admitted.

"Okay," Mike said, pulling out his sat phone. "We'll probably go in on my lawn, then."

He'd left another satellite phone with Nielson for general communications and he speed dialed that.

"Keldara House, Dinara Mahona speaking, how may I help you, sir or ma'am?" a female voice answered in Georgian.

"God I love Vanner," Mike replied, smiling. "Hi, Dinara, it's the Kildar. I'm up over the valley in a chopper. Could you wake up somebody from the duty squad that knows how to lay in an LZ and ask them to put one on the lawn?"

"Yes, Kildar," the Keldara said. "I will do that immediately."

"Thanks," Mike replied. "We'll just tool around up here until you call."

"Pilot," he said, switching back to the intercom. "There's somebody getting up to lay in an LZ, but it will be a few minutes. You've got fuel?"

"Enough for another hour, Kildar," the pilot replied. "More than enough for twenty minutes or so up here and then flying back."

"Take a turn around the valley, then," Mike said. "I'll show the lady the sights."

Using the chopper, Mike pointed out the houses of the Keldara, who were probably wondering what the hell was going on, the new roads that were being laid in, the ranges, where the dam was under construction and Alerrso. Finally, the sat phone rang.

"Kildar, this is Killjoy," the former Marine said. "We've got chemlights laid out on the lawn. Best I could do at the moment. One blinking strobe at the end. Wind is more or less from the north, recommend come in from the south and set down at the lower end of the lawn. That will give him plenty of room to pull out over the house."

"Will do," Mike said, passing the orders on to the pilot.

"Hey, Killjoy," Mike said as he pulled back the doors to the chopper. "How they hangin'?"

"Still one lower than the other," Killjoy replied, his eyes widening at the sight of Anastasia. "What, you didn't have *enough* women in the house?"

"She's a manager," Mike replied. "Give me a hand with her bags?"

He shook the hand of the pilot and co, then helped Anastasia across the lawn. She was wearing four-inch spike heels and they sank in the cut grass. Finally, he just picked her up and carried her to the paved walkway.

"Welcome to Keldara House," Mike said as he set her down. They were by the door to the harem garden, which was standing open, so he led her in that way. "This is sort of the side door. Sorry."

"It is very beautiful," she said, looking around in the moonlight. Hard work on the part of the Keldara had cleaned up the garden so it was presentable again. The fruit trees and roses had been trimmed and the trees were in bloom, filling the garden with a heady scent.

"It is nice," Mike said. "It's the harem garden, technically. But since I don't lock the girls in anyone can come in here. Nice place to have a party."

"It would be," Anastasia admitted.

"Oh, introductions," Mike said. "Anastasia Rakovich, Corporal Lawrence Killjoy. Call him Larry."

"Pleased to meet you, ma'am," Killjoy said, setting her bags down and shaking her hand.

"A pleasure to meet you, Mr. Killjoy," Anastasia said, formally.

"You don't generally get introduced, do you?" Mike asked.

"No," Anastasia admitted as they headed for the house.

"Would you prefer that I not?" Mike asked. "It's considered impolite in my culture. But so is having a harem."

"No, I would prefer to be introduced to people," Anastasia admitted. "If you're not, it makes you feel like a piece of mobile furniture. I want to meet people."

"Plenty of people to meet in the house at the moment," Mike replied. "The seven girls we picked up, the four I'm renting, about twenty trainers, the cook, the housekeeper and the girls that help out. Then there's all the Keldara, the people in Alerrso like Vadim, who's the local cop. You're going to be meeting a lot of people."

"That will be . . . different," Anastasia said, nervously. "But, I think, nice."

"Tomorrow, though," Mike said, yawning. "Tonight I'm for bed. Killjoy, any idea if anything's been done to set up for her?"

"Not as far as I know," the corporal replied.

"In that case, we'll just take her stuff up to my room," Mike said. "She can sleep with me."

"Bastard," Killjoy muttered.

"For the time being, Anastasia is taken," Mike said, definitely. "Pass the word. Later she can make up her own mind, but she's going to have to get used to the idea."

"Will do, sir," the corporal replied.

CHAPTER NINETEEN

"Shower and bath through there," Mike said, pointing to the adjoining master bath. "If you don't mind, I'll take one in the morning after I work out."

"I do not mind," Anastasia said. "Would you mind if I took a shower?"

"Go for it," Mike replied.

He usually slept in the nude during warmer months but for her sake he put on a pair of running shorts and crawled into bed.

He had fallen asleep to the sound of the shower but woke up when she climbed in next to him. He reached over to tell her he was there and his hand hit a naked abdomen. Immediately, he was massively horny.

The shorts came off as he slid across the bed and one arm went behind her as the other lifted to her firm breast. He slid his tongue down the side of her neck, causing a moan of either real or expertly feigned pleasure, but when his hand crept down between her legs she was wet.

He'd been married and been with hookers, but this was something different. Having a woman around who was just there for the screwing, no questions, no headaches, no negotiations, was amazingly exciting. Despite that, he took his time. Aware of her professed preferences he pinned her arms over her head and added nips and bites to the licking, the whole time manipulating her clitoris. Her labia had spread of its own will, another sign that he was on the right track, and her body was quickly covered in goose bumps. He ended up nipping and sucking at her nipples, his finger moving in a medium fast motion that seemed to be her preference, and then, almost without warning, she came with a hissing shriek and a whole body clench.

With that he let go of her arms and lifted her legs in the air, sliding into her hard and reaching up to pin the arms down with his hands on her wrists. As he pounded her hard she panted and moaned, finally reaching up to bite him, hard, on the left shoulder. She stayed attached there, moaning into his shoulder, until she came again, almost simultaneous with his own climax.

"Oh, my God," she whispered as he regretfully slid out of her and fumbled a tissue between her legs.

"Are you okay?" Mike asked.

"I am far, far, *far* more than okay," Anastasia whispered, rolling over and sliding her arms around him. "Can I hug you? Please, Kildar?"

"I take it Otryad did not spend much time pleasing you?" Mike asked, sliding his arm around her and cradling her into his shoulder.

"I had never realized that sort of thing *could* happen," Anastasia said, somewhat bitterly. "He was the only man I had ever been with and he was nothing like that. He was there for his pleasure and a girl got whatever she could from that. Thank you for being different."

"Thank *you*," Mike replied. "I won't promise to work on you as much every time; sometimes I'll just want a quickie. But that was pretty quick, I have to admit."

"I will be jealous when you are with other women," Anastasia admitted. "I will want you all to myself. I could have fun with you many times every day."

"Too much else to do, alas," Mike replied. "Among other things, I have seven girls to introduce to sex. Care to help?"

"If you insist," Anastasia said, sleepily. "But I don't think two at once in the same bed is a good introduction. Start as you mean to go on. I need to clean up. Talk about it tomorrow?"

"Whenever you want," Mike said.

"You look like shit, Mike," Adams said, his fingers just touching the weight bar.

"Long day yesterday," Mike admitted, struggling to lift the weights. He'd gotten up to fast repping two-seventy-five and heavy lifting three-fifty, but at the moment he could just barely lift the two-seventy-five.

"And a very short night from the sounds of it," Adams said. "The squeals from your new girlfriend kept waking me up."

"It was really amazing," Mike said, setting the weights into their holder. They'd ended up screwing at least four times during the night, despite the time they'd gotten in. He really should have slept in today, but he'd been up at six for PT instead. "And I am officially worn the fuck out."

"You've got seven more to go, man," Adams pointed out. "What the hell are you going to look like in a couple of weeks?"

"Probably dead," Mike admitted. "But what a way to go."

"Equipment issue starts in an hour," Adams said. "You going to be there for it?"

"Wouldn't miss it for the world," Mike replied. "But I need breakfast first. And coffee. Lots of coffee."

"You're going to need lots of oysters, bud," Adams said, chuckling as he tossed the former SEAL a towel. "And Viagra stock."

"Chief, they're teenage virgins," Mike said, toweling off. "Viagra is not going to be necessary."

▲   ▲   ▲

Three buildings had been completed as part of the construction. The issue was taking place in a building that would later be
converted to a weapons and storage building. At the moment the
lower floor was simply an open shell with a solid counter made
of tables hooked together running down the middle.

The Keldara were entering through the north door and being
issued their uniforms, boots and field gear by Keldara females
who had been chosen for the job. The militiamen had already
been broken down into six mixed platoons and assigned their two
primary instructors. The instructors were already in field uniforms,
Canadian digi-cam, with their rank badges, the badges of former
units, specialty badges and subdued flags marking country of
origin. They were standing by to answer questions as the Keldara
got their issue but the issue was proceeding without a hitch.

As the Keldara entered they were each given a large duffle for
their gear. Instead of being a standard seabag it had a zipper down
one side and folded out. The bags were a civilian design from
L.L. Bean that Mike found far superior to the standard seabag
the military used, especially in these circumstances. They then
proceeded down the tables, being issued hygiene items, uniforms,
boots, underwear and basic field gear and cold weather gear. Mike
had checked the duffels and all the gear would fit, if placed in
carefully. The women had been instructed on how to load the
gear and all the militiaman had to do was slide his bag down
the counter and have it loaded. Each station had a list that had
the name of the militiaman and his sizes in clothes and boots.
Since the men were known to the women it was easy enough for
them to issue the material. At the end the bag was zipped, the
integral backpack straps came out and the Keldara was ready to
go get it set up.

Once Team Oleg was completely issued, the two primary instructors, Matt Randolph and Duncan McKenzie led them off to their
barracks. Mike followed the team over to the open bay barracks
and watched, leaning against the wall, as each of the militiamen
was given a designated bunk and footlocker.

"Right," McKenzie said when all the troops were in place by their bunks. "Open your duffels. Remove one bath towel, one hand towel, the small container of shampoo, the bar of soap, one uniform blouse, one uniform trousers, one pair of socks, one pair of underwear, one T-shirt, your forage cap and one pair of boots." As he gave the orders, he held up each item from a pile on the table at the end. "Ensure you don't disturb all the other crap in there, or you'll be all night sorting it out. Don't touch the envelopes on your bloody beds; we'll get to them in time." The senior NCO of Team One was a veteran of the Black Watch and had a noticeable brogue even in Georgian.

Each of the items was in a plastic wrapper and there was quickly a large quantity of plastic scattered around the room.

"Efram," the senior NCO said to the closest troop. "Grab a trash bag and get that all sorted out. Each of you pick up your litter and stuff it in the bag as Efram goes by."

Once the litter was collected the NCO had them get out of their civilian clothes until the entire platoon was standing in the bay naked, then had them wrap the bath towels around their middles.

"Most of you lads don't know what a bar of soap is for," McKenzie said, striding down the runway in the middle of the barracks. "We will now conduct a class on the taking of the shower. Bring your hand towel, the shampoo and the soap."

He led the platoon into the bathroom and had Oleg get in one of the four stalls.

"Right, two controls," the NCO said, brusquely, pointing to them. "The left hand is usually the hot and will be marked, as this is, in red. The right is the cold. Upon one holder is a bar of soap. This is for use on the majority of your body. In the other is a bottle of generic shampoo. Shampoo is for use on the hairs of the head. In a pinch, soap can be used for shampoo and vice versa but we won't get into advanced hygiene at this time.

"Oleg," he continued, stepping back out of the stall, "ensuring that the majority of your body is *out* of the stream of water, turn the *left* control, the hot water control, in a clockwise motion to *full*. Wait until the water is running hot, then turn the *right* control, the cold, to a position of desired temperature. This may require turning *down* the hot, depending upon the *relative* thermal characteristics of the waters involved."

He led the team through the class on taking a shower, including washing behind their ears with the hand towel.

"In general, you will be under time for showering," McKenzie said when the whole team was done and standing around in their towels. "The term is shit, shower and shave. We will conduct a class on the use of a razor, which few of you are old enough to need, later. For now it's time to get your pretty new uniforms messed up."

For many of the Keldara the uniforms were the first completely new clothes they'd ever had and for now they found the clothing exciting rather than a pain. There was a fair amount of conversation as they changed and McKenzie got redder and redder as they took their time.

"Dawdling over clothing is for *women!*" he finally bellowed. "Anyone not in uniform in fifteen seconds is going to give me fifty push-ups to show they can *motivate!*"

As it turned out everyone made it by the timeline and McKenzie nodded in satisfaction.

"Now, on each bed, if you lads haven't fucked off with it, is a sealed paper envelope, you will open the envelope and place all the items on your bed, carefully."

In the envelope were two lengths of 550 parachute cord, a short length and a long one, dogtags, rubber dogtag mufflers and ID card. The latter was a heavy plastic card slightly smaller and thicker than a credit card with their picture, name and vital statistics on it.

"Right, this is the ticklish bit," McKenzie said. "First of all, everyone ensure that it is *their* picture and name on the ID card. If you're not sure, ask the lad next to you if that's your face.

Remove the thin cords from the long section of 550 cord, then slip the longer chain into the sleeve thus created."

He led them though the process of setting up their dogtags, with the ID card hanging on the chain as well.

"The ID card is the Kildar's innovation," McKenzie said, glancing over at Mike. "Besides the writing on it, it has a microchip inside to hold other information. As if anyone is going to be going around with a microchip reader."

"The medics will be issued one," Mike said, calmly. "As will a doctor if we ever have one assigned permanently. And the hospital in Tbilisi is going to get one as well. Having medical background info will be useful. Better than carrying around a bloody file."

"We will now, carefully and precisely, transfer the material from your duffel to your bloody footlocker," McKenzie boomed. "And you will do it by the numbers or I will have your ass. After that you will be taught to properly make a bed and square this ratty ass barracks away to *my* satisfaction."

Mike spot checked on the teams for the rest of the day, watching them get settled in. The instructors were firm but not particularly hard; that would come later. At the moment the Keldara were just getting used to their lives being regimented and instructed in *very* basic living standards. The Keldara took baths from time to time, mostly in the streams, but they had never had access to running water, or light switches for that matter, so every little item had to be explained. Mike and Nielson had, they thought, carefully thought out the introductory period, but it turned out there were various small problems that cropped up. Some of them the instructors handled, but a few Mike had to consult on. He also passed information from one team to the others as the problems cropped up and were dealt with.

The Keldara were fascinated by everything. Mike had had a washer and dryer installed in each of the barracks with power from heavy generators set up near the gravel pit. The fact that they could be used for washing clothes was a novel innovation to the Keldara. Light from light bulbs they'd seen in town, but had rarely had the opportunity to turn on and off. Mike found one of the instructors nearly apoplectic at a young recruit who had been turning the lights in the bathroom on and off just for the fun of it.

The training in equipment and barracks maintenance continued into the night but Mike had been firm. Until they got into full-scale training the recruits were to bed down at a normal time. By ten-thirty everything but a fire-guard light was off in each of the barracks and the trainers were back up at the caravanserai by eleven.

"Looks okay so far," Mike said as the trainers gathered in the living room for a late-night beer.

"Looks good," McKenzie said to nods from the other trainers. "Not many who are completely brain-dead, none really. A bit confused but they'll get past that."

"And they all think we're *nice* fellows," Vanner said in a mock brogue.

"Big party this weekend," Mike pointed out. "Everybody ensure they have a good time."

"So when do you start training *your* draftees?" Killjoy asked, grinning.

"Oh, I think Monday will do," Mike replied. "And on that note, I'm going to get to bed. See you bright and early tomorrow."

When Mike got to his room, Anastasia was already there.

"Do you mind if I sleep here, tonight, Kildar?" the girl asked. She was dressed in a nightgown and robe and sitting on a chair.

"Not at all," Mike said. "But I think I need to actually get some sleep tonight. Would a quickie be okay?"

"Whatever the Kildar desires," the girl said, standing up and slipping quickly out of the robe and nightdress.

"Whatever?" Mike asked, smiling. "I don't have the bondage dungeon set up yet."

"There is always the belt," Anastasia said, smiling in return.

▲   ▲   ▲

"First call, bucko," Adams said, banging on Mike's door.

"Go away," Mike muttered, pulling the pillows over his head.

"Actually, it's breakfast call," Adams said, opening the door. "It's damned near nine, buddy."

"Christ," Mike snapped, rolling over and looking at the clock. Sure enough, it was eight-forty. "I forgot to set the alarm."

"You needed the extra sleep," Adams said, grabbing a pair of shorts off a chair and tossing them at him. "But it's range day; I know you don't want to miss that."

"Was that a whip I heard last night?" Adams asked as Mike sat down at the kitchen table. The breakfast on the main dining table had already been cleared.

"Don't ask, don't tell, buddy," Mike said, chuckling. "And, no, it was a belt. Consensual I might add."

"Don't ask, don't tell is right," Adams said, shaking his head.

"For that matter, in the breaks I seem to remember a memory of another bed moving somewhere nearby. And since you're the nearest room . . ."

"You should have named Bambi, Thumper," Adams said, shrugging. "Boy does she ever. But you're looking better; I take it you actually got some sleep last night."

"Some," Mike said, sipping his coffee and digging into breakfast. "Mother Griffina, you are a treasure."

"You are too easy to please, Kildar," the woman replied. "And it appears I must keep your strength up."

"Not you, too?" Mike said, shaking his head. "Is my love life common knowledge in the whole house?"

"The whole valley is more like it," Adams said, grinning.

"It's like living in a fishbowl," Mike grumped. "I think we're going to miss first issue."

"It's under control," the chief replied as Vanner came in the kitchen.

"Sorry, Kildar," the sergeant said, waving a coffee cup. "Just getting the morning brew."

"Make yourself at home, Vanner," Mike said. "Good job getting the commo set up so fast. How are the Keldara women taking to it?"

"I picked out a half dozen who could read and write pretty well," the commo specialist said, filling his cup. "They're smart. I'd figured it would be the regular red-neck story you get in most of these tribes, but not with the Keldara. They're smart as a whip. Good looking, too."

"You're keeping more than one around at all times, right?" Mike said. "Where *is* the commo shack, anyway?"

"First-level cellars," Adams said. "West side."

"How in the hell did you rig it from there?" Mike asked. "And when?"

"You've been busy," Adams said, shrugging. "We took a look and that looked to be one of the more secure areas. It's down the hall from the armory and there's a room across from it that would make a good spot to put a duty team. Anybody coming in the caravanserai has to fight through to the back cellars and then down. The cables are run through the walls on the next level up, then trenched to the hill. From there it's armored cable up to the antenna farm. We're going to put in redundant antennas on the caravanserai itself and one of the other peaks."

"Probably unnecessary, but go for it," Mike said. "Among other things, if we get hit hard there's nobody to call. And, yeah, that bothers me."

"There's a room down the hall that has a bunch of junk in it," Vanner said. "You could put in a pretty good command room there. There's enough room, that's for sure. Run some commo through the walls and you'd be set. All in one nice neat little position. I could train up some of the ladies to make decent CIC personnel; they're already doing well at map reading."

"You probably won't get hit heavy," Adams said. "But if someone starts dropping mortars on your head, it would help to be at least one level down."

"Go for it," Mike said. "Good idea."

"Your wish is my command, Kildar," Vanner said, waving his coffee mug in salute.

"How'd you run the satellite phone down there?" Mike asked after a moment's thought.

"We set up an antenna and a booster box at the antenna farm," the former Marine said. "If you've got the codes, you can connect direct to the Iridium relay satellites in geosync, and I do. Took a firmware hack on the hardware, but that was easy enough. Just a spare chip I had lying around and a few lines of code."

"Did you understand any of that?" Mike asked when the commo specialist was gone.

"Something about an antenna," the chief said, shrugging. "It works, don't fuck with it."

"What happens when it breaks?" Mike asked.

"Call Vanner back over," the chief said, with another shrug. "Or somebody like him. You're probably going to need a commo geek around anyway."

"More permanent residents," Mike sighed. "I didn't think this all the way out. Everything made so much sense when I came up with this brilliant idea. Little did I know . . ."

"Yours not to reason why," Adams said. "Yours is but to get out there and act like you have a clue what is going on."

CHAPTER
TWENTY

The weapons issue and zero was going well.

Each of the Keldara had been issued a weapon and taught to find and memorize the serial number. After that they were run through a brief class on aiming and trigger control, then taken down to the range. There they were taken to the line and walked through zeroing the weapons. Since the leaders had already been issued and zeroed, they acted as firing coaches when the militiamen actually fired. Since they hadn't really been drilled in safety, Mike had insisted on a trained firer at each position. But between the team leaders and all the trainers assisting the Keldara were being run through the firing quickly.

"We'll be done before noon," Adams said, looking at his watch. "A couple of hours for training in stripping and cleaning and we'll be done."

"Just as well," Mike said. "They're going back to the family bosom for the weekend, so they should get off early today. Plenty of time to stress them after the festival."

"Kildar," McKenzie said, walking over. "The lads have asked

about getting off early today, something about this festival that's coming up. Apparently there's a bit of work to get ready."

"We were talking about that," Mike said, nodding. "Figure we'll cut them loose at sixteen hundred."

"I can live with that," the Scot said. "What is this festival anyway?"

"You know about as much as I do," Mike said. "I just got here in the winter. All I've picked up is that it's a planting festival, more of a spring festival. Not Easter, that was a couple of weeks ago and they barely noticed it except to go to church. And apparently the Sunday celebration this week will be at the homes."

"Mayday was two days ago," McKenzie said, frowning. "But this falls in the time of Beltane. That can be any time from Walpurgis to May Third or so."

"Beltane?" Adams asked.

"Celtic celebration," Mike said. "Falls between the spring equinox and midsummer. It's going to be interesting to see how they celebrate it."

Over the sound of the firing, Mike heard a heavy truck in the distance and turned to see the cement mixer headed over to the gravel pit.

"Been a while since I looked at the dam," he said, waving at Adams. "They don't get released until the weapons are clean. Then they can go."

"Works," the chief said.

"I'm going to go check on Meller and Company," Mike added, getting back in his Expedition.

The small stream was dry, a combination of the lack of snowmelt and a small dam and channel that had been cut to divert it to the main stream to the south. Later the channel would be reversed to bring the heavier stream over.

Where the stream had been there were now wooden forms, marking out the weirs that would control the flow of the water. At the moment it was just the wooden outline and a small amount of concrete poured into the bottom. Some of the older Keldara were moving the concrete around so that it would be even across the bottom while the mixer went back for another load.

Meller was down in the form with the others, spreading the concrete with a wide metal shovel. They had to work in and out of the reinforcing metal rods that had been laid down in the bottom of the foundation trench.

"Hey, Kildar," the engineer said, grinning. He had been standing on a platform to keep out of the knee-deep concrete, but he'd still managed to cover himself in concrete splatters. "Going good."

"How long to fill the first forms?" Mike asked.

"At this rate, a few days," Meller replied. "No problem with layering, though. Unfortunately, we're going to have to keep going during the festival. The concrete truck drivers aren't from around here so that's no problem. But I'm going to have to hire a few laborers from town to help while the Keldara are off."

"Not an issue," Mike said. "Since we're paying the Keldara for this, paying laborers isn't that big of a deal. The militia are getting off early. Any problem with letting the guys go?"

"Nope," Meller said. "I'd already arranged for shifts through the night. We'll have to keep pouring until this section is done so we don't get layering. But the guys to replace them are standing by. They're going to get here at seventeen hundred."

"What about you?" Mike asked. "You're not going to work straight through the pour are you?"

"Prael and I are trading off," Meller said. "I'll be around for part of the festival. Did you know there's a bonfire?"

"No," Mike admitted.

"They're gathering the wood for it tonight," the engineer said. "That's why they want to leave early."

"I wonder if I should help?" Mike mused. "Kildar and all. Or do I sit up on my throne and watch?"

"Only one way to find out," Meller pointed out. "Ask."

Choosing who to ask was the question on Mike's mind as he drove over to the Keldara compound. Father Ferani was oldest but there was more deference paid to Father Kulcyanov, which was why Mike always addressed him first. However, in this case, he probably wanted to talk to Father Makanee. He just got along with the guy better than the others, maybe because he was a tad younger. Or maybe it was just that they looked alike enough to be brothers.

He pulled into the compound and got out, digging in his safari jacket pocket as the children gathered around. He'd ordered a bunch of bags of hard candies and made it a habit to pass them out to the Keldara kids whenever he came to the compound. He'd pointed out that it was only once a day, and one per kid, but it made him popular with that segment of the Keldara, at least, and something of the effect wore off on the older Keldara.

"No, Varlam," he said, shaking his head at one of the kids as he tried to grab a piece of candy Mike had been handing to one of the younger girls. "This one is for Khava. *This* one is for you," he continued, handing the boy a candy.

The ritual took about ten minutes every time he arrived at the compound, but he considered it time well spent. And Mother Savina always made sure he had pockets full of candy when he went out the door.

"Justinas," he said, as he handed out one of the last pieces. "Do you know where Father Makanee is?"

"By the barn with the others," the boy replied, stripping off the wrapper of the candy and shoving it in his mouth. He pocketed the scrap of wrapper since Mike had been furious the first time the kids scattered the ground with litter. "I'll show you."

The boy led him through the tangle of small gardens that now littered the compound and around a couple of cow biers to the Ferani barn. There Mike found the elders and most of the males that weren't with the militia or working on projects gathered in one spot. At the moment, two of them were throwing axes at a target.

The axes the two were throwing were the standard wood-cutting axes that the Keldara used before he got replacements. They were a traditional European design, much lighter than the standard wood-cutting axe that was familiar in the U.S. Europeans had used the axes from time immemorial since most of the woods of Europe were relatively soft. It was only after arriving in the new world that a heavier axe became a necessity to cut the massive oaks of the American woodlands.

These axes had a thin, light, head and a round barrel connection to the haft, which was circular instead of oval as in most American axes. With the exception of the haft being longer, they looked a good bit like tomahawks and could be thrown like them.

"Father of All be with you this day," Father Kulcyanov said when Mike approached the group. Mike was surprised by the sight of the elder. He had on what Mike would call "Sunday-Go-To-Meetin'" clothes, a fine pair of pants and shirt that he usually wore to church on Sunday. But what really got Mike's attention was the tiger skin. The head had been hollowed out to make a sort of hat and a portion of skin trailed down the elder's shoulders like a short cape. Both the head and the cape showed signs of wear, but it was apparent they had been kept carefully; there was much less moth-eating to them than the occasional heads and skins he'd seen in the houses. Kulcyanov wasn't the only one so dressed, for that matter. All of the elders had their best clothes on and similar hats and capes. Father Shaynav was wearing a bull's head and cape, Fathers Mahona and Devlich were wearing wolf heads, Father Ferani was wearing a stag's head and Father Makanee was wearing a boar's head. It was pretty apparent that this was part of the rites of spring. The first test, probably.

"Father of All be with you all," Mike replied. "I would take a moment of Father Makanee's time, if he is available."

"Of course, Kildar," Father Makanee said, walking over from the group. "How can I assist you?"

"A word," Mike said, walking to the far end of the barn. "I wanted to ask about the festival," Mike continued when they were out of sight. "I should have gotten more information earlier, so

I could plan to participate. Tell me about what is going on, if you would, please?"

"Tonight the wood for the fire is gathered," Father Makanee said, frowning slightly and apparently choosing his words. "And it will be gathered on the tun," he continued, pointing out into the fields at one of the small hillocks that dotted the valley. This one was near the road, just north of the turnoff for the caravanserai. "Tomorrow morning the turf will be cut to make seats and the fire constructed in the middle. That will take most of the morning, but other things will be going on at the same time. The children will play games and the women will cook special foods. Starting at midday, the men will compete for the Ondah and that will take until in the evening."

"The Ondah," Mike said. "The test of strength? Wrestling?"

"There is wrestling," Father Makanee said. "And tests of strength. There are five tests: the test of the stone, the test of the wood, the test of the bull, the test of the fire and the test of the man. The test of the stone is carrying a heavy stone as far as you can. The test of the wood is picking up a large log and throwing it as far as you can. The test of the bull is how well you can first taunt and then throw a bull in a ring. The test of the fire is how high you can leap over a fire pit. And the test of the man is wrestling."

Mike blinked for a moment and then shook his head.

"That's interesting," was all he said. He realized that at least part of it fitted well with what were now called "Highland Games." Certainly the rock carrying and the log throwing, what was called the cabar toss if he recalled correctly. But the bull and the fire jump were different and he didn't know if wrestling was in the highland games. "Can anyone participate in these events?"

"Yes, Kildar," Father Makanee said, frowning in turn. "But the men prepare for them all year and the only ones who can truly compete for the Ondah are chosen by the axe toss. You are speaking of the trainers?"

"And I might want to try a couple," Mike said. "The reason I ask about the festival is to find out what I can do to be a part of it. Can I contribute food? Can I participate in the events? The wood cutting?"

"There are nine wood cutters," Father Makanee said, wrinkling his brow. "They are chosen from among the young men, at least one from each family. They throw the axe to see who can throw the hardest and most accurately. But one must be from each family."

"I don't want to interfere in that," Mike interjected.

"But if you want to cut the wood, that would be acceptable," Father Makanee replied. "You will be the ninth cutter. It would be an honor. It is a long time since we had a true Kildar, but the tradition is that the Kildar often was a wood cutter. It would be good. But . . . do you know how to throw an axe?"

"As a matter of fact, yes," Mike said, smiling faintly. "But not like those. I would have to practice with them."

"Come practice with us," Father Makanee said, drawing him back to the group. "We are only waiting for the young men on the range to join us."

Mike was drawn back to the group and handed one of the axes amid some half-hidden smiles. The range was about ten meters long, with a point at which you had to stand and throw at a target that was constructed of large logs set up in a pyramid with the flat ends facing the thrower.

Mike did, in fact, know how to throw an axe. It was one of those oddball spec ops methods for silent takedown, popular with Russian Spetznaz especially. The weapon of choice, however, was much shorter than the axe he was holding, with a much heavier head and a flat, hammer, back. And Mike had only learned it enough to get proficient, not expert. He'd met some Spetznaz on a training mission and only learned it to the point of "well, I can do it, too." American spec ops were firm believers that the best way to take down a sentry, silently, was to shoot him in the head with a silenced weapon.

So he stepped up to the line and swung the axe for a moment, thinking. The important thing about axe throwing was to get the spin of the axe just right. It had to spin a certain number of times so that the head was lined up with the target when it arrived. But this longer axe was going to rotate slower than the one he was used to using, both because the head was lighter and because the handle was longer.

He tossed it once, lightly, just to get a feel for the rotation. The handle hit the target instead of the head. So he retrieved the axe, knowing the Keldara were judging him carefully, and tried again. That time was just about right with the head impacting backwards. A bit more emphasis on rotation would get it.

The third time he threw the weapon lighter than he could, but got the spin just right. The handle hit with a distinct "bong" and the head thunked in an inch or so. He knew he could do better, but no reason to show that off, yet.

"Good throw, Kildar," Father Ferani said, frowning. "You have thrown axes before."

"Not like this," Mike said, going downrange to retrieve the weapon. "I will try again when the young men get here."

He gave the axe to one of the Keldara and waited with them for the younger men. In the meantime, he listened as the men talked about the festival. There would be games and competitions during the day, then a feast in the evening.

"There are oxen that are supposed to be stalled for the Kildar, aren't there?" he asked Father Makanee. "Would it be appropriate to donate one to the feast? There are not just the Keldara to be fed, but the trainers as well."

"Yes, Kildar," the elder said, smiling. "That would be excellent. We could slaughter it in the morning and then have it cook all day for the feast in the evening."

"Do it," Mike said. "If I'm going to be the Kildar, I should be the Kildar all the way. What are you doing with the other oxen that are no longer being used for work?" Oxen were male cattle that had been gelded, effectively steers. They made for the best beef if properly fed up.

"They are turned out to pasture," Father Makanee said, gesturing towards the pastures on the east side of the valley.

"I'll get Genadi to get some feed for them," Mike said. "We can partially graze them and partially feed them up, then slaughter what we don't eat this year in the fall. I like a good steak. And with all this unused beef trotting around, it seems a shame not to have plenty. Not to mention contributing to other festivals. Are there more I should know about?"

"There are four major festivals that we celebrate," Father Makanee said. "One for each season. There is another in midsummer, then a harvest festival and the winter festival. They are called Balar, Laman, Samnan and Imbol."

"Crap," Mike muttered. "Do you burn fires at the summer festival?"

"At each, with the largest being at Imbol," Father Makanee said, looking at him askance. "What is wrong?"

"Nothing," Mike said, frowning. "Okay, let's just say that it reminds me of something, strongly, and that something doesn't add up. Plenty of societies have . . . festivals at each of those points. But the specific practices vary and the names vary a lot. The names you just gave, and some of the practices, match closest to the Celts. Which has one of two reasons: Either you're displaced Celts or originals. The Celts came from somewhere in Eastern Europe back in the Neolithic." He looked at Father Makanee and shrugged. "I'm not making any sense, am I?"

"Who are the Celts?" Father Makanee asked.

"Wow, ask an easy one," Mike replied. "The Celts were a tribe that probably exploded out of Eastern Europe back when people used stone tools. They spread through northern Europe as lords over the population that was originally there and founded various separate tribes. The Gauls were Celts, as were the Irish and the Scottish. There's some argument that the Germanic tribes, including the Norse, were a Celtic offshoot. They're best known, though, in Wales, Scotland and Ireland. The point is that when people got around to studying their seasonal festivals, they found that they had four major ones: Imbolc, at the point between the winter solstice and the spring equinox, Beltane, around May first or now, Lammas, between the summer solstice and the fall equinox and Samhain, what's celebrated these days as Halloween, between the fall solstice and the winter. Imbolc, Beltane, Lammas and Samhain. And yours are Imbol, Balar, Laman and Samnan. That *can't* be coincidence. For that matter, the fires in Scandinavia at Lammas are called 'Baldur's Balar.' Baldur's Balefire. Of course, by the time anyone got around to recording things like that, they'd converted to Christianity and the old reasons for the fires had faded."

"You speak of Baldur?" Father Mahona asked, curiously. "What do you know of Baldur?"

"Baldur was the Norse god of the spring and summer," Mike said, dredging out his memory of the Norse mythology. "His symbol was the mistletoe because it was the one plant that could kill him. Loki tricked . . . someone, Frey maybe, into throwing a spear made of mistletoe at him and it killed him. His mother was so grief stricken that she turned her face from the world and brought winter. The gods bring him back for six months every year, though, and that is spring and summer. When he is in the underworld it is winter. The Celts had a slightly different take on it, but the Norse and Celts celebrate similar rituals at similar times. Heck, there are similarities to the Adonis myth, for that matter, and Persephone."

Father Mahona and Father Makanee traded a look for a moment which Mike caught but couldn't interpret. The locals were regular Sunday churchgoers at the small church in Alerrso and there was no reason for them to celebrate Norse or Celtic rituals. The similarities had to be coincidence. Practically every society in the Northern Hemisphere had similar seasonal rituals. Of course, most of them dated back to prehistoric rituals involving the old gods. But none of the societies maintained the actual religion.

"How is the training going?" Father Mahona said, clearing his throat.

"Too early to tell," Mike replied, willing to change the subject. "The guys are just getting zeroed today. Ask me in a couple of months."

"Much like the planting," Father Makanee said. "The seed is in the ground. Ask us in a couple of months if there will be a good crop."

"Well, the seed is good and the planting went well," Mike said, smiling. "The crop should be excellent."

"There could be a late frost," Father Makanee said. "Or a sudden storm as it is about to be brought in. Many things can happen to ruin the crop."

"I was actually talking about the militia," Mike said, smiling again.

"So was I," Father Makanee replied.

"I'm worried about the actual crop," Father Mahona said, unhappily. "I know that Genadi thinks we'll get more from these new hybrids, but we haven't planted as much land as last year . . ."

"With the new plows we planted *nearly* as much," Father Makanee replied, shaking his head. "And we were able to leave more fallow, which is good. You know we've been overusing the Sardana field. It's just not producing like it did once. Let it lie for a while . . ."

"But we *put* a crop in the Sardana," Mahona snapped. "Bloody clover if you can believe it! What's wrong with just turning the cattle out on it?"

"Genadi says we will later in the season," Makanee said, soothingly.

"We'll never get enough food in for winter, you'll see," Mahona said, balefully. "What with all that junk he had us spray the fields with . . ."

"Weed killer's only going to help," Mike said. "We're trying to grow wheat and oats and barley and peas, not thistles. What do you think the barley crop will do?"

"Well, the barley's our own," Father Makanee said. "Not a hybrid. We've used the same barley for generations and the women won't let us change. So we'll have to see what we see with that. But I think the wheat and peas will do well. Next year, we're going to see about soybeans."

"And what can you do with soybeans?" Father Mahona said, throwing up his hands. "Eat them? I don't think so."

"Make tofu?" Mike said, smiling, then shook his head when both the farmers looked at him in question. "It's a . . . not particularly good food that can be made from soybeans. I was joking."

"Normally we understand your jokes, Kildar," Father Makanee said, smiling. "That one we were lost."

"At least I've avoided the farmer's daughter's jokes," Mike pointed out.

"The ones with the traveling salesman?" Father Mahona asked, frowning. "I've heard them."

"What, all of them?" Mike asked. "Did you hear the one about the traveling former SEAL who got caught in a snowstorm?"

"No," Father Mahona said, puzzled.

"That's because we're living it," Mike replied. "When we get to the punch line, I'll tell you."

CHAPTER
TWENTY-ONE

"Here come the youngsters," Father Makanee said a few minutes later, gesturing to where the troops were walking up from the range. They'd turned in their weapons and were obviously discussing the zeroing with enthusiasm. Mike thought they'd probably be less enthusiastic by this time next week.

"Oleg," Mike said, shaking the hand of the Kulcyanov family militia leader. "It was going well when I left."

"Oh, it went well, I think, Kildar," Oleg replied, nodding at him. "I'm not sure about Shota. He had trouble hitting the mountainside."

"There are things to be said for simply being a pack mule," Mike pointed out. "And later we'll see how he takes to heavier weapons. Some people do better with machine guns than rifles. If he's one of those, he'll be perfect."

"Are you here to watch the competition, Kildar?" Sawn asked, walking over to the axe range. There were four ranges set up but it was still going to be a while before everyone could be run through.

"The Kildar wishes to participate," Father Mahona said, formally. "He would be one of the woodcutters. If he can throw well enough."

"He got the axe in the target," Father Makanee pointed out. "For one who is not a Keldara, to get the axe in on only three tries is a feat."

"On the short range," Father Mahona responded. Mike noticed that everyone was backing up and gulped as Sawn took a position that was twice as far as the previous line.

The Makanee militia leader spun the axe with the fingers of his right hand for a moment and then in one continuous motion brought it up to shoulder level and let fly. The axe spun hard and true, making a series of turns that were a blur, and then buried itself in the wood. The head was very near the center of the top log, the one painted in white as a target.

"Crap," Mike muttered. He *never* wanted to fight a Keldara with just an axe, that was for sure.

Some of the young men lined up to contest the throw while others simply gathered around and shouted encouragement. Mike noticed that all six of the militia leaders participated. He'd mostly talked with Genadi about who would be a good potential leader of the militia, but the six were, effectively, the designated heirs in their generation for the Families and the Keldara were careful about that. You had to show intelligence and wisdom and physical prowess to be considered for the spot of a Father of the Family. And the six had all three in abundance. Hell, most of the Keldara had all three, the six were simply exceptional.

And they all turned out to be exceptional with the axe throwing. Mike wasn't sure to what extent they were simply showing off for the Kildar, however. He had to consider that when Oleg ended up breaking the axe handle and burying the head so deep that it took a few minutes to work it out.

It took about an hour to run all the men who were contesting through the course and Mike had to admit that he didn't have a chance. Even the regular Keldara were very good at the skill while the leaders were fucking masters. That meant the six Families were all represented of course. There were a few misthrows, Shota in particular had hit the target so hard, and at such a bad angle, that the axe bounced back practically to the onlookers. But Mike was easily going to be in the bottom ten percent.

"Kildar, will you try your hand, now?" Father Mahona said, smugly.

"I'm not nearly as good as any of these fine young men," Mike said, nonetheless taking the axe from a slightly smirking Sawn. "But I will give it a try."

He considered the range as he spun the axe in his hand, much as Sawn had. The distance was about twice what he'd thrown before, so if he simply kept the same spin and threw a bit harder, it should at least hit. He spun the axe a bit harder and then brought it up, hurling it as hard as he could at the target.

It had to be luck. He *knew* it was luck. But luck had been with him more than once and She smiled on him again. The axe ran true to the target, the handle impacting hard enough that it came damned near breaking as Oleg's had, and the head buried itself in the target. It was slightly to one side, but deeply embedded. And instead of being in the bottom rank of throws, the toss was very near the top.

"Lucky," Mike said, shrugging, as the Keldara applauded by slapping their thighs.

"A very good throw," Father Makanee said, glancing at Mahona. "I think that the Kildar has proven his worth."

"For poplar, perhaps," Father Mahona replied.

"Poplar would be a good choice," Father Kulcyanov said, having overheard the exchange. "The tree of spring, the fire that we burn upon the hearth, the tree of quicklife."

"The rites must be explained," Father Makanee pointed out. "May I?"

"It is yours to explain," Father Kulcyanov said, nodding.

"Kildar," Father Makanee said, formally. "Choose nine young men to accompany you. You should go to the poplar stands along the river. Choose three trees that are crowding the others, trees that are high and straight but unlikely to cause damage if removed. They must be cut by the light of the moon only and you have until dawn to finish the task. Only you must swing the axe. When the trees are cut, you and the other nine return them to the tun along with the top cuttings. In the meantime, the other young men will scour the woods for branches for kindling. The branches of kindling must be gathered and not cut. At dawn, the nine who cut the trees must make the first cuts of the turf for the fire, but they do not have to complete the building of the pit. After cutting out the circle, they can retire and rest until noon, when the rest of the competitions begin. No one is required to participate in any of the competitions, so you can feel free to rest as long as you'd like. In fact, you don't have to do the cutting, although it would be an honor."

Mike hadn't realized he was being set a task that would take all damned night. But at this point, he really didn't see a way to back out.

"I'll do the cutting," he said, mentally kicking himself. "I can tell a chainsaw is out, but can I use a regular axe? One of the ones I had brought in? They cut better."

"The axes to be used are not these," Father Kulcyanov said. "They are kept by the Families, forged upon our fires and remade as necessary. We would . . . prefer you use those."

"Can do," Mike said, nodding. "Father Kulcyanov, I have lived among the Keldara for only a short time. I would have you choose the nine men to accompany me."

The detailing didn't take long and before dark had settled, Mike and his group, along with several others, had gathered in front of the Kulcyanov house. Father Kulcyanov entered and returned in a few moments with four axes; he was apparently the keeper of the spares. Each of the axes was subtly different; one was fairly light with a single, broad, edge, one was single sided and much larger, the third was about the same size with a pick back and the third was a monster with two heads. He set all four on a table by the door and then picked up the smallest.

"This is the axe Camaforn," the father said, formally, handing it to one of the winners. "Bear it with pride."

"I bear it with pride, in the name of the All Father," the young man said, bowing.

"Your tree is the pine, the evergreen, the fragrant boughed," Father Kulcyanov said. "Bring three logs, of the size of a man's thighs, to the tun by morning, that the blessing of the Father of All may be upon us."

"I shall in the name of my Family," the Keldara said, nodding and turning away.

The ritual, and there was no question that it was a ritual, continued through the other two groups. Oleg got the second to the largest axe, leaving the monster to Mike. He wasn't sure he could swing it for any time at all, much less cut down three trees "of the width of a man's thigh." His thigh? Vil's? Father Kulcyanov's? He guessed, however, that questions were not encouraged at this point.

"This is the axe Culcanar," Father Kulcyanov said, holding out the axe across outstretched hands. "Bear it with pride."

"I bear it with pride in the name of the All Father," Mike said. He wasn't particularly religious, but he'd come to the firm conclusion that they weren't talking about a Christian god.

"Your tree is the poplar, the tree of spring, the tree that burns upon our hearth, the quick lifed," the Father continued. "Bring three logs, of the size of a man's thighs, to the tun by morning, that the blessing of the Father of All may be upon us."

"I shall in the name of the Keldara," Mike said, formally. He'd thought about what he should swear by as he watched the ritual, and decided that, as the Kildar, he could only support the whole group. He'd *thought* about doing it in the name of the SEALs, but if Adams heard he'd never give him a moment's peace.

Father Kulcyanov nodded in approval, so apparently he'd chosen right.

Mike gathered his group up and headed down to the stream. The nearest serious stand of poplar was about a kilometer and a half away. The night was a tad cold for how he'd dressed, but he figured he'd be warming up in a bit.

The axe was not nearly as heavy as it looked; the head was actually fairly thin. But it didn't look like an axe for cutting trees, it looked like an axe for lopping off heads. If it was actually a battle-axe, the light weight made sense. You'd have to swing it for a long time in a fight; having a super heavy axe would make you wear out faster than your opponent.

The moon was past halfway and there was enough light to examine the axe, to a degree. It looked, hell it *felt*, old. It might have been reworked, but it had probably been reworked over centuries. And the original design appeared to be intact, as if each craftsman that had worked on it had been careful not to change a line. The whole festival was making him furiously curious about the origins of the Keldara.

"Okay, guys," he said to the group as they approached the stand of poplar, "I'm new here and I haven't been fully briefed. Hell, I've never chopped a tree down of any size. What the hell am I doing?"

There were chuckles from the mostly faceless group in the darkness, but one stepped up next to him and pointed at the poplars.

"There is one that is of a size," the Keldara said, stepping forward. "The limbs will make it heavy to the north, yes? It has grown out that way for light. Cut here," he continued, pointing to a spot on the side where there was a barely visible discoloration. "Cut into it about halfway. Then cut on the other side. When you start to hear it creak, drop the axe and run like hell."

"This is a special axe," Mike pointed out, spitting on his hands in preparation. "Should I really drop it?"

"Culcanar will understand," the Keldara said, cryptically.

Mike stepped up to the tree and started cutting as the young men in the group spread out through the trees, picking up fallen limbs.

Mike considered the ritual as he cut. The poplars along the stream were obviously kept there as erosion control and a ready source of firewood. They had been thinned out from time to time, there were stumps visible, but they'd been treated with care. He wondered how much the ritual had to do with care of the trees and how much to do with spring planting. Even the gathering of the wood from around them was a form of care, since it reduced the possibility of a wild fire. And cutting out certain trees, each of the cutters had been given a different wood to gather, meant that the clearing was widespread.

The entire festival had a very old feel to it. There were touches of Norse, touches of Celtic, but very little that he recognized from Georgian or Russian. "All Father," for example, was a name for Odin, the Norse father of the gods. But certain names, the name of the axe for example, Culcanar, sounded more Celtic. And very unchanged. There was no "ov" or "ich" to it. Culculane was a Celtic warrior myth. He seemed to recall it meant "Dog of Culan." So the axe's name, if it was from Celtic, would be something like "Dog of Canar." But the Keldara had referred to it in first person. That might refer to the axe or the original owner. He simply *had* to get to the bottom of "the mysteries." It was like an itch he couldn't scratch.

Poplar was a soft wood, but he could feel himself wearing out by the time he'd cut halfway through the tree. And he had two more to go. He felt sorry for Oleg, who had gotten oak, which was much harder. Presumably, someone was cutting maple which was hard as rock. That person was in for a hell of a night.

He'd gotten seriously warmed up on the first half, but he didn't stop as he moved to the other side of the tree. He was on a time limit and the moon was well up. He started in on the other side, getting into the rhythm again, one cut down, one up, chopping out a wedge in the side of the tree. But before he'd really gotten in the zone he heard a creaking sound and, taking the advice of the Keldara, he dropped the axe and ran like hell.

The tree seemed to be puzzled for a moment, swaying slightly as all the Keldara backed away hurriedly. Then it bent over and crashed to the ground with a slight twist, easily missing everyone.

"Do I top it now, or do that later?" Mike asked.

"Now," the same Keldara answered. "If you will, Kildar."

"Trim it up?" Mike asked, picking the axe back up and walking to the end. "Cut it in half or what?"

"Just top it, Kildar," another Keldara said. "We can carry it, topped, to the tun. And others will drag the top up. Later it can be cut in half."

Mike chopped the top off, leaving a log that was about twenty-five feet long. As big around as it was and filled with sap, it was going to be a fun time carrying it.

"Next tree, if you will," was all he said.

He was well into the first cut when he heard a group approaching and looked up. From the shapes in the moonlight, he saw that the girls had arrived with food and beer. What he really wanted was some water and the river was right there. But he knew better than to drink unfiltered river water; damned giardia cysts were everywhere and caused a rather raging case of Montezuma's Revenge.

"Kildar," one of the women said, walking over to him. "The cutting is going well."

"I guess," Mike replied, taking the beer bottle that she handed him and flexing his hands.

"I have brought you gloves," the woman continued.

"Thank you," Mike said, taking them from her and tucking them in his belt. "Is it Irina?"

"Yes, Kildar," the girl replied, smiling.

"Sorry, didn't recognize you at first," the former SEAL said. "How's the scar?"

"Healed," she said. "I thank you for my life."

"And I hope the Fathers took my little lecture to heart?" Mike asked. "You're not considered . . ."

"Unmarriageable?" she asked, giggling. "No, they accepted your command. In fact, I am to be promised to Jitka Ferani. We will be wed next fall, if the jadan can be worked out."

"Is that a dowry or a purchase?" Mike asked, having to use the English word for "dowry."

"When a woman is wed, she must bring certain money and things with her," Irina said, shrugging. "It is our custom."

"Dowry," Mike said, nodding.

"It is much money," Irina continued, unhappily. "It is very hard on the Family."

"Things will get better," Mike pointed out. "More planting and I'm thinking about other ways the Keldara can make money. And, besides, this is spring. Aren't you supposed to be happy?"

"You're right, Kildar," the girl said. "Drink your beer and eat your bread and meat, that you may have the strength to fell the trees of the spring. We'll leave this here; we go to gather flowers."

"Let's see," Mike said, smiling. "Girls gathering flowers, boys gathering wood. My, there might even be chance meetings."

"There may," the girl said, giggling again. "A few."

"What about all this careful separation?" Mike asked.

"It's spring," Irina replied, shrugging. "On the nights of the spring festival, things are . . . different."

"And here I am chopping down a tree," Mike said, shrugging ruefully.

"It makes you one of the Nine," Irina said, smiling in the moonlight. "You will be able to challenge for the Ondah, the King of Spring. The Ondah chooses the Queen."

"I'm not even going to try," Mike pointed out. "After this is over, I'm just going to crash."

"You will find the day is long, but fun," Irina promised. "No one will sleep tonight, except the young children and the old people. And tomorrow there will be feasting and games and dancing. And tomorrow night is the Lighting, and no one will sleep at all."

"Sounds like Hell Week," Mike said, grinning. "I'd better eat and drink my beer so I can finish cutting down this tree."

Some of the girls hung around after Irina left, ostensibly

looking for flowers in the woods and mostly hanging out with the boys, who began bringing in less and less wood. Mike didn't care, though. He was busy cutting down the tree, thankful for the gloves Irina had brought. He had calluses, but not the right kind either in depth or position to help him with the axe.

As it turned out, he finished all three trees well before dawn. That only left getting them to the hill. That was where the others had their place. Five of them could lift one of the logs over their head, and Mike joined the second group, despite the weariness of his arms, lifting the log onto his shoulder and carrying it up to the hill.

They were one of the first groups in but as it turned out there was a particular spot that the logs had to be laid. Chocks were placed on the hill and then Father Kulcyanov, who was looking mighty worn, carefully had the poplar logs laid perpendicular to the slope at a particular point on the side of the nearly round hill.

When Mike returned to the hill, following the last poplar log and with the other four dragging the crowns, Father Kulcyanov stepped over to him and nodded.

"Kildar, you would do me a great honor if you could cut down one more tree before dawn," the elder said. "Givi can show you the proper tree. It must be a fir tree, of the width of a thigh and at least as tall as two normal men. Again, it must be cut before dawn and should be in the village by dawn."

"That's not much time," Mike said, estimating by the moon and then checking his watch.

"The young men assure me that you can do it," Father Kulcyanov said. "I would send Oleg, but he has had trouble with the oak. He has not yet cut his last tree."

"Okay, okay," Mike said, feeling hard done by. "I'm on it. Any idea where to find a fir nearby?"

"Givi will lead you," the elder said, gesturing to one of the Kulcyanov boys.

"Lead on, Givi," Mike said. "Come on, boys, one more tree to cut down. You want it in the village?"

"Yes, Kildar," Father Kulcyanov said. "In front of my house."

"Let's go," Mike said, trotting off. They didn't have a lot of time, if the tree was going to be there before dawn.

Givi led them to the hill behind the compound and up a steep path to near its summit. Mike could hear cutters in the woods as they passed and the sound of laughter from the girls who were "looking for flowers." At one point he also clearly heard the sort of gasp you only got when two people were entwined. So much for all of the girls being virgins.

As they neared the summit, they came to a grove of firs. Mike could see that there was some sort of crosstree set at the top of the ridge, but the guide led him off to one side and it dropped out of sight. Givi led them through the grove to a tree that looked identical to the others. But he definitely felt that was the one to cut.

The fir tree had branches that reached nearly to the ground, making it hard to get the axe in.

"Is it okay to cut away the branches?" Mike asked.

"Yes," Givi said. "It's really the only way."

Mike crawled under the boughs and hacked away a couple of branches, giving himself enough room to get at the trunk on one side at least. One of the lads had a sharpening stone with him and Mike quickly honed the blade—it had obviously needed it—and then started cutting the tree.

The spot where he was cutting had had branches on it so there were tough knots to negotiate. And the fir was much harder than the poplar. But he felt the urgency of time so he laid in as hard as he could, really hammering it so that chips flew. In about fifteen minutes he'd cut halfway through and crawled under the other side to give himself some room to cut there.

In less than an hour he had the tree felled and took a few minutes cutting away some of the larger branches so that the Keldara could get the tree up on their shoulders. When it was all ready, they started down the path as fast as they could, safely, racing the approaching dawn with those not carrying the tree gathering up the fallen branches and following. It was already pre-dawn, Before Morning Nautical Twilight as they'd say in the military, with the air a ghostly blue. The moon was down and the sun not yet up and the visibility sucked. There was also a slight ground fog, giving the woods an eerie feeling. It combined to really slow them down.

Mike wasn't sure if Keldara dawn counted as the sun over the horizon or the traditional "telling a white thread from a black thread." But whichever counted, they were in the village in time. When they got to the spot outside the Kulcyanov house, all eight of the other axemen and their parties were gathered around a hole dug in the hard courtyard.

The men carrying the tree laid it gently on the ground and the other axemen fell on it with a will, cutting away the branches until there was only a bit of green at the top. Then the whole group gathered together to set it in the hole and pull it vertical with ropes and pushing. When it was vertical, the earth that had been dug out of the hole was shoveled back in and tamped down hard so that the tree stood firmly upright.

Several of the cuttings from the tree fellings had been gathered in the same area and as soon as the tree was erected, the axemen started chopping them up. They cut the boughs from the woody portions so that there was soon a huge heap of greenery on one side of the courtyard.

As this was going on, the younger children and old people of the village started to come out, bringing breakfast for the whole troop. Mostly it was cakes with some sort of a wash on them and eggs, with buttermilk instead of the usual beer. Mike was so thirsty from the previous night that he ended up drinking about a gallon of the milk. He also started to wonder when he could leave to go get some sleep.

Besides whatever else they had been doing, the girls from the village *had* been gathering flowers. They proved it by coming forward, as soon as the boughs were cut, with baskets heaped with wildflowers. Using twine and vines they began tying the flowers all around the tree, getting boosts from the boys to get the upper sections, which involved a certain amount of grab ass and lots of giggling. At the top, which involved standing on shoulders, the girls hung small oatmeal cakes and brightly colored eggs like Easter eggs from the branches that had been left.

It was at that point that Mike finally realized that what he had cut was a Maypole.

Some of the girls who hadn't been involved in decorating the Maypole had taken the boughs and gone around the houses of the Keldara, hanging them from the doorways until the entire village was decked in green. They added their wildflowers to the doorways and gathered more eggs and cakes from the women at the houses.

These were added to the doorways or hung from the Maypole. The children ran around trying to cadge them from the girls and Mike could understand why. The cakes were primarily oatmeal, but seasoned with honey and some fruit. They were pretty good; he'd eaten three when they were offered.

After the Maypole was decorated, the men trooped off towards the hill where the wood had been laid out. Mike figured he had to be in on this, too, so he followed along, noting in passing that "his" group had waited until he headed out.

When they got to the hill, he saw the point of the careful arrangement of the poplar logs. There were four sets of logs perpendicular to the hill, with the spaces between filled by four more sets parallel and the last set of three logs in a pyramid at the top.

Many of the men had carried shovels up to the hill and now one of them was offered to Mike.

"You must help in the first cut of the turf," Givi said quietly, holding a hand out for the axe. "Stand by the base of one of the logs in the triangle and when Father Kulcyanov says, cut into the turf in a sort of circle towards the next log over, moving to your right. There will be one of the other axemen halfway between. Just cut to where he has started. Try to make it even."

Mike did as he was told, watching Father Kulcyanov for the signal. The old man was standing under the pyramid of logs in what looked almost like a trance, looking to the west. At a certain point he raised his arms, held them for a moment, and then dropped them.

Mike had been looking in the same direction and realized that the sun had finally hit the tip of one of the distant mountain-tops. He ignored it, though, as he dug down into the hard turf, making a cut in it and then moving on towards the next man over. It didn't seem to be a race, but Mike hardly wanted to be last so he hurried while paying attention to getting a nice even curve. When he reached the point the other man had started at, he stopped.

"Kildar, we thank you for your assistance in the Rite of Spring," Father Kulcyanov said, formally. "The other men will complete the circle while the Burakan retire to rest for the events of the day."

"What do I do about the axe?" Mike asked, gratefully handing over the shovel. He was in decent shape but the exertions of the night had used muscle groups that were different from those he'd primarily been working.

"Keep it near you through the day," Kulcyanov replied. "You may choose a champion to carry it for you in the tests. I ask that you be in the village again at noon for the first feasting. The women of the village will prepare the food. You will choose the food of one among them to eat."

"Okay," Mike said, going over to Givi to get the axe. "Givi, a moment of your time?" he asked, taking the Keldara by the elbow.

"Yes, Kildar?" Givi asked when they were well away from the group at the top of the hill.

"Make sure that Katrina makes one of those lunches," Mike said. He looked at the raised eyebrow and shrugged. "I only know a few of the Keldara women by name, and most of those are taken already. I know Katrina's not going to have anyone ask for her lunch basket or whatever. And I don't want to step on toes."

"If you are chosen as Ondah, would you ask her to be your queen?" the Keldara asked, askance.

"I'm not going to be Ondah," Mike pointed out. "I'm going to throw in the towel, even if I get close. That's for people like Oleg or Vil, not me. I'm the Kildar. So it won't come up. Okay?"

"Of course, Kildar," Givi said, nodding.

"I'm going up to the serai until noon," Mike said, looking up at the sky and wincing. "I doubt I'm going to get much sleep."

"Mike," Adams said, walking up the hill. "Where the hell have you been?"

"It's a long story, man," Mike replied, walking down towards him. "You're just wondering now?"

"Mother Savina said you were with the Keldara last night," the chief said, glancing at the axe. "Nice. Buy it?"

"It's a loaner," Mike said. "I hope like hell you brought wheels. I'm not up to the climb up the hill at the moment."

CHAPTER
TWENTY-TWO

"So you've been up all fucking night?" Adams asked as Mike was sipping coffee.

"I've been up all night cutting down trees," Mike replied, working his back and shoulders. "And now I've got to be back down in the compound in . . ." He looked at his watch and shook his head, " . . . an hour and a half. And there's events all afternoon I'm supposed to compete in."

"Endurance test," Nielson said, nodding. "Nine men are chosen the night before, worked all night, given a short break, and then they have to compete all day. The winner is the king for the year."

"I hope like hell I don't get sacrificed in winter or something," Mike said.

"You've been reading the Golden Bough," Nielson said, chuckling. "Unlikely. Actual human sacrifice is pretty much gone from these rituals. But, you're right, this is very interesting stuff, especially since much of it isn't similar to local rites."

"Hey, Kildar," Vanner said, wandering in the kitchen for

coffee. "You don't look so hot. Another tough night with the new manager?"

"Bite me, Vanner," Mike said. "What do you make of that?" he asked, pointing at the axe. Since dawn he'd been able to see it better. It was definitely old, but very well maintained, with a silver edge to the blade and deep carvings on the head and haft that were distinctly Celtic looking.

"It's an axe," Vanner said.

"Is that all our intel specialist can dig up?" Adams asked, laughing.

"Okay, it's a big battle-axe," Vanner said, picking it up and looking at it. "Celtic? Where'd you get it?"

"It's part of the Keldara spring ritual," Mike said. "Take some pics and see if you can find anything similar on the Web. Originals, not modern. That's as original as they come, unless I'm much mistaken."

"This is a Keldara piece?" Vanner asked, puzzled.

"There are nine of them. Father Kulcyanov keeps four and the rest are with the other families," Mike replied. "That's the largest. They're all named. That one's called Culcander or Culcaner or something."

"*Not* Culculane?" Nielson asked, sharply.

"Not Culculane," Mike said, nodding. "But similar, don't you think? Anyway, see what you can find."

"Will do," Vanner said. "Although I was hoping to go to this festival today."

"Just see what you can find fast," Mike said. "And get pics. I've got to be out of here, with it, in about an hour."

"Can do," Vanner replied, getting his coffee and leaving.

"Why are you so worked up about where the Keldara come from?" Adams asked.

"I over analyze," Mike told him, grinning. "You said so yourself. I need a favor from you guys."

"My wife, sure. My toothbrush, maybe. My knife, never," Adams said, grinning.

"I need you to carry the axe for me," Mike said. "It's supposed to stay near me all day but it can be carried by a 'designated champion.' You're so designated."

"Thanks buddy," Adams said, glancing at the weapon. "I'm a spear carrier now, huh?"

"That would be you," Mike said. "And I don't want to bring the ladies with *me* since I think I'm treading on really shaky ground. But they should be able to participate. Get someone as an escort for each of them and bring them down to the village at noon. That's when the festivities mainly begin. Have a picnic lunch packed. Nielson, if you'd escort Anastasia, Adams maybe Klavdiya, etcetera. Make sure they're briefed that I probably won't be able to spend much time on them. I'll try to get a chance to explain to Anastasia myself."

"You'd better," Adams said. "She looked all pouty last night when you didn't come home."

"She's supposed to *reduce* my stress," Mike said with a sigh. "Nielson, you explain it. I've got too much on my plate."

"She'll be fine," Nielson said, grinning. "And if she's not, I've got a belt."

"Oh, brother," Mike moaned, dropping his face into his hands.

Mike took his Mercedes back to the compound since he was damned if he was going to walk the hill. He had to stop short of the raised area, though, since it seemed the entire Keldara tribe was out in force.

Children were running around at random, with a shouting, milling throng damaging the flowers on the Maypole by trying to get the eggs and cakes off the top. The women and teenaged girls, however, were lined up by the houses, most of them holding baskets, while the men stood opposite them. There didn't seem to by any order to it, either by house or station, but Mike wedged himself in near Vil.

"What now?" he asked the other Burakan.

"Father Kulcyanov figures out when it's noon," Vil said, pointing to the old man who, alone among the adult males, was standing by the Maypole. "Then he gives a blessing and we head for the women whose baskets we want to eat from."

"Okay," Mike said as the elder shooed the children away and considered the shadow of the pole. After a moment, Kulcyanov raised his hands.

"Father of All," the man boomed across the square, "we ask that you bring us fertility and good crops this year and that you bless the food that you have given us. Bless, too, this celebration of the return of your son and bring us a king that is worthy to stand in his stead."

When he lowered his arms the men moved forward, homing in on the ladies whose baskets they preferred. There was a certain amount of jostling for some of the girls who weren't effectively spoken for, but none around Katrina, who was looking a bit forlorn.

"Hello, Katrina," Mike said, stepping over to her. "Mind if I share your basket?"

"I had hoped you would," the girl replied, smiling like the rising sun. "But with women of your own, now . . ."

"They are not Keldara," Mike pointed out. "Where do we eat?"

"There is a nice spot up the hill," she said, gesturing to the rise behind the village.

"More hills," Mike muttered, but followed her.

The girl led him up the hill to one of the streams that speckled the ridge. About a hundred meters above the valley, there was a small spot where the stream fell through a moss-filled crack then over a ridge of granite and another short fall. The ledge of granite continued on either side, flat and smooth from flooding, to banks of earth. The banks were currently covered in flowers of a type he didn't recognize. There was just enough dry sand on one side of the ledge for the picnic to be laid out. He could see the compound through the trees and the caravanserai clearly and there were other couples in the woods in their own chosen bowers. But the screening trees, the banks and the babbling stream gave a feeling of intimacy. Too much intimacy in his opinion.

"I'm surprised you're allowed up here like this," Mike said as Katrina began unpacking the basket. "All that stuff about unmarried girls not being around men and all that."

"The spring festival is different," Katrina said, laying out the food. There was the inevitable bread and cheese and beer. She set out one bottle and tied the others with string to dangle in the stream. Besides the basics there were some more of the oat cakes and brightly painted eggs. "Things are allowed that are not allowed the rest of the year."

Mike considered a discussion of fertility rites and then decided it would both go over her head and be a very uncomfortable discussion. He was remarkably attracted to the little redhead. He knew a good bit of that was his other head thinking, but there was something about her that appealed to him immensely. She just . . . fit in a way that most women hadn't.

"The spring festival is about fertility," she continued, looking up at him shyly. "That is why we set up the Maypole and decorate it with the colors of the season, that we can have good crops for the year. It's said that a girl who is pregnant can touch it and her delivery will be easy. And . . . a girl who gets pregnant will have a boy."

"Lots of reasons to get pregnant today, then," Mike said, frowning. "But not if you're unmarried."

"I would not get pregnant today," she said, not looking at him. "It's not my time. Not that I'm in the bleeding," she continued, quickly, looking up at him. "Just that I'm not at my time. So . . ."

"No," he said, although it took a lot to drag it out of him. "It wouldn't be good for you and you know it. And it would be bad for me, as well."

"You're just in love with that blonde witch you brought in," Katrina said, angrily.

"I'm hardly in love with Anastasia," Mike said, smiling faintly. "Pretty as she is. And she's not nearly as pretty as you. So there."

"You say that, but you never do anything about it," Katrina said, pouting. "I could do the thing with the mouth."

"Don't go there," Mike said, shaking his head and telling himself to get down. "Let's just eat lunch and avoid that particular subject. If we can."

"Very well, Kildar," the girl said, primly. "If you insist."

"I do, I do," Mike said. "What do you think the women would think of selling their beer?"

"We already do to the village," Katrina said. "Not the best, mind you."

"I'd noticed," Mike said, opening the bottle and pouring some for each of them. "But I was talking about a lot of it. Enough to ship overseas. That would take a full microbrewery at least. We'd have to make thousands of bottles for it to be worthwhile."

"I don't know about that," Katrina said, frowning. "I don't know how you'd do that. We just make it in the home."

"I don't know how to do it either," Mike admitted. "But that's what consultants are for. But if we started making Keldara beer as a microbrewery we'd probably be able to sell it in Europe or the States. It's outstanding beer. And the money, most of it, would flow to the Keldara. I'd have a stake as well, but I'd just take a small cut of the profits."

"Mother Lenka would be the person to talk to about that," Katrina said. "She knows all there is to know about making beer."

"But Mother Lenka is not here," Mike replied, smiling. "You are, so I talk to you."

"I like it when you talk to me," Katrina said. "You don't treat me like I'm strange or someone to be avoided. You pay attention to me for me."

"Well, being gorgeous helps," Mike pointed out, smiling. "But you're not all that strange at all. You're just strange to the Keldara. And they're not used to much strangeness."

"And you are?" Katrina asked.

"Trust me," Mike said. "You're not a patch on some of the girlfriends I've had. I won't get into the list, don't know if I could remember all of them, but you're not nearly as strange as half of them. But I do care for you, a great deal. It's one of the reasons I won't sleep with you; I don't want you to get hurt. And here we are back on that subject."

"If you hadn't brought all those girls into your household there would be a place for me," Katrina said, sadly. "But you did. And that foreign witch."

"I needed Anastasia because of the rest," Mike replied. "But, trust me, if you were in the household it would be a special place. I'd like you to make your home among the Keldara, though, if you can. And if it turns out you can't . . . we'll talk. But not this spring, it's too soon. You're far too young . . ." He held up a hand to forestall the response. "I know, among the Keldara you should be married already. But among *my* people you're far too young. And, yes, some of the girls that we picked up are younger. I had them thrown on me, I didn't have much choice. And I don't intend to . . . open them until they're a bit . . . older. Besides, there's more out there than just me. I'd like you to try to live life before you throw yourself at me. And if you can't . . . we'll talk. That's all I've ever promised and it's all I will."

"You are the most stubborn man," Katrina said, exasperatedly.

"Get used to it," Mike said. He'd been eating as they talked and he wiped his hands. "I hope like hell I can just watch for the rest of the day but I get the impression I'm supposed to participate in these contests."

"You are one of the Burakan," Katrina said, shocked. "Of course you have to compete."

"More luck me," Mike said, laying back and looking at the sky. "I'd rather just lie here and sleep. This is a nice spot."

"I like it very much," Katrina said, crossing the blanket and lying down by him. "Is this permitted?"

"Very much so," Mike replied, putting one arm under her head. "But that's all the touching we're going to do."

"I think this is where the water sprites come to play," Katrina said, snuggling into him. "In the spray and the falls of the stream. It is a very pretty place."

"Pretty girl, pretty place to snuggle and I've got to go, what? Throw a bull? I've never thrown a bull in my life. Carry big rocks? Done that in SEAL training. Toss a big log? Wrestle?"

"And jump the fire pit," Katrina said. "You must play with the bull, also, not just toss it. The Burakan are judged on their artistry in playing with the bull."

"Great," Mike grunted. "I should have been in the rodeo. Maybe I'll play the rodeo clown, I saw one of them one time. It looked like a hell of a way to make a living."

"Whatever you do, do not let yourself get directly in front of the bull's horns," Katrina said. "It will gore you for sure."

"Hold on," Mike said, sitting up. "It's got *horns*?"

"Of course," Katrina said, sitting up as well. "It is a fighting bull."

"You could get *killed* that way," Mike pointed out, realizing how fatuous the statement was after he said it. "Are they *nuts*?"

"It is a test of courage," Katrina said, her eyes narrowing. "You're not afraid are you?"

"Of *course* I'm afraid," Mike said, then frowned. "In *my* culture it's not a shame to admit fear. You just work through it. Sure, there's times you don't mention it. In a sub comes to mind. But you just do the damned job. But fighting with a *bull*? With *horns*? That's nuts!"

"You admit to being afraid?" Katrina said, amazed.

"I've been flat terrified more times than I want to remember," Mike said, thinking about a corridor stinking with dead bodies, not to mention spraying poison gas in a closed room. "There was one time," he said, avoiding those particular, highly classified, events, "when I had a double failure on a jump. You know what a parachute is?"

"No," Katrina said, frowning.

"It's a device for jumping out of airplanes," Mike said, picking up one of the napkins and holding it by the corners. "Imagine this as a very big piece of fabric," he said, pulling it through the air. "You jump out of the plane and then pull a ring so that the big fabric, attached to strings, comes out. And you float down through the air."

"That must be exciting," Katrina said, her eyes wide. "You have done this?"

"A couple of thousand times," Mike said. "I used to instruct in it. But one time, on a training jump, the chutes wouldn't come out of the bags they were in. You use two, for safety, but neither one would come out. I had to struggle to get the reserve deployed. It didn't open until I was a couple of hundred feet off the ground and we'd jumped from higher than the mountains," he said, gesturing at the peaks around them. "Now *that* was frightening. But there was a reason for me to be doing it." He thought about it for a moment and then shrugged.

"Okay, I'll admit it, I'd still be jumping for fun if I was in the States." He thought about it some more and shrugged again. "So maybe fighting a bull isn't so nuts after all. But I don't know *how*."

"Grab it by the horns," Katrina said, holding out her hands. "Get to the side and pull down on the horns to the side. Twist the head and force it to the ground and the body will follow."

"Sounds easy," Mike said, grinning. "And it's not, is it?"

"No," Katrina admitted. "Do not let it get you in front of its horns or it will hook up and you will be done."

"Thanks for the handy safety tip," Mike said, standing up and holding out his hand. "And on that note, I think we'd better be getting back."

"Yes, we should," Katrina said, unhappily. But she took his hand. However, when he hauled her to her feet she continued up, swarming on him and planting a kiss on his lips.

Mike leaned into it for a moment, their tongues tangling, then pulled himself away. More like pried her off.

"Very nice," he said, setting her back on her feet reluctantly. "But I'm going to be late."

"You are so very stubborn," Katrina said, shaking her head. But she started to pack up the lunch.

The first test was the test of the stone. A course had been laid out, about thirty meters long, with a line at the end and one huge fucking stone at the beginning.

"In the test of the stone, the contestant must pick up the stone and carry it to the far line, then back," Father Mahona said for the benefit of the visitors. Most of the Keldara were gathered to watch, along with the trainers and the women from the castle. Mike was glad to see about five of the trainers were missing, which meant Adams and Nielson had kept a reaction team around. He'd worried that if the Chechens got frisky today, nobody was in a position to do anything about it. He also wondered when would be a good time to point out to the Keldara that future festivals were going to be interrupted by personnel being on duty. "A count is kept starting from when they cross the first line until they get back to the line. He who makes it to the far line and back fastest wins. If you drop the stone you are permitted to pick it back up and finish."

The Burakan weren't the only ones participating in the test; in fact they went last. A few of the Keldara men were lined up to try their hand and as Mike watched the first one lift the stone, Russell wandered over to get in the line.

"Going to try your hand, Russell?" Mike called.

"Going to show them how it's supposed to be done, Kildar," the former Ranger called back.

The first Keldara hefted the stone on his legs, then up to hold it with it mostly across his forearms, and staggered forward. As he crossed the line the whole group of Keldara began clapping, in time, on their thighs with a few of his friends yelling encouragement and trying to speed the clapping up. He dropped it halfway back, had to get it back up, and finished in about a minute and a half.

The other Keldara went one by one, most of them dropping the rock at one point or another and only one finishing in under a minute.

Then it was Russell's turn. The massive former Ranger had found some chalk somewhere and first chalked his hands, then bent at the knees and got the rock up, getting his hands all the way under it and twisting them in a complex fashion. Once it was in place, he took off.

Instead of the stagger that the Keldara effected, he did the first part of the course at a fast walk, the stone held all the way off his legs and freeing them up so he could really move. He finished in less than forty seconds, which the Keldara seemed to find amazing.

When he finished the course, despite blowing hard at the effort, he hefted the stone up and over his head, finally tossing it away from him and stepping back with a bow.

"Show off," Mike said when the Ranger strolled over. He was still breathing in and out slowly and deeply, but the effort clearly hadn't significantly strained him.

"The thing's about five-fifty," he said, handing Mike a block of chalk. "Strongman competitions use one that's about eight hundred. This is easy time. The thing to do is get it all the way up and hook your fingers," Russell whispered, demonstrating the finger lock. "You have to let the weight fall mostly on your right index finger; it keeps the fingers locked that way. Then just *go*."

The Burakan were next and Mike watched carefully. His competitors used the same technique as the regular Keldara and mostly made about the same time. The exception was Oleg, who hefted the stone nearly up to his chin and took off at a fast walk like Russell. He just had the muscles to hold the damned thing up that high, even without using the finger lock. He made the course in just under fifty seconds. Still not as good as Russell, but Mike's time to beat.

Mike suddenly realized that his competitive streak had taken over as he walked over to the stone. All SEALs had a competitive streak; you had to have one to make it through BUDS and on the teams. He wasn't intending to win the trial; if it came down to cases he'd throw one of the competitions. But he was damned well going to hang in as long as he could.

Mike looked at the stone, slowly chalking his hands and considering the course. When his hands were well chalked he bent at the knees and got the thing up on them without much of a struggle. He'd worked with weights that were heavier but not much and this thing was just *awkward*. He hooked his fingers under the rock as Russell had shown him and then stood up. It was solid. Sure that he had it, he stepped off as fast as he could.

He was fine on the first length but something about the turn made his fingers start to slip. He still managed to keep a hold on the stone but he had to slow down to keep it from slipping. He still made it across in respectable time, just about the same as Oleg.

He still had enough of a hold to heft the thing up in a clean jerk over his head and toss it off like Russell.

"Very impressive, Kildar," Father Mahona said. "The next test is the test of the wood."

CHAPTER
TWENTY-THREE

"Caber toss," McKenzie said, quietly, as the Keldara moved over to the next course. "I'll join in. The technique is like what Russell showed you on the stone, but you have to get a run going and really *toss* it. Watch me."

The log was about ten feet long and "the thickness of a man's thigh." Mike wasn't sure if it had been cut the night before by one of the other Burakan or if it was an old log, but it had been stripped of bark and sanded. There was a line on the ground and a flat area behind, apparently for the run up. Although Mike was trying to figure out how you were supposed to run with the damned thing.

A few of the Keldara lined up as Father Ferani explained for the non-Keldara.

"The contestants will pick up the log with their hands and run up to the line. Then they will toss it as far as they can. The first point that any part of the log lands on is the distance and that is the measurement for this competition. The competitor must not cross the line either before or after they release the log or the toss is disqualified."

The first Keldara got the log up vertical then bent down and got it up on his right shoulder. He backed up with the thing precariously balanced on his shoulder and ran forward, stopping at the line to throw it out. The log went forward still more or less vertical and the bottom touched the ground about ten feet out. It looked pretty respectable to Mike.

The rest of the Keldara tossed one by one, leaving divots from seven to eleven feet out, with one of them dropping it on the run; then it was McKenzie's turn.

Like Russell he had chalked his hands and at the beginning he started much like the Keldara, getting the log vertical. But he put it on his left shoulder and balanced it carefully, his hands locked underneath, before starting off on a run.

He ran faster than most of the Keldara but the big difference was in the toss. He turned at the last, throwing the thing backwards, his feet just at the edge of the line. The log, instead of staying more or less vertical, described a parabola in the air with the end impacting first. It gave him a good six to eight feet beyond the longest toss of the Keldara.

"Don't go as close to the line as I did," McKenzie said, walking over to Mike. "But toss it from your left and over. The body helps you get the lift on it and you can flip it over that way. The arms are also more suited for that sort of toss with a weight that strong. Put more strength into your right arm, too. Walk the distance off before you start and turn one step before the line."

The other Burakan went one at a time. Most of them were around the same distance as the other Keldara. Oleg was the exception. The massive Keldara still used the same technique, but he had the strength to really loft the damned thing, getting it to turn over like McKenzie and getting it nearly as far.

Mike ignored the eyes on him as he walked off the course, getting the distance just right and trying the turn. He marked the spot to start on the turf with his heel and then went over to pick up the log. He got it up easily enough, but balancing it was a different story. He was afraid he'd drop it on the run but put that out of his mind.

He carefully walked to the starting point, then staggered forward as fast as he could, keeping the log balanced, turning at the marked point and tossing it over his back like McKenzie.

When he turned around he had to grin. The divot that his log had dug was right on top of Oleg's.

"Looks like it's you and me, buddy," Mike said to Oleg as they walked to the next test.

"You are formidable, Kildar," the Keldara admitted. "As should be. It will be an honor to beat you."

"That's the spirit," Mike said. "I think you're going to lose a Kildar on the test of the bull."

"Watch me, carefully," Oleg said, seriously. "The other tests have their dangers. But the test of the bull is the true test of courage. You must first play with it and then stand your ground, letting it come to you before grasping the horns. That is the moment of truth; if you flinch you will be badly injured or killed. I would hate to see that happen."

"Me too," Mike admitted, waving to Adams.

"Got something for me?" Adams asked.

"Get with Doc Forgate," Mike said. "The test of the bull is coming up. Make sure he's standing by to give aid. Including advanced aid. If anybody gets really gored, he's going to have to stabilize them so we can get them to the hospital."

"Will do," the chief said, walking back over to the trainers.

The next test, though, was the test of fire. A large triangular area had been dug out and a fire laid on it. The fire had burned down, leaving only coals.

"This is the test of fire," Father Makanee said, waving at the coals. "The contestant must jump the coals, barefoot. He must choose the widest place he thinks he can jump. It is a test of both courage and wisdom. Knowing your limits is the true test."

"Point of order," Adams said, holding up his hand. "Does the contestant *have* to jump the coals?"

"To win they must pass from one side to the other," Father Makanee said, frowning. "The one to cross at the widest point wins."

Adams looked over at Mike and winked. It was all he had to do.

The military sometimes went through bizarre periods. During the previous administration, there had been a brief fad for bringing in oddball "motivational specialists" to "improve the understanding of the military." The guys were mostly idiots, or parroted stuff the military had dreamed up first. A few had had some useful things to say. But the one that Mike knew Adams was thinking of was the firewalker.

The teams, one by one, had been sent through this guy's "motivational course." Most of it was right out of the military handbook for using physical tasks to build confidence. The problem being that his "physical tasks" had been extremely basic from a SEAL point of view. He'd even had an "obstacle course" that was so laughably easy the SEALs had played through the whole thing.

But at midnight the fire walking had started. They'd had the theory explained to them carefully and it worked. You really *could* walk over coals just like these. You had to step carefully and, most of all, have absolute confidence. Nobody really had figured out *why* you had to be confident and calm to do it, but you did. However, Mike was "in the zone." He knew he could cross the widest part. And, best of all, in a way that nobody among the Keldara would believe.

He didn't pay much attention as the Keldara jumped the fire pit, letting himself fall into an alpha state that was much like autohypnosis. He simply envisioned himself walking across the coals and the fire not touching him. He dropped out a bit when Oleg came up, watching in disinterest as the Keldara backed up and ran at the pit. He didn't make the widest jump, that had been Vil, and when he landed his heel came down in the fire. He rolled over, grasping at his heel and grimacing.

Mike watched it all in disinterest then removed his boots carefully. He dragged his feet on the grass as he walked to the coals, ensuring that nothing was sticking to his feet, and then paused at the side of the fire.

"Kildar," Father Makanee said, quietly. "You cannot possibly jump here."

"I'm not gonna jump," Mike said, distantly but distinctly, his voice carrying across the buzz of the Keldara. Which immediately silenced as everyone turned to watch. He raised his face and hands to the sky and stepped off onto the coals, his mind adrift.

Slowly and carefully he walked across the hot coals. Each foot was placed perfectly, much like when he was doing a sneak, and his mind was sitting on another plane. When he stepped off onto the grass on the far side instead of applause there was stunned silence from the Keldara.

Mike lowered his hands and face and just rode the endorphin rush. It was amazing what doing the fire walk felt like when you finished; one of the SEALs had let slip that it felt like doing a line of coke. When he finally looked up the first eye he caught was Katrina's, who was looking at him as if he'd walked over water instead of fire. He couldn't help it, he winked.

"Are you well, Kildar?" Oleg asked, limping over.

"Very," Mike said, grinning at him. "It's an amazing rush. I'll show you how to do it sometime. It's like the thing with the bull; you have to know how and be supremely confident."

"You're not burned?" Oleg asked, amazed.

"Not a bit," Mike said, lifting up one sole to show him. The skin wasn't even red.

"The Kildar is the winner of the test of fire," Father Makanee said, clearly and distinctly.

"I've got to throw one of these," Mike said to Adams as they walked to the bull pen.

"Just checking out of this one might be a good idea," Adams said, quietly. "I took a look at that bull. It's a monster."

The bull was, indeed, a monster. It stood about five feet at the shoulder and must have weighed over a ton. This time there were a few Keldara baiting it from the solid stone walls, but nobody was getting in to play.

"The test of the bull," Father Shaynav said, standing on a platform to one side of the ring. He was wearing his bull cape and holding a stick with a hook on the end for controlling the bull through the ring in its nose. Evidently, if things went wrong it was the elder's job to control the bull. "Each contestant must bring the bull's body fully to the ground and hold it there for three seconds to pass the test. The contestant will be judged upon both his defeating the bull and his skill and prowess in working with the bull in the ring. The test is a test of courage, skill and wisdom. Those who do not know their ability will fall to the power of the bull."

Vil was the first to enter the ring. He leapt lightly off the wall, on the bull's offside, and ran around the ring to get behind it.

The bull saw him out of the corner of his eye, though, and turned in place, snorting and pawing the ground. As the Keldara continued in a circle the bull continued to spin in place, trying to get a good read on the adversary.

Vil trotted around the more or less circular enclosure once, then darted in to touch the bull on the flank. The beast spun quickly when touched and charged at him but Vil dodged out of the way, laughing, and touched it on the other flank.

He continued to play with the bull, touching it on the flanks and back and even once on the head. But it was clear the Keldara was running out of steam by the time he really confronted the animal, darting in just at the base of the neck and grasping the horns in both hands, then stepping forward and down.

The bull resisted the twist, trying to shake off his gadfly and then falling over on his side.

Vil held him down just long enough for the count, then darted up and raised his hands in victory as he ran to the wall.

Most of the rest of the Burakan duplicated the performance, running the bull in circles and then darting in at the end to throw it. The good part about it from Mike's perspective was that they were wearing the animal down; it was covered in sweat by the time Oleg got in the ring. But the bad part was it was also getting angrier.

Oleg was still limping from the fall in the fire and he wasn't as fast as the rest. The bull was able to line up on him more than once and charge. The second time required a roll away from a head sweep that surely would have gored the Keldara badly. That time Oleg was clearly done and leapt to his feet, getting behind the sweeping head and throwing the bull with a massive heave. Mike wasn't sure how well he counted against the rest; his throw had been almost effortless but his "play" time had been mediocre.

Unfortunately, it was Mike's turn. He decided that the only choice was to simply be confident that he could duplicate the performance but get it over with as soon as possible. He leapt off the low stone wall and waved at the bull.

"Come on, big guy," he said, taunting the thing to charge. "Come and get me."

The bull seemed confused by an adversary that didn't run in circles.

"Come on," Mike repeated, waving his hands. "I'm right here."

The bull swung his head from side to side, looking at the human doubtfully, then quickly put his head down and charged.

Mike was taken aback by the speed. He'd been watching from the wall but that was different than being the one on the ground. The charge was lightning fast and he half instinctively stepped forward. He tried to get to the side but the bull corrected at the last moment and he suddenly found himself right where he wasn't supposed to be: directly in front of a charging bull.

But the step forward had gotten him inside of the bull's intended charge. He grabbed the horns desperately, holding them off of him as the bull hooked upward for a gore.

Again, by instinct as much as anything he jumped as the bull hooked up, riding the gore instead of being thrown by it. He suddenly found himself heading upward at a tremendous rate and let go of the horns. The throw of the bull tossed him up and over like an acrobat. He'd been in the air before, though, in freefall and he quickly adjusted his body position for a landing, hitting the ground actually *behind* the bull and rolling into a perfect parachute landing fall that actually rolled him to his feet.

He hadn't intended anything like that but he dusted off his left shoulder nonchalantly as the bull spun in place, looking for its adversary. He wasn't about to try to replicate the feat, however, so he stepped to the side quickly, keeping inside of the circle of the bull's turn and out of sight.

The bull could hear him and it quickly turned back but Mike reversed course, still staying to the side. The bull was wearing and couldn't turn as fast as it had at the beginning so Mike was able to repeat the move a couple of times as he figured out exactly how you got your hands on the horns in the right way.

His first attempt, however, was nearly his last. He stepped forward to the base of the bull's neck like the others and grabbed at the horns but only his right hand connected. The bull reacted with a massive head toss and Mike, again, felt himself yanked through the air as the incredible strength of the bull made nothing of his weight.

The toss pulled him across the bull's neck, half wrenching his right arm out of its socket. He rolled with it, though, landing on his feet on the far side of the bull and letting go with his right. Just for shits and giggles he grabbed with his left and, sure enough, the bull dragged him across its neck again to land on his feet.

Mike reached forward with both hands this time but the bull had had enough and actually jumped half sideways to line him up for another charge.

Mike grabbed the horns more to keep them away from him

than anything and found himself in the air again, this time in a flat toss across the bull's shoulder. There wasn't much he could do with that but take it on the chin. So much for points for grace.

He got up much more slowly this time and by the time he was on his feet the bull was charging again. He darted into it and caught the horns, first dropping his weight to try to pull it down and then, when it was clear he was about to be killed, leaping up.

This time he was ready for the ride through the air and managed a flip that landed him on the bull's rump. He only touched, jumping off immediately, and landing on both feet behind the bull again.

He quickly spun in place, into the bull's turn, and this time got both hands on the bull's horns with his weight down. He wrestled with the bull much less smoothly than the Keldara but in a moment he had it on the ground.

He'd had enough of fucking around with the damned thing, though, so as soon as he let go he was out of the enclosure.

"Impressive, Kildar," Father Shaynav said, walking over to him.

"Luck," Mike said, knowing the truth of the statement.

"You said you'd never wrestled a bull before," Oleg said, walking over to him. "You are, without doubt, the winner of the test of the bull. If you win at the test of the man you will be Ondah."

"Which is why I'm going to step out of the competition," Mike said, looking at Oleg and the elder. "I do not want to be Ondah. And I'm afraid I *do* have special training that would be unfair to use in the test of the man. Perhaps after we have done more training with the Keldara it would be a fair test. But after the test is complete, I will give a demonstration with Chief Adams."

"This is . . . not right," Father Shaynav said, frowning. "If you are the best, you should be Ondah."

"I am *Kildar*," Mike pointed out. "It is not right that the Kildar be the best, without being the Ondah? Which is the higher honor? Should I take the honor from my . . . retainers by taking their one chance of glory? If you wish me to compete, I'll compete. But if the test of the man is as lacking in rules as the other tests, I'm afraid I will do damage to the Keldara that I fight."

"We are strong," Oleg protested.

"You should compete," Father Shaynav said, definitely.

"Get the other elders," Mike snapped.

When the group had gathered together, with the rest of the Keldara held back from what was clearly an important discussion, Mike raised his hands.

"I will not take the honor of Ondah," Mike said. "With the other tests, frankly, I had hoped I would fail. But I strongly doubt, even against Oleg, that I will fail the test of the man. I have seen the Keldara in fights, I know my own ability and I doubt that I will lose. But I *refuse* to take the position of Ondah. What does Ondah mean to the Kildar?"

"If you do not, you take the honor of the position from the one who it goes to," Father Mahona said, angrily. "I have been Ondah. I knew that I was the *best*. You would take that from your people, Kildar."

"Yes, *Kildar*," Mike pointed out. "You have said before, is it not good that you have a 'true Kildar' again? Is it not good, correct, that the Kildar be the best? But why should he take the Ondah from such as Oleg or Vil? What is such an honor to the Kildar? And, understand, when I fight, without rules, damage is done. I'm a *trained* fighter. I am a *trainer* in hand-to-hand combat. SEAL hand to hand, which is dirty, brutal and short. If you wish, when the others have fought, I will either demonstrate with Chief Adams, who I know will not be seriously hurt, or I will fight against the winner. But if I fight against an untrained Keldara, they will be in Doc Forgate's care. Trust me on this."

"We must discuss this, Kildar," Father Kulcyanov said, formally. "The elders."

"Very well," Mike said, nodding. "I'm going to get a beer."

"What's going on?" Adams said when Mike walked over to the group of trainers.

"I'm in the running to win the medal or whatever," Mike said. "I don't want it. It's for the Keldara. I never should have been in the competition. I assumed that I'd get beat at some point. But I didn't. Hell, I even managed the bull."

"You were wonderful," Anastasia said, her eyes glowing. "You were much better than the others. Is this bull jumping an American thing?"

"Nobody, not even rodeo clowns, is stupid enough to do that," Killjoy interjected. "Were you fucking nuts?"

"I didn't *mean* to do it," Mike said. "I was just trying to stay alive. It was luck and some training in other stuff. But the point is, if I fight the Keldara—"

"You're going to kick their ass," Adams said, nodding. "And take the medal or crown or whatever."

"And not only is that their prize," Mike said. "But you know how I fight."

"You'd put them in the hospital," Adams replied.

"So I don't want to," Mike said. "I told them I'd demonstrate with you."

"What, you want to get your ass kicked?" Adams asked, grinning.

"You're out of shape and getting old, fuckwad," Mike replied. "I'd put *you* in the hospital. But *you* I can lose for a while; the Keldara start training on Monday."

"I'd put *you* in the hospital," Adams said. "You've been out of the teams too long to be any good anymore."

"Bets?" Mike asked. "The point is, I probably wouldn't put you in the hospital or vice versa. But I don't want to fight a damned Keldara. He doesn't know how to block for shit."

"There's that," Adams admitted.

"Here they come," Mike said as the huddle among the elders broke up.

"The Kildar has said that he does not want to take the title of Ondah," Father Kulcyanov said, facing the gathered groups. "The Ondah is a title for the Keldara. But to show that he is not fearful of the test of man, he has agreed to fight the winner. Not for the title, but simply for honor. As he has said, the Kildar *should* be the best. But the Ondah is a title for the Keldara."

"Thank you for this ruling," Mike said, waving at the elders. "Let's continue."

Two circles had been marked out on the ground in front of the Keldara houses. The competition was double elimination, with the losers facing losers and the winners facing winners until one person was victorious. The rules were rather basic, no kneeing of the balls and no gouging. Anything else, up to and including biting, seemed to be allowed. A fall was counted as any point other than the feet or hands on the ground, best three falls won. Anyone stepping out of the circle stopped the competition and twice out of the circle counted for a fall.

The Keldara were brawlers. In general, the two contestants would close, punch for a bit and then get into a grapple. They used backing and hip throws in the main. Oleg had a tendency to just pick up his opponent and toss him down on his back. Vil and Oleg were the last two fighters after about an hour of competition. Oleg got a good hold on Vil a couple of times and tossed him but the lighter Keldara was quick and landed on feet and hands. Oleg finally got him down three times, one on a hip throw and the other two by literally throwing him to the ground so hard it overcame Vil's ability to keep himself up.

"Oleg is the winner of the test of man," Father Kulcyanov said. "Oleg is the Ondah. But before he is crowned, he must face the Kildar."

"Crap," Mike said, stepping in the ring. "Oleg, you up for this?"

"I am well, Kildar," the Keldara said, crouching with hands half closed and his feet spread in what Mike would call a cat stance. He had a bleeding lip from a previous blow and a shiner forming on his eye. And his nose was bleeding. And he still had a slight limp from the fire. But he seemed pumped rather than battered. The guy just liked to fight.

"Well, try not to hurt me too much and I'll try not to hurt you too much," Mike said, standing on the balls of his feet in a horse stance. "Let's get this over with."

Oleg charged the Kildar and Mike let him come. The Keldara threw a strong roundhouse, which Mike blocked and then leaned into, grabbing him by one wrist and his shirt and continuing the rush over his outstretched leg. Instead of putting him facedown, though, Mike pulled back hard on the wrist, pressing down into the throw so the Keldara landed, hard, on his back. At the last minute he caught himself as he was about to break the arm across his leg. It was hard not to; it was a conditioned response, but he managed it. Oleg hit the ground, hard.

"Point to the Kildar," Father Kulcyanov said.

"Someday I'll show you what just happened," Mike said, helping the winded Keldara to his feet. "And how to fall."

Oleg waved his hands for a moment to get his breath and then got into his crouch again, closing much more slowly. He jabbed at Mike a time or two, which Mike easily blocked, and then closed.

Mike reacted automatically with a forekick to the Keldara's abdomen, following it up with a round kick that snapped Oleg's head to the side in a spray of blood and then a full flying kick to the back of the head that put the Kulcyanov on his face.

"Jesus," he said, darting forward. "Oleg, you okay?"

"I have never been beaten, Kildar," the Keldara said, getting up to his knees and hands and shaking his head as blood poured from his mouth. "But I am now. You hit worse than a bull. Where did you learn to kick like that?"

"I'm a damned *SEAL* instructor," Mike said, helping Oleg to his feet. "SEAL hand to hand isn't about fighting for fun. It's about doing so much damage to the other guy, he can't fight anymore. I was pulling my blows and not following through; you should be in the hospital with broken bones now. Or dead."

"And we will be taught this?" Oleg asked, wiping at his mouth.

"As much as I can," Mike said.

"Then next year, Kildar," the Keldara said, "I will purely kick your ass, as the instructors say." He spit out a mouthful of blood and worked his tongue in his mouth. It was obvious there were some loose teeth.

"Look forward to it," Mike said, laughing.

"I don't feel right taking the position of Ondah," Oleg admitted as the Keldara pressed forward. "You are the better."

"I'm the Kildar," Mike said. "I *should* be better."

CHAPTER
TWENTY-FOUR

The sun was setting by the time the last test was complete and the Keldara gathered in the yard of the houses, setting out tables and bringing out an evening feast. Mike had been smelling the steer roasting all afternoon and he was looking forward to the dinner.

The men and women sat separately, with the women doing the serving. The whole steer was brought into the space among the tables and set on a separate table to be carved. It had been roasted, whole, in a pit and looked and smelled wonderful.

The elders handled the carving with the help of the Burakan, Mike being excepted. The senior women, Anastasia being included in them as the de facto "woman of the Kildar" were actually served first with choice cuts from the ribs. The butt and withers were served to the younger men and women, the men getting the choicer cuts, the rest of the rib portion was served to the Burakan and the trainers. Last the elders, Mike and the senior trainers were served from the tenderloin. Each of the Burakan, including Mike, had their designated axes in front of them.

Mike was actually served dead last, which he found odd, but it was a huge hunk of the center of the tenderloin. There were potatoes and huge loaves of heavy bread as well as boiled cabbage and choice spring greens gathered from the woods. To drink there was the inevitable Keldara beer in pitchers. Mike was thirsty but he went light on the beer.

"You need to introduce broccoli," Nielson said as he dug into his own filet. "It grows fast and it's packed with vitamins."

"I'll talk to Genadi about it," Mike said, looking around for the farm manager. He was with the younger men, just below the married males in pecking order.

When most of the diners were finished, Father Kulcyanov stood up and raised his hands for silence.

"The tests of spring are complete," he said. "The Ondah has been chosen, Oleg of the Family of Kulcyanov. He is crowned the King of Spring," the elder said, simply.

He had carried a bag to the table and now dipped into it, removing a laureate that appeared to be made of some yellow vegetation.

"Crap," Nielson said.

"The Golden Bough," Mike replied in English, shaking his head as he recognized the distinct outline of dried mistletoe. "How fucking *old* is this ritual?"

"What are you talking about?" Adams whispered in English, leaning across Father Ferani as Father Kulcyanov placed the laureate on Oleg's head.

"Too long to explain," Mike whispered back. "There's a whole damned book about it. But we might be watching the oldest—"

"And most original," Nielson interjected.

"And most original spring rite in the world," Mike finished.

"What do you talk about?" Father Ferani asked suspiciously.

"This is a great honor," Mike said in Georgian, gesturing at Oleg who now stood up and held his hands up to applause. "This ritual is written of in books, but it was thought to be lost in time. The Keldara seem to have kept it, with some additions that might be . . . I don't know. But this is something that I never thought I'd see."

"Where did you hear of the mysteries?" Father Mahona interjected, sharply.

"There is a book," Mike said. "It lists many of the rites of spring around the world. But the giving of the Golden Bough has not been done, as far as the book is concerned, for centuries. The King of Spring, is he also called the King of the Wood?"

"This is something we do not speak of," Father Mahona snapped, sitting up rigidly and turning away.

"Sorry," Mike said, shrugging. "Shit," he added, closing his eyes.

"What?" Adams asked, ignoring the frown on Father Ferani's face.

"The rock pickers," Mike said. "The chant they used. It had something about Sybellios in it, I think."

"The Cebellian Mysteries?" Nielson said, excitedly. "You don't think . . . ?"

"I think we should stop talking about it," Mike said, looking at the expression on the elders' faces.

Oleg had left the high table and now walked down among the women, rubbing his chin in thought. He deliberately walked right past Lydia, looking over the young women and pausing by Irina, who was seated near her friend, then darting back and seizing Lydia, pulling her to her feet and kissing her in front of the whole group.

The girls gathered around Lydia, covered her in necklaces made from wildflowers and put a wreath on her head of flowers to match the one on Oleg's head.

This appeared to be the signal for everyone to get up from the table. As the women, with Lydia being the exception, started to clear the feast, Lydia and Oleg were led back to the main table and given a place of honor next to Mike.

"Congratulations," Mike said to the grinning Lydia.

"Oleg has tried for the last two years to win the Ondah," she admitted, beaming. "Last year he was beaten by Vil."

"That's hard to believe," Mike said.

"He did better on the test of the stone and the test of fire," Oleg said, leaning over to explain. "I always overestimate how far I can jump. Last year I was so badly burned, I had to stop."

"After I teach you how to walk on the fire, it will be a test of distance," Mike said, smiling.

"Everyone was amazed," Lydia said. "No one had seen anyone walk on fire. We'd heard of it, but..."

"It's really not that hard," Mike said. "Anyone can do it, even the women."

"That would make the test interesting," Oleg said, grinning.

"When do we light the bonfire?" Mike asked. "No, let me guess. At midnight, but the fires in the houses have to be extinguished first."

"You know our ways," Oleg said, his brow furrowing.

"I'm having a lovely time watching them," Mike admitted. "When your reading is a little better, I'll show you why. But... are there things that happen after the bonfire is lit?"

"There are mysteries that we don't even share with you, Kildar," Oleg said, formally.

"That's okay," Mike said. "I'd be surprised if you did."

When the feast was cleared, the group got up and headed for the hill with the bonfire laid on it. The other Burakan picked up their axes so Mike did the same.

"Kildar," Oleg said, walking beside him in the darkness. "We must bring the fire from the wood."

"Do you use the drill method?" Mike asked. "Or flint and tinder?"

"The drill," Oleg said, looking over at him in the moonlight. "Your reading again?"

"The needfire," Mike said. "*Teigin* something?"

"Yes," Oleg said, shaking his head. "I see the mysteries are not so mysterious."

"There are some," Mike said. "How do you do it?"

"There is an axletree set up," Oleg said, "with the drill protruding from it and into a plank of oak. Two of the Burakan hold the drill steady while the other six turn the axle. The Ondah is supposed to blow the fire to light. I think that you should do it. You are the true Ondah."

"Forget that," Mike said. "Getting the fire started is important and you're probably better at it than I am. You do it."

"As you wish, Kildar," Oleg said, clearly unhappy.

"You've started a fire with a drill before," Adams pointed out as the Keldara continued up the hill and Mike slowed down.

"Let him have his moment," Mike said.

A circular theater of turf benches had been set up around the fire, with four openings to let people through. Mike took a quick read on the stars and was pretty sure they were at the cardinal points of the compass. The axletree had been set up to one side and as the whole group filed into the area the nine Burakan stepped forward to bring the fire. Mike looked over at the caravanserai and, sure enough, somebody had turned off all the lights; the valley was in total darkness save for the moon. The duty squad was probably pissed as hell. On the other hand, Vanner had ended up wiring the whole cellars so they were probably down there playing cards and watching TV on the satellite.

The women had arranged themselves on the north side of the circle and the men on the south. As everyone settled into position, Father Kulcyanov carefully aligned the spokes of the axletree with what Mike assumed was ritual significance. But Mike, frankly, was ritualed out. He'd had a good meal and a long day. At this point, all he really wanted to do was sleep.

He took his designated position, however, and started turning the spokes on command. The drill was supported by a plank laid across two mounds of cut turf, drill held by Sawn and Vil, with Oleg crouched waiting for the fire.

Turning the spokes was boring at best. Mike wanted to get into the game but he was just too worn out to care. Finally, though, there was a flare of light from under the plank and Oleg waved for the whole assembly to be removed.

The fire was small, but Oleg carefully built it up with twigs until there were a few solidly burning brands. Then he transferred it to the kindling of the bonfire. In moments, the kindling had caught and started to work on the main logs.

"The *taigon-tar* is come," Father Kulcyanov said, raising his hands to the sky. "The Father of All looks upon us with kindness and will bring us good crops and a well people for the year. Let the *bannach caillean* be chosen."

"Dead on," Nielson said as Mike settled on the turf next to him. "Even the same pronunciation, which is surprising."

The older women went around among the men, passing out cakes. There was a brief discussion with Father Kulcyanov and a cake was given to Mike, but not to the trainers.

"Nine knobs," Mike said, showing it to Nielson.

"Bet you get the black bean," Nielson replied, grinning.

When all the cakes had been distributed to the men, Father Kulcyanov raised his hands again and then lowered them.

Mike followed the actions of the rest of the men and raised the cake to his mouth, biting into it. In ancient Scotland and England, each year a person would be chosen among the people for ceremonial purposes. There were various methods of choosing, but a bean in a cake, a "bannock," was one of the most common. The term that was used, the "bannach caillean," was just about dead on to what he recalled from reading about the ceremony lo those many years ago. Originally, the person had probably been sacrificed to propitiate the gods. Later they were simply subjected to various humiliations and mock sacrifices, such as being cast in the river or mock thrown in the fire. He *hoped* the Keldara weren't *absolutely* authentic; he wasn't about to stand by and allow an actual human sacrifice.

He fully expected a solid bean to be in the middle. But he didn't encounter anything on the first bite so he kept munching.

It wasn't hard, the oat cake had been made with a sweetener, probably honey, and covered with a sweet coating; it was quite good.

When he was about half way through the cake he heard a voice cry out on the left side of the fire and saw a Keldara he couldn't quite place spit out something on his hand.

"Gurun has the bean!" Vil called, laughing. He and another of the Keldara grabbed the sheepish man by the arms and pulled him to his feet. "Into the fire with him!"

"Into the fire!" the rest chanted as the man was dragged to the edge of the blazing bonfire.

"Kildar," Nielson whispered, seriously.

"Wait," Mike said. Everyone was grinning at the man's evident discomfiture; he couldn't believe even the Keldara would be grinning if Gurun was really going to be sacrificed.

As it turned out, Vil and the other Keldara simply pushed him at the fire, three times Mike noticed, and then pulled him back. After that they sat back down, with Gurun ruefully shaking his head.

"A year of bad luck," Father Mahona said, leaning over and pointing at the man with his chin. "That's the fate of the *caillean*. Do your books speak of this as well, Kildar?"

"Yes," Mike replied. "And that in the very old days the *caillean* was sacrificed for the promise of a good harvest."

"So it is said," Father Mahona said, sitting back with a blank look on his face.

"I'm glad to see that you've dispensed with that practice at least," Mike said. "I need every militiaman I can get," he added with a disarming smile.

The choosing of the *caillean* seemed to be the signal for the party to really commence. The two kegs that had been set on the hilltop were broached and as the younger men lined up on one, the women poured mugs from the second and started to serve the seniors, including the trainers. Mike, naturally, was served first and he used the first mouthful to wash out the last of the oat cake. It had been good, but it was a bit of a mouthful to eat without anything to wash it down.

After everyone had a beer, Sawn, Vil and two Keldara Mike didn't know gathered between the men and the women. Sawn was carrying a musical instrument that looked something like a small bagpipe while one of the unknown Keldara held a harp and the other a drum. Vil stood between them as they began to play.

"I wonder what McKenzie makes of all of this?" Mike asked. "Get him."

By the time the Scottish NCO had made his way over to Mike, the players had started to play.

"That's not a bagpipe, is it?" Mike asked. The instrument was softer and sweeter than any bagpipe he'd ever heard, but had the same continuous undertone.

"Uillean pipe," McKenzie said crouched behind him. "Similar but it hasn't got the full throw of a bagpipe. It was for playing indoors. The reason the Scots stuck to the bagpipe was the English outlawed both. You could play the pipe on the moors, get the damned Brits in an uproar and then run away."

"Or ambush them," Adams said.

"That too," the NCO admitted, grinning, as Vil began to sing. "The drum's a classic bodran, though."

"What the hell language is that?" Mike asked. He couldn't catch a word of it.

"It is very old," Father Makanee said from beside him. "We don't even know the words anymore. But it is traditional to be sung on the festivals."

"I wish Vanner was here," Mike mused. "He might be able to get something from it."

"He doesn't have to," McKenzie said, his voice low and sad. "It's the Gael. Oh, it's corrupted, but I recognize the Gael. Even some of the words." He hummed for a moment and then sang along. "Far is this land we come to, held in thrall by our king. We have followed the flight of the birds and come to this land of mountains. Our duty to guard the something something against the enemy. We only want to go back I'd guess is that word, to our land of water and green."

"They're *Irish*?" Mike asked, aghast.

"I wonder how old the term 'follow the wild geese' really is?" Nielson mused. "Most people place it from around the potato famine. But these guys—"

"They're bloody damned *Irish*?" McKenzie said, amazed.

"Ah, ah, ah," Nielson said, shaking his head. "They didn't come here in any history I know. That means they probably go back far enough that they're Scots. Remember—"

"We mostly changed places, I know," McKenzie growled. "You mean they're Scots?"

"They're Gael for sure," Nielson said. "Scots and Irish is quibbling at that antiquity. But *how* long ago? And how in the *hell* did they wind up in Georgia?"

"Wait," McKenzie said, holding up a hand as the song continued. "They traveled from their homes through . . . I don't get that part. Into heat and darkness? Many fights they were in, ever victors, and they took much gold. But they were defeated and . . . I think that's enslaved but it's not a Gael word. Their lord was cast down and they were sent here by . . . someone to be guards. Now they await the day they can return. They are the Keldaran, the homeless ones. They are . . . I don't recognize that one."

"Varangi," Nielson whispered, having caught the word clearly. "They're God-be-damned Varangians."

"What the hell had you and Nielson so worked up last night?" Adams said, sitting down across from Mike.

"Something God damned interesting," Mike replied.

After the song, the ritual had broken down into party including more singing, but most of that had been in Georgian. He'd ended up with Katrina and Anastasia on his knees, holding a conversation that he tuned out. Probably a bad idea, and Anastasia hadn't liked it when he more or less ignored her on getting back to the caravanserai. But it had been a long day and he passed out as soon as he hit the bed.

"You were completely checked out last night," Adams continued. "You and the colonel. You going to give?"

"Yeah," Mike said. "Call a meeting for around eleven. I'll try to get you guys to understand it then."

"The Keldara are the last remnant of the Varangian guard," Mike said when the whole group of trainers were gathered at the table.

"You're sure?" Vanner said, excitedly.

"Positive," Nielson replied, nodding. "Absolutely positive."

"Fucking *cool!*" Vanner spat.

"Okay, somebody going to explain what's got Vanner so excited?" Sergeant Heard asked.

"I think you guys should understand," Mike replied, nodding. "But you need to *really* understand. Okay, who's heard of the Selous Scouts?" He nodded when practically every hand went up. The Rhodesian group was a legend in the special operations community. "Okay, how about the battle at Thermopylae?" Fewer hands at that. "Spartans?" More hands. "Vikings?" Every hand shot up.

"I want you to think in those terms," Mike said. "But I gotta lecture, so try to stay awake. After the Western Roman Empire fell, it more or less moved to Constantinople, what's currently Istanbul, and the Byzantine empire was founded. One of the problems of the original Roman Empire, towards the end, was that the guards of the emperors, the Praetorian Guard, ended up picking and choosing who was going to be emperor. And they didn't always do a good job."

"Sort of like coups?" Russell asked.

"Sort of," Mike replied. "They were the kingmakers. To keep that from happening, the Byzantine emperors hired foreign mercenaries as their guards. The Vikings had started to move into Russia, conquering it, and they were in contact with Byzantines.

The Byzantine emperors hired those guys, 'fierce fighters from the north,' to be their guards. They were called the Varangi, which meant foreigner. They formed the Varangian Guard."

"We come from the land of the ice and snow," Adams half sang. "From the midnight sun where the hot springs blow, the hammer of the gods. So you're saying the Keldara are Vikings?"

"That's where it gets weird," Mike said. "McKenzie was able to translate one of their songs and, no, they're not Norse. They're Celts, Scottish or Irish, back then it didn't really matter. There *is* a lot of Norse in there, that's probably where the blonds and redheads and such come from."

"There are plenty of Irish redheads," Meller interjected.

"They got that from being repeatedly invaded by the Norse," Vanner said. "Back then, they were all dark hair and eyes."

"So what *probably* happened was that this group of foreigners was wandering around the Mediterranean," Nielson said. "Doing the usual rape, loot, pillage and burn. And they ran smack dab into the Byzantines, somehow. The survivors were probably given the choice of working for the emperor as Varangians or death."

"And since they weren't quite right to actually defend the emperor," Vanner continued, nodding, "he sent them up here to guard the toll booth. Along with a smattering of real Varangi. Ergo the blond hair and blue eyes."

"Keldara," McKenzie said. "The Kelts. Sawn, Padrek. Hell, Kulcyanov is probably a corruption of Culcyan. Maybe even Culculane."

"The point is that it's like running into a fossilized group of Spartans," Mike said, looking around at the trainers. "These guys, their stock at least, are warriors who descended on civilization, so far back there's not even many records, and ended up stuck in this valley as guards. They came from Ireland or Scotland—"

"Ireland," McKenzie said, firmly. "But before the Irish invaded Scotland, so they're Scots as well..."

"Following the wild geese. And now they're here."

"And this changes the training ... how?" Russell asked.

"Don't think in terms of farmers," Nielson said. "You guys watched those contests. And you missed the axe throw. Think in terms of . . . Gurkhas."

"That good?" Sergeant Heard asked.

"That good," Nielson said. "I'm going to up the rate at which they train, based on it. Put it that way."

"But they've been here for . . . how long?" Russell asked.

"Say a millennium and a half," Vanner said.

"So we're changing the training schedule based on that?" the former Ranger continued, surprised.

"Yeah, they've been here that long," Mike said. "But they've *kept* the warrior tradition that long. These aren't Iraqi sheep. These guys are like the Gurkhas and the Kurds. You can just push them harder. They'll respond. Treat every single one like a potential Ranger or SEAL candidate. And I bet you're amazed how fast they catch on."

"I don't want just a militia anymore," he continued, looking around at the whole group and catching each of their eyes. "I don't want a decent company of American-quality light infantry. I don't want just fighters. By next fall, I want a company of commandoes."

CHAPTER
TWENTY-FIVE

"You are tense," Anastasia said as she worked on his back. She was straddled across his butt, pressing hard into the push-up muscles. All she had on was a lightweight blue silk nightgown that had ridden up to her hips. Mike didn't even have that much on.

Mike had taken an easy day on Sunday, not even working out after the stresses of Saturday, mostly spending the time talking with Nielson about changing the training schedule and Vanner about archaeology. The Marine MI guy turned out to have a mass of unrelated information he'd picked up in a dozen odd places and the two of them had examined the architecture in the foyer again, comparing it to data on the web. The worn carvings on the pillars, as well as the essentially cruciform layout of the floor, argued for Byzantine design. There were differences, but some of them could be related to climatic conditions. He still couldn't find anything definite indicating when the building had been constructed.

He'd also taken the opportunity to poke around in the lower cellars. On the west side, towards the mountain, they were in pretty bad repair, with the plaster flaked off and seepage water puddled on the floor. He wasn't sure how much damage there was, structurally, but the caravanserai had lasted for hundreds of years, if not thousands, so he was inclined to dismiss it. He made a mental note, though, to have Prael or Meller check on it.

Near the stairs there was an old well with a metal cover plate, probably put there by the Soviets. He managed to drag it aside just enough to get a ear to it and heard rushing water not far below. There was apparently an underground stream or river that passed under the serai. In the event of a total FUBAR like a siege, they were good for water. He made another mental note to get a hand pump for the well.

On the east side the cellars were in pretty good condition. The damp had gotten to them as well, and the plaster was flaked, but not as badly. There was a very old wooden door to the last room and he had a fairly hard time forcing it open. But he decided that he'd found his bondage dungeon. The room was the longest in the cellars, the ceiling domed up to about ten feet in the center with four domes down the length. On the walls there were small discolorations about a meter off the ground that when he examined them seemed to be the remnants of something metal. Probably shackles from the look and very very old.

The cellars were remarkably free of litter, but they were very dusty and in places in the corners there were small piles of decayed stuff. Most of it was essentially soil, it had been down here so long, but he found bits of wood in some of the piles. A forensic archaeologist might have made something of it, but he wasn't planning on calling one in. He'd left word to have the Keldara get a detail down to the east side to get it cleaned out and left it at that.

What he hadn't found was any indication of the original builders. He'd hoped to find some graffiti or a foundation marking or something. But all he'd found was just dirt and crumbling plaster.

"I found out something about the Keldara," Mike said, shrugging.

"It makes me interested in the serai. And I'm worried about the training. They need to get good, and they need to get good fast."

"You worry too much," Anastasia said. "Turn over."

Mike rolled over and she mounted him, tightening down when he was in her, and began moving up and down.

"There," she said, huskily. "You can stop thinking now."

Mike pushed the nightgown up and over her head, pulling it down to pin her arms with a quick twist of the fabric, and rolling over so he was on her.

"I also found a good dungeon," Mike said, stopping for a moment in her.

"You're still thinking?" Anastasia gasped. "And you stopped."

"I can't let you think you're in charge," Mike said, chuckling. "If I let you think you're in charge before long you'll be running the place and then it'll be nothing but work, work, work all day long."

"If you don't start working soon . . ." Anastasia said, trying to lean up to bite his shoulder.

Mike ducked back with a laugh and grinned at her.

"If I don't start working soon, what?" he asked, teasingly.

"I can get . . . my arms . . ." the girl replied, struggling to get an arm loose.

"Ah, ah," Mike said, dropping his weight on her and clamping a hand over her mouth. "Don't think so!" He still didn't start moving, though, just stayed in her, grinning faintly and looking her in the eye.

Anastasia glared over the clamped hand, then closed her eyes and bore down, trying to push him out.

"Ain't gonna happen," Mike said, firmly, pressing back. The harem manager had some of the strongest muscles he'd ever encountered and it wasn't exactly easy, but he was already in place. Pushing him out wasn't in the cards.

Finally, Anastasia went limp, looking pleadingly at him over the hand and muttering into it.

"That's better," Mike said, starting to stroke. "Time to prove who's boss."

Normally he either worked on her with tongue and finger to bring her to climax or simply took his own and figured he'd owe her. Tonight he did neither, instead pounding at her like a steam press, hard, fast and constant. He slid his left hand up behind her, grabbing her left wrist and pinning it up behind her back, then began pounding, keeping his hand clamped over her mouth.

Anastasia fought back, wrapping her legs around his hips and trying to pull him out while wrestling to get a bite on his hand. But he had her fully pinned—she wasn't going anywhere—and he had a thumb under her chin, holding her mouth firmly shut, her head pressed back into the pillow. After a few moments the girl lay back, half exhausted from the struggle, letting out a low moan and closing her eyes.

Mike took this as a signal to redouble his efforts, keeping the speed constant but pounding in harder. As the girl started to pant he removed his hand from her mouth and grabbed her hair, turning her head to the side brutally and sliding his tongue up her exposed throat, then biting down on it like a vampire.

At that Anastasia climaxed, letting out a shriek of pleasure and clamping her legs powerfully around his waist. Mike didn't slow up, though, he just kept pounding.

"You're not done, yet?" Anastasia moaned as the last of her shudders passed.

"Not even close," Mike replied, not even out of breath. "I figure I can keep this up for about, oh, six hours."

"Oh, God," Anastasia whimpered, lying limp.

Mike just chuckled, evilly, and kept going.

"You're looking chipper this morning," Adams said as Mike walked into the kitchen, whistling. "You didn't wear yourself out last night, did you?"

"Only for crunches," Mike said, getting a cup of coffee. It was just a bit after four o'clock in the morning, o-dark-thirty in military

parlance, on the first day of training. First call was five but the trainers were going to be at the barracks at four-thirty to wake up the
trainees, most of whom had partied well into the previous night.

"Think I should go down and join the rest for first call?" Mike
asked.

"Nah, let them have the fun," Adams said, chuckling.

Vil let out a groan as the lights in the bay went on and grabbed
his head at a bellowed: "FIRST CALL!"

"It's before dawn," Edvin muttered from the bunk above him.

"ON YOUR FEET YOU KELDARA WANKERS!" Sergeant
McKenzie bellowed. "PT UNIFORM! FALL OUT IN FIVE MIN-
UTES!"

"Crap," Vil muttered, rolling to his feet and clutching his head
again. "Which one's the PT uniform?"

"The gray one," Dutov said, stumbling out of his bed and
opening his footlocker. "And we're to wear the new shoes, the
'running' shoes."

"They want us to *run*?" Edvin asked.

"Apparently," Vil said, looking around for the sergeant and
belatedly realizing he was supposed to be in charge. He shook
his head for a moment against the hangover and then stood up.
"ON YOUR FEET! GET IN PT UNIFORM! NOW!"

"Oh, what a bunch of sorry looking sons of bitches." Adams
chuckled, walking down the blocks of recruits who were stumbling
through their first class in calisthenics. Jumping jacks did not
require a high degree of physical coordination, but from some
of the green faces most of the Keldara didn't *have* a high degree
of physical coordination this morning.

"Teach them they can push through a hangover, anyway," Mike
said, trying not to smile. "I'll probably cut back on the run this
morning, though."

"About time for that," Adams said, considering the series the
Keldara were supposed to go through this morning.

"Call it when you're ready," Mike said.

Adams looked over at Sergeant Heard, who had the nearest set of Keldara. They were deliberately going to let some of the female trainers work with the militia so they could see that women could "hang." The female Keldara were going to be their heavy weapons support, not to mention positional defense. They were going to have to learn that they could depend upon females for support in combat. Showing them the examples of the trainers would work to that end.

Heard nodded over at Adams and turned back to her group.

" . . . Two-three-twenty-nine," she called. "One-two-three and HALT! Attention in the ranks!" she shouted as one of the Keldara bent over, gasping. "You think that was *hard*! You don't know what *hard* means, *boys*!" The last word was said with such a note of bitter contempt even Mike flinched.

As the other five teams halted their jumping jacks, Adams took a center position on the formation.

"Company, ten-shut!" he called. "Platoon guides. Post!"

The trainers waved the team leaders over to take their places in front of the team formations and trotted to the rear. The team leaders had hastily snatched their guidons from their holders. Each was a field of blue with the name of the team on it. When they were in position, Adams spun in place.

"Kildar! The company is formed."

Mike walked over and saluted Adams who, in turn, trotted to the rear of the formation.

"Good morning, boyos," Mike called to the Keldara. "I think some of us drank a bit too much last night. The traditional method for dealing with that in the military is to sweat the liquor out. Which we're now going to accomplish. A *soldier* has to learn to deal with discomfort. Fatigue, pain, cold, lack of food and sleep. That is what we're going to teach you to do, to keep going even when you think you can't. Because when you're in mission mode, there's no excuse. You either do the job or you die and your squad mates die with you. So when you think you can't go any farther, you'd better find it inside or you're not going to be any damned good to anyone except as pig-slops. Company! Left-FACE! Quick-time, march . . . double-time . . . MARCH!"

"What's wrong, Oleg?" Mike asked, sympathetically, trotting over to the team leader, who was looking pretty shaky.

The run was light from the point of view of the U.S. military: only going on three miles and no more than a seven- or eight-minute mile. Of course, the Keldara weren't trained runners. They did, however, have the basic soldierly trait of being able to handle pain and fatigue. What he wasn't sure was that they had the right "drive on" mentality that had to accompany those.

"Not . . . used . . . to . . . running . . . Kildar," the team leader gasped.

"You can fall out, you know," Mike purred suggestively. A few, not many, of the Keldara had done so. Most of them puking by the side of the road and then trying to catch up. "Of course, I'll have to find someone else that can actually *lead* your team . . ."

"I will stay, Kildar," Oleg said, firmly.

"But you don't even know how far we're going," Mike pointed out. "I can keep going, faster than this, for kilometers and kilometers. You Keldara watch me, you've seen it. We could be running all day."

"I'll . . . run all . . . day . . . Kildar," Oleg said, weaving a bit.

"Okay," Mike said. "We'll just run all day. Nothing important on the training schedule, anyway." He trotted back to the side of the formation, which was turning off the road and down the slope to the Keldara compound, then sped up and headed to the front where Adams was leading the formation.

"I've got it," Mike said. The formation area for the militia was down on the flats near the houses and Mike turned the Keldara towards it. He headed into the formation area, where most of the Keldara expected the, to them brutal, run would end, then continued through it to one of the graveled roads that led to the training areas.

He didn't look back as he passed through the formation area but he heard Adams grunt.

"How many'd we lose?" Mike asked as they crossed the nearest bridge.

"'Bout a third," Adams growled.

"Go back and round 'em up," Mike said, chuckling. "And there'd better not be any team leaders."

"Doesn't look like it," Adams said, peeling away.

Mike led the group about fifty meters past the bridge, enough room to turn around, then trotted in a curve onto the verge and back. The trainers chivvied the group into the turn and headed back to the barracks.

Mike passed the barracks *again*, though, heading back towards the road and turning around again. The Keldara were fixated on the run ending and expected it to end at the barracks. He wanted them to get their hopes up and then lose them as the expected stopping point didn't occur.

Finally he brought them to a "quick-time" march up on the road and walked them back to the barracks for a cool-down. When they were back in formation in front of the barracks, he brought them to at-ease and faced them.

"You're used to looking forward to the end of work," Mike said, looking over the formation of blowing Keldara. "For the beer at the end of the day of picking rocks. For the sun to fall on the harvesting or the last stand of wheat cut and the party to follow. But a soldier cannot be looking for the end of work, for the end of pain. Your mind starts to focus on that and it will betray you. As you return from a mission, anticipating a beer and rest, you could be ambushed. You might be sent on to another mission, and another and another. You cannot focus on rest, on peace, until you *are* at peace. You have to exist in a state of mind without a goal of the end of pain. You must learn to accept the pain, to revel in it, to make a brother of pain. To be a soldier *is* pain! It is suffering and loss and sacrifice. You must learn to pray for chaos and pain! This is one of the many things you're going to have to learn if you want to be soldiers. And if you turn out to be lousy soldiers, which it looks like this morning, then I'll just get some people that know how to do the damned job, to revel in the pain, and you can till the damned fields if that's all you're *good* for! Sergeant Major! Post!"

"They're looking pretty good," Mike said, walking past one of the barracks as a footlocker sailed out the window. He spoke quietly, his face stern and contemptuous of the nervous troopers standing at attention outside the barracks.

"Gotta agree," Adams said, raising his voice slightly to overcome McKenzie's trained bellow as an armful of uniforms followed the footlocker. "The trainers say they're having to look *God* damned hard to find defects. *Much* better than standard recruit material. These guys are neat, thoughtful, strong and they've got stamina from hell. It's scary."

"I think I should have gotten some Gurkha trainers," Mike mused. "They're used to top-notch entry material."

"Well, we're not being as choosy as they are," Adams pointed out. "There are a few that aren't quite up to standard. One of 'em's Gurun. You know, the guy who got the bean or whatever. Killjoy says it's not that he's not trying, it's that the rest don't want to have a damned thing to do with him."

"In some societies, the guy who's in his position gets referred to as dead," Mike replied. "We might have to pull him out. It'd be hell on him, though."

"Does that mean we lose one guy per year?" Adams asked, frowning. "That's going to play hell with manning. We don't have all that many guys as it is."

"Think of it as a casualty," Mike said. "We also need to be looking for replacements for the team leaders. We *are* going to be engaging in combat at some point and the guy with the shortest life expectancy is the team leader. So make damned sure we have the right guys in the assistant team leader slots."

"Will do," Adams said, frowning. "What are you going to do if they won't accept Gurun?"

"Find another job for him," Mike said, musingly. "I don't know him from Adam. If he can't fit in, though, send him to me and I'll look him over."

Mike spent most of the day watching the "training." It really was training, but what it seemed to be was purest abuse. The trainees weren't being taught to shoot or blow things up or even kill people, although many of them probably wanted to kill the trainers. They were being taught a series of skills, all of which could be lumped under the heading "soldierly conduct." The idea was to break their normal methods of doing things, of thinking, of living, and teach them new ones.

The *way* this was being done was the "abuse." The troops were made to fall into the square in front of the barracks while the instructors went through and inspected their gear. They'd been given a class in how it was to be prepared, how it was to be laid out, how it was to be cleaned. Most of it was brand new, but "military" clean was different from "civilian" clean. If there was lint or a bit of thread in the crease of an ammunition pouch, it wasn't "clean." The point here was attention to detail, absolutely zero defect. There were many tasks that soldiers performed where the slightest mistake would lead to death. Learning to do things *perfectly* was the point. If they could learn to make their beds *perfectly*, to clean their gear *perfectly*, to lay out their gear *perfectly*, then when they had to lay in a charge of explosives *perfectly* or clear a mine *perfectly* they might actually survive.

Furthermore, the conditions were designed to be stressful. It might actually work to have gunfire and explosions going off, randomly, while they were going through this stage of training and Mike had considered it. Hell, he could do the training any way he wanted. But the instructors screaming at them and having them do the same tasks over and over again, never willing to accept even true perfection, was stressful enough. And they'd be doing it well into the night. By the end of the week the recruits would be so mind numb, they'd be doing the tasks in a haze of unreality. And they'd eventually be doing them *perfectly* in that state of mind. Which was the point.

"You've got some training of your own to do," Adams pointed out, grinning.

"And I'll start tonight," Mike replied. "I've been considering how to do it. Right that is. Gor . . . isn't the right way in my opinion."

"It's got its attractions, though," Adams said with another grin. The Gor books were still classics of bondage fantasy, emphasis on fantasy.

"I'm going to go check on the dam," Mike said. "Not much to see here for a while. Call me if there are any problems."

"Will do, boss," Adams said. "You go . . . check on the dam."

Mike headed for the Expedition, rolling his eyes as he went.

"Got the pour done," Meller said, gesturing at the weir. The concrete structure was about six feet high and thirty feet long, a rectangular box with rectangular openings in the bottom and a broad, triangular, concrete platform in front of it. "It will take about a week to set enough to start dumping on it, but we're starting with the edges now."

He spoke over the sound of a truck as it climbed up the grade to the dump point. The broad platform above the dam had been partially dug and partially blasted out and was now wide enough that the truck could make half a three-point turn so its load would dump over the side. As Mike watched, it backed into position and dropped a load of loam over the side. As soon as the dirt was dumped, it dropped the cargo bay and began turning to go back down the hill.

As the truck drove away, the older Keldara men who were working on the project began spreading the dirt out. Some of that was done with a small bulldozer but mostly it was spade work. As soon as the dirt was spread out evenly, three of the Keldara started pressing it down with hand compactors.

"As long as the rain holds off we can keep this up," Meller continued.

"Know anything about microbreweries?" Mike asked, distantly.

"Not a thing," Meller said, frowning. "Except I like their beer. The Keldara beer is better, though. Why?"

"I want to build one," Mike said. "I had Genadi plant most of the new fields in barley. I'm not sure if that will give us enough to run a decent microbrewery, but it will be a start."

"I can build the *building*," Meller said, definitely. "But I have no idea how it should be laid out and I don't know anything about how they work except that they have big copper vats."

"Same here," Mike said, sighing. "I guess I'll just have to do some research."

"Delegate," Meller said. "Vanner's underutilized at the moment. If you get him to find a design, I'll put it together. I suppose the Keldara women can figure out how to increase their output."

"I'd better go talk to Mother Lenka about that," Mike said. "You got enough people?"

"For now," Meller said, shrugging. "This is more or less make-work until the concrete sets."

"Okay, see you later," Mike replied.

CHAPTER
TWENTY-SIX

"Hello, Mother Lenka," Mike said, finding the Keldara woman in the back of the Devlich house.

"Kildar," Mother Lenka said. She was seated on a stool in the kitchen, watching the younger women work.

"I've got a question for you," Mike said. "Care to go for a ride?"

"Of course, Kildar," Mother Lenka said, getting to her feet. "I can explain to you how to train your women."

"Pass," Mike said, grinning. The old woman was a terror about "explaining" things.

"Larissa," Mother Lenka continued, "keep these lazy bones at work; the men will be wanting their food on time."

"Yes, Mother Lenka," one of the Keldara women, presumably Larissa, replied, nodding at her.

Mike drove the old woman up to the bench over the Keldara compound.

"What are we looking at?" the old woman asked as they got out of the SUV.

"How much beer do you make every year?" Mike asked, walking through the brush covering the bench. Something had been up here within the last fifteen years or so, judging by the size of the saplings that grew on the bench.

"About three thousand liters," Mother Lenka said, frowning. "And let me tell you, it's not easy. We start after the harvest and work on it most of the winter."

Mike nodded and continued down a game trail to the end of the bench. There was another of the innumerable streams where the bench curved into the mountainside. He made a note to ensure it was spring fed, but most of them were. They trickled off in high summer, he'd been told, but never quite went away.

"I'm thinking of trying to make enough to sell," Mike said, coming back out of the brush to where Mother Lenka was standing.

"We already do," Mother Lenka pointed out, gesturing at the town.

"More than that," Mike said. "Much more. Enough to export."

"Never happen," Mother Lenka snapped. "You are talking about . . ."

"Ten thousand liters, minimum," Mike said. "Over what is usually made."

"There isn't enough time in the world," the woman protested. "Or enough stoves to bake the barley!"

"We'll build a brewery," Mike said. "Up here. With water on tap. The barley will be automatically fed to the *very* large ovens. And the women will work it, which will give them a source of income."

"Ah," Mother Lenka said, giving him a toothless smile. "Now I understand. But there is a problem."

"And that is?" Mike asked, raising an eyebrow.

"There is an undertaste to the brew, yes?" Mother Lenka asked, walking into the brush. "This bush," she said, lifting a low growing bush that looked something like a blueberry bush.

"This makes the tiger berries. We put some of them, crushed, in the mix. That is what gives it the slight tang you don't get with true beer. Very old Keldara secret. But we'd have to have . . . very much of these berries. The women gather them in fall, but we could never gather enough. Without the berries, it won't be the beer you know so well."

"For this year," Mike said, musingly, "we'll just have to have an all-hands evolution to gather them. Get as many as we can gathered. I'll talk to Genadi about planting some more. I don't know how fast they grow, but we can have fields planted if we have to."

"The best come from the wild mountains," Mother Lenka sniffed.

"But it's not for the *Keldara*," Mike said, smiling. "It's for barbarians that don't know what *real* beer tastes like."

"Well, I suppose barbarians will drink anything," Mother Lenka said with a sniff. "I have tasted a can of something called 'light beer.' It is . . . bad."

"Love in a small boat beer," Mike said, cryptically.

Mother Lenka raised an eyebrow then cackled.

"Yes, Kildar," the old woman replied, still chuckling. "I get it. Fucking close to water, yes? Well, we will give them something that is *not* close to water. The tiger berry is a . . . what you call it? Aphrodisiac, yes? *That* will give them some zip in their peckers."

"Vanner?" Mike asked, sticking his head in the commo room.

"Intel," one of the Keldara women on duty said, pointing to the next room.

Mike frowned and stepped down the cellar hall. The next door was locked.

"Vanner?" he asked, tapping on the door.

"Hi, Kildar," Vanner replied as he opened the portal. "Welcome to the intel room." There were two Keldara women in the room, seated at a table reading something.

Mike had devoted about sixty grand to general "intel" items. Vanner had apparently been shopping. The room was crowded with electronics gear including scanners, a couple of *very* large printers and three computers with oversized monitors. One of them displayed a portion of a topographic map that Mike could make out was the northeast end of the valley. It was marked with roads that had just been put in and the new training ranges and their buildings.

"Very nice," Mike said, dryly. "What's going on?"

"I'm training Lilia and Stella in the basics of updating maps," Vanner said. "I pulled a couple of satellite shots off the commercial net and we're updating the valley map using a commercial topography program. What we're doing right now is looking over the output and doing an eyeball comparison since the program has a tendency to get details wrong. I also got Prael's survey data and we're using that to double-check the satellite data. After that I'm going to ask Colonel Nielson for funds for a full area satellite sweep. We can use that to get better maps of the Area of Operations. I got two map printers, cheap, so when we have better maps we'll be able to produce them for the Keldara. And I ordered the most comprehensive mapset available from Janes so we'll be set for most potential deployments, even though I know the Keldara aren't designed for deployment."

"What the hell are those?" Mike asked, pointing to a couple of what looked like very large radios.

"Oh, well . . ." Vanner said, clearing his throat. "I didn't use the full budget getting the primary gear, so I pulled a couple of those off E-bay. They're last-generation intercept gear. German. I've been teaching the girls about intercept. Most of the Chechens that use radios speak Russian and most of the girls know Russian. So we've been listening in on the Chechens from time to time, trying to figure out their operational pattern. They don't use encryption systems, but they do occasionally use codes and their transmissions tend to be cryptic anyway. I got a freeware program that gathers codes and looks for patterning so we're picking out some of their code words and we're getting a feel for their shorthand. I've been using a remote site for triangulation, trying to get a feel for the movements. Most of them don't have radios, anyway, or use sat phones. I can't do much with those; you need a ferret satellite to pick up sat-phone transmissions. But we're picking some stuff up. Nothing we can use, yet, but we're establishing some patterns."

"Oh," Mike said, blinking. "Good." When he'd budgeted for an intel setup he'd expected a bit of improvement in the maps and maybe a stab at pattern generation. Not this.

"I don't get many indicators that there's any special activity directed at the valley at the moment," Vanner continued. "Only three out of sixteen indicators that the Keldara are a target. The term has come up twice, both in reference to changes in movement away from the valley. There may be a force forming near the Pankisi Gorge for an incursion into Chechnya, that's got about a nine-point indicator rate with an almost three hundred percent increase in traffic in a localized region. I dropped that through our Russian conduit since it doesn't affect us."

"Okay," Mike said, grinning.

"Is this a social call?" Vanner asked.

"No," Mike said, shaking his head. "I want to set up a micro-brewery so the Keldara can look at exporting their beer. I'd like you to do the initial research. Think of it as . . . intel gathering. I need a design for a microbrewery, how to run one, what goes into it, maybe a few consultants to contact."

"Okay," Vanner said, his eyes going distant as he nodded. "I'll get started on it right away."

"Thanks," Mike said, grinning as the intel NCO turned away. "Have fun."

Mike walked to the harem next, opening the door to the area carefully. Anastasia had started classes and he didn't want to interrupt if she was lecturing. However, it seemed most of the girls were working on something when he came in.

The girls were seated on cushions, using short desks. He saw that Katya was frowning as she wrote something. The girl had been picking up reading fairly fast but her writing ability still left a lot to be desired.

He waved to Anastasia and walked to the small room on the ground floor she'd set up as an office.

"Yes, Kildar?" the girl asked as she followed him into the room.

"Three things," Mike said, grabbing a chair in front of the desk and letting her have the swivel chair behind it. "I want to get computers in here, for one. Knowledge of how to use a computer, if not programming, is pretty much a necessity in modern life."

"I don't know anything about computers, Kildar," Anastasia said, frowning. "I don't even know how to turn one on."

"You'll have to learn, too," Mike pointed out. "When we get them, I'll have Vanner set up a network. They can be used for learning, too. Maybe I'll just get each of the girls a laptop and a wireless card. But that brings me to the second item; we need to get a tutor for the girls. I know you're used to instruction, and you might be better for basic instruction. But I'd like some of these girls to get to at *least* advanced high-school level by the time they leave. Not just basic reading and math but history, science, what have you. I'd like you to look into that. Look around Tbilisi. Female, obviously, and open-minded just as obviously."

"Very well, Kildar," Anastasia said, her brow furrowing. "I can find someone; I have hired people for the hareem before."

"Great," Mike said, one more detail handled. Hopefully well. "Last item: the girls. I'll have a session with Klavdiya tonight. I'd rather spend some time with each, rather than deal with them assembly line. Does that make sense to you?"

"Very much so," Anastasia said, relieved. "I would suggest that you spend quite a bit of time with each of them for at least a week."

"I don't know how much time I'll have, day to day," Mike said.

"But I'll figure something out. Now, any problems you can't deal with?"

"Katya is, yes, very much a bitch," Anastasia said, frowning. "Also smart and manipulative. I would have her out of here as soon as possible; she poisons all around her."

"I told her if she gave me any trouble, I wouldn't bother selling her, I'd just put her down like a rabid dog," Mike said. "Is it that level of trouble?"

"Not . . . quite that bad," Anastasia said, hastily. "But she is poisoning the new girls. She is a problem, but I don't think she should be *killed*."

"Don't put a huge value on her," Mike said, shrugging. "Her problem is she's underutilized. I don't mean sexually; all the trainers think she's the greatest thing since sliced bread. But she's got one hell of a mind. A rabid one, admittedly, but she's intelligent and fast-thinking. Unfortunately," he sighed.

"She has virtually no education," Anastasia said. "So you can't put her in the intelligence and communications section."

"Wouldn't think about that, anyway," Mike said. "She'd figure out a way to knife *me* in the back. Let me talk to her after we're done."

"I think we are," Anastasia said, smiling faintly. "I guess I'll be missing your company for a while?"

"I think I'll be a little busy, yeah," Mike said, grinning sheepishly. "I don't hold you as monogamous, though. Feel free to trip up a trainer if you're of a mind. I know you think I own you, but I *don't*. You're a free agent."

"I think I'll wait my turn," Anastasia said, sighing. "The rest would be a come-down, I'm sure."

"Can't find out unless you check," Mike pointed out. "I'll go get Katya and have a little chat. Have Klavdiya meet me in my suite at dinner."

"Damnit, Kat," Mike said when the obviously apprehensive hooker was seated in his office, "do you *want* me to have to put you down?"

"I am *trying* not to be a problem, Kildar," Katya said, sniffling and dropping her head.

"Oh, quit the act," Mike said, sharply. "We both know it is one. I won't ask you the last time you *actually* cried."

"A long time ago," Katya said. Her head came up and she gave him a poisonous look. "It doesn't do you a bit of good."

"Well, you're screwing up my harem and I won't have it," Mike said. "But that's the only place where there are classes you can attend . . ."

"I *hate* them," Katya said, angrily. "All the other girls are so *slow!*"

Mike started to open his mouth, then closed it. He gave the situation some thought and then blew out, angrily.

"Okay, in addition to a dozen *other* duties I have, I'm making you my personal project," Mike said. "That does not, by the way, mean that you're going to be having sex with me. But *I'll* under-take to instruct you. How far along are you in reading?"

"I can read well in Russian," Katya said, carefully. "I don't know all the words . . ."

"Ever heard of a dictionary?" Mike asked. "I'm not going to be *nice* about teaching you, by the way."

"We don't *have* a Russian dictionary," Kat snapped back. "Or, yes, I'd look the words up."

"I know we've got one around *somewhere*," Mike said, making a note on a pad. "But I'll order a few. What about English?"

"Only speak little," Kat said in broken English. "Not read well."

"Next project," Mike said, nodding. "You need to get English *down*. It's the de facto international language. As of now, you're my assistant. Did you understand that?"

"Yes," Katya answered in English.

"I need a list of the girls who have not been broached," Mike said. "I want to spend a week with each of them. Make up a list and a calendar. I'm going to run it by Anastasia before I go with it, though. If you figure out some way to make trouble doing that, and it's obvious, I *will* beat the hell out of you. Understand?"

"Yes, Kildar," Katya said, frowning.

"Here's a Day-Timer," Mike said, digging in his desk and finding one he'd picked up free with some office supply orders. "I want you to, in general, have the girls lined up in reverse order of age, that is the oldest ones first. None who are under sixteen. Did you get that?"

"Yes, Kildar," Katya replied.

"Repeat it," Mike said. "In English."

"To make schedule," Katya said, carefully. "Oldest girls to go first. One per week. Younger be sixteen."

"The *youngest* to be sixteen," Mike corrected. "Start with Klavdiya, though. And after lunch, meet me in the workout room. If you're going to be my assistant, you're going to be training with me all the way. Go work on the schedule for now. When you're not working with me, go down to the intel section and talk English with Vanner in his free time. Got it?"

"Yes, Kildar," Katya said.

"Take off," Mike said, turning to his paperwork. "And don't get in trouble."

Mike ate a sandwich for lunch and then changed into workout gear and headed down to the weight room. When he got there, Katya was waiting.

"I have the schedule, Kildar," Katya said, handing him the Day-Timer. "I have listed all the girls in reverse order of age, with Klavdiya first."

"Okay," Mike said, flipping through the book and sighing. "We're going to work out together, then we'll go do some shooting. Go change into shorts and a T-shirt for this. I suppose you *could* work out in a skirt, but it's not normal."

Mike was through his warm-up when the girl got back to the room. He looked her over and nodded.

"Your thighs are pretty solid," Mike said. "We'll start today working on upper body."

"Yes, Kildar," Katya said, puzzled.

"You need to warm up, first," Mike said, leading her over to the cross-trainer. He showed her how to use it and set it for a fifteen-minute light course. "When the time runs out, we'll start warming up your upper body; this is just to get your heart working."

He moved over to the circuit training and dialed in his settings, then started pumping. He'd barely gotten through the triceps workout when Kat was done. He showed her how to reset the Nautilus machines and gave her a general weight range to work with. She noticed that he was moving at least five times her workout weight.

"Are you set me low to keep from making strong?" Kat asked, looking at him coldly.

"You have to start low," Mike said just as coldly. "I'll build you up to the max you're good for. But if you think you're going to pump my level, ever, you're sadly mistaken. You can go ahead and try if you'd like," he added with a grin.

They worked on the circuit for an hour, a light workout for him but about as much as Kat could take on her first day.

"Arms tired," Katya said, working her shoulders. She had sweat dripping down her face and wiped at it with a towel.

"You just thought you were in shape," Mike said, grinning. "Come on."

He led her down the corridor to a room at the far end from the intel room that had been set up as a dojo, where there were punching bags and floor pads.

"I'm going to show you a few fight moves," Mike said. "If you use them on the girls..."

"I'm in trouble," Kat said, nodding.

"When I start working the girls, I'll bring them in for this as well," Mike noted. "But you'll be doing this most of the time. In time, you'll be helping to train."

"Yes, Kildar," Kat said. "Thank you."

"Most people, when they fight with hands, use a closed fist," Mike said, handing her a pair of fighting gloves. "Like this," he said, punching a bag with his fist. "And they punch *to* the target. Try to hit the surface. You understand?"

"Yes," Katya said, frowning.

"Better to use the open palm," Mike said, opening up his hand and pointing to the base of the his palm. "Curve the fingers, hit at the base of your palm. That has the bones of your arm lined up with the target and it transmits more power. It also won't break your fingers, which hitting with a closed fist will do. And hit *through* the target," he continued, striking the bag hard. "The important thing is the speed of the strike. You must do it over and over again, learn to strike very fast, like a snake, and hard. Work on that for now," he said, stepping away from the bag. "Hard and fast."

She stepped up to the bag and punched it, hard, with an open-hand right hand.

"Harder," Mike said. "And faster. Think of someone you hate, me if you want. And punch *through* the bag," he continued, pointing to the middle of the bag. "Try to get your hand through to here."

She hit again, harder, then again, her face working.

"Gets some of the mad out, don't it?" Mike said. "Now the other hand, alternate the two. Hard, fast and through with both. Go."

She started hitting with both hands and then shifted around on her feet uncomfortably.

"You noticed you weren't standing right, good," Mike said, tapping at her ankles with his foot. "Right foot there, left foot forward. Cat stance is what it's called, coincidentally. Hit twice, one each hand, then pause."

When she'd finished the strikes he had her move one foot then the other, circling the bag.

"Keep your body centered," Mike said, running his finger down an imaginary line. "Bring your butt forward a bit; you're leaning away from the target. If you know where your center is, you can bring more power to the strikes. Don't kick, just strike, then move. We'll work on kicks later; most kicks are for show-offs anyway."

"You kick in Ondah contest," Kat said, panting. She hit twice, then moved, circling the bag.

"I was showing off," Mike said. "And Oleg was a big SOB. Kicks have more power than hand strikes. But there are more counters, too. Keep going."

He worked her on strikes and moving for about an hour until she was dripping with sweat.

"Go take a shower," Mike said, when the girl was pretty much worn out. "Then meet me at the office in regular uniform."

Mike was back at his desk, showered, when Kat turned up. She'd spent enough time to get makeup on but she wasn't much slower than he had been.

"Have you worked with a computer?" Mike asked, pulling his laptop out of its case.

"No, Kildar," Katya said, her eyes widening.

"This one doesn't have anything secure on it," Mike said, opening the computer up. "I was working on my typing, though. I'd never learned to touch type. So it's got a teaching program on it." He brought up the program and led her to the room he'd set up as a conference room. "This program will run you though how to touch type. It's about the most boring thing in the world, but it's important to learn. And it's in English, so you'll have twice as much to think about. It should keep you occupied," he added with a smile.

Mike ran through his bare minimum paperwork and then headed out to the household range. As part of the whole improvements program, Meller had bermed the walls of the range and Praz had upgraded the range and included a small tactical range.

Mike ran through a program circuit with M-4 and pistol, which was his scheduled shoot for the day, taking up most of the rest of the afternoon. By the time he was done the sun was starting to set. He dropped the weapons in the armory—Latif had been trained in cleaning so he could leave it to him—and washed up for dinner.

He stopped by the conference room and found Katya still plugging away at the computer.

"Dinner time," Mike said, walking over to look over the girl's shoulder.

"This not hard," Katya replied. She'd run through the first four levels of the training program, which had taken Mike most of a week of solid work. Given that it wasn't in her native tongue, it was doubly impressive. And the program wouldn't let you move on to the next level until you'd passed the requisite test.

"You're doing very well," Mike said, shaking his head. "I think you were being severely underutilized. If you keep to this rate, I'll be using you as a secretary in a week," he added with a grin. "I won't *keep* you as a secretary—you'll get bored to tears after a while—but you'll learn some useful skills."

"Would like learn more about computer," Katya said. "Am have trouble with pad," she said, pointing to the touchpad on the laptop.

"The only way to learn is to do it," Mike pointed out. "There are games on there, simple ones. If you play those you'll learn to use it faster. I'll show them to you sometime, not now. It's time for dinner."

"And time for Klavdiya to learn, yes?" Katya said maliciously.

"Unlike for some," Mike pointed out, "I'm planning on having it be a *good* time."

Mike had had some changes made to the rooms upstairs. He'd had the master bath opened out into one of the adjoining rooms, adding a large shower and Jacuzzi tub, used the rest of the room to make a small office and sitting area, increased the size of the closet, had a gun safe installed in it and converted one of the rooms adjoining his suite into a small dining room with attached kitchen. Effectively, he never had to leave the suite.

When he got to the sitting room, Klavdiya was sitting on the couch awaiting him nervously. She was wearing a light-blue, low-cut dress he hadn't seen before, presumably the fruits of her purchasing. It suited her well.

"Mother Savina was supposed to bring up a light dinner," Mike said, smiling at her. "Let's eat."

"Okay," Klavdiya said, standing up.

The small table had been set with two places and candles for lighting. Mike lit the candles and turned down the lights, then lifted the covers off the plates to see what they were having for dinner. Chicken in a creamy sauce with a side of rice and mixed vegetables. Light enough.

"Wine?" he asked, lifting out a chilled bottle of a local white.

"A little," Klavdiya replied.

"And only a little for me, too," Mike said, pouring for her. "Shakespeare said that wine giveth the desire and taketh away the ability. Truer words were never writ."

"Who is Shakespeare?" Klavdiya asked, picking at her food.

"An English playwright and poet," Mike replied. "You'll read him eventually, I hope. Very good plays. He had the human nature down. Are you reading much, yet?"

"Only a little," Klavdiya said. "I am not so good, yet."

"It takes practice," Mike admitted. "You'll get better. You can learn a lot about the world from reading. Of course, living in it helps as well."

As they chatted the girl began to relax, which was the whole point. Dessert was a chocolate confection with coffee to wash it down. At which point, Klavdiya started tensing up again.

"Come on," Mike said, standing up and holding out his hand. "No worries."

Klavdiya got up uncertainly and followed him to the sitting room.

"Not there?" she asked, pointing to the bedroom.

"In a bit," Mike said, sitting down on the couch and pulling her lightly down to sit beside him. He'd set out a bottle of mead beforehand and pulled the cork, pouring two small glasses. "This is just a bit stronger than the wine. It will relax you so I can have my way with you," he said, smiling humorously.

"I am yours, Kildar," the girl said, taking the small glass.

"In one gulp," Mike said, tossing his off. The mead was strong and warming.

"That is good," Klavdiya said, pulling her legs up onto the couch to tuck under her.

"Made from honey," Mike said, putting his arm on her shoulders. "I don't think you make it around here, much, which is strange. Is there anything you want to talk about?"

"No," Klavdiya said, looking up at him from lowered eyes that were still a bit frightened.

"Then let's try doing," Mike said, leaning over to kiss her.

She stiffened at first but then slid into his arms with a moan. He flicked his tongue against her lips and hers parted for him to enter. He ran his tongue around her mouth, but when his hand slid onto her thigh she stiffened up again.

He kept his hand away from taboo zones, sliding it up her side and eliciting another moan, then down to her thigh again. This time when it slid up it was inside the dress sliding up her nylon covered thigh. Klavdiya wriggled around so that he could get his hand further up and he slid it up, pushing the dress up at the same time, until his hand was on her ass. He rested it there for a time, just stroking, then ran the other hand under the dress and had it up and over her head before she realized.

She sat back at that, biting her lip, as he tossed the dress onto the coffee table.

"Kildar," she said, uncertainly.

"Shhhh," Mike replied. She was wearing light blue bikini panties and a matching front-opening bra, and nylons supported by a garter belt. The panties had been put on outside the garter; he presumed she'd had help in dressing from Anastasia. "Now's not the time for words."

He started over, holding her gently and kissing, then slid his tongue down her throat as she lay back and writhed under his hands. He slid his hand up and down her sides as he kissed and licked on her neck, getting a mouthful of perfume in the process that he ignored. He also had to spit out some hair, but that was a small price to pay. She had a lovely body, young and taut and firm. He slid his tongue down onto her chest, then reached up and opened up the bra. This time she didn't stiffen, just moaned and arched as he took one of her nipples in his mouth while gently tickling the other.

He slid his left hand away from the nipple and up behind her head, then slowly lowered her onto the couch, sliding his right hand down her side and along her leg as he continued to nuzzle at her luscious breasts. They were very firm, just fully swelled out and not even starting to sag. He could feel himself getting aroused and firmly told himself to calm down. The wonderful part about it was that he *could* take her any way that he wished. He *owned* her; she had no recourse but to do his will. It was a heady feeling of absolute power that he had to carefully control.

He slid his right hand under her ass as he nuzzled at her and slid the panties down, gently. She did stiffen at that, clamping her knees together. That excited him enough he couldn't help yanking them down between her clamped knees, then sliding his hand up between her legs, roughly, sliding a leg over to spread them and then slipping a finger into her warmness.

She started to draw back at that but he pinned her in place with his weight and forced his finger into her, rubbing gently. She moaned and writhed to get away but he pressed her down, continuing to nuzzle at her breasts and neck, slipping his tongue down onto the juncture of her neck and shoulder and pressing in hard. He could feel a wave of goose bumps cover her arms and stomach and she began to moisten as he gently manipulated her.

He still didn't take her, continuing to stroke her with tongue and finger, slowly spreading her legs as she loosened up under his expert touch. Finally, she arched and gasped, letting out a squeak of surprise as much as pleasure as she orgasmed.

He quickly pulled his pants off at that, **spreading her wide** and taking her as she was still shuddering. She was tight as hell and he had to work to get in but she let out a shriek of combined pleasure and pain as her hymen broke, rocking into him as he took her. He didn't worry about her pleasure, now, simply stroking hard. But he held back as well as he could, giving her a good, hard, long fucking for her first time until she was shrieking with pleasure and bucking under him. Then he came into her, hard, pinning her down and biting into her shoulder muscles to keep from shouting himself.

"Oh, Kildar," Klavdiya said, crying, as she wrapped her arms and legs around him. "That was . . ."

"There aren't words, love," Mike said, gently, stroking at her face.

"Oooh," she moaned as he slid out of her.

He'd planned for that as well, and picked up a cloth from the table, sliding it between her legs gently.

"Are you hurt?" he asked.

"It hurt a little," she said. "But not so much. I must go clean up, Anastasia told me how."

"Meet me in the bedroom if you will," Mike said.

When she was gone he cleaned up the small amount of mess and wiped himself down, then went to the bedroom. He pulled the covers partially down, got undressed and was waiting for her when she came in. She was looking nervous again.

"Come on," Mike said, holding up the covers. "We're not even *close* to done, yet."

"Yes, Kildar," the girl said, uncertainly. She was still wearing her stockings and high-heels. She started to take them off but Mike gestured for her to stop.

"Leave them on," Mike said, grinning. "They're cute."

"Yes, Kildar," she said, uncertainly, but hopped into bed anyway.

"Now to show you the other ways you can please me," Mike said.

"I am told one," she said, smiling shyly. "Can I try?"

"Go ahead," Mike said, his brow furrowing.

The girl bent over and slid her head under the covers, one shoe-clad foot sticking out as she started giving him head, the foot waving back and forth thoughtfully as she worked.

She'd clearly been instructed in giving blowjobs by Anastasia, and Mike wondered if he should audit some of the "special" courses the harem manager was giving. She took him slowly at first, licking his dick like an ice-cream cone and getting it extended before she took him in her mouth. Once it was in she began working her head up and down, going faster and faster and sucking hard. At one point she went all the way down, taking him in the back of her throat and swallowing but that caused her to choke so she backed off and continued with her stroking.

Finally, Mike couldn't take it anymore; he reached down and pulled her back up on the bed and onto him. He lifted her legs to straddle his body and then inserted with her on top of him. She was quite moist; apparently giving head had excited her but it was still a struggle; the girl was still tight as hell. She bounced on him, working her hips and biting her lip as her fingers dug into his pectorals painfully.

"Oh, yes!" she said. "Oh, Kildar! OH GOD!"

As she came Mike rolled her over and slammed her, pinning her hands over her head to keep her from scratching any worse and pile-driving her as she screamed in ecstasy. He dug his elbows into the top of her shoulders to pin her in place against his thrusts and pounded for all he was worth until he came again.

"Kildar," she said as he rolled her onto his shoulder to cuddle. "I have never been with another man, but I cannot imagine it being better."

"Different men are . . . different," Mike said, sliding in to make contact with as much skin as possible. "Some are better than others. I pay attention and I care, it helps. Are you still okay?"

"I *am* sore," Klavdiya said. "But when you are in me, I don't care. But . . . I'm tired," she added, yawning.

"They call orgasm 'nature's tranquilizer,'" Mike said, smiling. "The problem with most men is they go to sleep right after they get theirs and they don't give the woman hers first."

"You don't go to sleep?" the girl said, sleepily, with another yawn.

"I'm a SEAL," Mike said, grinning. "We're supermen, hadn't you heard?"

Mike listened to her breathing for a bit and then yawned.

"But I could sleep," he admitted, drifting off.

He woke up in the middle of the night and as he felt the warm bundle against him, he was instantly fully awake. He thought about it for a second and then just pulled her over and spread her legs and took her.

It was hard getting in; she was dry and tight. As she woke up she struggled a bit but he clamped his hand over her mouth and forced it into her tight slot with a grunt of effort. He pinned her hands again, keeping his hand over her mouth, and simply took her, hard. He could see her eyes by the light from the window, wide and frightened, and it excited him tremendously.

"I'm taking you," he said, roughly. "I can take you any time I want. And I'm going to. I'm going to take you, again and again, whether you want it or not."

He felt her moisten instantly at that and her eyes closed and her head rolled back as she began to pant and buck. He didn't worry about her needs this time, though, simply taking what he wanted and coming into her again.

"That's the other side of me," Mike said, taking his hand off her mouth and pulling out of her. "The rough side of me. Sometimes it will come out."

"I liked it, Kildar," Klavdiya said, still panting. "I like you inside of me, taking me. Even when it hurts."

She cleaned up sketchily and then curled into him again. This time Mike was the first one to fall asleep.

CHAPTER
TWENTY-SEVEN

"Carting your girls around with you, now?" Meller asked as Katya and Lida walked over to watch the building dam. The engineer had hired three dump trucks from the area and some other equipment so the dam was building swiftly. The south side was about seventy percent filled in and the north about halfway with a building mound in the center. Besides the Keldara with hand compactors there were two rolling compactors, which looked somewhat like steam rollers, working the dirt.

"Sort of," Mike said. "I'm teaching Kat to be an assistant. Not for me, not long term, but it's something I think she could do as an occupation if she could keep from knifing her boss in the back. And it's a good way to learn how things work. Lida I'm keeping close as a bonding thing."

It had been three weeks since training, of the militia and the girls, had started and Mike was on his third young lady in as many weeks.

"And you've been doing a good bit of bonding," Meller said, grinning.

"This is a weird situation," Mike said. "At least for me. Not that I'm knocking it or anything. The sex is great."

"Well, fortunately with the training rotation we're not missing Kat," Meller said. "But the moans from down the hall are interesting. I guess she enjoys her new status."

"Apparently," Mike said, chuckling. Meller was not the first to comment on the sounds, by a long stretch. "How long?"

"Two weeks," Meller said in a satisfied tone. "Once we're finished with the main dirt laydown, all we have to do is cover it with clay and start filling. I figure about another two weeks for that. I'm going to turn over to Prael next week and get started on the electric."

"Don't forget my brewery building," Mike said.

"I haven't," Meller said. "Prael's going to start clearing the foundations tomorrow. Father Mahona's going to be in charge of the construction; it's going to be straight Keldara construction for the most part. Vanner's gotten a design for it and he's working with Mother Lenka on the brewing cycle."

"Works for me," Mike said. "I'll need someone to do the sales, though. I'm thinking of getting the Keldara town brew as an example so we can get some sales lined up for when we have our first batch done."

"You're assuming your first brew is going to be good enough for market," Meller pointed out.

"I'm trusting Mother Lenka on that one," Mike admitted. "I think she could get a saleable brew out of a stone. Time to go collect the girls before they distract the workmen too much. I'll be glad to have power from this thing; those generators I had installed are costing like crazy."

"So is this," Meller pointed out. "But it's capital expenditure. You'll have power from it for a century."

"I doubt I'll last that long," Mike said, chuckling.

"Mike, got something to discuss with you," Nielson said when he got back to the serai.

"Lida, go to classes," Mike said, patting the girl on the butt. "I'll come fetch you later. Katya . . ."

"I'll go finish my spreadsheet," Katya said, nodding.

"Projections on beer sales," Mike said, following Nielson to the latter's office. "Might be cart before the horse, but I figure we can start looking at what we might get."

"And it keeps her occupied," Nielson said, chuckling.

"And it keeps her occupied," Mike admitted. "I'm having a hard time finding work for her."

"Toss her over to me," Nielson said, sitting behind his overloaded desk. "I could use an assistant that can do spreadsheets."

"And her typing's improving," Mike said. "What can I do for you? How's the training going?"

"Good," Nielson admitted. "As far as I can tell at this point. With one exception."

"Gurun," Mike guessed. "What's happening?"

"He's really being . . . put on," Nielson said, frowning. "Not really his fault. Stuff happens and it all gets blamed on him, whether it's his fault or not. Even when it's clearly someone else's."

"Standard thing with the *caillean*," Mike said, grimacing.

"The problem is it's causing a real rift in his team," Nielson said. "I've spoken to Vil but he just shuts down on the subject. And none of the other team leaders are willing to let him transfer. It's like the whole clan has shut him out."

"They have in a way," Mike said, sighing. "I hate to lose a fighter, but they're not going to accept him no matter what." He thought about it for a second and then shrugged. "I don't know him from Adam. What's he like?"

"Smart," Nielson said, shrugging. "I don't know him well, either, but I've talked to Peters about him and he says he's actually very good. If he wasn't having this other problem he'd consider him for the team assistant slot. As it is . . ."

"Let me talk to him," Mike said, sighing. "Bring him up this evening. If we pull him we'll do it tonight."

"Will do," Nielson said.

▲   ▲   ▲

"Kildar," Katya said when he got to his office. "I've prepared the spreadsheet on beer sales and a report on potential distributors I pulled from the internet. Two in Europe and six in America. Also . . . Sergeant Vanner and I disagree on something. I would like you to talk to him about it."

"He's the intel head," Mike said, frowning. "I don't think you should go over his head."

"I thought about that," Katya replied. "But I also think it is important."

"Okay," Mike sighed. "Call him up here."

"Hey, Kildar," Vanner said when he got to the office. "What's up?"

"I hear you and Katya disagree on something," Mike said.

"Yeah," Vanner said, frowning. "But I was going to bring it up. I'm starting to think her way on it."

"Don't make me pull teeth to find out," Mike said, smiling thinly.

"It's the usual intel mess," Vanner said. "I've started working on a Humint side as well. I got with Vadim and he's feeding me everything that his men pick up along with gossip from the town that the girls pick up. Then I'm piecing that together with what we're getting from intercepts. Katya? You want to cover the rest?"

"The Chechen force that was going into Russia appears to have gotten intelligence that they were to be intercepted by the Russians," Katya said, pulling out some sheets of paper. "We got that from rumors from Nakosta, which is a town south of Alerrso. They also appear to have been told that it was *we* who told the Russians they were coming."

"Crap," Mike said, shaking his head. "I hate the fucking Russians."

"Agreed," Vanner said. "A Spetznaz team, operating in Georgia by the way, got a piece of them. The Spetznaz reported at least two KIA and some WIA, but they only got a small piece. The group was last reported headed west deeper into Georgia and the Spetznaz were recalled, choppered out. The rest of it is surmise from intercepts. The Chechens change frequencies, but they're really bad at it. They keep coming back to the previous freq, or one that was used recently, and broadcasting. So you get these scraps of intercept that might mean something and might not."

"The leader of the Chechen force that was going into Russia was called Breslav," Katya said. "And we got an intercept, two days ago: 'Breslav, have you reached Turdun.'"

"Turdun's a valley to the southeast," Mike said, frowning. "A couple of small farms. Are they going to raid there, you think?"

"There's an old trail from Turdun to here," Vanner said. "Kat, you got a map?"

"Here," she said, rolling out the old Soviet map. It had been marked up, however, with trails.

"It's a mule trail, only," Vanner said. "But they could set up a rally point in Turdun and then cross it to Alerrso; it ends just below the pass coming in one of the small off-shoot valleys. I've been trying to figure out the movement rate, but I'm not sure. If they pushed after leaving the Russian AO they could be there already. Or they could be still on the way."

Mike sat back and considered the situation for a moment.

"How many?" he asked.

"The Chechen assault force was about two hundred according to rumor," Katya said. "But that number has two separate sources and what the Spetznaz saw of it confirms. And it accords with what the Russians know of Breslav. He's a Chechen warlord with about a hundred to two hundred followers. He calls it a battalion."

"Pretty small battalion," Mike mused. "But larger than I'd like to tackle at this point. Any chance this is disinformation?"

"Could be," Vanner admitted. "But it feels real if it's anything at all. If it was disinformation I'd expect *more* indicators, especially Humint. All we really have is this one intercept. As far as I know, Breslav never responded. He might have used a sat phone, though.

I'm getting side-band twitches on those from time to time. One of the twitches was from the general direction of Chechnya, but inside of Georgia. It could have been Breslav calling in. I didn't get a good fix on it, but it was well inside of Georgia, southeast of Turdun, though. That was yesterday. I can't tell *how* far from Turdun, though."

"Okay," Mike said. "Prepare a more definite brief. I'm not doing anything important right now. I'll take a team out and do a recon, see if there's anything to it."

"Don't get yourself whacked," Vanner warned.

"I won't," Mike said. "On your way out, ask the colonel to come see me."

"So, it looks like the Chechens might be coming to visit," Mike said. He'd assembled the full team of instructors along with three of the Keldara hunters who were going to be designated team snipers. He'd waited until Vanner was done with his dog and pony to take over.

"First, I'd like to know where we are on potential defense. Sergeant Heard, how are the ladies coming along?"

"Pretty good," the former MP said. "We skipped the hoo-rah stuff and went straight to weapons training. They've all qualified with small arms and we're working on medium and heavy machine guns at the moment. We still haven't worked on mortars, though."

"Leave the mortars at the serai for now," Mike said. "If we need to use them, we can use our heavy weapons instructors to man them from here and they've got range for the whole valley. Get some equipment up here and dig them in, though. Don't mess up my lawn too much."

"Will do," Sergeant Greer said, grinning. He was one of the basic instructors but when they went to advanced training he was the designated mortar instructor. "I'll get the ladies to help if you don't mind; no time like the present."

"Works," Mike said. "I'm going to take a small team up to try to see if there's anything to this. Praz, what's your best weapon at about a thousand meters?"

"Seven millimeter," Praz said. "Or fifty."

"Praz, Russell and Killjoy," Mike said. "And the three Keldara. Praz and I will take sniper rifles, the rest will take SPRs. We need to get zeroed in tomorrow. Pack tonight, we'll leave tomorrow night. Accelerate the militia weapons training; they need to be able to do positional defense as soon as possible."

"Will do," Nielson said, making a note.

"Vanner, commo?" Mike asked.

"If you can pack some microboxes along, that would be good," Vanner said. "That way you can keep your transmission power down." The small "black boxes" worked on a distributed network and only weighed two pounds.

"We had a ruck march scheduled for day after tomorrow," Adams said. "We're going to move that around for rifle training, but we can only run three teams through the range at a time. What say we take the other three, with their instructors in charge, and go place boxes behind your route? Do that for two days, take them back and run them through the range?"

"That's going to be a big movement," Mike said. "Take one team and make it look like a training exercise. Send one team up behind us, one south and one up into the hills to the east. That way we'll have full coverage anyway. Rotate the other teams in behind them. Do some patrol training. Set it up and pre-train tomorrow, move out the day after. Get the other teams as dialed in on engagement as possible in three days. Then rotate the first teams out."

"Do we send the first teams out armed or unarmed?" Nielson asked, thoughtfully.

"Armed," Mike said. "I know they're only familiarized, but always bring a gun to a gunfight. No magazine in the well, but full load on their gear. No frags, no heavy weapons. One of the instructors can bring a machine gun if they choose and load up as they please. The Keldara can carry spare ammo."

"Works," Adams said. "We'll get it set up while you're gone."

"Taking one of your girls with you?" Vanner asked, grinning. "Gonna get cold up in the hills."

"Not even Katya," Mike replied.

As the Expedition rolled to a stop, Mike stepped out trotting and ran to the rear.

"Gear up," he said, quietly. They were less than seven kilometers from the Turdun Valley. Of course, it was on the other side of a high ridge, but the Chechens could have gotten to this point already.

It didn't feel like an ambush, though. It felt . . . right. Like he was back in his element. There was an owl calling off to the west and the trees were moving in a high wind across the pass. It sounded good, like home. He wasn't juggling training schedules or budgets anymore, just going out to find and localize some bad guys. And, with any luck, neutralize them.

He still wasn't sure how to do that, though. The correlation of forces was . . . severe. The Chechen force was filled with experienced guerilla fighters and his militia was severely outnumbered. The trainers, if he centralized them, would be a formidable force, but they hadn't trained together. If he had a Specter or an F-15 loaded with JDAMs he wouldn't think about how to take out the Chechens. He'd sincerely considered calling Washington to scream for help but he figured this was a personal fight. Let the Chechens learn not to fuck with the Keldara.

He shrugged on his ruck and hefted his rifle, stepping aside to let the others load up as he drifted to the woodline. The opening of the trail was clear in the faint light and he didn't even turn on his Night Observation Device. After a moment, though, he keyed on the thermal sight on the 7mm sniper rifle and scanned the woods. Nothing, not even a deer.

"We're geared up," Praz said from the edge of the woodline.

"Lasko, Killjoy, Vanim, Praz, Me, Otar and Russell," Mike said. His voice was pitched low but not a whisper, which would carry farther.

He waited for his position in the team and then rolled in, following Praz into the darkness. The team was camoed up in ghillie suits and floppy "boonie" hats, the latter with strips of glowing tape on the rear. As they entered the woods the light level dropped and Mike flipped down his monocular NOD, using it to find his way through the dark. Through the NOD the team was clear, especially the faintly glowing strips. The Chechens very rarely used NODs so they were probably fine.

The night was clear but high cirrus clouds presaged rain for later. If so, it would just be in the nature of the mission. Rain would actually be good from his point of view; it would make it less likely the Chechens could move fast and less likely the team would be detected. The other two spec ops types were going to eat rain up and the Keldara needed to learn.

They moved slowly up the mountain, getting their gear in position and stopping to check on rattle. The Keldara were good stalkers and trackers, but they were unfamiliar with the gear and needed some adjustment. But by an hour into the mission they were all good, moving up the mountainside like camouflaged ghosts.

When they reached the saddle at the top of the ridge, Mike halted the team and sent Killjoy and Lasko to the top. Killjoy had a set of thermal imaging binoculars for reconning. After fifteen minutes the two came back down and Killjoy got close enough to make a negative hand gesture. If the Chechens were coming they weren't in the Turdun Valley yet. At least, not in view.

There were two trails entering the valley that the Chechens could be using. The left-hand one was more direct, but they could have come in on the right-hand one that was more to the south. However, the two valleys paralleled a ridge running between them. Mike had mentally designated an observation rally point on the top of the ridge. They'd have to find a good hide and be discreet, since they'd be in view of both trails. But that was their target.

He waved the team forward and they moved out, cautiously but quickly. They'd spent about three hours getting to the top of the ridge and they had less than that until dawn. They had to get down into the valley, cross it undetected, and get up on the next wood-covered ridge before dawn. At that point he'd probably call a halt, detail some lookouts and catch a nap during the day.

As it turned out, the trail they were on was more complicated than it looked on the map. After a couple of switchbacks it had entered a narrow defile that was parallel to the slope. The up side of the defile on the north side led into the tree-covered slope but the down side on the south was a high dike of granite. A small stream ran at the base of the granite, obviously unable to penetrate, while the trail, which was fairly wide at that point, followed the stream. The dike of rock led them well off to the east from the direction they were headed and Mike more than once considered trying to climb out of it. However, the walls were granite and smooth with moss from the stream climbing up their sides; getting out would be problematic. Finally, the ridge of rock that formed the defile fell away and the trail cut back to the west, the stream falling through a series of cascades towards the valley floor. At that point, he called a halt since the sun was damned near up. There was a group of large boulders not far from the trail and he figured they could lay up there.

He motioned them to the bivouac and picked a spot for himself. Russell handled the Keldara, making sure the positions they'd chosen were out of sight from the surroundings.

Mike pulled out his poncho liner, all the snivel gear he'd brought, and makings for dinner.

"Have you worked with this, yet?" he asked Lasko, quietly, as he pulled out a folding stove that fit in with his canteen.

"No," Lasko said, looking at the device curiously. "Sergeant Russell gave me one but I don't know how it works."

"With these," Mike said, pulling out a packet of chemical tablets. He set one of the blue tablets on the ground in the middle of the stove, then pulled out his canteen cup. Filling the latter with water he set it in the stove and cautiously lit the chemical tab, shielding the light with his hand. "You don't want light or smoke, but these can't be seen for more than a few yards. You can smell them from that far."

"I noticed," Lasko said, waving at the acrid scent.

"The smell dissipates fast," Mike said. "I've had ragheads walk by no more than fifty meters away and not smell them." He pulled out a pouch of Mountain House chicken and noodles and waved at Lasko. "Go fix your own."

"Shouldn't someone be watching?" Lasko asked.

"Russell," Mike said, waving towards the trail.

"Where . . . ?" Lasko said, then grunted. "I could barely find him." The former Ranger had settled by a bush and his ghillie suit blended him in perfectly.

"Now you know why we're using these," Mike said, waving the enveloping coverage. "They're hot as hell and catch on the brush, but when you wear one you fucking disappear. Go get some chow, you'll be on watch soon enough."

When the water was heated he put the stove away and dumped the noodles in the water. They mixed rapidly and he ate them while they were still close to boiling. As soon as he was done he finished off the water in the canteen, took a piss and crawled over to Russell's position.

"Got it," Mike said, sitting up slowly to look out over the valley.

"Thanks," Russell said, getting up slowly.

"Have Praz do the schedule," Mike said. "I've got first."

"Will do," Russell said.

Mike leaned back against one of the boulders and let his mind go open. It wasn't numb by any stretch of the imagination, just open to the whole environment. He listened to each of the sounds in the environment, categorizing them as his eyes ceaselessly swept the valley. The clouds were definitely moving in; there'd be rain by nightfall. There was one farm in view in the small valley, the usual high mountain setup much like that of the Keldara. This one ran goats, though, and he was a bit worried about that. But they were tending to stay down in the valley today; with the look of imminent rain the goatherds clearly didn't want to be far from shelter.

Lasko came out to join him shortly after he got in position and Mike let the Keldara watch and listen to nothing. He wasn't going to do instruction except instruction in remaining silent and alert. The Keldara, though, had that down from hours of hunting. The two of them stayed side by side for two hours until relieved by Killjoy and Vanim.

Mike woke up to a stirring in the camp at dusk. He'd shown Lasko how to attach his poncho to the poncho liner and had done so himself. He'd been glad for it when a light rain started to fall about an hour before. He hadn't done more than wake up to the rain on his face and pull the poncho up over his head.

It was still raining when the team started to stir but he ignored it. The boonie caps shed most of the rain off his face, anyway. He didn't even bother pulling out his Gortex, just set about making "breakfast" and doing his makeup. He'd given the Keldara a quick class in camouflage makeup the night before and now he had them redo it. It wasn't the method that was generally trained; he preferred a simple tiger-stripe diagonally down the face. Russell did his makeup precisely according to the book, dark makeup on highlights and light on shadows. Killjoy effected the "Braveheart" look, with one side done in dark brown and the other striped. Praz actually made himself up like a figure from Kiss except in camouflage. Mike had never seen that any of the various ways of putting on the makeup made any difference as long as it reduced shine.

As soon as it was full dark they started off, swinging wide away from the farm and keeping to the eastern woodline to cross the valley. There was a swift-flowing stream at the base and they rigged a rope-line across it for the crossing. After that obstacle there wasn't anything hindering them except the woods. They were dark and tangled and the team went in line ahead, cautiously moving through the brush. They were approaching one of the trails the Chechens might use and it wouldn't do to stumble into them.

When they got near the trail Mike called a halt. He had the team array itself in a line parallel to the trail, then he doffed his ghillie suit and most of his gear, designating Vanim and Lasko to bring it up, then ghosted forward silently through the woods to the edge of the trail.

He was just in sight of Praz as he reached the trail and checked it out. There wasn't anything moving in view and no noise, although that would be muffled by the rain. There also weren't any tracks. Given that the rain wasn't heavy yet, there probably would have still been some sign of two hundred guys and some mules moving through.

He waved the team forward, keeping an eye on the trail until they were across, then joining up with them at a rally point on the far side.

From there it was a climb up the ridge. There weren't any useful trails in their area so they had to make their way through the brush. It was heavy going; the hill was steep and the brush thick. More than once they had to form a human chain to get over some obstacle. But by midnight they were on the top of the ridge and looking for a good observation point.

They'd been able to see the easternmost trail most of the way up the hill, but it wasn't until they got to the top that they could see the western one. They stopped for a time when they reached the top and Mike and Praz scanned both trails looking for signs of the Chechens. The rain had increased but Mike ignored it, searching the west trail for any glimmer of heat signs. He picked up a few, but they were all animals. The Chechens weren't here.

It was likely, frankly, that they weren't going to show. The intel was light, to be honest, and there was no real reason for a "battalion" of Chechens to attack the Keldara. Such a heavy attack might force the government of Georgia to finally react. And it was a long way from their real enemies, the Russians. On the other hand, they could be reacting to being stung by the intel

Mike had passed. It wasn't smart, but the Chechens weren't usually described as "smart."

However, they weren't here. Vadim had been talking to the farmers in the area and if the Chechens had passed down the valley they couldn't have missed them. Hell, the farm probably would have been a smoking wreck. And there really weren't many trails they could have used to the east. So either they weren't coming or Mike's team was in place ahead of them.

After ensuring their quarry wasn't on the trail, Mike led the team up along the spine of the ridge towards a high prominence. He'd spotted it from their first OP and it looked like a good place to set up, a group of rocks at a high point on the ridge. From there they should have a good view of both trails.

It took about an hour to make it up to the designated OP but when he got there he found it was nearly perfect. Erosion had worn away underlying rock, leaving a series of large granite boulders that had fallen in on themselves. There were even a few dry semi-caves under the rocks and the team crawled into their shelter gratefully.

"Okay, same list as last night," Mike said. "Lasko and me, then Killjoy and Vanim, Russell and Otar. Praz gets a double day-shift. No fires tonight, not even chem fires."

CHAPTER
TWENTY-EIGHT

Mike took the opportunity to pull out his Gortex rain-gear and showed Lasko how to use it, then the two of them took up a position overlooking the trails. Mike had Lasko watch the western trail, which was less likely to be used, while he watched the eastern. Both of them stopped from time to time to check their surroundings as well. Mike figured even with the rain they would hear anyone coming before they were in view.

When Mike's shift was over he tried the radio. The box was designed to be used with the microboxes and instead of sending out a strong signal designed to bounce off the ionosphere or use ground conduction, it sent out a light signal, slowly increasing, as it hunted for what was, essentially, an internet router. They'd set up a box on the far ridge and it should be in range. Finally the signal strength went to nearly full and he keyed the mike.

"Keldara Base this is Six," Mike said. The radio was frequency agile and encrypted, meaning that it switched frequencies repeatedly, staying on one for less than a second, and digitally scrambled the voices. All that a very good intercept system would pick up would be random hisses on various frequencies. He wasn't sure that even Uncle Sam could listen in. And localizing it, because of the frequency changes and the distributed system, was very difficult.

"Six, Base," a female voice answered.

"We're at point 274," Mike said. Prior to setting out, he and Vanner had marked up the old Soviet map with a series of location points and 274 was very near their present position. "Negative contact, negative sign."

"Roger, Six," the female voice answered. "Team Sawn near point 618." That would put them up on the first ridgeline. Mike hoped they were being careful. On the other hand, if the shit hit the fan there were something like supports handy.

"Roger 618. Six, out," Mike said. Just because nobody should be able to listen, it didn't mean he should take chances.

This set up the program for the next few days. The team checked in hourly—that way if they were surprised or there was a radio malfunction somebody would know they were cut off—reported negative contact and checked back out. They had enough food for four days and there was a spring not far off so they had water. They were bored out of their gourds, but Mike thought it was good training for the Keldara sniper designates.

He'd reconned the area with an eye to a possible ambush of the Chechens. They had a good view of both trails from their OP, but egressing, running away, would be difficult. On the second day, with no one in sight, he had the three Keldara start clearing the trail along the ridgeline. Both the east and west trails snaked back and forth. If they engaged from up here, they should be able to engage and then run down the ridgeline, more or less straight, to the valley. He could either bring up a vehicle on call or do the two-step boogie across the valley.

On the third day they were there, Team Oleg moved up to supporting position, fresh from a couple of days on the range. They weren't exactly what Mike would call trained but they were better than Sawn's group, which only knew which end the bullet came out of. Adams was with them, as well as McKenzie and Porter, his assistant trainer.

Late on the third day, just as dusk was coming on, Praz stuck his hand out of his ghillie suit and made a motion of men walking.

Mike slithered over to the lookout and peered through binoculars at the trail. There were three men moving down the trail. The men wore civilian clothing but they were carrying AKs so they were legitimate combatants; Mike had checked with Vadim about friendly forces and there weren't any active in the area. The three weren't being particularly cautious and looked, frankly, bored. They stopped at a place where a stream crossed the trail and the area widened out. One of them crossed the stream and went into the woods on the far side, then came back out.

As he did, a larger group moved into the area and spread out, most of them flopping to the ground at the tree line. The men weren't wearing packs, they only had their weapons and some of them wore ammunition vests, so Mike couldn't figure out why they looked so tired. Moving through the mountains, even in the rain, wasn't all that hard.

The second group was followed by a third, smaller group, one of whom began to gesticulate and apparently shout angrily. The men that had flopped got up and moved into the woods as more men and now mules flooded into the area. Gear was unpacked, the men in the woods came back with wood and in less than an hour a camp was in place. They'd lit fires for warmth and to cook their food and were acting anything but tactical.

The mules appeared to be carrying stores, spare ammo and, notably, heavy weapons. There were five that carried, between them, two 80mm mortars, some ammunition cases for them and a half a dozen RPGs and ammo. All the mules were heavily overloaded and looked just about at the end of their rope. But, then again, mujahideen mules always looked at the end of their rope.

Mike did a count on the group and determined that there were quite a few short of two hundred, closer to one-eighty. He wasn't sure if that meant another group or that the intel estimate was wrong. They might have detached a group to take the wounded to a base somewhere, for that matter. Figure five wounded based on the Spetznaz report, two or three seriously. Four stretcher bearers per, a few guards for support. That might be it.

By full dark the group had been fed and were bedded down, propping up scraps of plastic against the continuing rain. There were a few guards on duty, but the group didn't appear to expect trouble. Given that they were deep inside Georgia, that said it all about their ability to move freely in the country.

Mike moved back to the hide and picked up the radio.

"Base this is Six," Mike said. "SEAL REP. ECHO, One Eight Zero. Two Eight Zero Mike Mike. Six Romeo Papa Golf." There were one hundred and eighty bad guys, heavy weapons were two eighty millimeter mortars and six RPGs.

"Six, Base," a female voice replied. "Copy Echo, One Eight Zero. Two Eight Zero Mike Mike. Count Six Romeo Papa Golf."

"Roger," Mike said. "Get Five. Contact in Three Zero Mike."

"Roger, Six," Base replied.

"What we gonna do, boss?" Russell asked.

"We're gonna kill 'em all and fuck their old ladies," Mike said.

"Six this is Five, over," Nielson called over the radio in thirty minutes.

"Five, what is the status of Team Vil?" Mike said. As he recalled, Vil and Oleg's groups were both through initial training.

"Deployed south near point 625," Nielson said.

"Redeploy mounted to 738," Mike said, moving the team to a point north of Alerrso near the opening to the valley. "Redeploy Team Oleg to point 618, offset five hundred meters south for ambush tomorrow. Bunker up. Will lead Echo element to ambush point. Upon ambush, Vil to redeploy to near point 274 to catch leakers. Clear?"

There was a pause as Nielson obviously considered the map and the plan.

"Clear," Nielson said after a moment.

"Will send guide to Team Oleg, leave team in place to guide in Vil," Mike continued. "Prepare to implement by NLT 0900 tomorrow. Six out."

"Russell, Otar," Mike said. "Pack up. Head for the defile we passed through. Make contact with Adams and have him lay in an ambush for the defile. Have him dig in deep; they're probably going to try to fight through. Leave the back door open, though, and make damned sure that nobody kills us when we come a-running. Clear?"

"Clear," Russell said, grinning.

"Killjoy, Vanim, move down the trail to near the base of the ridge. Find a good hide point. After we initiate the ambush, Vil will move up with his team in vehicles. Bring the vehicles to the west trail, then put them in position to engage the enemy as they retreat. Clear?"

"Clear," Killjoy replied, smiling. "Fuck their old ladies, huh?"

"We'll see," Mike said. "Take most of the spare ammo and gear with you; we're going to be moving light. Get going."

Mike snuggled the stock of the Mannlicher into his shoulder and took a light breath, then let it out. He and Praz had carefully measured the distance to the camp, which was starting to unhurriedly break down in the morning light, and designated targets. The mortars had been unloaded at one point and they'd managed to designate the mortarmen and, most importantly, their leaders. He definitely wanted the trained mortarmen out of the equation; the mortars would be hell on the ambush no matter what.

He'd also figured out who Breslav probably was but he was leaving him for last. He wanted the Chechens to pursue aggressively and he figured they'd need leadership to do that. The snipers intended to take out the mortarmen, especially the team leaders, and as many of the mules as they could before moving out.

"Lasko, keep an eye on the targets and call," Mike said. "If either one of us goes down, you take over."

"Got it," the Keldara said, quietly.

Mike lined up one of the mortar team leaders and carefully stroked the trigger.

The 7mm round took about a second and a half to cover the distance, by which time Mike had switched targets to the mule the team was loading and Praz had engaged the other team leader.

"Kildar left and up," Lasko murmured. "Mortarman in cover behind a log. Praz, left, down, bucking mule. Kill, for Kildar, right and down, mule. Kill for Praz, left and up, mortarman."

The two snipers steadily worked the camp as it exploded in activity.

"Kildar, Praz, down and right, team trying to get mortar up," Lasko said. "Track right, team attempting to get mortar up."

"What's the rest of the group doing?" Mike asked.

"One group, about twenty, is working over to the left," Lasko said. "Track left, machine-gunner setting up."

Mike tracked left and spotted the team with the assistant gunner just closing the top on the machine gun. The gunner was tracking back and forth, looking for the snipers that were engaging from the hilltop but clearly unable to find them. Mike lined up on his prone body and watched through the scope as the gunner's head exploded. The assistant gunner tried to get the machine gun in action but Praz took him out with a shot to the body.

"Track right," Lasko said. "They're still trying to get the mortars in action."

Mike looked at the mortar team, which was surrounded by dead bodies, and shook his head.

"Stupid brave," he said. They should have moved the mortars out of the open area. He ignored the crew that was slewing the mortar their way and shot the sight away, killing the gunner in the process. Then he hit the AG just as he was lifting one of the rounds into the tube. The round dropped and headed downrange, but it landed well to their right and short, far enough away that the explosion of the round was muffled by the trees.

"Fuck this," Praz muttered. Shortly afterwards the ready box of ammunition by "his" mortar exploded, sending shrapnel all over the camp, knocking the mortar over and killing most of the crew.

"Good point," Mike said, lining up the box that the crew had set out by the mortar. There was another box under it for good measure and both were laid far too close to the weapon itself. He put two rounds into the boxes, as the shaken crew was just getting to its feet, before the box finally went up at the third hit.

"Time to boogie," Mike said, sliding backwards out of the hide.

They'd sent most of their gear with Killjoy and Otar so the packs were light. They tossed them on and headed down the cut trail towards the valley.

Mike paused at one point and took up a position by a rock, well in sight of the Chechens. They were starting to get their act together and he wanted none of that. He doffed the ghillie suit and leaned against a boulder, in full view of the group in the distance. He knew he wasn't much of a figure to pick out but it was possible.

"Lasko," Mike said, "can you see Breslav?"

Lasko tracked around the camp with the spotting scope and then paused.

"Upper right quadrant," Lasko said. "South of the stream. Talking with someone."

"Got it," Mike said. He lased the two men and got a range of twelve hundred meters, tough downhill and with a crosswind. He carefully lined up the man Breslav was talking to and engaged. He had to time the shot between heart pumps since his heart rate was way up.

"Target. Kill," Lasko murmured. "Breslav has gone to ground behind the tree trunk."

Mike shot the tree a couple of times just to make his point.

"We've got company coming up the hill," Praz said.

"Good," Mike replied.

"They're engaging," Praz pointed out.

Mike couldn't hear any bullets nearby, which was fine by him. But he did see an RPG land short of their position and heard a following crack from Praz's rifle.

"Got the RPG," Praz said.

"Let's go," Mike replied. "They know where we are at least."

"They're following," Praz said as they headed down the hill.

"Good," Mike replied. "Anybody see the main group?"

"Negative," Praz said as they scrambled down the hill. When they hit the flats they were going to be in the open, fair targets for the pursuing Chechens.

"Oleg, Oleg, this is Kildar, over," Mike panted into his mike.

"Kildar, this is Team Oleg, over," Adams replied.

"We're being pursued by two groups of Chechens," Mike said as they hit the bottom of the hill and crossed the small stream there. "One group is on our hill and in direct pursuit. The main body should be behind them. We'll try to engage from the far tree line and get the two to close up. The mortars might or might not have been taken out. One is definitely down, the other is a possible."

"Roger," Adams said. "We're in position."

"Don't let Vil move, yet," Mike said. "We need to have both groups across the valley before he moves."

"We've got a good view of the valley," Adams said. "You're in view. Speaking of which, so are the guys behind you."

They were crossing a plowed field with a hint of green showing on it. The farmer was out of his house, plowing in another field. When he saw the camouflage-covered men burst from the trees he dropped the traces of the plow and began running for his house. But not as fast as Mike, Praz and Lasko were running.

"I am . . . getting tired," Lasko grunted.

"Gimme your pack and weapon," Mike said, dropping back and pulling the pack off.

"I can . . . make it . . ." the Keldara replied, struggling to hold onto the pack.

"Fuck that," Mike said, snatching the pack off the older man's back. "I'm younger and in much better shape for this. Praz, how you doing?"

"I'm going to die tired," Praz grunted but kept moving.

"Kildar, be aware, the pursuing group is in view of you," Adams said.

Mike heard a round crack overhead but they were most of the way across the valley, at least three hundred meters away, and muj shooting was notoriously bad. All they had to do was make it to the tree line.

"Fuck," Praz grunted, stumbling to his knees and then back up. "Took one in the body armor."

"You okay?" Mike asked as he slithered down the bank of the main valley stream. It was wide and shallow, easily fordable, instead of the mountain torrent they had crossed on the hillside. For that matter, it offered a moment's cover but they couldn't stay there.

"Fine," the sniper said, shaking his head. "Let's go."

They scrambled up out of the stream with rounds cracking around them and darted across the last open area to the woodline, reaching that concealment without anyone getting hit again.

"Spread out," Mike said, handing Lasko his gear and moving to the east. "We're going to have to shoot and move towards the trail." He dropped behind the stump of a fallen tree and started searching for targets. The Chechen force had moved out into the valley and was running towards them but they were more than four hundred meters back.

He lined up one guy who was gesticulating and pushing some of the laggards, taking him down. He jacked another round into the Mannlicher and shot the next guy in view.

Praz was engaged as well and Mike had taken down five targets when the Chechens hesitated and then began running back for the opposite tree line. By the time they'd gotten there, Lasko was finally shooting and before they reached the trees there were twelve bodies scattered on the green field. The farmer's ox, meanwhile, had wandered away to the west, away from the gunfire.

"Lasko," Mike called. "Move up the hill to the east. Stay concealed as much as you can. Move about thirty meters, find an overlook spot, then call."

"Yes, Kildar," the Keldara said. Mike could hear him move out, barely; the hunter was remarkably stealthy.

Mike spotted a Chechen moving on the far hillside and lined him up. He fired and saw the man drop out of sight, dead or at least wounded. Okay, maybe just scared and fast.

Some of the men on the ground were only wounded and one was crawling back towards the tree line. Mike let him get about thirty meters from the tree line and then carefully shot him in his remaining good leg. The man waved at the tree line for help, dropping back to the ground, then lifting himself up.

"You're a bastard," Praz said.

"Wait for it," Mike replied. Sure enough, a Chechen darted out from cover, running to the man's side.

"Yours," Mike said.

There was a crack from Praz's rifle and the "rescuer" fell to the ground.

"Kildar," Lasko said, over the radio. "I am in position."

"Go, Praz," Mike called. "Leapfrog past Lasko."

There was a sudden fusillade of shots from the far tree line and another Chechen darted into view. Mike ignored the shots, most of which weren't even making it to their position, and again waited for the Chechen to reach the injured man in the field. This time, though, he shot him as he lifted the man up.

"You are a bastard," Praz said over the radio. "I'm in my spot. Lasko's well up the hill; don't get in his line of fire."

Mike pulled out of his position, moving slowly up the hill from bush to bush. The trees gave plenty of concealment but he wasn't willing to take chances at this point.

"Kildar," Lasko called. "I can see the main force of the Chechens at the opening to the trail. They are closing on your position."

"Roger," Mike said, swearing faintly. "I'm heading for the trail. You two, keep the second body under fire. When the main force gets fully in view, head straight up the hill to the first switch-back."

CHAPTER
TWENTY-NINE

Mike quit trying to move slowly, instead going as fast as he could on the steep hillside, moving from one handhold on a tree to another. In a few minutes, he reached the trail and looked out towards the south.

The main body of the Chechen force was deployed in the field with a machine gun setting up to the west. He dropped to his knees and lined up the machine gun, taking out the gunner and AG and then darting onto the trail. At this point he was about five hundred meters from the Chechens and while he was in sight he was depending upon the distance and moving to avoid being hit. The machine gun might have gotten him, they were better for long distances, but so far the Chechens' personal shooting had been no great shakes.

He stepped onto the trail and looked back at them, waving his rifle over his head and then putting it to his shoulder. As the group opened fire, he carefully lined up one of the fighters and shot him through the head. Then he turned and ran up the trail. The first bend was less than twenty meters away but by the time he reached it the trees around him were dropping leaves from the flurry of shots.

The trail was steep and any time he came in view of the valley he took fire so he had to hurry. By the time he got up to the area of the defile, he was puffing and blowing hard.

"Adams . . ." Mike gasped. "You see me?"

"Got you in view, man," Adams replied evenly. "Come on through."

Mike looked up the hillside from the defile as he ran through but even knowing there was an ambush up there, it was hard for him to spot the positions. Adams had apparently spent the night carefully laying in the ambush and the Keldara positions were fully covered and bunkered. The most noticeable thing was that much of the vegetation on the uphill side of the defile was gone. But even the places where there had been scrub had been filled in with fallen leaves so it looked nearly natural; the fact that they were firelanes was almost impossible to spot. A few lumps at the base of trees were probably claymores covered by fallen leaves but Mike couldn't spot so much as one bit of wiring or detcord. It was unlikely the Chechens would spot the ambush until it was triggered.

"When you get to the next switchback, Otar will guide you into your hide," Adams said.

"Where are the bad guys?" Mike asked, slowing down. The high rock wall gave him all the cover he needed.

"There are three groups," Adams said. "The group that was to the west that was chasing you is moving over to the main group. That's split with one group headed for the trail and another heading straight up the hill. I don't see any sign of the mortars."

"Russell, you there?" Mike asked.

"Here, boss," the Ranger replied.

"Can you see what's going on?"

"Negative, we're on the back side of the hill to lead Vil in."

"Send Vanim on a sneak over to the other side of the hill," Mike said after a moment. "Tell him to see if he can spot the mortars. If they open up, definitely try to spot them. We don't want them engaging Vil's group, especially. You two may have to take them out."

"Will do," Russell replied.

Mike trotted through the rest of the defile, reaching the switch-back in a couple of minutes.

"Kildar," Lasko said, rising out of the bushes as he reached the bend.

"Good to see you," Mike said. "Where's Otar?"

"He is in the hide," the Keldara replied, turning up the trail. "With Sergeant Praz."

Mike followed the Keldara up the trail until he paused and turned down the hill. They slid down a steep portion which stopped at a level spot. As Mike hit the level spot, he realized it was hollow. The bunker was so well camouflaged, he hadn't realized it was there until he was standing on it.

"Nice," he said as a spider hatch opened in the back.

"Come on in," Praz said, grinning. "All the comforts of home. These Keldara can dig like motherfuckers."

The bunker was deep and wide, with a central firing area and two basementlike wings. It was a sizeable construction to be completed overnight. The top was covered with tree trunks and the firing holes were small; Mike wasn't sure even a mortar could do much to it other than from a direct hit on delay. Maybe not even then.

Despite its size it was crowded with Praz, Lasko, Killjoy, Otar, the two Keldara who had apparently constructed it and Mike. The Keldara were loaded down with ammo vests, body armor and helmets, ready for a solid fight. They didn't look scared, however, just eager.

"Good to see you," Mike said to the Keldara in the bunker. "Nice place you've got here," he added, shaking their hands.

"It is much like the shelters we make when out tending the sheep in summer pasture," Lasko said, looking around. "Stronger, but much the same."

"All it took was a little digging," one of the Keldara said, shrugging. "We worked in teams with one team cutting trees and bringing them down to the bunkers and the other team doing the digging."

"Adams," Mike said, peering out of the bunker and seeing nothing but the end of the trail and trees, "I'm blind up here. What you got?"

"Main body is on the trail," Adams replied. "The second group is moving up the hill. They're not moving very fast. They shot up the woodline before they got there and have been crawling up ever since. I think the main body will get to the defile before they do at this rate."

"I should have brought up the mortars," Mike said over the radio.

"Nielson thought of that," Adams said, somewhat smugly. "They're up on the ridgeline with the heavy instructors, a team of females to handle them and a security team of instructors."

"Glory be," Mike said. "Russell, you hear that?"

"Heard it, boss," the Ranger replied. "When's Vil going to move?"

"Not until we spring the ambush," Mike said. "What's the status with Vanim?"

"I am on the far side of the hill, Kildar," the Keldara answered, quietly. "One of the mortars is set up in a clearing near the end of the trail. I do not know how to say it better than that."

"Peters, you on this circuit?" Mike asked.

"Roger, Kildar," the heavy-weapons NCO answered.

"Talk Vanim over to another channel," Mike said. "Then use him to adjust the mortars. Can do?"

"Can do," Peters replied.

Mike ignored the conversation as the NCO carefully explained how to change frequencies. He was blind as a bat and that bothered him. All he could see was the end of the defile.

"Kildar," Adams said. "The main body has reached the defile. The second group is heading up the hill but they're about a hundred meters below it and the slope is steepening out. You're actually one of the security positions and I'm a little worried about that group. Don't let them sweep around you."

"Got it," Mike said. "Have Vil's group start moving. By the time they're in view, we should have the main body's full and undivided attention."

"Vil's moving," Nielson said over the circuit.

"Guys," Mike said to the two Keldara who were looking out their firing ports nervously. "Is there any way we can dig out a couple more shooting points? It seems a shame to have six guns in here and only two able to shoot."

"Yes, Kildar," one of the Keldara said, setting his rifle against the side of the hole. "Right away."

"Main body is fully in the defile and moving to the ambush point," Adams said a couple of minutes later. The Keldara had found points they could dig through and Vanim and Killjoy had spots to shoot from at least. Mike put them on the points since their SPRs, a highly accurate M-16 variant, would be better in a firefight than the sniper rifles. "All positions, stand to. Initiating."

There was a thunderous roar from the defile as the claymores detonated, followed by screams from humans and mules. This was followed by a growing roar of fire from the hillside as the Keldara poured fire into the defile.

There was a crack from one of the Keldara rifles and then another as the Keldara cursed.

"He is hiding behind a tree," the man muttered, angrily. "Coward."

"There's another," Vanim said, firing. "Got him."

"I'll just sit here and twiddle my fingers," Mike said, doing just that. "Keep an eye to the right, guys. We're expecting company that way."

There was an explosion to the left of their position, a mortar round Mike was pretty sure. Then he, faintly, heard the rumble of shells overhead.

"Peters just counterbatteried their mortar," Adams said. "It's out. I'm shifting him to your control. Go to channel three."

"Peters?" Mike said on that channel. He peered past Lasko, looking for the men working their way up the slope.

"Go, Kildar," the mortar NCO replied.

"I don't have anything here, yet," Mike said then paused. "Stand by. Right, from my position, two hundred meters, azimuth . . ." He checked the compass in his binoculars. "One eight three."

"Shot over," Peters said no more than five seconds later. "We had that laid in already."

"Shot out," Mike replied. He could see the group of Chechens struggling up the steep hill. The granite that created the defile made the hill nearly vertical along its length.

"Splash over," Peters said a few second later.

"Splash out," Mike replied. There was a tremendous explosion in the trees between his position and the struggling Chechens.

"Polar," Mike said. "Azimuth One Eight Three. Drop fifty, fire for effect. Troops in open in woodland. Mix delay and quick."

"Roger," Peters said. "Incoming."

In a few moments rounds started to drop among the Chechens of the second group, some of them exploding in the trees to rain shrapnel down on the exposed fighters while others penetrated on delay to explode on or near the ground. Otar and one of the original Keldara had engaged the group of Chechens and before long Mike could see the survivors turning and skidding down the hill on their butts.

"Cease fire," Mike said over the circuit. "Switching to command freq."

"Padrek, on your right!" "I got him, I got him!" "Father of All, where did he come from? Yakov, to your right there, behind the oak, I can't get him . . ." "CUT THE CHATTER!" "Where did that last one go?"

The main freq was jammed with the excited Keldara passing word back and forth and Adams trying to settle them down.

"CEASE FIRE!" Adams shouted over the net, getting stepped

on twice. Mike could hear him blowing a whistle at the same time. Finally, the fire died down and the Keldara cleared the command net.

"Team Oleg," Oleg said, as soon as he could be heard. "By odd numbers, up out of your positions and take over watch for evens."

"That is us," one of the Keldara said.

"Stay here," Mike replied. "The rest of us will get out. You guys keep this door closed."

Mike, Lasko and Praz crawled out of the bunker and looked towards the defile. The ground was hazy with propellant and the remnants of the dust from the claymores, but he could see the trail was littered with bodies.

He'd expected the Keldara to be whooping it up, as a group of muj probably would in similar circumstances. But they weren't. Teams were up out of their bunkers and prone, pointing their weapons into the defile.

"Even numbers, out of your bunkers," Oleg said, grunting as he apparently was climbing out of his. "Prepare to sweep across the objective."

"Team Vil is in position," Vil's voice said on the circuit. "There are Chechens filtering out of the woods."

"Shag ass," Adams growled over the radio. "Push the rest out of the woods before the others get to the other side of the valley. When you're firing into the valley, aim *low*. Don't hit your buddies on the other side."

Mike spotted the chief sliding down the hill to his left and angled that way, sliding towards the defile himself. The Keldara were moving forward in pairs, with one covering the top of the defile as the other headed down.

When the first group reached the defile, they ignored the few wounded Chechens, moving in pairs to lift one another up to the top. When most of the group was on top, they continued down the hill.

Mike caught up to Adams in the defile and shook his head.

"Was this training or what?" Mike asked.

"We rehearsed twice," Adams said. "After we had the bunkers in but before we camouflaged. Training, I guess. And some natural talent. You were right; these guys are *good*."

"I'll give you a leg up," Mike said, making a stirrup of his hands.

He and the chief made it up and over the wall, following the Keldara down the hill. The Keldara were moving fast but carefully, occasionally trading shots with some of the Chechens on the hill. But the Chechens were mostly just trying to run away.

When Mike got to the base of the hill he could see the Chechens reversing his earlier course across the fields, running for all they were worth. One group was nearly at the far tree line, with the main group of survivors, no more than fifty of them, halfway across.

"This is an awful way to make a living," Mike said, sliding to a halt and keying his mike. "Vil, engage."

A burst of fire came from the far hillside, raking the Chechens that had nearly made it to the tree line. Mike could see a line of machine-gun bullets pock down the field and into the group which, at the unexpected fire, stopped and began firing back, most of them still standing. There had been about fifteen in the group when the fire started and the first burst killed more than half of them, spotting more bodies onto the green field.

Mike switched frequencies to the mortar freq.

"Peters, you have the field zeroed in?" Mike asked.

"I've got Reynolds up on the ridge, spotting for us," the NCO said as there was a clap of explosion from a firing mortar. "We're on it."

The Chechens were caught between two fires, some of them taking refuge in the cover of the stream but most caught in the open field. A few broke towards the farmer's house but they had barely made it ten meters in that direction when a mortar round went off over their head, scything shrapnel down into the group and throwing them all to the ground.

More mortar rounds fell in the main body, one of them hitting the ground between two of the Chechens and throwing their dismembered bodies through the air. The rounds quickly walked down to the streambed, however, shifting to airburst and slaughtering the mujahideen that had taken shelter in the cover of its banks.

In no more than five minutes, between the mortars and direct fire from both woodlines, there were no more Chechens moving on the field.

"Cease fire mortars," Adams growled. "Team Vil, sweep the field. Team Oleg, up the hill again; make sure there aren't any fighters left functional. Take prisoners if you can, but don't let them get froggy. Colonel, if you could call Vadim in, please, to take charge of the prisoners."

"On it," Nielson replied.

It took far more time to clean up the mess than to make it, as usual. Vadim, along with a group of trucks from the Keldara, showed up about thirty minutes after the fighting was over. When he spotted Mike standing by the stream he walked over, shaking his head.

"How many?" he asked, looking at the bodies scattered across the field.

"At least a hundred and fifty," Mike replied. "They're scattered from here back up both trails," he continued, gesturing in both directions. "There might have been some leakers, but not many."

"And you did this with how many?" Vadim asked.

"Two teams," Mike said, shrugging. "About forty. And some women to run the mortars."

"Women," Vadim said, shaking his head again. "The Keldara are tigers, yes?"

"Very much so," Mike said. "Which gives me an idea."

"You've done well," Mike said, looking over the assembled Keldara militia.

They'd gathered the Chechen dead using the trucks and the few surviving mules and buried them in a mass grave at the end of the farmer's field. Vadim had spoken to him about it but the man and his family hadn't come out the whole time the Keldara were there.

When they got back to the barracks, Mike had the militia clean their gear and authorized two beers per man. The trainers had joined in, which was unusual, but Mike considered it in keeping with the action. The fight had been over before noon, but it had taken most of the day to clean up the battlefield, get back and clean their gear. When they were done, Mike had told them to take a day off and go home to their families. He hadn't said anything to them except that they'd done a good job. The day off gave him time to get some stuff made up at the serai.

On the day after, he'd had them assemble in front of their barracks at 0900 for an address.

"Despite being barely into training, you met the enemy on the field of battle and defeated them," Mike continued. "Very handily for that matter." One of the Keldara from Vil's force had been hit in the arm, but other than that and a few bruises from rounds hitting body armor, the teams hadn't taken a single casualty. "Training *will* continue," he said to groans. "But as of this moment, you are *soldiers.*"

He turned and waved towards the headquarters and the senior trainer for each of the teams came out, bearing new guidons. They were still blue, but instead of the name of the team being prominent, each of them now bore a snarling tiger face with the team name below it. Behind the trainers, a group of Keldara women came out bearing new uniform blouses. On the shoulder of each was the same patch.

"In keeping with that, I give you a new designation," Mike said, as the trainers marched to the front of each team and traded guidons with the team leader. "You are no longer the militia of the Keldara. You are the Tigers of the Mountains. And we will show the *world*, that you had better not fuck with the Mountain Tigers."

▶ END ◀